UNDER THE WINTER SUN

ELEMENTAL ENCHANTERS SERIES

3

CARRIGAN RICHARDS

also by carrigan richards

Standalone Novels
Pieces of Me
Black Dove

Elemental Enchanters Series
Under a Blood Moon (#1)
Under the Burning Stars (#2)
When Darkness Fell (#2.5)
Under the Winter Sun (#3)
Under an Onyx Sky (#4)

January Dreams Series
January Dreams
Silent Dreams
Shattered Dreams

UNDER THE WINTER SUN

ELEMENTAL ENCHANTERS SERIES

3

CARRIGAN RICHARDS

Carrigan Richards Publishing, LLC
PO Box 3782
Suwanee, GA 30024

First published in the United States 2014
This paperback edition published 2024

Copyright © 2014 Carrigan Richards

All rights reserved. No part of this publication may be
reproduced, distributed, or transmitted in any form or by
any means, including photocopying, recording, or other
electronic or mechanical methods, without the prior
written permission of the publisher.
The story, all names, characters, and incidents portrayed in
this production are fictitious. No identification with actual
persons (living or deceased), places, buildings, and products
is intended or should be inferred.
Cover Art by Jake @ J Caleb Design

ISBN: PB: 979-8-98582-25-9-5; ASIN: eBook: B00OX69NR8

Printed and bound in the USA

To my brother who taught me how to stand up for myself.

Will the winter sun keep us warm
in these dark times?
—Dishwalla

PROLOGUE

Havok inhaled the crisp winter air. From the high rampart of the ancient castle, the hills rolled endlessly, their trees ablaze in reds, oranges, and yellows. The snow-capped mountains on the horizon, with their jagged peaks, stood as a testament to the wild, untamed beauty of his homeland. To his left, miles away, a rocky cliff sent water cascading into the shimmering Crystal River below, the sound a faint murmur on the wind.

A smile tugged at his lips. After so many years, he was finally home.

Caprington. His family's legacy. The town stood as proud as ever, though its people were long gone. Victims of countless wars or the quiet decay of old age. Only he and Savina remained now, the last remnants of a once-mighty lineage.

But not for long. Soon, Savina would die too.

"Happy to be home?" Xavier Holstone asked from behind.

Havok turned, regarding the young man who had been at his side since childhood. In many ways, Xavier was more of a son than Colden ever could have been. The thought of his real son's sacrifice stirred the faintest flicker of sorrow. Colden had died to bring him back, and that sacrifice had been for the greater good.

"Yes." Havok inhaled a deep breath. "I had forgotten how clean the air is here. How peaceful. Not a single Ephemeral for miles."

"We've been clearing them out for years," Xavier said, pride coloring his voice.

"Good. Soon we will have all of the Elementals, and the Ephemerals will finally be wiped from this world."

"We're ready to begin."

"Excellent." Havok followed Xavier inside the castle, the air growing cooler as they stepped into the shadows of the stone corridor. Built in the 1200s, the fortress had withstood a myriad of attacks and storms. Its ancient stone walls, once battered by time and war, now stood strong, with the faint hum of modern lights added to their ageless grandeur.

They walked in silence until they reached a pair of towering double doors. Xavier pushed one open, and they stepped through into a grand hall. Havok's gaze traveled up to the high, arched ceilings, admiring the intricate patterns carved into the wood beams above.

They strode down the center aisle, flanked on both sides by crowds of his followers, who kneeled as they passed. At the front of the room, his prisoners stood bound. Their faces were familiar to him: Melissa, Jeremy, Joss, Maggie, Kira.

Melissa held his gaze, calm and calculating. Jeremy's nervous fidgeting betrayed his fear. And Joss... Joss glared at him with those striking violet eyes, her defiance evident even in chains. A small but mighty woman stepped forward, joining Xavier beside Havok as he spoke to his followers. Trudy. Loyal, fierce, and sharp as a blade.

Havok gave her a slight nod, and she returned it, her gaze flickering over the bound prisoners with a detached curiosity.

A cold, satisfied smile spread across Havok's face. "It is so lovely to see you all. I do apologize for the barbaric means of your captivity." He nodded toward Xavier and Eve, the dark-haired woman at his side, who began untying the prisoners. "Welcome to Caprington. I trust you will come to find it much like home. It is a beautiful place, after all. Alas, I brought you here because Savina has poisoned your minds, and I wish to show you the truth."

"You betrayed us, Colden," Joss said. "How could you?"

Havok's smile faltered for a fraction of a second. *Colden.* The name grated on him, a reminder of a son who had never met his expectations. "Colden is gone. I am Havok now," he corrected, his voice low and cold. The truth was far more complex, of course. His soul now resided in Colden's body. But there was no need to dwell on that.

Joss's jaw clenched. "You're a monster," she hissed.

Maggie raised her chin, her dark eyes unwavering. "Savina has led us for years, but I've often questioned her motives. Perhaps ... there's truth in what you say."

Havok's brows lifted. "Oh? I was under the impression that the Elders were all so loyal to her."

Maggie hesitated, a slight frown touching her face. "Loyalty to Savina has never been easy, and there are those of us who've wondered if she's kept things hidden for her own benefit. Even now, I can't say I truly understand her intentions."

Perhaps she's useful after all.

"Perhaps you're right, Havok. Perhaps … she's manipulated us all."

"I never trusted the Elders' rules either," Melissa said. "Even with Savina's side of the story, I couldn't understand why she never sided with you."

Havok turned his attention to her, surprised by her calm tone. The Earth Enchanter. Tall, blonde, and powerful. She was a gifted warrior with a talent for invisibility and the ability to turn her body into stone. He had been particularly impressed with her skills in the past.

Havok's interest sharpened as he studied Maggie and Melissa, his gaze lingering on Maggie. "So, you both suspect Savina of treachery? You'd be willing to consider my side of this war?"

Maggie let a faint smile ghost cross her face. "If it means protecting our people, I will consider anything. We were working undercover. Savina only looked out for herself. She's the one who killed many of our people."

Havok narrowed his eyes, stepping closer. He probed their minds with a delicate touch. They weren't lying. They truly meant what they said. "Interesting," he murmured, as a smile crept onto his face. "I had hoped to gather all the Elementals here with me."

Xavier nodded. "We can gather an army and go after them. Sorcha has already weakened them. It'll be easy."

Havok's lips curled in irritation. "The Elders still have their powers, Xavier. Or have you forgotten?"

"No. But we can trick them."

Havok raised his hand, silencing him. "No. Savina has declared war, and they will come. I am a patient man,

Xavier, and when they do, I have plans for them. Ones they won't survive."

"We're supposed to just sit here and wait?"

"We will train our new members. And once we have all of the Elementals, we will force the Ephemerals and the renegades to obey us. We will build a better world. The Ephemerals have ruled long enough. It is our time and anyone who stands in our way will be obliterated."

As applause filled the hall, Havok swelled with pride. He would finally complete his family's mission, once and for all.

As the cheers quieted, his gaze swept over the prisoners and his followers. "The Elementals have always believed their power lies in their talents. But real power lies not in brute strength, but in the mind. And I know their minds better than they do."

He turned to Joss, whose defiance wavered. "By the time they arrive, they'll barely know who they are. A nudge here, a whisper there, and they'll doubt their own memories, question their thoughts. Their emotions … their loyalties … all so easy to twist."

Joss's glare faltered, and Havok's smirk deepened. He cast a sidelong glance at Xavier, whose eyes gleamed with understanding. "And that is why we wait," Havok continued. "Let them come here, drawn by loyalty they don't even realize is fragile. They'll shatter without a single spell or weapon lifted."

Xavier leaned in. "They'll be easy prey."

"Precisely," Havok replied. "When they arrive, they won't even know they're already lost."

Havok's words hung in the air, and the hall erupted once more, the applause echoing off the stone walls. He could almost taste it: the quiet satisfaction of a game he had already won.

1

TENSION

The wind howled, tearing through the cemetery like a beast unleashed, scattering leaves into a wild, frenzied swirl. The sky, a dull gray, cast everything in a cold pallor, while bare branches clawed upward like skeletal fingers into the thick fog. The gravestones rose from the earth, forcing Ava Hannigan to step carefully between them, each one a jagged reminder of lives cut short.

Ava hugged herself tighter, her teeth chattering as the wind bit through her layers. The November chill seemed to seep into her very bones. She stood behind a small crowd of mourners, heads bowed in black.

Peter hadn't wanted Ava to be there muttering something about how she "didn't know Seth very well" and didn't need to be there.

But she was there anyway, and as she caught a glimpse of Peter's face, pale and worn from grief, she hoped he'd understand. Maybe she hadn't known Seth the way he had, but she was here for Peter, for whatever he needed. Still, his quiet, distant gaze told her he was dealing with this alone.

A piercing scream split the air, and Ava looked up, startled.

Seth's mother was sobbing, her body trembling as her husband held her close. A wave of agony washed over Ava. Seth had died in the war, but his parents would never know the truth. Savina had made sure they believed it was a car accident. They had no idea their son had been one of the Ephemerals, transformed into a half-Enchanter, or that his best friend, Peter McNabb, was a Paramortal—a protector of Enchanters.

Peter stood beside her, silent and still, but his guilt pulsed through their empathic necklaces. Ava reached for his hand, her eyes drifting to the fallen leaves at their feet. One vibrant red leaf lay on the ground, stark against the brown and gold. A brittle, crumpled leaf landed beside her boot, so fragile it looked like it would shatter if she so much as breathed on it. Like everything else in her life.

She didn't want to be there. She was eighteen, and her life felt like one long funeral. Just last week, they'd buried Alena, Esteban, Zhan … and Colden. Colden, who had betrayed them, or rather, the monster Havok who had taken his body. Havok, who had murdered her mother, Luci. Who had destroyed her family home. Who had manipulated everything she held dear into something unrecognizable.

And all of it—her mother's secrets, her friends' deaths, the fractured pieces of her life—was her fault. She had sought out the Necromancer, desperate to understand Luci's lies. Instead, she'd released Havok. Her stomach churned, remembering that single moment of stubbornness that had shattered everything.

Clutching her garnet pendant, Ava willed it to show some sign of life from their missing friends. But there was only silence, as if the world had been drained of color and sound. All that was left was the cold. She was powerless now, like all the others. Sorcha had made sure that in the final moments of battle, she'd stripped them all of their abilities except the Elders, and Peter, whose regenerating gift kept him whole. Losing her powers left a gaping hole in her, like a piece of her soul had been torn out.

She gritted her teeth. Havok had to pay. Her soul might be promised to him, thanks to Luci's betrayal, but she would find a way to kill him. She had gotten her friends into this, and she would get them out.

A gust of wind slammed into her, whipping her fiery hair around her face like flames, but no heat reached her. Only the numbing cold, pressing down on her like a shroud.

Peter squeezed her fingers, and she relaxed for a moment. He'd always been her anchor. But even that felt tenuous now, with his guilt, her constant screwups, and the distance that had crept between them.

Beside them, Mr. McNabb, Link, Nicole, Lance, and Thomas stood huddled together, their faces drawn. She was surprised that Thomas, her ex, had come to Seth's funeral. They had all changed. They were all broken, each carrying wounds that wouldn't heal. Lance stood rigid, barely holding himself together in Melissa's absence, while Gillian, too distraught over Jeremy's disappearance, had blamed Peter in a heated moment.

The priest's sermon ended, and the crowd began to disperse.

Seth's mother approached, her eyes red and swollen. She placed a trembling hand on Peter's shoulder. "Thank you for coming. He was lucky to have you as a friend."

Peter's sorrow radiated through their necklaces. "Yeah … he was a great friend."

A tear slid down his cheek, and Ava wrapped her arms around him, holding him as his grief broke free. There were no words for this kind of emptiness.

Mr. McNabb turned to Peter, his voice rough with grief. "May you never forget what is worth remembering, nor ever remember what is best forgotten."

Peter wiped his eyes, clearing his throat. "Thanks, Dad."

"Are you riding with me or Ava?" Mr. McNabb asked Peter.

"I'll ride with Ava. She can take me home later."

His father nodded, squeezing his shoulder one last time before walking away.

Peter loosened his tie, his hands trembling as he shook his head. "I've gotta tell him. He needs to know what really happened. He needs to know what I am."

Ava's heart clenched at the vulnerability in his voice. "I know. I can help. If you want me to be there, I'll be there."

"Maybe," Peter murmured, but he didn't sound convincing.

Link and Nicole shifted closer, their faces weary. "I haven't told my parents either. I'm not sure I even know how."

Nicole nodded, her cheeks flushed from the cold. "Same here. How do you explain that you're … different? That you've been changed into something else?"

Link took her hand, his eyes softening as they met hers. "We'll figure it out."

"My dad can help," Ava said. "He's … been through this." She tried to muster a smile, sensing their relief, however slight.

Relief softened Nicole's face. "That would be great."

"Let's go." Thomas glanced up as another icy gust swept through. "It's freezing out here."

They walked toward Lance's SUV, the biting wind following them. The drive back to the Manor was silent, each of them lost in their thoughts. Ava stared out the window, her own guilt gnawing at her, ever-present. She had gotten them all here, to this moment of loss and fear, and now it was up to her to fix it.

The car pulled up to Blackhart Manor, its towering spires and gothic architecture rising against the bleak November sky. The pine trees surrounding the estate were the only trees still holding color, vibrant against the gray. Beyond the wrought iron gates, the garden burst with life—holly berry bushes, snow-white chrysanthemums, orchids, roses, and lilies in full bloom, as if untouched by the season.

Ava paused, taking in the colors, feeling the beauty like a pang in her chest. The garden had been Kira's domain, a living canvas of her care and precision. But she was gone, taken like so many others. She let the brief moment of beauty sink in, then turned toward the Manor's imposing arched door.

The Manor's cathedral ceilings and grand staircase no longer held the same awe. The halls had become a place of grief.

The past week had been a blur of funerals and sleepless nights. Ava had spent the first two days after the battle drifting in and out of sleep, too exhausted to do anything else. She hadn't eaten much, either. On the third day, the Elders had tried to reassure them that Havok wouldn't kill them. But how could they know that for sure? Had Havok sent them a message saying, "Hey, don't worry. We made it to Caprington in one piece"? On the fourth day, she'd retreated to her room, perched on the window bench in the alcove, clutching her pentagram necklace, desperately hoping to feel something from Melissa, Jeremy, or Joss.

All she wanted now was to sleep, to let the grief and guilt fade away, but she knew it wouldn't. Without her powers, without her friends, she felt like a ghost, chained to a world that barely recognized her.

Ava's necklace warmed, a familiar sign of Peter's anguish.

"I'm so sorry." He rubbed his eyes. His disheveled brown hair brushed against the collar of his shirt, his choppy bangs falling just above his thick eyebrows. He was a few inches taller than her, his lean build made stronger from months of training.

"Peter, please stop apologizing. You're not responsible for Seth's death or the kidnappings. And I'm so sorry about Seth."

He took her cold hands in his, cupping them between his warm palms. "Your hands are freezing." His thumbs brushed over her knuckles.

She tried to smile, savoring the warmth, but the tightness in her chest wouldn't ease. He'd always been her rock, but now, after everything they'd lost, he was slipping away, like a tether slowly unraveling.

"I don't know what I'd do without you," she whispered.

Peter looked at her, his eyes clouded with pain. "I don't know what I'd do without you either." His words were empty, burdened by the sorrow that had permeated his entire being.

She squeezed his hands tighter, hoping it would be enough to keep him close.

"All of my friends are gone, Ava." he said.

An aching stab of guilt shot through her. Valerie and Amanda's memories of Seth and Peter had been erased after Trudy McVaine's attack. Seth was dead, and Peter had lost every piece of his old life except for his father. If she hadn't brought Peter into this world, maybe his friends would still be around. Maybe Seth would be alive. "I never wanted this for you. I was selfish when I asked you to become an Enchanter."

"I wanted this. Even now." He reached up, brushing a loose strand of her hair behind her ear, then leaned in, his lips finding hers. His kiss was warm, familiar, like something precious they'd almost lost. But each touch, each gentle caress, felt more fragile than ever, a reminder of how close they'd come to losing it all.

"I love you, Peter." Ava rested her forehead against his.

"I love you. I never want to lose you. You're all I have left."

"You won't."

Tears welled in his eyes, and his grip tightened. "If they had taken you, I would've done anything to get you back. Anything."

Ava stroked his cheek. "They didn't take me. And they never will."

They kissed again, but this time, the flood of sadness, anger, and regret hit Ava like a wave, drowning out the moment. Peter's guilt, Gillian's sadness was all too much. She grasped her necklace, desperate to control the connection, to stop feeling everything at once.

He drew back with a sigh. "Do you think she'll ever forgive me?"

Ava hesitated. "I don't know. But you can't let it consume you. This isn't your fault."

He lay back on the bed, and she curled up beside him, resting her head on his shoulder. She wanted to sleep, but she feared the nightmares that haunted her every night since the battle. Peter used to stay with her, protecting her from the darkness, but he hadn't stayed since that night.

"I miss Colden," she whispered.

He squeezed her. "I know. How are you dealing with that?"

"I don't know. I feel responsible for all of it. If I hadn't gone to the Necromancer, none of this would have happened."

"You don't know that for certain. Didn't Colden convince you to go?"

"It wasn't him. It was Havok. I don't even know if it was ever really Colden," she said. "He could've been Corbin the whole time, manipulating me."

"I'm sure it was Colden most of the time. Did he ever seem ... off?"

"No. Not once. But this is such a mess. How could Corbin's soul have lived inside Colden for so long?"

"I don't know, Ava. I didn't even know any of this was possible before I met you."

She looked up into his eyes. "How are you handling it?"

He hesitated, looking away. "I keep thinking I could've been stronger. Maybe I could've saved Seth." His voice grew rough, guilt flashing in his eyes. "I ran, Ava. I got scared, and I ran."

"You saved me," she reminded him. "Twice. If anything, it's on me for what happened to Colden. It's my fault, Peter."

"You're not to blame for any of this." He took her hand, his eyes searching hers. "You never did find out why your mom pledged your soul to Havok, did you?"

"No," she said bitterly.

"Do you think Savina knows?"

"I don't think so."

"Are you still having nightmares?"

She didn't want to admit it. She didn't want Peter to feel bad for not staying with her. "They're not that bad," she lied. In truth, the nightmares had worsened. Luci's spirit convincing her to join Havok. Colden's eyes turning dark as Havok emerged. The feeling of venom coursing through her veins. Melissa being taken away. Tears pricked her eyes.

"You're lying."

"I just wish you'd stay with me."

"I hate staying here, Ava."

"So do I."

"I'm sorry. Maybe you and your dad can move soon."

"Yeah." She straightened the silver bracelet Peter had given her for her birthday, the words *Without you, I'm nothing* engraved on the inside. She wished he would ask her to stay with him. Just for one night.

He reached up and brushed his knuckles against her cheek. He leaned in, as if to kiss her, but at the last moment, he pressed his lips to her forehead instead.

Someone knocked on the door, and then it opened.

"Ava," her father said, stepping into the room. His gray hair, now more prominent, made him look older than he was. His lanky posture and the small protruding stomach were a far cry from the half-Enchanter he used to be. The wrinkles etched into his face weren't only from age; they were from raising a rebellious daughter who had thrown herself headfirst into danger more times than he could count. His eyes landed on Peter, and his expression tensed, not pleased to see them alone in her room. "Dinner's ready."

Her heart sank at the thought of another dinner without Colden, Melissa, or Joss. Colden had always cooked for them. The familiar ache in her stomach intensified, and food repulsed her. "I'm not hungry."

"You're eating dinner," her father insisted. "Now, come on."

The lump in her throat grew, but she swallowed hard, determined not to let herself cry.

Peter stood and helped Ava to her feet. "We should eat."

They followed her father down to the great dining hall. He joined Aaron and Gustav at the long table, but Ava had no desire to sit with the Elders. She and Peter settled in chairs near the exit, across from Gabriel, Natalia, and Eric. The closer to the door, the better.

But she couldn't escape Natalia's burning glare. To some, Natalia was the picture of perfection with her olive skin and perfectly bobbed black hair. Her Siren abilities made her powerful enough to bring any enemy to their knees. But to Ava, Natalia was cold. She had never shown Ava any kindness, especially after what had happened to Colden. Not that Ava deserved it.

"Hey," Gabriel greeted Ava, his crystal blue eyes showing the same tiredness she felt. His short black hair lay flat except for his raised bangs, and his smooth, pale face now bore a five o'clock shadow. Leaning his muscular frame forward, he rested his elbows on the table.

"Hey," Ava said, though she could feel Natalia's eyes drilling into her.

"I can't believe you have the nerve to sit near me," Natalia hissed, her cold gaze locked on Ava.

Heat rushed to her cheeks. "I'll eat fast if that makes you feel better."

"Let me make something clear," Natalia snapped. "After everything you've done, you don't belong here. I'm surprised you haven't been banned for what you've caused."

Ava's temper flared. "I know exactly what I've done. But don't think for a second that I don't care."

Gabriel leaned forward, his calm gaze hardening. "Natalia, that's enough. We've all lost people, and none of us is blameless in this. I suggest you remember that before pointing fingers."

Natalia stiffened, her glare icy, and the surrounding chatter quieted as people turned to look.

Peter squeezed Ava's hand under the table.

She looked down at her plate, her emotions a tangled mess of relief, gratitude, and guilt. Gabriel didn't have to defend her. He hadn't owed her anything. Yet he'd chosen to speak up when no one else did. Someone still believed in her, even when she was struggling to believe in herself.

But the guilt crept back, whispering that she didn't deserve his support. Still, every instinct told her to get up and leave, but she forced herself to stay seated. She wouldn't let Natalia bully her.

Slowly, the conversations resumed around them.

"You okay?" Peter whispered in her ear.

She nodded, though the tension still churned in her stomach.

Konstantin Volodin, the telekinetic Enchanter, dropped down in the chair beside Ava with a small, polite smile.

"Good evening." His thick Russian accent made it hard for Ava to understand him sometimes, but she had learned to follow the rhythm of his speech over the months they had known each other.

"Hi," she said.

"How are you doing?" His pale blue eyes were filled with quiet understanding.

"Okay, I guess."

"I know what you mean."

As they waited for the food to be served, the oppressive feeling of everyone's grief and loss filled the air. Ava knew it overwhelmed Peter. His shame trickled through their bond, and every time Ava's thoughts wandered to her missing friends, Peter's guilt deepened. She needed to learn how to shield her emotions better, for his sake.

Anastasya Grigoryev and Katarina emerged from the kitchen carrying kettles of soup, followed by Ilya with baskets of fresh bread. Ava's eyes drifted around the smaller group of people gathered at the table. The absence of Colden, Joss, and the others hung like a dark cloud over them. It felt like a shadow of what their family had once been.

The silence as they ladled soup into their bowls gnawed at her. Every clink of a spoon against a bowl made her nerves prickle. She couldn't stand the stillness, the small talk. It was as if they were all pretending that everything was normal when nothing was.

She stirred the reddish-brown soup in front of her, her thoughts drifting back to Joss. Ava missed her bright smile and the way her violet eyes lit up when she laughed. She had been one of the few who understood Ava's complicated feelings for Peter. And now she was gone. A searing pain gripped Ava's stomach, as if someone were wringing it out.

A loud clink drew her attention. Peter had set his spoon down and dragged his hands down his face, his shoulders hunched over as remorse radiated from him. Ava hadn't meant to think of Joss. She didn't want to remind him of everything they had lost. Guilt washed over her for adding to his pain.

"You should eat," Gabriel's low voice broke through her thoughts.

"I'm not hungry." Ava pushed her bowl away.

"It will replenish you," Gabriel said. "Your body needs it."

"He's right," Peter added, picking up his spoon again.

Ava sighed and brought a spoonful of the warm soup to her mouth. "Happy?" she muttered, feeling bad for snapping at Gabriel. He had saved her life more than once, and he was one of the few people who still stood by her. "Sorry," she added.

"It's okay," Gabriel said, his tone as forgiving as always.

Natalia shook her head in disgust and shot Gabriel a pointed look before crossing her arms over her chest.

The Elders' leader, Savina Geddes, rose from her seat, clasping her hands in front of her. Her commanding green eyes were now filled with a deep sadness that Ava had never seen before. Savina had been different since her brother Colden's death, as if a part of her had been extinguished. Her red hair, long and flowing, seemed to dull from grief. "I would like to say a few things before we disperse," she said, her voice monotone and somber.

Aaron, Savina's mate, watched her with unwavering affection, his russet eyes never leaving her. Their bond was centuries old, and yet the love between them seemed eternal. Ava wondered what it was like to be with someone that long and still love them so deeply.

"Firstly, all of you are still welcome to stay here," Savina said. "But I know some of you have homes and families to whom you'd like to return. I assure you it is safe to do so. Also, I believe the young Enchanters—" her gaze swept over Ava, Peter, and the others— "will return to school on Monday."

Ava's jaw dropped. "School?"

A spoon clinked against a bowl, followed by a few murmurs of surprise. "Are you serious?" Thomas asked, his blue eyes flashing with irritation. He had become aggressive and angry ever since killing his father under the Cimmerians' influence, his old self almost unrecognizable. He ran a hand through his strawberry-blond hair.

"There is nothing we can do until you are all healed, and your powers have returned," Savina said. "Returning to school will keep you busy and give you something to focus on."

"We're supposed to go on acting is if nothing happened?" Ava asked.

"Ava," her dad warned.

Link leaned back in his chair with his arms crossed. "Can't we home school? I don't see the point in going back."

Natalia let out another exasperated sigh.

Aaron stood, his presence commanding the room into silence. He was always kind, but when he spoke, there was no mistaking the authority behind his words. "You will all listen to Savina. You will return to school because it is the right thing to do. There is nothing anyone can do until we are all ready to train again. You will obey these rules."

Great. She wasn't sure she could handle the stares or whispers at school. Students had been disappearing for months. Some died like Seth, Drew, and Jonah. And there were those who had left, like Valerie and Amanda. The Ephemerals had blamed Ava and the others for the bombing, and now they'd have to face that judgment once more.

"This will help strengthen your minds," Savina added.

Ava suppressed a sigh, her frustration bubbling to the surface. "I don't understand," she blurted. "Why can't we go after them now? By the time we get there, won't our powers be back?"

"Ava, enough," her father cautioned.

"We must be prepared before we leave," Aaron explained. "There will be no more discussion about this." His stern tone prevented her from arguing. "Furthermore, we will start training in the evenings, so you are welcome to join us."

Link crossed his arms. "How are we supposed to train without our powers?"

"You will learn fighting techniques useful with or without your abilities," Aaron said.

Lance and Thomas nodded in agreement, but Ava wasn't sure how training would help when she was so weak and powerless. But what choice did she have?

"That is all," Aaron said.

Everyone began to scatter from the table, but Ava couldn't make herself move. She needed to keep her emotions buried deep, far enough that Peter couldn't sense them. She had to learn to hide her feelings better. She needed Gabriel to teach her how.

Peter sighed beside her.

"Are you okay?" she asked, though she already knew the answer.

"I can't be here," he muttered, rubbing his eyes. "Would you be okay if I took your car home? I'll bring it back tomorrow." He no longer had a car since Ava had totaled his while driving back from the Halloween dance. An invisible Trudy McVaine had attacked her from the backseat, leaving Ava shaken and filled with guilt.

The tightness in her stomach returned. Why didn't he want her to drive him home? "Sure," she said. "You don't want any company?" She hoped for once he would say yes. She didn't want to be alone again tonight.

He shook his head, his expression distant. "I just want to be alone."

Ava tried to mask the disappointment that surged within her. "Yeah, of course."

"Sorry." He kissed her forehead, a gesture that once brought comfort, but now felt like a barrier between them. And just like that, he left.

Ava shut her eyes, taking deep, controlled breaths. She wouldn't cry. She couldn't let herself feel sad or disappointed, not now. Pushing herself to her feet, she left the dining room, hoping the fresh air would calm her.

Lance, Thomas, and Gillian stood near the stairs.

"Hey," she called, walking toward them.

Lance offered her a sad smile as he pulled her into a gentle hug. "Hey." His scruffy dark hair and tired brown eyes told her he wasn't doing much better.

Gillian stood next to Thomas, hugging herself. Her black curls were matted, and her big blue eyes were clouded with anger and sadness. Ava missed the cheerfulness Gillian used to radiate, the carefree innocence that had always made her feel lighter. Things had changed between them since Peter came into the picture, and Ava couldn't help but wonder if she had become the kind of girl who chose a boy over her friends. She vowed to herself she wouldn't let that happen. They had to find Jeremy and the others. She would do whatever it took to get them back. Who knew what Havok was doing to them?

"You all right, Ava?" Lance asked, pulling her from her thoughts.

She blinked, realizing she hadn't responded. "Yeah," she muttered. "What were you guys talking about?"

"Are you staying here?" Thomas asked. His muscular frame filled out his black sweater, and his hair brushed against the neckline.

Ava shrugged. "I don't really have much of a choice. What about you?"

"Yeah. My mom wants to stay with everyone, though I'd rather be anywhere else," Thomas replied, his irritation clear.

"Sorry, man," Lance said. "I think I'm gonna head home tonight."

Ava turned to Gillian. "What about you?"

Gillian's icy gaze met hers, and Ava felt a sting of hatred beneath it. Gillian turned on her heel and walked away.

Ava sighed, her fractured friendship pressing harder against her chest.

"Just give her time," Lance said.

She shook her head, needing to change the subject. "I can't believe they want us to go back to school. This is ridiculous."

Thomas rolled his eyes. "Seriously. What do they expect us to do?"

"I get it," Lance said. "But maybe it'll help. Or maybe I'm just hoping something will."

Thomas rubbed the back of his neck. "I'm gonna go check on my mom. See you guys later." He gave them a quick nod and walked away.

Lance turned back to Ava. "How's Peter doing?"

"Not great. I can't believe I dragged him into all of this."

"You didn't," he said. "He knew what he was getting into."

"Did he, though? Did he really understand? Because of me, all his friends are either dead or missing. He blames himself for not protecting everyone, and he can feel all the grief, all the time. It's eating him alive."

Lance frowned. "He hasn't had much time to adjust. Give him some space. He'll come around. Besides, they were going to come after him eventually, because of who he is."

Time. That was all everyone said to her these days. *Give it time, you just need more time.* Time to grieve. Time to get their powers back. Time to find their friends. She was sick of hearing the word. Time didn't fix anything.

"I hope you're right," she said.

After Lance left, Ava wandered back upstairs to her favorite spot in the Manor. The window bench, with its arched roof, felt like a small, enclosed haven. Sitting down, she peered out at the garden below, remembering Kira always tending to the flowers. Kira had been a bright spot, uplifting in every brief conversation they'd had. Now she was gone, too, taken like the others.

Ava sighed, clutching her necklace as the sense of Peter's remorse washed over her again. She was hurting him. She needed to stop.

A knock on the door startled her. "Come in."

Her father stepped into the room. "Hey, sweetie."

"Hey, Dad."

He closed the door behind him and crossed the room, sitting on the edge of her bed. "You know Savina's offered for everyone to stay here, but our apartment is ready if you'd rather move into it. I wanted to ask what you prefer."

She looked away, feeling torn. She wanted to leave, to escape the reminders of Colden, of her mistakes, but a part of her didn't want to abandon Gabriel and the others. Still, Peter was right. "I want to go."

"Are you sure?" her father asked. "It's safer here, and most of your friends are staying."

She shook her head. "Peter's right, Dad. Being here makes it worse."

Her father sighed. "I understand, Ava. But don't let this situation consume you. You blame yourself for Colden's death, but Savina said it was inevitable."

Ava nodded, but her heart didn't believe it. "I know. It's just ... I miss them all. I don't know how to make sense of any of it." Her throat constricted, and tears blurred her vision. Before she could stop them, they spilled over.

Her father moved beside her, wrapping his arm around her. "I miss them, too."

And for the first time in what felt like days, Ava allowed herself to cry into her father's shirt, her grief too much to hold back.

2

HURT

Ava turned the faucet to hot. Steam rose, curling into the air and fogging the antique oval mirror above the sink. The warm mist clung to her skin as she ran her hands under the stream of water. Staring at it, she fixated on the way it splashed into the porcelain basin and swirled down the drain. She wanted to move it, to bend it to her will like she had before.

But nothing happened.

Her brow furrowed in concentration as she tried harder, urging the water to lift, to ripple at her command. She focused on every drop, willing it to respond.

Still, nothing.

Ava sighed, gripping the edge of the counter until her knuckles turned white. *You can do this.* She took a deep breath, forcing herself to calm down. *Focus.* Her gaze traced the water's path again as it flowed into the sink with a mesmerizing rhythm. *Listen to it. Feel it.*

She moved her hand above the stream, her fingers trembling as she tried one last time to make it obey.

Nothing.

Her shoulders slumped, and frustration surged through her like a hot wave. She slammed the faucet shut, grabbed a towel, and dried her hands before flinging it at the mirror. The soft thud of fabric did little to ease the anger bubbling inside her.

She stared at her reflection in the fogged glass, barely able to make out the shape of her face. *What's wrong with me?*

She wanted to sleep, to escape the feeling of failure, but it was impossible. The Manor's grand halls felt suffocating, and the weight of everything that had happened crushed her with every step she took. There was one place that might bring her comfort tonight. A place where the world felt smaller, where she could think.

Ava made her way downstairs to the library, her footsteps swallowed by the thick silence of the house at this hour. The only light came from the blazing fire in the stone fireplace, casting a harsh, flickering glow across the towering shelves. Shadows clung to the walls, stretching like phantom memories, pulling her back to places she desperately tried to forget. She crossed the room and sank down onto the stone hearth, feeling the fire's heat seep into her skin, a comfort she couldn't quite hold onto. Without her powers, she was always cold. Tonight, even the heat from the fire couldn't reach the chill beneath her skin.

As she stared into the flames, they seemed to shift and morph, twisting into shapes that were achingly familiar. Luci's face flickered in the embers, her eyes cold, distant, until Ava heard her mother's voice, an echo that felt almost real. *This is your destiny. Join them.* The words were a whisper, yet they hit Ava with the force of a scream. A ripple of panic crawled through her. She shook her head, trying to push the image away, but Luci's betrayal clung to her, suffocating.

How could Luci promise her soul to Havok and still ask Savina to protect her?

Ava wrapped her arms around her knees, her fingers digging into her skin. But the memories surged forward, unstoppable. She was back in the flames of her own house fire, watching everything she'd ever known burn. Her mother's spirit appeared again, stepping through the fire with a serene, almost haunting expression. Ava's heartbeat thundered in her ears, a cold sweat prickling her skin despite the heat. She struggled to breathe, feeling trapped between the past and the present.

"Ava?"

She flinched, startled out of the memory, her gaze snapping to the figure beside her. Gabriel was there, sitting on the floor, his back against the hearth step, watching her with that steady, knowing gaze. He always seemed to pull her back from the edge, and this time was no different. Even when she wasn't sure she wanted him there, he was there.

"Can't sleep?" she asked.

"No. How are you holding up?" His voice was gentle, but there was an intensity in his eyes that made her look away, unable to hold his gaze.

Ava shrugged, hugging her knees to her chest. "Frustrated. Missing my friends. And Colden…" The loss was a blade that never dulled. It cut into her all over again.

"Me too," he whispered.

Her vision blurred with tears, and her necklace warmed. She lifted her head, trying to fight back the flood of emotions, but they surged forward like a wave she couldn't hold back.

"You don't have to hide it," he said. "It's okay to cry."

"It's not that. I need you to teach me to hide my feelings. I know you said it takes time, but I have to learn."

His brow furrowed, a shadow of concern darkening his expression. "Why the urgency?"

"I have to be strong for Peter and everyone else." She bit her lip, a fresh wave of guilt rising inside her. Peter already carried so much guilt. She couldn't let him feel her grief, too. It was easier to pretend, to bury it all, than to let him see the cracks in her façade.

He sighed, his eyes studying her with an understanding that made her feel exposed. "Ava, it's okay to let people see your emotions. It's okay to feel."

"You don't."

A rare flicker of vulnerability softened his crystal-blue eyes. "I do. I've just ... learned how to manage them. But it's not the same for everyone."

"Teach me how. Please."

"Why do you want to block it all out?"

"Because Peter feels ashamed every time I think of Colden or my friends. I don't want to make things harder for him."

"You aren't the one making it harder, Ava. Peter needs to learn that none of this is his fault. It wasn't his job to save everyone, especially in his first fight."

"But he still blames himself. And I ... I did this, Gabriel."

"No, you didn't. He made his choice."

"How do I block my feelings?" she asked, desperation creeping into her voice. "I need to do this for him. Please."

Gabriel's expression softened, a mix of empathy and something else. A sadness she couldn't quite place. He sighed, looking at her as though weighing his words. "It's not easy. It takes practice, and a certain willingness to let go of things … to push them aside, even if they're painful."

"Push them aside?"

He nodded, his gaze distant. "When emotions get overwhelming, I force myself to compartmentalize. It's like … locking things in a box, somewhere deep inside. I focus on the here and now, on the task in front of me, rather than letting feelings cloud my mind." His eyes flickered to the fire. "It's not that I don't feel them. I just don't let them out."

"But doesn't that make them worse?" She leaned closer. "How do you keep it all from breaking through?"

"Sometimes, it does break through. There are nights I … I can't sleep. Nights where the things I thought I'd buried come back, and it's like they never left." His voice grew softer, as if he were sharing a secret. "But I've learned to pull back when I feel it coming, to control my breathing, to focus on something else entirely."

Her heart ached at the vulnerability hidden in his words. "So, you're saying … it's a matter of will?"

He met her gaze, a flicker of sadness in his eyes. "It's a matter of survival. It's not easy, and it's not something I'd wish on anyone. But if you're determined to learn, I'll help you."

Her shoulders dropped as she took in his words. There was no magic fix, no spell to make the pain vanish. Only patience, control, and the strength to face it alone even when it felt impossible.

"You're strong. You'll figure it out."

She looked away, her gaze fixed on the fire, the flickering light stinging her eyes. "If I were strong, I wouldn't have ... killed Colden. I wouldn't have gone to a Necromancer for answers."

Gabriel reached for her hand. "You didn't kill him, Ava. You did what you had to for the answers. You shouldn't carry this guilt alone."

She swallowed hard. The steady strength of his hand calmed her. "But it cost lives."

"You're blaming yourself for the war?"

How could she answer that? How could she not?

"You didn't start this war. This was going to happen, no matter what."

"But I released Corbin."

"Corbin would have been released eventually, with or without you. You need to let that go before it tears you apart."

His words washed over her, a tide of truth she wasn't ready to face, but one she needed to hear. Inhaling deeply, the tension in her shoulders eased. Her focus sharpened. She had to get her powers back. She had to stop Havok. For Colden. For everyone.

"I miss Colden. I just wish I could talk to him."

"I miss him too. He and Aaron were like fathers to me."

"Really?"

"Yeah. Colden was selfless. Aaron's more ... rational, tough. But I've learned a lot from both of them."

She smiled. "I see a bit of both in you."

"I wasn't always this good at hiding my feelings, you know. There was a time when I couldn't control anything. My anger, my sadness, even my fear."

"You?"

He nodded as a sad smile crossed his face. "I lost someone … a long time ago. I shut everyone out, tried to pretend I didn't feel anything. It took me years to learn how to manage it. But I guess I never really stopped hiding."

Hearing Gabriel had cared so deeply for someone else sent an unexpected pang through her chest, but she pushed the feeling aside. "I'm sorry."

"Thanks. I just … wanted you to know that you're not alone in this. We've all been through things we don't always talk about."

His expression shifted almost like a shadow had passed over his face, a heaviness that wasn't there moments ago. She wasn't sure what it was, but she'd caught these glimpses of him before.

He was always so calm, so composed, but there were moments when she sensed something deeper lurking beneath that quiet exterior. Something guarded. She wondered what it was he wasn't telling her.

"You're not alone either, Gabriel," she said, meaning it with every fiber of her being.

He glanced at her, his lips curving into a faint smile, but it didn't quite reach his eyes. He looked down at his hands, his fingers tracing the grain of the stone beneath them. "Sometimes it feels like I am."

She wanted to ask him about it, to push him to open up. But she stopped herself. Gabriel was always there for her, though there was a part of him he kept hidden from everyone including her. Maybe that was why she felt drawn to him, why he was so different from anyone else. He understood her in ways that no one else did, yet there was a piece of him she couldn't quite reach.

He rubbed his hands together in a repetitive motion. She wondered what he was thinking or feeling, not that he ever showed it. She moved closer to him and caught his gaze. Her heart skipped a beat. She wasn't sure why it did that sometimes. He had a way of making her feel as though he could see right through her. She didn't know what it was about him that made him so familiar and comfortable to be around, but when he looked at her with such intensity, she had to avoid his gaze.

"How are you really?" she asked.

"I'm okay. I guess. I miss Colden, Joss, Maggie, and Kira.

"Do you think they're all okay?" she asked, hearing the hopefulness in her voice.

"They're alive."

Ava's chest tightened. She wanted to believe it, but the doubt lingered. "I just ... I don't know what we'll do if we can't get them back."

"We will."

She glanced down, feeling a pang of something she couldn't name. She didn't know when he'd become so important to her, but there he was, carrying her burdens even when she couldn't carry her own. "Thank you. You've been ... more than I deserve," she whispered.

He squeezed her hand, his gaze unwavering. "You never have to thank me, Ava. I'd like to think we've become good friends."

"We have. I hate that I've caused a rift between you and Natalia."

He rolled his eyes and smirked. "I can be friends with whomever I want. She and I have been friends for ages. She may not like you, but she'll get over it. And she would never stop being my friend because we're friends. She's not like that."

"Why have you stood beside me all this time?"

"Because even though you do dumb things, you care deeply and you're loyal. Believe it or not, you're a great friend and you're fun to be around."

Ava looked down at their intertwined hands, feeling a strange ache as she prepared to tell him. "I should head up and try to get some sleep. Tomorrow … my dad and I are moving into the apartment."

She expected Gabriel to nod, to offer some casual words of encouragement, but his hand went still against hers, and a shadow flashed across his face, there and gone before she could read it.

"You'll still be around sometimes, right?"

She bit her lip, feeling the pull between what she wanted and what she knew she needed to do. "I… I don't want to be here until my abilities come back."

Gabriel's gaze lowered, his fingers fidgeting with the edge of his sleeve. "At all?" His voice was controlled, though the heaviness in it made her pause.

"I can't … I can't face everyone here with what I've done. And seeing Colden … the battle … it's like all I see are my failure staring back at me."

He nodded slowly, but his silence spoke volumes.

She could see the quiet disappointment, a flicker of something deeper he held back.

When he met her eyes, he forced a small, understanding smile, but it didn't reach his eyes.

She didn't want to hurt him. She had lost so many people already, and the thought of distancing herself from someone who had been there for her felt … wrong. Even if she didn't feel like she deserved his support, she wasn't ready to lose it either.

"You're welcome to visit me … if you want."

His lips curved into a small smile, but it was tinged with something bittersweet. "Of course. If you don't feel like coming back, I'll train with you elsewhere. Or…" He paused, a faint vulnerability showing through. "We could just hang out."

Ava blinked at him, surprised at how much relief his offer brought her. She didn't know when she'd feel like herself again but knowing that Gabriel didn't expect her to be perfect … it made her feel a little less alone.

STARTING OVER

Mr. Hannigan set his suitcase down beside the door of their new apartment. The complex was large, with swimming pools, tennis courts, and a park for little kids. The landscaping was meticulously maintained with colorful flowers, but they didn't compare to the garden at the Manor or the rose bushes in front of Ava's old house.

He slid the key inside the lock and turned it. "Ready?"

Ava nodded, shifting her weight as she adjusted her bag on her shoulder. The breezeway was dark and cold, sending a shiver down her spine. She couldn't wait to get inside. Her eyelids were heavy from staying up all night with Gabriel, but the anticipation of stepping into a new chapter of her life kept her alert. "Yeah."

"You sure?" her father asked, his tone teasing.

She tilted her head and gave him a look. "Yes."

"I'm not hearing the enthusiasm." A playful smile tugged at his lips.

Rolling her eyes, Ava smiled back. "Dad, come on."

"That's better. Sort of." He pushed the door open and flicked on the light switch. The apartment opened up into a modest kitchen connected to a dining room, both covered in gray hexagonal tiles. They stepped into the living room, where a white fireplace stood with a space above it for a TV. A half bath was tucked off to the side, and the two bedrooms, each with their own bathroom, were located in the back.

It was nice, but it felt so compact, so small, almost claustrophobic compared to the Manor. It was a far cry from the openness and warmth of her old house.

They had no furniture yet, but her father had promised to furnish it by the weekend.

Ava crossed the living room to her new bedroom. Her heart sank. The room was small and plain, its beige walls stark and unfamiliar. She shouldn't complain. At least they had a place to call home. But standing there, she couldn't help but miss her old room with its familiar corners, the space where she'd grown up.

The memories of her old life, the house, her mother, flickered in her mind, but she pushed them away. After learning what her mother had done, after all the betrayals, Ava knew she had to let go. The apartment was a fresh start. It had to be.

After getting somewhat settled, Peter came over, and for the first time in what felt like ages, they cooked dinner together. Ava couldn't remember the last time they had done something so normal, something so … easy. Probably not since the summer before her powers manifested.

While they ate, the low hum of the TV filled the quiet between them.

"Can I talk to you?" Peter asked, breaking the comfortable silence.

Her father held a puzzled expression. "Sure."

Peter fidgeted with his napkin before speaking. "It's my dad. I'm running out of excuses, and I'm not sure what to tell him when we leave for Caprington. Did you ever tell your parents what you were? I'm scared he'll abandon me."

Taking a deep breath, her dad leaned back. "It was easier for me to hide it longer since I was in college, so there were times when I didn't talk to my parents. It was still hard, though. I had the same fears as you."

Peter's brow furrowed. "How'd you tell them?"

"I just sat them down and explained everything. I was patient when they asked questions. At first, my mom was scared but she accepted my choice. Dad took it a lot better than I ever imagined."

"What if my dad disowns me? I mean, how do I tell him I'm an Enchanter and oh yeah, I'm about to leave and may not come back?"

"Don't say that," Ava said.

"I have to look at every possibility," Peter replied, his voice edged with frustration. "This isn't some normal situation, Ava."

Her father leaned forward. "Your father loves you. I know these things can scare people, but I can't see him abandoning you."

Peter exhaled, the tension easing from his face a little. "I've gotta tell him the truth. I don't want to scare him, but what if I never make it back?"

"You can't think like that," her father said. "I'm sure he already has worries about something happening to you. That's what parents do. I can help talk to him if you'd like."

Peter nodded. "Thanks. That means a lot."

"Anytime."

After dinner, Ava and Peter retreated to her room, sitting against the wall on the floor. Ava drew her knees to her chest while Peter rested his arms on his knees. They had sat like that before, both eager to touch each other, but tonight felt different. The distance between them, and she didn't know how to bridge it.

"Why didn't you tell me about your fears?" she asked.

Peter's gaze stayed fixed on the floor. "I didn't want you to worry. You have too much to think about already."

"You can still talk to me."

"I know."

She hesitated, then reached for his hand. "Peter, you're brave. You've been through so much. Becoming an Enchanter, losing your friends, fighting in a war. Just keep being strong for your dad. He'll love you no matter what."

A wave of emotion surged from Peter, and his lips were on hers. She pulled him closer, trying to hold onto the connection, but another feeling intruded. Gillian's anger, sharp and biting.

He broke away. "We shouldn't do this."

"Peter—"

"I don't want to upset anyone." He ran a hand through his hair, frustration clouding his expression.

"She can't dictate what we do. You have to ignore her."

"I can't. It's hard enough that I blame myself."

Ava reached for him again, and he drew her close, draping an arm over her shoulder.

"Every minute I'm with you, I want to hold you," he said. "But then I feel guilty, because others can't be with the people they love."

She rested her head on his chest. "I spent so much time hiding my feelings for you before. Now that we're together, I don't want to do that anymore. We shouldn't have to."

"I know," he murmured. "But her anger is always there, cutting in. It kills the mood, knowing she blames me."

"She's always been angry with us. But she can't stop me from loving you."

Peter kissed her again, but the affection had faded. "I wouldn't want your dad to walk in on us anyway," he teased, but his tone was distant.

"Do you think we're being selfish?"

He paused, not meeting her eyes. "Part of me thinks we're not. But the other part…" He trailed off. "Maybe we should talk to Savina."

"I don't want to go back. Not until I have my powers."

Peter's guilt surged through their connection, sharp and overwhelming.

"Peter, don't."

"Sorry." He jumped to his feet. "I need to go."

Her heart sank. "Why?"

"I really need to talk to my dad."

"Right now?"

"Yeah."

"I'll come with you," she offered.

He held her face between his hands. "I appreciate that. But I think this is something I need to do on my own."

"Okay."

Walking him out to his car, Ava shivered as the cold wind swept over her. Peter wrapped his arms around her, warming her.

"It'll be okay," she whispered, though she wasn't sure if she believed it herself.

"I might need to hear that more often. Will you be okay tonight?"

"Yeah, I'll be fine," she lied, not wanting to admit how much she needed him to stay. She kissed him. "I'll see you tomorrow."

As soon as he released her, the cold returned. He drove away, and a hollow ache settled deep in her chest. For a moment, she thought about texting Gabriel, but she shook the thought away. *He wouldn't want to hang out with me like this.*

She turned back to the empty apartment, her footsteps echoing off the walls. The silence in her room was suffocating. She missed Melissa's playful comments, missed the sound of Joss's laughter. Missed Jeremy's talks.

Sighing, Ava spread out the flannel sleeping bag and curled up inside, feeling the loneliness close in around her like the walls themselves were crowding. She took a deep breath, forcing herself to bury her grief, her loneliness, the gnawing self-hatred that seemed to grow each day. She pushed it down until there was nothing left but a hollow ache.

Ava bit her lip as she hesitated before the door. The hallway behind her seemed to stretch into darkness, but the pull to enter was irresistible. She pushed the door open. The room was dim, the curtains drawn, suffocating any light. A stale, cold air lingered.

Colden lay in the bed, bundled beneath layers of blankets, his pale face nearly swallowed by pillows. He'd always looked delicate, but now he was drenched in sweat, his eyes bloodshot from illness.

Tears streamed down her face.

"Ava," his voice was barely a whisper, but it still carried that familiar warmth. "Do not cry, my dear."

"I did this to you," Ava sobbed. "I'm so sorry."

"Do not blame yourself. It is my time." His hand reached out to her, pale and shaking.

She hesitated but took his cold fingers in hers. A shiver ran down her spine. No matter how hard she tried, she couldn't warm herself.

His eyes softened for a moment, but something changed. Slowly, his expression shifted. His gaze grew darker, more sinister. The corners of his lips stretched into an unnatural grin.

Her heart raced as she tried to pull her hand away, but his grip tightened.

"Your soul belongs to me, Ava." Colden's voice was gone, replaced by Havok's deep, rasping tone. "I have your mother to thank for that."

Her blood ran cold. She yanked harder, trying to break free from Havok's grasp, but his hand was like iron. His menacing grin widened as he dragged her closer, his breath hot against her skin.

The room plunged deeper into darkness, shadows contorting and writhing like living creatures. She screamed, but no sound came out. She was trapped. His hold was unbreakable. Panic surged through her as she fought to escape, but there was no escape.

Havok's eyes glinted with malice as he whispered, "You'll never be free."

4

SLIPPING AWAY

Gray light seeped through the blinds, barely cutting through the darkness of the room. Heavy clouds crowded the sky, casting the world in a somber, unrelenting gloom. Rain tapped against the window in a steady rhythm, the sound filling the silence that hung thick in the air.

The sleeping bag rustled as Ava shifted, her back stiff and cheeks damp. She blinked, disoriented, her body aching from another night on the floor. She rose and crossed to the window, peeking through the blinds. Black clouds gathered in layers, swallowing any trace of the sun. It had been days since the world had seen light. Only this endless, oppressive rain.

When will it ever stop?

The memory of the dream, Colden's pale sickness followed by Havok's menacing smile, left a knot of tension in her chest. The pain of losing Colden, of everything she had done, threatened to overwhelm her again. But she couldn't let it. She wouldn't. *What would Melissa do?*

Ava took a deep breath, remembering what Gabriel had taught her. *Breathe in, breathe out.* Focus on something else, on the present. She could almost hear Melissa's upbeat voice in her head, telling her to shake it off, that today was a new day, and that she could handle anything. She had to be strong for Peter.

With trembling hands, she tried to channel that energy, pushing down the wave of emotion that threatened to overtake her. *No time for tears. I'm stronger than this.*

The sounds of dishes clinking together in the kitchen gave her something tangible to focus on. She decided to join her dad.

Ava stood up, straightened her shoulders, and took a deep breath. "Come on, Ava," she whispered to herself. "You've got this."

It was what Melissa would have said, and Ava repeated it in her mind, over and over, as if saying it enough times might make it true.

As soon as she made her way to the kitchen, her dad looked up from stirring his coffee. "Good morning."

"Morning," she replied, trying to push a bit of warmth into her voice.

"I thought maybe we could go furniture shopping today."

"That would be great. I'm too old for a sleeping bag." She forced a laugh, the sound hollow even to her own ears.

Her dad chuckled and shook his head. "You've been eighteen for all of two weeks."

"The last few weeks have felt like several years."

"I know. Get dressed and we'll go."

They spent most of the day shopping, and for a few hours, Ava enjoyed herself. Being with her father kept her mind off everything—Colden, her powers, and the darkness that always seemed to be creeping in. Peter came over later, and they all had dinner together again.

"How did it go?" she asked Peter once they were inside her room.

Peter leaned against the wall, his expression tired but lighter than usual. "Pretty awkward and stressful in the beginning. But the more we talked, the better it got." He gave her a small smile. "You were right, though. It was okay."

Ava smiled and hugged him. "I'm proud of you."

"Thanks." He pulled away too soon. "Nice room, by the way."

"Thanks." She looked around at the new full-size bed and matching dresser. It wasn't much, but it was cozy, and she felt a small sense of pride in the new space. "Wanna watch a movie?"

"Yeah, sounds great."

She put on a random comedy and curled up next to him on the bed. They didn't touch more than cuddling, and she tried to focus on the movie. But all she wanted was to feel something other than grief. *Maybe if I hold him tighter...* She took a deep breath, forcing the negative thoughts down. But she had to be patient and strong for him. He needed time.

Peter groaned beside her, rubbing his face. He looked drained, his eyes red-rimmed and tired. His exhaustion radiated off him, and her heart sank. She missed the way he used to smile, missed the way his eyes would light up when he saw her. Now they only held sadness, and Ava couldn't help but feel it was her fault. She had dragged him into this life, into this mess.

"Morning," he yawned.

"Morning. Did you sleep well?"

"Not really."

"I'm sorry."

"For what?" He raised an eyebrow.

"Making you sleep here when you could've been in your own bed."

He sighed. "I don't mind. I probably wouldn't have slept any better at home."

She studied him, searching for any trace of the boy she'd fallen in love with. She leaned over and kissed him, needing to feel close, even if for a moment.

He hesitated, his lips unmoving at first, but he eased her down, his hands moving to her sides.

A flicker of hope sparked in Ava's chest. Maybe it would help, maybe it would bring them back to where they were before everything fell apart. She kissed him harder, desire flooding through her as his hands slid across her stomach. She shivered, craving that connection, wanting to lose herself in him and forget everything else.

His lips grazed above her collarbone, then up to neck. Her heart couldn't find a steady rhythm. She reached to remove her top, but he stopped her.

"Ava." He hesitated.

"It's okay." She lifted her top above her head, trying to keep the moment alive.

But his body tensed, and the warmth between them vanished.

Ava felt it too. Gillian's anger, sharp and bitter, flooded through the connection.

Peter rolled back onto his knees, rubbing his face in frustration.

Ava's heart sank, and she quickly pulled her top back down, masking the sting of rejection. She knew what he was about to say before he spoke.

"We shouldn't do this."

"Peter—"

"We should get ready for school."

She nodded, swallowing her disappointment. *Push it down.*

The silence between them was thick with everything they weren't saying. Peter stood, moving toward the door as if the tension was too much to bear.

"Ava, I don't think we should do this anymore." His voice was heavy with guilt

Her heart stopped. "Do what?"

"You know. Kiss ... touch each other. I just can't stand feeling everyone's sadness and anger. It's too much, and with Seth gone ... I just can't."

Ava clenched her teeth, fighting against the lump rising in her throat. *Why am I losing him?* "Okay."

Peter crossed the room and caressed her cheek. "I love you, Ava. I swear it has nothing to do with you. I just need time to grieve, to figure out how to block these feelings."

"I know." She swallowed the tears.

He pressed a quick kiss to her lips and turned to leave. "I'll be out here."

As the door closed, Ava stood frozen in place, the hollowness in her chest expanding, pressing into every part of her. She wanted to cry, to scream, but instead, she took a deep breath and forced it all down. She couldn't afford to fall apart. Not now.

Dressed in a thick blue sweater and jeans, she slipped her feet into boots that came up to her knees. She wrapped a scarf around her neck and pulled a beanie over her head. *It's so weird to be wearing so much.* She couldn't remember the last time she cared about being warm. Back when life was simpler, before powers, before battles, before grief.

She walked out of her room, and her dad leaned against the kitchen counter, sipping coffee. Peter stood by the door, his hands tucked into his pockets, looking as tired as she felt.

"Good morning." Her father eyed her.

"Morning." She hoisted her backpack on her shoulder. "I'll see you later."

"Ava?" Her father stopped her as she reached for the door.

"I'll warm up the car," Peter suggested and walked outside.

"What's up?" Ava turned to her dad.

"I know things have been hard lately." He hesitated, trying to find the right words. "But I'm not too keen on Peter staying overnight. At least not in the same room."

He didn't seem to mind when we stayed at the Manor. Then again, maybe he never realized they stayed in the same room. "Dad, nothing's going on. It's okay."

Her father raised an eyebrow, his expression firm. "He sleeps on the couch, Ava."

"Okay," she muttered, irritated but knowing Peter wouldn't care since he didn't want to touch her anyway. "Is that all?"

"Yeah. Have a good day." His tone softened as he added, "I love you."

"I love you too, Dad." She hugged him and headed outside. The cold hit her like a wall, biting through her clothes as she slid into the passenger seat of Peter's car.

"Everything okay?" he asked, his breath fogging the air as he glanced at her.

"Yeah." She took off her beanie, tousling her red hair. "My dad doesn't like us staying in the same room."

"After this morning, can you blame him?"

She rolled her eyes. "He says you have to sleep on the couch. I don't think he realizes how much it helps having you there." She stared out the window, biting the inside of her cheek. *It's the only time I feel remotely okay.*

Peter took her hand, his touch warm but distant. "I know. It helps me too. But your dad's just looking out for you. Making sure I behave," he said with a lopsided grin, trying to lighten the mood.

"I guess you'll be behaving from now on," she muttered, her gaze still fixed outside. *I'm the one who needs you. Why can't you see that?*

He sighed. "Ava, please try to understand."

"I'm trying. But it feels like you're punishing me."

"I told you not to take it personally. It's hard for me to concentrate on being with you like that when Gillian's anger consumes me. Or Lance's depression. They can sense us too, Ava. They feel what we feel for each other, and it hurts them. It just ... feels wrong."

She swallowed her anger, her heart aching with pain. *What about what I need?* Being with Peter was the only thing that helped her forget the endless pain inside, but how could she say that without sounding selfish?

"We'll get through this."

She nodded but couldn't shake the feeling that things were falling apart. "We could always skip today," she suggested, almost desperate to cling to the one thing that made her feel grounded—being with him.

"Let's just see how it goes. We only have a few weeks until winter break."

"I don't want to go," she groaned, slumping back in her seat.

"No one does. But maybe it'll help keep our minds off everything."

The almost bare trees and buildings blurred into streaks as they drove. The thought of school felt so far removed from her life now. What was the point? She couldn't even remember what they were studying. *The last time I went, Trudy tried to kill Peter's friends, and Savina had to erase their minds.* She chewed her lip, resentment bubbling beneath the surface. *And now we're just supposed to pretend like none of that happened?*

Her mind drifted to the Ephemerals. They still hated her. Berated her for wearing her necklace and for her supposed involvement in the bombing. *They have no idea what's really going on. They didn't even know I killed two of them.*

Ava shook her head, staring out the window. Maybe she'd go today but skip the rest of the week. What difference would it make? She didn't want to be around the Ephemerals, and she didn't want to be reminded of everything she'd lost.

As Peter pulled into the parking space, Link and Nicole were waiting for them.

"Hey." Link stubbed out a cigarette. His blond hair had grown into a shaggy mess, and stubble shadowed his face. Link had never been so rough around the edges, but Ava guessed being kidnapped by Cimmerians, forced to become an Enchanter, then thrown into war would change anyone.

"Since when do you smoke?" Ava asked.

Nicole rolled her eyes, tucking a few strands of hair behind her ear. "He just started."

"Takes the edge off."

Ava glanced at the building while students shuffled inside as though nothing had happened. Just last week, she'd been warring against dark Enchanters, and now she was back at school, like it was any other day.

"Would Savina really notice us not being at school?" Link asked.

"Probably not," Ava said. "She's been holed up for a while."

"What else are we going to do?" Peter asked. "Sit around and think?"

"Good point," Link muttered.

As they walked inside the brick building, the sudden rush of heat hit Ava like a wave. She walked beside Peter, and they moved through the familiar gray corridor, the red lockers on both sides almost mocking her with their normalcy. Students leaned against them, chatting, laughing, ignoring Ava and her friends for the most part. Quite the contrast from the past few months.

Lance, Thomas, and Gillian stood frozen, staring at something. Whatever it was, it upset Gillian.

When they reached the group, Ava's stomach twisted. A few lockers had been decorated with notes, flowers, and mementos. Gillian covered her mouth, her shoulders trembling as she tried to contain her sobs. Ava knew why. Gillian had convinced Trent to shoot up a mall and then kill himself, manipulated by the Cimmerians. Ava's gaze moved to Drew and Jonah's lockers, bile rising in her throat as the memories clawed their way to the surface. Fighting to keep it in, she gritted her teeth.

"Oh my God," Gillian whispered before breaking into a run, heading toward the bathroom.

Ava wanted to follow her, but Peter's rage hit her like a blast of heat, surging through their connection.

"Should I go after her?" Nicole asked, glancing between them.

"Yeah. You guys go ahead," Ava said. Nicole nodded, and the others followed her down the hall.

Peter lunged for the locker, his movements violent, tearing the notes and pictures from it. His foot shot out, kicking the flowers into the air. "They didn't know him!" he screamed, his voice raw and filled with fury.

Several students stopped to stare, their eyes wide, whispers already starting. Ava's heart raced. She'd seen Peter upset before, but not like this.

"Stop, Peter. You're scaring me." She reached for his arm, but he jerked away from her, his eyes wild with grief.

He didn't stop until the locker was stripped bare. Torn pictures, ripped notes, and shattered flowers littered the hallway.

Ava's breath caught in her throat. She didn't know what to say. The onlookers began to move on as Peter slumped against the locker, his forehead resting on the cold metal. He took deep, shuddering breaths.

She reached for his hand again, and this time he let her take it, his fingers trembling.

"Sorry," he rasped.

Wrapping her arms around him, she held him close, but his grief pressed down on both of them. "It's okay," she whispered, though deep down, she wasn't sure if it was. She didn't know how to help him. Didn't know if she could.

"No one knew Seth. Not like I did. So why would they leave that stupid stuff on his locker? Saying how much they'll miss him and how they were such good friends. They knew nothing."

Her chest ached as she looked into his eyes. He was unraveling. "We'll get through this. You and me." But even as the words left her mouth, doubt gnawed at her. *Will we really get through this?* It felt like everything was slipping away, and she didn't know how to stop it.

The bell rang, shattering the fragile moment between them.

"I'll see you at lunch," Peter muttered, his tone distant, like he was already pulling away.

Ava's heart sank like a stone in water as Peter walked away. Would they survive this?

Sitting through English wasn't any better than sitting at the Manor. Ava stared at the empty seat in front of her, the one Drew Foley used to occupy. A sharp pain gripped her stomach. He and Jonah were dead because of her. *I killed them.* It had been self-defense, but the knowledge never made her regret go away.

Time crawled by, each second an eternity as the teacher's monotonous lecture on *The Great Gatsby* tortured her. Ava couldn't care less about the green light or what it symbolized. *What's the point of school when we should be searching for the rest of the coven?* But they were stuck waiting. Stuck until their powers returned and they were strong enough to fight again. Ava hated the waiting. It meant doing nothing. And doing nothing meant thinking and overanalyzing.

Whispers floated from the group of students nearby, their voices low but not low enough for Ava to miss.

"Maybe they joined Xavier," one girl said.

"Totally into drugs," a boy whispered. "I mean, look at her. She totally looks drugged out."

"Maybe Melissa and Jeremy had to go to rehab," another girl added.

The boy laughed, and Ava clenched her fists under her desk. Her necklace warmed against her chest, reacting to her anger. *How dare they?* Their cruel words cut deeper than she wanted to admit. The Ephemerals had always acted like they were better than her, and it still hurt, no matter how much she tried to tune them out.

When the bell rang, Ava gathered her things and hurried to her next class. *I will not cry. I won't give them the satisfaction.* She slid into her seat and put her head down on the desk. It was all too much—the noise, the whispers, the constant pretending that everything was fine. Her necklace warmed again. *Peter.* He was always there, his emotions pressing in on hers.

After class, she found Peter, and together they walked to the cafeteria where Gillian, Thomas, Lance, Nicole, and Link were already seated. Ava hoped for a brief moment of peace, but the tension was there.

Gillian looked up from her untouched salad and glared at Peter. "I can't believe you're sitting here." Her short curly hair frizzed around her face like she hadn't bothered to brush it.

Ava had thought things would be better between Gillian and Peter, now that the Cimmerians' manipulation had been exposed. But it was worse. Much worse.

Guilt radiated from Peter, and Ava took his hand, but he pulled away. "Lay off, Gillian."

Gillian narrowed her eyes, her glare cutting through Ava.

"It wasn't your fault." Lance tore up a napkin.

"How can you say that?" Gillian spat. "It was his job to protect everyone, and he failed."

Thomas leaned back in his chair, his large feet propped up on the swivel chairs. "Would you give it a rest?"

Link shook his head. "Instead of blaming him, can't you be glad that the rest of us are here?"

Gillian turned her glare to Link. "Yeah, I'm thrilled. Everyone else is here while these two rub their happiness in our faces."

Ava sighed. "We aren't rubbing it in your face. I'm sorry that you're hurting, Gillian, but I'm not sorry for how I feel about Peter."

"You're so selfish, Ava."

"Gillian, enough," Lance snapped. "Just stop, okay? They haven't done anything wrong. You can't sit here and say you wouldn't do the same if Jeremy were here."

Lance's words silenced the table. No one spoke, no one ate. The tension in the air was thick and suffocating.

After what felt like an eternity, the bell sounded. Gillian stood up, fixing Ava with a glare. "Don't bother sitting with us tomorrow. Or ever again."

Ava's anger surged, her heart pounding. "You need to chill out. This wasn't Peter's fault."

"He was brought into this because of his protection ability. Not because of your stupid love for each other," Gillian snapped. "And now, he's useless. We all are, because he couldn't do his job."

Ava's vision blurred with fury. "You are such a bitch, Gillian. I can't stand this anymore. You blame everyone else for everything that's gone wrong, but we've all lost someone. Not just you."

"Yeah." Gillian's eyes filled with tears. "And you're the reason Colden's dead. You started the war. And now Jeremy's gone, and who knows what's happened to him." She stormed off.

A painful tightness gripped Ava's chest. *I can't do this anymore.* Her necklace warmed as the anger coursed through her, hot and violent. She grabbed the nearest lunch tray and hurled it across the cafeteria. It slammed onto the floor, food scattering everywhere.

"Hey!" a cafeteria worker shouted. "Clean that up!"

Ava glared at her, her blood boiling. "You clean it up. Isn't that your job?"

"Do you want detention?" the woman snapped.

"Is that supposed to teach me a lesson?"

"Ava," Peter warned.

"Go to the principal's office," the woman said, her eyes narrowing.

"Make me," Ava retorted.

The woman stared at her. "What's your name?"

"Ava Hannigan. Want me to write it down for you?"

"Sorry. I'll take her." Peter grabbed Ava by the arm and pulled her outside. He spun her around. "What the hell was that?"

Ava shrugged, the cold air hitting her face. "What? I thought it was funny."

"Why did you do that?"

"Are you really mad at me?"

"Why did you do that?"

"Because I can't take this anymore!" Ava exploded. "I'm so tired of Gillian blaming us for everything. And I feel like things are changing between us. Don't you feel it too?"

Peter's expression softened, his anger fading. With a gentle push, he pressed her back to the brick wall. "You can't listen to her. You know how I feel about you."

"I know, but I need to *feel* it, Peter. I need to know we're okay. You're the only thing keeping me together right now. Don't take that away."

"I'm going through a lot, too. Maybe from now on, we'll sit at our own table, away from Gillian."

"I'm not coming back. School isn't helping. It's just making everything worse."

"You're not even trying."

She looked away. She knew she was being ridiculous

Peter studied her, his expression thoughtful. "I have an idea." He took her hand in his. Ava hesitated but let him lead the way.

Peter drove down the two-lane road toward Blackhart Manor. Ava tensed, her mind racing. She wasn't ready to go back. But before she could object, he turned left, pulling the car to a stop in front of a familiar wooden cabin.

The last time she'd been there was the morning she woke up possessed. The memory of it was like being trapped inside a glass box. She'd witnessed everything her body did, but she couldn't stop it. Couldn't scream. Couldn't reach Peter. She remembered screaming for him in her mind, desperate for him to save her. But he couldn't hear her. *No one could.* Being possessed was a nightmare, and the disappointment from her father, Savina, and Gabriel had made it worse.

As they exited the vehicle, the barren woods surrounding them fell into an eerie quiet. Ava followed Peter, her heart beating faster the closer they got. Leaves were sparse on the trees, except for the pine needles that dotted the evergreens. The sound of crashing water grew louder, cutting through the silence. Peter pushed through the branches, and the waterfall came into view.

It was as beautiful and calming as she remembered. Water cascaded into the deep, clear pool below, surrounded by rocks and boulders. The ground beneath them was soft and damp from all the rain, leaves and pine straw embedded into the earth.

"I want to try something." Peter brought her closer. He leaned over a rock and dipped his hand into the water. Ava hugged herself as a gust of wind swept through the clearing. A few seconds later, he looked up at her, grinning, his eyes bright with excitement.

"What?" Her heart fluttered in response to his smile.

"Take off your coat. And scarf. And gloves," he instructed, already pulling off his shirt.

Ava removed her layers, her body trembling with the chill. The tank top under her sweater offered little protection from the wind, but she trusted Peter. He took her hand, and heat spread through her, soothing her like a blanket.

Her heart pounded in her chest as Peter led her toward the water, guiding her over the slippery rocks.

He edged into the pool, still holding her hand. As Ava stepped in after him, the freezing water took her breath away. But, seconds later, it turned warm, wrapping her in a comforting embrace.

He wrapped his arms around her as the waterfall sprayed them both, pulling her to the center of the pool. "I know being around water makes you feel better." His lopsided grin returned. "I remember the first time you took me to the beach, and you made the water warm for me. Thought I'd return the favor."

Ava smiled, the warmth sinking into her bones as she closed her eyes. The calm settled in, pushing back the storm of emotions inside her. "Are you making it warm, or protecting me from the cold?"

"Both?"

Her smile widened as she rested her head against his shoulder. It was ages since she had felt even a semblance of tranquility. "Thank you," she whispered. "Thank you."

Peter kissed her, his lips soft against hers, and for a moment, the world around them disappeared. "Anything for you," he murmured against her lips. "I can't take away all your pain, but I'll do whatever I can. And I'm sorry about this morning. I've just had so much going on, but you're right. We can keep each other together."

She kissed him again, her heart swelling with gratitude, though deep down, the guilt still lingered. *How can I feel this happy, even for a moment, when everything is falling apart?*

They swam together, laughing as Peter held her close, the water flowing around them, warm and inviting. For now, she let herself forget, let herself be there with him. They crossed behind the waterfall to a rock ledge that curved inward like a shallow cave. Pulling themselves out of the water, they lay on the cool rocks, their bodies pressed close. He wrapped his arm around her, his breath tickling her hair as he held her.

"Can we come here every day instead of school?" Ava asked.

"I wish. Maybe after school."

"I'm not going back."

"Yes, you are. I'm going to need you there with me."

"Then skip with me," she teased, though there was a hint of seriousness in her tone.

He chuckled. "We should do what the Elders want. They seem to know what's best."

"They just don't know what to do with us. I probably got myself suspended anyway."

"I'm sure the lady won't mention it to the principal. But you can't lash out like that."

"I know." Ava sighed, staring up at the sky through the mist of the waterfall. "Gillian just got to me."

Peter kissed the top of her head. "You've got to work on your anger."

Ava held back a response, feeling a small pang of hurt. *Maybe he's right,* she thought, even though his words stung. It wasn't easy keeping all of the emotions bottled up inside. He seemed to be managing his own struggles better than she was, and now he was telling her she needed to do the same.

I'm making everything harder for him. She was leaning on Peter for stability, for comfort, for everything. But he had his own burdens to bear, and she wasn't helping.

She felt awful, like she was drowning in guilt. *I need to stop relying on him so much. I need to bury my emotions better, keep it all together.*

Swallowing the rising lump in her throat, she forced herself to smile at him. "Yeah, I'll work on it." Though she wasn't sure how much longer she could hold everything in.

5

GOING UNDER

The nightmares left Ava shaken, flashes of Colden's death and Havok's menacing grin lingering even as she lay awake. The few times she slept, fragments of Melissa's capture haunted her. She needed to find a spell, something to take the nightmares away, but there wasn't time to think about herself. She forced herself out of bed, hoping that making it through another day at school would make her feel better. Besides, Peter had promised they'd go to the waterfall, and she doubted he'd follow through if she didn't show up.

Her father stood in the kitchen, scrutinizing a box of waffles with a suspicious look. "Waffles?"

"No, thanks." Ava forced a smile back, fighting the urge to tell him she wasn't hungry.

"Good, because I think they're expired." He tossed the box into the trash with a chuckle, then glanced over. "How was school yesterday?"

"It's ... school." She leaned against the counter. "Not easy showing my face there."

"I know it's hard, but sitting here all day would only make it worse."

A knock at the door ended the conversation. Peter.

With a quick kiss on her father's cheek, Ava grabbed her bag and left. She willed herself to feel lighter, telling herself today she'd let the rumors roll off her.

At lunch, they sat with the group, minus Gillian. Ava dropped in the seat beside Peter. Her gaze landed on Lance. Dark circles shadowed his eyes, and his easygoing demeanor was weighed down by exhaustion. She hated seeing him like this, seeing any of them like this. They were all suffering in different ways, carrying their own invisible burdens. She wished she could do something to take away their pain, even though her own felt overwhelming.

But she kept her expression neutral, determined to stay strong for them. They didn't need her adding to their grief, and she couldn't let them see how much it was eating at her too.

"Where's G?" she asked.

"Stayed home. Said she wasn't feeling well," Lance said.

"Should we check on her?"

"She'll be fine."

A wry grin tugged at Thomas's lips as he leaned in. "So, did you really punch the lunch lady yesterday?"

Ava groaned. "No, I threw a tray."

Thomas barked out a laugh. "Even better."

"Gillian pissed me off, okay? She's just ... overdoing it."

Lance frowned. "She's hurting, Ava. Jeremy's gone. She's dealing with it in her way."

"I lost Jeremy too."

Thomas cut in, "Let's all go to the Manor tonight. It'll be good for us. What do you say?"

She shook her head. "No."

"Why not?"

"I just don't want to."

The bell saved her from more questions, and as the others left, Nicole lingered, giving her a soft smile. "If you ever need to talk, I'm here. I know things have been hard."

Ava nodded, touched by her kindness. She envied Nicole's sense of purpose. "Thanks. I hope training goes well."

"I'll let you know." Nicole smiled again before leaving.

As she walked away, Ava couldn't shake the feeling that everyone was moving forward, while she was stuck unable to face the past, but too broken to look toward the future.

When they reached the waterfall, the air was crisp and the water colder than the day before. Ava waded in, the chill biting through her skin. She took Peter's hand as he eased her into the water, but she let go after a moment.

"I want to try this alone," she said.

Peter hesitated. "Are you sure? You could start by just warming yourself up. You can—"

"No, I want to go under."

He didn't protest, though concern lingered in his eyes.

She ducked her head beneath the water. The cold swallowed her, pressing against her skin like icy needles. Taking a breath felt wrong. The water rushed into her nose, burning her throat and chest as she fought to rise back up, gasping and choking, the sharp pain spreading through her lungs.

He pulled her to the shore. "Are you okay?"

"I'm fine." She forced the words out, though they felt tight in her throat. *What's wrong with me?* She took a breath, swallowing her disappointment. *Push it down. Don't let him feel it.*

They stayed as the sun sank lower, casting long shadows over the pool, but nothing worked. Ava tried making herself warm, tried moving the water. Anything. Everything slipped through her fingers, the frustration building with every failed attempt.

"Don't get discouraged, Ava," Peter said as they walked back to the car. "It could be too soon to try. Why don't we come back tomorrow?"

"Okay." The word tasted hollow, her hope diminishing with every step.

Each day after school, they'd head to the waterfall, and every attempt was another failure. And lately, Peter seemed to cut their time there shorter and shorter. He'd glance at his watch, offer a rushed excuse, and suggest they try again tomorrow. Ava's disappointment built, but she buried it, unwilling to let her frustration seep through their connection. She couldn't blame him, she told herself he was dealing with so much already. Still, the sessions felt like they were slipping away, like he was.

One evening, after another fruitless attempt, Peter glanced over at her as they climbed into the car. "Why don't we go to the Manor tonight? Maybe Savina can help."

Ava's hands went cold. "I'm not ready."

He started the engine and turned on the heat, casting her a sidelong glance. "Would you be upset if I went? I'll come back afterward."

She swallowed hard, fighting the flare of anger. It hurt that he wanted to go, but she couldn't stop him. "No."

"Are you sure?"

"Yes."

Push it down. Bury it.

When she got home, her father had dinner ready, but she barely touched it, escaping to her room as soon as she could. The silence pressed in around her, amplifying the ache of Peter's absence.

She flicked on the bathroom light. The blue shower curtain and matching towels felt foreign, and a wave of longing washed over her. She missed the candles and Monet paintings from her old bathroom. She missed everything that used to feel like home.

Turning on the shower, she sat on the edge of the tub, her chest tightening as tears threatened. When they came, they flooded over her, overwhelming and unstoppable. She stepped into the shower, letting the hot water pour over her, muffling her sobs. It was the first time she'd allowed herself to cry since that terrible night. The water soothed her, but it couldn't wash away the ache inside.

She dressed in black pajamas and curled up under her blankets, the emptiness around her thick and suffocating. She checked her phone for messages, though she didn't expect any.

A text appeared.

Why don't skeletons ever fight each other?

Ava blinked, wiping her eyes as she opened the message. Gabriel. A mix of surprise and relief flooded her.

Because they don't have the guts.

She smiled despite herself, the tension in her chest easing. She typed back, *you're such a dork,* but hesitated, deleting it and setting her phone aside. She would talk to him later. Just ... not tonight.

A few hours later, she woke to Peter standing over her. His eyes were bloodshot, his face drawn. "Hey." She smiled.

"Hey." He kissed her, a brief touch, then lay beside her with a heavy sigh.

Even as he held her, Ava felt the distance. She sensed the weariness and sadness he was carrying, the growing chasm between them. "What's wrong?"

"Just tired." He rubbed his eyes. "I was practicing with Gustav and Aaron. It's ... frustrating."

"How so?"

"I can handle things when I'm prepared. But if I get caught off guard ... I lose control." He paused. "What if I let everyone down again? What if ... I lose you?"

"You won't."

"Katarina was helping me tonight. She says she has to turn her feelings off. It becomes a job to protect people. But I can't just turn it off like she does."

Ava's heart broke at the fear in his voice. She leaned in, kissing him, desperate to bridge the distance. But even as she pulled him closer, the emptiness remained, an invisible wall she couldn't break through.

Over the next few weeks, their lives fell into a rhythm. School, the waterfall, and evenings with her father or Peter's dad. Every night, Peter asked her to join him at the Manor, and every night, she said no. She didn't feel ready, and the more he pushed, the more she resisted.

On one of the coldest days, she let go of Peter's hand at the waterfall. "I want to try by myself today."

"Ava…" He reached for her, but she pulled away.

"No." She took a deep breath, fighting the biting cold that spread through her body. *You can do this.* But the chill overwhelmed her.

Peter's concerned gaze burned into her. "Ava, stop."

"No." *Concentrate. You can do this.*

"For chrissakes, your lips are blue." His hands wrapped around hers, filling her with warmth, but the cold inside her lingered, sinking deep into her bones.

"It's not working," she whispered.

"It will. We'll keep trying."

But as they drove home, Ava knew she was losing something vital. Every day, Peter grew more distant, slipping further out of reach.

She turned to him as they pulled into the driveway. "Will you come over later?"

"Maybe." He glanced down, texting someone as he spoke.

Ava's heart sank. She forced a smile and got out of the car, but as he drove away, she felt more alone than ever.

That night, as she lay in bed, the shadows of her nightmares crept in, each one darker than the last. She reached for her phone, desperate for comfort, but the message waiting from Peter brought a hollow ache.

I'm sorry I won't be there tonight. Training drained me. I'll see you tomorrow. I love you.

As Ava stared at the screen, a single tear slipped down her cheek.

6

DISINTEGRATION

The blinding brightness of the sun felt almost cruel as Ava drove to school alone, her hands clenched tight around the steering wheel. The heater was blasting, but the chill in her bones wouldn't leave, the cold seeping into her like Peter's growing distance. She shook her head, attempting to dismiss the nagging thoughts. *I can't let it bother me.* But the tension coiled within her, growing tighter with each passing mile, like a wound refusing to heal.

Lost in thought, she almost missed the sudden stop ahead, her brakes squealing as she barely avoided the car in front of her. The sound startled her, a jolt of irritation bubbling up despite her efforts to stay calm. She took a deep breath, but it did little to settle her nerves. *Push it down.*

When she arrived at school, Thomas was waiting near the entrance, an unexpected sight. The last thing she wanted today was someone who thought they could help.

"Hey." As he smiled, the sunlight glinted off his pale blue eyes.

"Hi." She walked past him, through the double doors, each step a determination not to let him drag her down.

He followed her, undeterred. "You okay?"

"I'm fine." *Why does everyone keep asking me that?*

He fell silent, but when they reached her locker, he ventured again, "It's just, last night you seemed... I don't know, like something was bothering you."

"I'm good." Her fingers flew across the locker combination, spinning the dial with frantic speed.

"Do you want to talk about it?"

"Nope." *Push it down. Keep it down.*

Thomas paused, watching her. "Why don't you come to the Manor?"

Her fingers trembled as she punched the locker in frustration. *Not this again.*

Thomas touched her arm gently. "Ava, just ... calm down."

"Leave me alone," she hissed, pulling her arm away. "You don't get to tell me how to feel."

He sighed, stepping back. "That's not what I'm trying to do, Ava. I just—I miss them too."

Finally, the lock clicked, and she exhaled, staring into the empty space inside her locker, as if it mirrored everything she was trying to avoid.

Peter appeared as the bell rang, reaching for her shoulder with his usual quiet gentleness. "Why did you leave this morning? I was coming to pick you up."

Thomas slipped away, and she searched Peter's face for some sign of affection or concern.

"Oh, sorry," she mumbled, forcing a weak smile. "I thought I'd start driving myself."

"Why?" He frowned, the crease between his brows deepening.

"I don't know." *Push it down.*

"Are you mad at me?"

She bit her lip. "No." *Yes.* The lie was heavy on her tongue.

"I still want to ride together."

"Okay."

"Sorry about last night."

She waved her hand dismissively. "It's fine. You lost track of time."

"I know you're upset. The necklace doesn't have to tell me."

She crossed her arms. "I said I'm fine."

A flicker of frustration crossed his face. "What happened?"

"It's not that important."

"Do you want to go to the Manor after school?"

"No. I thought we were going to the waterfall."

He frowned. "It's not working, Ava."

She felt as if a rug had been pulled out from under her. He'd been the one telling her not to give up, to keep trying every day, reassuring her that her powers would come back with time. She couldn't shake the feeling that he was giving up. Not just on the waterfall but on her. Was he tired of trying, tired of watching her fail?

"Why don't we see a movie or something?" She searched his face, hoping he'd agree, hoping for a sliver of the closeness they used to have.

"That didn't go well last time," he muttered.

"Then how about a hike?"

"It's too cold for you."

Push it down. She swallowed her irritation. "Okay. Then come over."

He shifted, uncomfortable. "I want to go the Manor again."

Despite the boiling frustration underneath, she maintained an even tone. "Have fun."

The awkwardness between them lingered, thick in the silence. The rest of the day was a blur, her frustration growing with every passing hour, until all she wanted was to get home and collapse.

Once home, she tossed her backpack onto her bed, thinking she was alone until a knock echoed through the quiet. When she answered the door, her heart lifted at the sight of Peter. Maybe he'd changed his mind.

But the moment he walked in without his usual hug, without even a soft smile, her heart dropped. His expression was guarded, his body tense, and there was a flicker of worry in his eyes. He was there for something else.

"Hey." She fiddled with the edge of her sleeve.

"Hey." He glanced around the room as if he were looking for something to say.

"Did you ... decide on a movie?"

He finally met her gaze, regret crossing his face. "Ava, I'm not here to watch a movie."

The pit in her stomach grew. She wrapped her arms around herself, bracing for whatever was coming. "What's wrong?"

He sighed, a tired sound, as if he'd been holding back the words. "Ava, why don't you come with me to the Manor?"

She tensed, crossing her arms. "Peter, stop asking me. It's getting really annoying."

"Look, I know it's hard, but it could help. I want you there with me."

Does he even want to be here? The thought scraped against her insides, raw and sharp. "I've told you a thousand times. I don't want to go."

"Ava, you can't just avoid it forever."

"I'm not avoiding anything."

"Yes, you are. You're hiding from it."

"Why can't you understand?" Her voice cracked, and she hated the weakness she heard in it. "I don't want to be reminded of every mistake I've made. I'll go back when I'm ready. Are you that tired of being here with me?"

"Of course not."

"Then why do you keep pushing me to go there?"

He sighed, rubbing his temples. "Because ... because the more I practice, the stronger I get. I can't let what happened happen again."

"It wasn't your fault! All I feel from you is this guilt like it's crushing you. I'm the one who unleashed Havok. If anything, it's my fault, not yours."

"But that's why we should go to Blackhart. To prepare. To fix this."

"I have no powers to train with. I can't even get warm by myself. There's no reason for me to go."

"Being with everyone would help you. Maybe you could heal faster. Maybe you could even talk to Savina."

"I'm not ready to face all of that."

"Why are you so stubborn? I know you're in a lot of pain. But come on. Let's get out of here. Try different scenery. You can't be holed up here forever."

"I tried getting you to go somewhere with me, but you didn't want to. You're so fixated on training."

He sighed again. "I don't get why you are so afraid. You can't give up."

"You should go."

"Ava—"

"Go."

Peter's gaze softened, but he didn't reach for her. "You have to try. It's not just about the Manor. It's about you moving forward. We're all trying to … but it feels like you're stuck."

"Of course I'm stuck! I lost my friends. I killed Colden! And I don't even have my powers. You don't understand how hard this is."

He flinched. "My best friend died, Ava. You think I don't know that pain?" His face drained of color, his expression a mix of hurt and disbelief.

The flash of pain in his eyes was sharper than any blade, and for a moment, she couldn't bear the sight of the pain she had caused. She wanted to take it all back, but the words hung in the air, irreversible.

She reached out, but he stepped back, the space between them widening. Her hands fell limp at her sides, powerless, as she watched him retreat. He was slipping away, and no matter how desperately she tried to hold on, it felt like grasping at sand as it spilled through her fingers.

"I gotta go." He walked out.

The door clicked shut behind him, and Ava remained frozen, her feet glued to the floor. A hollow ache spread through her chest, as though someone had scooped out her insides. She wanted to call after him, to apologize, to say anything that could take back the words she'd thrown at him, but the knot in her throat—fear, guilt, stubbornness—held her silent.

Her hands trembled as she wrapped them around her arms, trying to steady herself. She wished she hadn't lashed out at Peter, wished she could undo the moment, but the words had slipped free before she could stop them. How could she have said that? She had tried so hard to keep her emotions in check for his sake, to avoid piling more guilt onto his shoulders. But it was too much. Keeping it all inside was suffocating.

Didn't Peter understand? Didn't he know that stepping into that mansion again would undo her? That the memories of her friends, the laughter, the fights, the love, were waiting to overwhelm her the moment she crossed the threshold? Blackhart wasn't just a place. It was a reminder of what they'd lost, of the people who weren't coming back. Of everything she'd failed to protect.

The silence in the room was deafening, but she stayed frozen, unable to face the storm she had unleashed.

Her phone buzzed and she pulled it out of her back pocket, hoping it was Peter, but it was Gabriel.

Wanna catch a movie? Or I can bring popcorn and we can just complain about everything instead?

Her fingers hovered over the screen, wanting to respond with more than a polite rejection. She wanted to tell him about the fight, about Peter, about how trapped she felt.

She could almost imagine his half-smile, the comfort he always brought.

She started to type a response, her fingers hovering above the letters.

I could use the company…

She hesitated, staring at the words.

What would she even say if he came over? Talk about the stupid fight with Peter? The guilt she couldn't escape? How terrible of a person she was? No. Gabriel didn't need to hear about all of her messy drama. She didn't deserve his friendship. She backspaced over the words and sighed. *Push it down.*

She gripped her phone tighter as the frustration built inside her. She wanted to scream, throw something, or … do anything to make the ache go away. Her vision blurred with tears, but she blinked them back. She wasn't going to cry. Not again.

Instead, she swallowed the lump in her throat and typed the only thing she could muster: a lie.

Not tonight. thanks.

Her phone buzzed again.

Okay. But I'm here whenever.

Short, simple, and yet it stirred something inside her. She wished she could take his offer, but even the thought of facing anyone right now felt like too much.

Ava tossed her phone onto the bed, the small thud sounding louder in the quiet room. She curled up under the covers, pulling them tight around her. The silence felt suffocating, but she didn't want to fill it. Overwhelmed by her emotions, she just wanted to lie there and let them consume her.

I'm fine. I can handle this.

She closed her eyes, letting the darkness take over, but sleep never came.

Ava jerked awake at the sound of the front door closing. Her father was home, and she heard him shuffle to his room, the familiar creak of the floorboards following him. A few minutes later, the muffled hum of the TV drifted through the apartment.

He tapped on her door and opened it, sighing when he saw her still in bed. "Ava, why are you always in bed? Where's Peter?"

"The Manor," she groaned.

"Why didn't you go with him?"

She didn't answer, pulling the blanket tighter around her shoulders. What could she say? That it was easier to hide in her bed than face the world? Her father lingered, but the knock at the front door saved her from an inevitable lecture.

"Good evening, Connor," Savina greeted him, her calm, melodic voice unmistakable.

Ava sat up, straining to listen.

"Hello, Savina. How are you?" her father asked.

"I am well. I came to see if I could speak with Ava for a moment."

"Please do. She's ... not coping well at all. Peter's been trying, and I've tried, but she won't listen to us."

"I will talk with her."

Moments later, there was a soft tap on Ava's door before Savina pushed it open. She stepped in, her presence as commanding as ever. Her long auburn hair was pulled back, and her black skirt and matching turtleneck made her seem almost regal, a figure out of another era.

"Good evening, Ava," she greeted, her smile warm and observant.

"Hi," Ava mumbled, feeling a sudden rush of nerves. Having Savina there in her bedroom was surreal.

"May I?" Savina gestured to the edge of the bed, and Ava nodded. The familiar scent of oranges filled the room as Savina settled beside her.

"I'm sorry I haven't been back," Ava blurted.

"Do not fret about that. Peter is worried about you, and so am I. And others. Why will you not come to Blackhart?"

Ava hesitated, the words lodging in her throat. "I don't have any powers. It's too painful." The confession dragged the air from her lungs.

Savina took her hand in hers. "I understand that. Everywhere I look, I still think I will see Colden. I spent too much time alone in my room after ... after everything. It did me no good."

"I feel powerless. I've killed too many people. And I try so hard not to make things worse for Peter."

"You carry too much burden on yourself, Ava. You are allowed to grieve," Savina squeezed her hand. "You did not kill Colden. When he reaped Corbin's soul, none of us knew what it would do to him. I tried to heal him, but nothing worked. We thought there might be a cure... I was so obsessed with finding it, I neglected you and your search for answers. No one blames you, Ava. Not even me."

"It's hard not to. I hate this. I hate what Havok has done to us."

"I do too." Her eyes darkened with shared pain. "And I understand that you may not be ready to return yet. I won't make you. The others are learning new ways of fighting, and until their powers return, they train. But please, do not be angry with Peter. If your powers were back, what would you be doing?"

"I'd be doing exactly what Peter's doing."

"I know you are scared. Pain and memories can be terrifying. But I want you to remember that being with those who understand, those who share your pain, can help. They have all lost someone, just like you. It strengthens them, and it could strengthen you."

Ava bit her lip, nodding slowly. The warmth of Savina's hand and the truth in her words comforted her, but the fear still remained.

"As I said, it is your choice when you return," Savina continued. "But when you need to talk, do not hesitate. You are not alone."

With a gentle squeeze of Ava's hand, Savina rose with effortless grace. She glanced back, her green eyes filled with quiet understanding, then slipped out of the room, leaving Ava in the stillness.

Ava stared at the door long after Savina had gone, her mind swirling with guilt, grief, and confusion. She hadn't heard from Peter all night, and a fresh wave of regret washed over her. Maybe it was time. Maybe she needed to face the Manor—and her demons—so she could stop letting them control her.

7

DETERMINATION

The darkened sky mirrored Ava's somber mood as she drove toward school. She was tired of feeling drained. Powerless. Useless. Tired of the grief clinging to her like a parasite, refusing to let go. Savina's words circled her mind. *Learn to fight without powers.* Maybe it could give her a purpose. Maybe it could help her channel all this anger and guilt into something useful.

She'd been unfair to Peter. Too needy, too stubborn. She needed to do better. *Be better.*

Pulling into the school parking lot, Ava's stomach knotted. Since her argument with Peter, the silence had left her nerves jagged and raw. Was he still angry? His guilt still lingered, but the sadness seemed lighter somehow. Why did that feel like a bad thing? *Because I'm still miserable. And I've made him miserable, too.*

She spotted him near his locker, staring down at his phone. Her breath caught in her throat. For a moment, she thought about turning around, avoiding the conversation. But she forced her feet to move.

"Hey," she said softly, testing the waters.

Peter looked up, sliding his phone into his pocket with practiced ease. Something in his body language shifted, a stiffness she couldn't quite place. Her stomach churned. *Why does he look guilty? Is he hiding something?* She hated the creeping thoughts but couldn't stop them. *No, don't do this right now. Focus.*

"Hey."

"Peter, I'm so sorry. I shouldn't have said those things. I've been selfish and stubborn. It's just—it's really hard for me, and I know it's hard for you too."

He exhaled and held out his arms.

Relief flooded her chest as she stepped into his embrace. But even as he held her, she couldn't ignore the small details. His grip wasn't as firm, his chin rested against her head. *Is he holding back?* Her breath caught, and she buried her face in his shoulder to hide the uncertainty on her face. *No. Stop. You're overthinking again.*

"I'm sorry, too," he murmured. "I haven't been very understanding."

She leaned back, studying his face. "Are you mad at me?"

He avoided her gaze, and her stomach lurched with anxiety. *Why won't he look at me? What's he not telling me?*

"No," he said. "I didn't know what else to do, so I talked to Savina. I was worried about you."

A mix of guilt and unease constricted Ava's chest. "Do you forgive me?"

Peter's eyes softened, and he gave a small nod. "Of course." He kissed her forehead, a gesture that felt warm but somehow distant. The moment should have brought relief, but it left her feeling hollow instead. *He's holding something back. Why won't he just tell me? Is he tired of me?* Her thoughts spiraled as he pulled away, and she tried to plaster on a smile to mask her unease.

"I talked to Savina last night. And I think I'm ready to come tonight."

A soft smile spread across his face. "Good."

He smiled like everything was fine, like they were fine, but the flicker of guilt behind his eyes haunted her. She clung to his small moment of approval, desperate for things to feel normal again, even as her instincts screamed that something was wrong.

As the last bell rang, Ava's stomach churned with anxiety. The whole day had passed in a haze of nerves. She barely remembered any of her classes. All she could think about was what it would be like to step back into the Manor after everything. But it was time. She couldn't hide forever.

Driving down the isolated gravel road, Ava's breath fogged the air as she stepped out of the car. The cold bit at her skin. Her feet moved on autopilot as she made her way to the arched door. She hesitated, looking at the vibrant garden that lined the path, the familiar flowers offering a brief moment of solace.

When she pushed open the door, a wave of heat greeted her, wrapping around her like comfort against the cold she couldn't shake. She tugged off her beanie and scarf, pausing in the foyer longer than she needed to, as if staying there might somehow bring back the past. For a fleeting moment, she half-expected to see Colden's familiar smile, him teasing her about tracking in dirt. A sharp, relentless pain constricted her chest.

She tightened her fists, the wool of her scarf still tangled in her fingers, and took a slow, shaky breath. Her stomach cramped, the knot of grief twisting deeper. *Not here. Not now.* She pressed her back against the door, trying to anchor herself. *Push it down.*

"Ava." Aaron emerged from one of the parlors, his russet eyes shining with a welcoming glow. "We've missed you. It's good to see you."

She gave him a small, strained smile. "You too."

"Peter's outside with the others. We've been teaching them a lot. You should join us when you're ready."

"Thanks. I'll be out soon."

Aaron nodded, squeezing her shoulder before he left. Lingering for a moment, the quiet of the Manor settled around her.

As Ava wandered into the library, an emptiness filled her, and she hesitated at the entrance. This place had always been her sanctuary, especially during those late-night talks with Gabriel. She could almost feel his presence in the stillness of the room, the warmth of their conversations remaining in the air. But now, it was quiet. Too quiet. She almost expected to see him leaning against one of the shelves, waiting for her with that familiar smirk, but the room was empty.

A knot formed in her chest as she moved along the rows of books, running her fingers over the worn spines. She paused in front of the section of Dostoyevsky and closed her eyes, remembering how Jeremy used to lose himself in his novels, his fingers playing with his lip as he read. Memories of her loss washed over her, bringing a sharp, agonizing pain to her chest.

She touched her amulet, desperate to feel some kind of connection to her friends, to Jeremy, to Melissa, anyone, but there was nothing. The emptiness deepened.

"Ava?"

She jumped at the sound of her name and turned. Her breath hitched at the sight of Gabriel standing in the doorway. For a moment, all the emotions she'd buried over the past weeks rushed to the surface. She hadn't realized how much she missed him until now. Seeing him there, with his striking blue eyes and familiar calmness, sent a wave of unexpected relief through her.

He looked different. More put together than the last time she'd seen him. His shadowed stubble was gone, and his hair was cropped short, his bangs standing up in that effortless way she remembered. His white button-down shirt fit him well, and the sight of his necklace peeking out from under his collar made her heart skip.

It was as if seeing him reminded her of everything she had been missing. The stable, calming influence he had on her. She relied on him to feel … well, anything but the crushing weight of loss.

"Hi," she said.

Next to him was Natalia, graceful and poised as always, though her hazel eyes softened ever so slightly at the sight of Ava. For once, Ava didn't mind Natalia, but it was Gabriel who held her focus. She hadn't expected to feel this surge of comfort by seeing him.

"Ava," Natalia said, a surprising concern in her tone.

Gabriel gave her an easy, familiar smile. "It's good to see you."

"You too," she replied.

"How are you?" he asked, his blue eyes searching hers as if he could sense the turmoil she was trying to keep hidden.

For a moment, she wanted to break down and tell him everything. How hard it had been. How lonely she felt. How lost. But she swallowed it down, managing a small smile. "I'm okay." The words felt hollow. "You?"

"Day by day," he said.

Natalia shifted beside him, looking impatient. "We should go back."

"Would you like to join us outside?" he asked.

Natalia rolled her eyes and walked away.

Ava hesitated, but something in Gabriel's voice made her want to say yes. "Sure."

As they stepped out into the cold, the bitter air stole her breath for a moment. Ava tugged her beanie down over her ears, clenching her teeth against the chill. Gabriel slid his hand into hers, and the icy bite of the air seemed to vanish. Her body relaxed, the warmth from his touch spreading through her, soothing something deeper than just the cold. It wasn't the heat radiating from his hand. It was the comfort of feeling connected again, a feeling she hadn't realized she missed so much.

Their fingers intertwined, and it didn't feel awkward or forced. It felt safe. For a moment, she wasn't alone anymore.

"Thanks," she whispered.

A knowing smile played on Gabriel's lips. "Anytime."

The air around them felt easier, like the tension she'd been carrying had lifted. But reality crept back in. "Wait. You have your powers?"

"Not completely, but close."

Why hadn't hers come back at all? What was wrong with her? The doubt gnawed at her, even as Gabriel squeezed her hand in silent reassurance, pulling her out of her spiraling thoughts.

His gaze met hers. "Just give it time."

She wanted to believe him, but the knot of fear in her stomach tightened.

Ahead, Natalia crossed her arms and strode toward Eric, Aaron, and Savina, her steps as graceful as always. Ava chewed on the inside of her mouth as her eyes scanned the vast field. Almost everyone was there, except for Lance and Maya's coven.

A group of the Enchanters stood in a line, observing Gustav sparring with someone. Katarina zipped around Gustav in a flash of electric blue. When the movement stopped, Konstantin clapped, and Katarina flashed a proud smile.

Memories of training with Ava's friends flooded back. She could still see Melissa's carefree laugh as they practiced together, Joss grinning as she shocked everyone around her, Jeremy engrossed in his books afterward. Even now, the echoes of their voices played in her head, the absence of them was like an ache that wouldn't go away. She choked back a sob as grief overwhelmed her.

Gabriel squeezed her hand. The quiet strength in his touch anchored her, keeping her from unraveling. She managed to force the tears back, burying the pain deep down.

Ava spotted Savina in the distance and offered a small smile in acknowledgment.

"Ava!" Peter's signature smoldering smile flashed. "You came."

When Gabriel released her hand, the cold rushed back.

She resisted the urge to reach for him again. "I did." She forced herself to smile back. "Does everyone have their abilities back?"

"Not yet. But it's coming back, little by little."

"I'll leave you two," Gabriel said, stepping away.

Ava's heart dipped, and for a brief second, she didn't want him to go.

A gust of wind ripped through her, sending an involuntary shiver through her body until Peter's hand closed around hers. Still, her thoughts lingered on Gabriel, on the way he made her feel so grounded in that moment.

"Where's Lance and Maya's group?" she asked.

"Lance has been going to Melissa's parents' house every day. He's been helping them out. It keeps him busy. Maya's group went home. They decided not to come to Caprington."

Ava blinked, guilt settling heavy in her chest. She had no idea Lance had been spending so much time helping Melissa's family. How much had she missed while isolating herself? "I had no idea."

"Do you wanna watch me practice? I'm about to go a round with Gustav. He's been teaching me a lot about protecting while fighting. It's harder than it sounds. Trying to focus on protecting and attacking at the same time."

"Maybe I should take lessons," she half-joked, but there was truth behind her words. Maybe that's what she needed. Something to focus on other than the constant ache in her chest.

"You could learn a lot from him," Peter said. "Did you know Gustav's older than Savina and Aaron? He's fought countless Cimmerians. His daughter was captured by Corbin, and he thinks she became a Cimmerian. They haven't seen each other in two hundred years."

Ava felt her breath hitch. Two hundred years.

"Oh, no—Ava, I didn't mean to—Mel won't—"

"I know," she cut him off.

Ilya called out. "Peter! Ava! Hello!"

Ava forced herself to smile, grateful for the distraction. "Hi."

Peter turned back to her. "I'm up next." He kissed her forehead, leaving her cold again as he joined the others in training. She stood awkwardly behind the group, watching from a distance, but Gabriel appeared beside her before the chill could settle too deeply into her bones.

Eric joined them, looping his arm through hers, adding another layer of warmth. "We've got you."

Even though she appreciated the gesture, it stung to feel so fragile. Everyone was taking care of her, like she was something that might break.

"You're fragile right now," Eric said, his voice gentle but direct. "That's why your powers haven't come back. It's like when you're sick. Everything feels harder, colder."

Ava swallowed, nodding. She hated it, hated feeling weak.

Peter moved with precision, aiming a swift kick at Katarina's legs, but she was too fast. She dodged easily, then retaliated with a powerful kick to his stomach, forcing him to double over with a grunt. He grabbed at her legs, but she leaped into the air, flipping with grace over him. Before he could recover, she was behind him, her hands lighting up like hot coals as they clamped around his throat.

A strangled cry escaped Peter as his neck began to smoke, the flesh burning beneath her touch.

Ava's heart lurched, and she surged forward, her mind screaming for her to intervene. But strong hands gripped her arms, holding her back. "No!" she gasped, eyes wide in horror as Peter collapsed to his knees, smoke rising from the burns.

Katarina's eyes widened as she jerked her hands away. She stared at them as if they had betrayed her. "I am so sorry. I didn't know my ability would work." She knelt beside Peter, panic flooding her brown eyes.

He coughed, his hand rubbing his neck, but to Ava's shock, the burns faded almost as quickly as they'd appeared. The skin healed, as if untouched by the scorching heat. Peter gave a weak smile. "Yeah, I'm good. It just … caught me off guard."

Eric released Ava, and she pushed past Ilya and Anastasya, rushing to Peter's side. Her hands hovered over his neck as she examined him, her fingers trembling. "Does it still hurt?"

Peter gave her a reassuring smile, though it didn't quite reach his eyes. "No, I'm fine. I promise."

Katarina shook her head, still pale with guilt. "I didn't mean to … I'm so sorry."

Peter waved off her apology, though his hand lingered at his throat. "It's okay. It happens."

A sudden cheer erupted from Gustav, his deep voice booming through the field. "Your ability is coming back, Katarina!" His large hands clapped together, a smile spreading across his face as he pulled Katarina into a bear hug, swallowing her with his massive frame.

Ava blinked, taken aback. She couldn't remember the last time she'd seen Gustav smile, let alone act so animated. It was strange, unsettling even. How could they be in such high spirits after what happened? The last time she had been there, the air had been thick with grief and tension, suffocating like a steam room. Now, it was almost celebratory.

"Ava," Gustav called, his green eyes gleaming with excitement, "would you like to give it a try?"

"Not today." She stepped back. The thought of trying, only to fail again, was too much to bear. Especially in front of everyone.

Gillian let out an exasperated sigh from the line. "I will." She strode forward.

Gabriel stepped up to face her, his posture relaxed, but his eyes sharp.

She threw a punch, but Gabriel sidestepped, causing her to hit nothing but air. Frustration flared across her face. She swung her leg toward his midsection, but he was already moving, dodging with fluid grace. Each missed attack seemed to fuel her frustration, her grunts growing louder with each failure.

With a swift motion, Gabriel caught her ankle mid-kick, yanking it hard enough to throw her off balance. She landed hard on her back, the wind knocked out of her.

"You have to be quicker," he teased, a playful smirk tugging at his lips. His eyes sparkled with amusement, though there was no malice behind it.

She scrambled to her feet, her face red with embarrassment and anger. "Let's go again."

"Nah, it's my turn," Eric said and faced Gabriel.

As Eric made his way to the front, an identical version of him stepped into the clearing.

Ava blinked, confused until she realized it was Ilya mimicking Eric's appearance with perfection. "That's creepy," she muttered under her breath.

The resemblance was uncanny, right down to the smirk and the confident stance. For a moment, it was impossible to tell them apart. The two circled each other, and then they lunged.

It was a flurry of movement, too quick to follow, until one of the Erics was flat on his back, while the other stood over him, boot pressed to the fallen man's neck.

The victor smiled, his features shifting back into Ilya's. "Havok will never know who's who," he said, offering Eric a hand to help him up.

Eric chuckled, brushing the dust off his pants as he accepted the help. "I know my own strength, Ilya. I'm stronger than that."

Ilya grinned. "But Havok won't."

Ava managed a small smile at their banter, though a familiar ache tugged at her heart. The camaraderie, the lightness in the air felt wrong to her. Her friends were still missing, and her own powers were nowhere in sight. She couldn't shake the guilt, reminding her of everything she had failed to do. *Push it down.*

"Hey, Ava." Lance's voice broke through her thoughts. His dark eyes held a sadness that mirrored her own. "You're here. Have you practiced at all?"

Ava shook her head, avoiding his gaze. "No. I'm just watching."

"Well, I'm glad you came."

As the twilight sky darkened into evening, Aaron's voice cut through the crowd, calling everyone to dinner. Ava hesitated, a pang of dread settling in her chest. She wasn't sure she was ready to face the Manor again, to be around everyone in the quiet, intimate atmosphere of dinner.

But she knew it would be good to stay.

Dinner was far livelier than the last one Ava had shared with them. It was almost surreal. Everyone seemed to be in high spirits, chatting and laughing, as if they'd all taken happy pills. Or maybe, Ava thought bitterly, they weren't wallowing anymore. Their confidence must have been growing, fueled by the slow return of their powers. She couldn't help but feel left behind, powerless, literally and figuratively. But she'd been trying. Trying to keep it together.

After dinner, exhaustion settled over her. All she wanted was to go home.

"Are you ready to go?" she asked Peter as they stepped out of the dining hall into the cool hallway.

He hesitated, his hand lingering near his pocket as if tempted to reach for his phone again. He avoided her gaze. "I think I'll stay a little longer. I want to hear more of Gustav's stories." The words sounded casual, but something in his tone didn't sit right. Like he was offering her a half-truth instead of the whole picture.

Why won't he just come home with me? The thought screamed in her mind, but she swallowed it down, forcing a smile. "Okay. Have fun."

"See you in the morning," he added, already turning toward the parlor.

Her heart sank as he walked away. It was like he didn't want to be around her. Even though she'd buried her feelings for him, he still didn't want to be near her.

Peter doesn't love me anymore. I messed up.

The thought sliced through her defenses. She shook her head, trying to push it away. *He's just tired. He's stressed. It's not about you.* Peter's lack of emotion was like chains wrapped around her heart with an iron ball weighing it down. She longed to feel his arms around her or his soft lips on hers. Or for him to hold her hand.

But she couldn't shake the image of him avoiding her gaze. Doubts gnawed at her, turning her insides to knots. *Maybe I pushed him too far. Maybe he's done with me.* Her fists tightened in her pockets as she battled the crushing feeling of self-loathing. *You're being paranoid. He's just giving you space.*

But a deeper voice whispered that she'd already lost him, that he was slipping through her fingers, and there was nothing she could do about it.

She turned toward the library, her steps slowing as the thought of Gabriel crossed her mind. He'd always known how to calm her, to make the chaos inside her seem less suffocating. She could almost hear him in her head, reminding her to breathe, to let go. Thinking about it made her shoulders relax.

But as she began to walk toward the library, her phone buzzed in her pocket. It was a message from her dad:

Could you pick up some flu medicine on your way home? Just in case. Thanks.

Ava sighed, pulling her beanie down over her head and turned toward the front door.

Her mind buzzed with everything she refused to think about. *Maybe Peter just needs time. Maybe he's still grieving.* She repeated the thoughts like a mantra as she drove toward the pharmacy, the harsh fluorescent lights of the parking lot casting long shadows across the pavement.

The edges of her emotions started to fray, threatening to spill over, but she took a deep breath. She couldn't let them take control. If she did, everyone would know something was wrong, and she wasn't ready to talk about it. Not yet.

With a long exhale, she pushed the feelings down like Gabriel had taught her and drove home.

Usually, Peter sent a message letting Ava know he was on his way to pick her up for school. But not today. Every time she called, it went to voicemail. She could feel him, knew he was fine, so why wasn't he answering? She didn't want to act like an obsessed girlfriend, but the silence annoyed her.

With a frustrated breath, she tossed her phone onto the kitchen counter. The hollow clink echoed in the quiet kitchen.

Her father shuffled in, still dressed in his pajamas, looking tired.

"Dad, are you okay?"

"I'm fine, just not feeling great." He grabbed the coffee filter.

"What's wrong?"

"Think I'm catching a cold."

"Do you want me to stay and take care of you?" She wished she could heal him.

He chuckled. "No, you don't have to fuss. I'll be all right."

She studied him, watching him rinse the coffee pot and move with his usual morning rhythm, but the unease didn't leave her. Every small movement felt like something more, a warning sign she couldn't ignore.

"You don't need to keep watching me, Ava." He glanced back, amusement flickering in his eyes.

"Sorry. The last time someone got sick, it didn't end well…"

His movements slowed, and he turned, towel in hand. "I promise, it's just a cold. You don't have to worry about me, okay?"

She nodded but couldn't stop her thoughts from racing ahead to worst-case scenarios.

"How was training last night?" he asked.

"I just watched."

"You'll get there. It takes time."

"Maybe… It just feels like everyone else is already getting their powers back. Must be nice." The bitterness slipped out before she could stop it.

"Ava, be happy for them. Yours will come back, too. Give it time." He glanced at the stove clock. "You might want to get going, or you'll be late."

She sighed, leaning over to kiss his cheek. "Call me if you need anything."

"I'll be fine, sweetie. Don't worry about me." He smiled but couldn't hide the weariness in his eyes.

Ava's fingers gripped the steering wheel as she drove toward school, her mind spiraling with questions. Where was Peter? He hadn't sent a single message, and every time she tried calling, it went straight to voicemail. She hadn't felt anything alarming through their connection, but his absence gnawed at her.

Arriving at school, she scanned the parking lot and hallways for him, but he was nowhere in sight. She waited by her locker, glancing down the hall every few seconds, but still no sign of him. The bell rang, cutting through her growing frustration. *Fine*, she thought, marching off to class alone.

Time crawled by, the silence of her phone unsettling her. Was Peter okay? Had something happened? She'd been through this before when he went missing, and the anxiety of those days crept back. By the time lunch rolled around, Ava's nerves were frayed.

As she walked toward their usual table, she spotted Peter sitting with the others, his tray already half empty. Relief washed over her, but it was short-lived. She slid into the seat next to him, her stomach twisting at the sight of his disheveled appearance. His hair stuck up at odd angles, and dark circles shadowed his eyes. He looked like he hadn't slept in days.

"Where've you been?" she asked, keeping her tone soft.

"Overslept."

"You couldn't tell me?"

"I just got here," he snapped. The sharpness of his tone cut deep, but she felt his regret through their connection. "Sorry," he muttered. "I'm just tired."

She forced herself to let it go. *He's just stressed. It's not about you.* "Were you at the Manor late?"

"Yes. Would you like a full report of my every movement?"

Her cheeks flushed, embarrassment mixing with anger, but she bit her tongue. Why was he acting like this?

Thomas barked a laugh. "I still can't get over how Ilya scared the crap out of you, G."

Ava tried to focus on the group, but Peter chuckled along with them, the earlier tension gone from his shoulders. She watched as he leaned in, joking with Gillian, his earlier sharpness now replaced with easy laughter. The knot in her chest tightened. *Why can't he laugh like that with me?* "What happened?" she asked, desperate to feel included.

"Nothing," Peter said flatly, dismissing her as he turned back to the others.

Her heart sank. *I don't belong here anymore.*

Her thoughts spiraled as she pushed the food around her tray. Peter pulled out his phone, his fingers flying across the screen. She stared at the side of his face, waiting for him to notice her, but he didn't even glance her way. It was like she wasn't even there. If she disappeared, would anyone care? Couldn't Peter see how much she was hurting? Couldn't any of them?

"Has anyone else had abilities return?" Thomas asked.

"None," Gillian spat.

Ava shook her head, muttering, "Nothing."

"Yeah, me neither," Thomas said. "We'll keep at it."

"Gustav's a good teacher," Peter said, still texting.

"So, did it hurt when Katarina burned you?" Thomas asked Peter.

"Yeah, but it went away as soon as she let go," Peter replied, absentmindedly.

"You seem to be getting better at the protecting thing," Thomas said.

Ava blinked, surprised. Was Thomas talking to Peter? Since when did they start having real conversations?

Thomas turned to her. "You coming tonight, Ava?"

"Yes."

"Are you actually going to do something this time or just watch?" Gillian snarked.

Ava avoided her probing gaze. "I don't know yet." She turned to Peter. "Are you ready for your exams?"

He shrugged. "Yeah, most of them seem pretty easy."

"I don't think I'll pass. Maybe you could help me study?" she asked, hoping to reconnect with him in some small way.

"Yeah, maybe," he replied, not looking up from his phone.

That was a no.

His phone buzzed again as he stood, and he glanced at the screen with a fleeting expression Ava couldn't place. Regret? Guilt? He muttered, "Later," and walked away.

She stared at the empty spot where Peter had been sitting, and a hollow ache spread through her chest. He used to look at her, touch her, hold her like she was the most important person in the room. Now, it felt like she didn't even exist to him.

The temperature dropped, and dark clouds gathered as Ava drove to the Manor, her mood as gloomy as the sky. She didn't want to sit around and watch the others practice; she wanted to spend time with Peter, to feel close to him again. As she pulled into the driveway beside his car, uncertainty gripped her.

She got out and caught him as he was shutting his door. "Hey," she called.

"Hey," Peter said. "You gonna practice today?"

"Maybe."

"Cool. I'll see you out there." He turned toward the door without waiting for a reply.

"Peter?" Her voice wavered.

He glanced back. "Yeah?"

"Can we talk?" She bit her lip.

He sighed. "About what?"

"Is something wrong?"

"No, why do you always assume something's wrong?"

"Because you're acting like you don't want to be around me."

"I'm stressed out, Ava. We all are. But I wish you'd stop assuming everything is about you."

His words stung, and she bit the inside of her cheek. "I'm just saying ... you've been distant."

"I'm trying to focus." He ran a hand through his hair. "I want to be a better Enchanter. You know this."

She wanted to hold his hand but was afraid. "Then why is it so awkward between us? And who do you keep texting?"

His eyes narrowed. "What are you talking about?"

"You're always on your phone."

"I'm looking stuff up online. Don't be so nosy," he snapped.

Ava fought back a retort. "Sorry. Will you come over tonight after practice?"

"Maybe. I'll see you later." He turned on his heel and walked inside.

She crossed her arms. Her chest felt tight, like she couldn't take a full breath. Something was wrong, but she couldn't tell if it was with Peter, or if it was her. The self-doubt started to creep in. She wanted to cry. Scream. Punch something. But she had to be strong. She needed to practice. Focus on anything but everything she had lost ... and was losing.

She stared at the grand, imposing Manor. Its warm, glowing windows offered no comfort. She was tired of feeling like she didn't belong there, like she was stuck on the outside looking in. She should go join Peter on the field, but her feet moved in another direction.

Instead, she wandered to the library, seeking solace among the quiet rows of books.

"Hey."

Ava jumped, her heart skipping a beat.

Gabriel lounged in his usual chair by the fire, a soft smile playing on his lips. The flickering light cast warm shadows across his face, making his blue eyes seem even brighter. "Sorry, didn't mean to startle you."

She let out a small sigh, sinking into the chair beside him, resting her head against the back of the chair. "It's okay."

"You seem ... tired."

"I guess I am."

"Are you sleeping okay?"

She shrugged, avoiding his gaze. "Everything feels ... off. I don't have my powers, I'm tired all the time, and Peter's so distant. It's like he's consumed by his guilt, and I'm just ... I don't know. No matter how hard I push it down, I still feel ... empty, guilty." Her voice trembled. "I can't help but feel like I'm making things worse. How can I stop feeling like this?"

"You don't have to figure it out all at once," he said. "But you can't keep carrying all of this alone. It's too much for anyone." His blue eyes searched hers. "I've been there,

Ava. I know what it's like to feel stuck, like nothing you do matters. But I promise you, it does."

"I know, but it's hard. I try to hold it all in because I don't want Peter to feel guilty, but it's getting to be too much. He doesn't even notice anymore. It's like I'm invisible."

The muscle in his jaw twitched. "You're not invisible. Not to me, and not to the people who care about you."

"It doesn't feel like that."

"I know." He leaned closer. "But I need you to hear this: you are enough. You're not failing anyone. Not Peter. Not anyone. Including yourself. You've been through more than most people could handle, and you're still standing. That matters."

Her eyes burned with tears, but she refused to let them fall. "I feel so … broken."

"You're not broken. You're hurt. And that's okay. But you don't have to go through this alone."

For a moment, the silence stretched between them, broken by the crackling of the fire. His gaze never wavered, a steady anchor in the chaos of her thoughts.

"Thanks. I don't know why you care so much."

He hesitated. "Because I see you, Ava. And you deserve to be seen."

A mix of emotions swirled inside her. Gratitude, relief, and something she couldn't quite name. She managed a small, shaky smile. "I don't know what I'd do without you."

He smiled back, the kind of smile that made her feel like maybe things could get better. "You don't have to find out." He paused. "When's the last time you did something for yourself? Something not about training or Peter or any of this?"

"I don't even know. There hasn't really been time for that."

"That's what I thought." He stood, offering her his hand. "Come on. We're going out."

She took his hand with a weak smile. "Where are we going?"

He shrugged. "Just for a drive. Trust me."

As they stepped outside, the cold air hit Ava like a wall. She stiffened, pulling her beanie down over her ears.

Gabriel unlocked his car and opened the door for her. She settled in the cold black leather seats.

Once he got in on the driver's side, she snapped her seatbelt in. "I had no idea you had a car."

He grinned as he clicked on his seatbelt. "Yeah, shocking, right? I usually just teleport everywhere, but it's hard to impress people when you show up looking like you stepped out of a magic trick."

Ava smirked. "I guess teleporting doesn't come with cup holders."

"Exactly. Plus, teleporting doesn't let me show off my great taste in mid-range vehicles." He turned the ignition, and the engine came to life with a soft purr. The blue glow of the dashboard lights created a calm, intimate atmosphere. He clicked on the heater, and the seats began to warm.

"Heated seats? Trying to impress me?"

"Absolutely. They're my secret weapon. How else am I supposed to convince you to go on more drives with me?"

Ava smiled at his joke, but the moment of levity faded. She stared out the window, the dark landscape whizzing by, but her mind was stuck in place, swirling with thoughts she couldn't control. She took a breath and glanced at Gabriel. "I just… I don't know how much longer I can keep this up. Everything feels so heavy, and I don't even know what to do anymore. I'm not getting my powers back, Peter's distant, and I'm just stuck. Feeling like I'm the only one not moving forward." She stopped. She'd been unloading on him again. It wasn't the first time she'd said something like that. And that's when the guilt started creeping in. She wasn't trying to dump all her problems on Gabriel, but it felt like he was the only one who actually listened. "Sorry, I don't want to make this about me." She rubbed the back of her neck. "You've got your own stuff to deal with."

"It's okay, Ava. You're allowed to feel that way. And you can talk to me. Don't apologize."

After a beat of silence, she sighed. "How are you handling all of this?"

"It's not easy. I'm trying to hold it together, to keep everyone calm and focused, but…" He paused, his lips tightening in a brief frown. "Some days, I feel like I'm running on fumes. Like I'm only pretending I've got it all figured out."

Ava blinked, surprised by the admission. He was always so composed, so in control, it was easy to forget he might be struggling too.

"But you're always so calm. It's hard to tell."

He glanced at her, his blue eyes catching the dim light of the dashboard. "Yeah, well, I've had a long time to practice. But that doesn't mean it's not hard. I just ... try not to let it show. Too many people are relying on me, you know?"

A pang of guilt settled in. She hadn't thought about how much Gabriel was dealing with, how much weight he was carrying on his shoulders. It wasn't just her. Everyone was relying on him. She'd been leaning on him too, without even realizing.

"I'm sorry." She looked down at her hands. "I didn't think about that. You've been holding it together for everyone, and here I am … adding to it."

"Don't apologize, Ava. You're not adding to anything. If anything, I'd rather you talk to me than bottle it all up. It helps … keeps me grounded, you know?"

She glanced at him. "Still… I don't want to make things harder for you."

"You're not." He hesitated. "Actually … you help me too."

She blinked, caught off guard. "How?"

He let out a breath, glancing out the window for a second as if searching for the right words. "It's … easy to get lost in all of this. Everyone looks to me like I've got all the answers, but sometimes, it feels like I'm just one wrong move away from losing control. But when I'm with you…" He looked back at her, his eyes meeting hers. "I don't know. It makes everything feel more manageable. Less heavy."

Her heart skipped a beat. She hadn't expected that. "I didn't know I … helped you like that."

Gabriel's lips quirked into a small, reassuring smile. "You do, Ava. More than you know. You carry too much on your shoulders, too."

The sound of waves greeted Ava as Gabriel parked near the beach. The soft roar of the ocean filled the air, mingling with the scent of saltwater and seaweed. The moon hung low in the sky, its silver light dancing across the waves.

"I thought you could use some fresh air." He cut the engine and turned to her. "I know the Manor feels suffocating."

"How did we get here so fast?" she asked.

"I drove really fast?" A sly smile played on his lips.

"Or you teleported?" she teased, glancing at him with a raised eyebrow.

"Maybe." He shrugged.

Ava stepped onto the sand, the cool grains shifting beneath her feet. She hesitated at the water's edge, the gentle waves lapping at her boots. "It's beautiful."

Gabriel stood beside her, his hands in his pockets. "The ocean's always been a good reminder for me. No matter how chaotic things get, it's constant. It just … is."

But the familiar doubt crept in. "I haven't been able to get anything back. Nothing happens when I try."

He faced her, his hands resting on her arms. "You *are* water. It's part of you. It's in your soul. But you can't force it."

She bit her lip, avoiding his gaze. "I've been trying so hard…"

"I know. But sometimes you have to let go of trying. Just … be."

"You make it sound so easy."

"Close your eyes."

"Why?"

"Just close them."

Ava hesitated but did as he instructed, shutting out the world around her.

Gabriel's hands slid down to hers, fingers brushing her skin.

She hoped he couldn't feel how fast her heart was beating, the pulse in her wrists quickening under his touch.

"Listen to the waves. Smell the air. Feel the breeze, calm and steady." His voice became a rhythm of its own. "Breathe in. Breathe out."

The salty ocean breeze filled her lungs as she took a deep breath. With each slow exhale, her tension eased, unravelling like a loose thread.

"Let it all in. Clear your mind."

For a fleeting moment, something sparked inside her—a rush of energy that felt familiar yet distant. The pulse of power tingled through her veins like the touch of a long-lost friend.

"Don't force it." Gabriel's fingertips grazed her wrists, the sensation sending a shiver down her spine, but not from the cold.

When she opened her eyes, she met his gaze. His heated stare held her captive for a moment longer than expected. He cleared his throat and released her hands.

"I felt it," she whispered.

"Wanna try it in the water?" His smile was inviting, hopeful.

She nodded, shedding her jacket and boots as the cool night air brushed against her skin. The sand beneath her feet felt cool, gritty, grounding her to the earth.

Gabriel pulled his shirt over his head in one fluid motion, the fabric sliding off to reveal his lean, muscular frame. The moonlight cast a soft, silvery glow over his pale skin, accentuating the contours of his shoulders and chest. The faint scars that traced his ribs caught her attention, subtle reminders of a past he rarely spoke about.

Heat rose to her cheeks, and she looked away, focusing on the water. But the image lingered, her mind flickering between admiration and unease. She wasn't sure what she felt, only that the moment felt different, charged with something.

He waded into the water with slow, deliberate steps before diving in, disappearing beneath the gentle waves.

Taking a few deep breaths, Ava followed suit, letting go of her thoughts—Colden, Melissa, Jeremy, the war, Peter.

She blocked it all out as she stepped into the water. It was warm, wrapping around her feet like a welcoming embrace.

She sighed, a small, relieved smile playing on her lips. "It's … warm," she called to Gabriel as he surfaced, water streaming from his dark hair. "Are you doing that?"

"I can't control the temperature of the water. Only myself," he said.

Her heart raced at the possibility. Were her powers coming back? The pulse of energy inside her stirred, pushing her forward into the water. Ava took another step, then dove underneath. With its gentle heat, the ocean cradled her like it had always belonged to her. When she surfaced, a sense of peace washed over her, more alive than she had felt in weeks. She still couldn't breathe underwater, but it was a start.

"That's the first time I've seen you smile in a while," he said, treading water beside her, his eyes twinkling with satisfaction.

"It's exactly what I needed." She hadn't felt this alive in so long. "How did you know this would work?"

He shrugged with that easy charm of his. "I just did. Come on, I'll race you."

"I don't know if—" She started, but Gabriel was already swimming ahead of her. Moonlight glinted on the surface of the calm water, causing gentle ripples. For a moment, she paused, letting the tranquility of the scene soak in. With a smile tugging at her lips, she pushed off and swam to catch up.

As they raced, Ava felt stronger, lighter, and for those precious minutes, all her worries faded away. The water set her free. After a few races, where she was sure Gabriel let her win, they sat on the beach, letting their clothes dry. The night sky stretched above them, brilliant stars twinkling against the dark canvas, some flickering as if unsure of their place in the vastness.

It was a perfect night, the serenity of the ocean, the stars, and Gabriel's company all blending together to create a brief escape.

She missed being around Gabriel more than she realized. He had a way of calming her and challenging her at the same time. "Thank you."

"You're welcome. But don't think I did it just for you. I needed it myself." His smile was easy, but there was something unspoken in his eyes.

"Of course. We should do this more often." Her words carried a vulnerability she hadn't intended, but she pushed through it.

"The water is always here for you."

Ava bit her lip, hesitating for a moment. "I meant us. Hanging out. I've missed you." The words left her mouth before she could stop them, and they sounded far too needy. She regretted speaking. His gaze burned into her, but she wouldn't meet his eyes, clinging to the texture of the sand as her sole comfort.

"I missed you, too." His hand slipped into hers, warming her.

Her body responded to his touch, tension melting away like snow in the sun. She exhaled, not realizing she had been holding her breath. "Thanks. I'm sorry I never called or anything. I guess I just got lost in my own mind."

"I'm not one to tell people 'I told you so.' But you knew it was a bad idea to keep it all inside. You deserve to feel those things, too, Ava. It's okay to be upset. To be sad."

"I know. I just didn't want to make things worse for Peter. He's been dealing with so much, and I didn't want to add to his guilt."

"That's something he's gotta figure out. He shouldn't punish you because he can't shut out everyone's emotions. It's not easy, but still, it's not fair for him to push that on you."

She dug her hand into the sand, feeling its gritty texture between her fingers. "I don't like sitting around thinking about all this. It's the waiting. It kills me to know they're out there and we're still here. I can't feel them anymore."

Gabriel looked out over the ocean, his expression hardening. "We'll find them."

Ava glanced up, her gaze locking onto his. In the moonlight, his blue eyes glowed like twin flames. "How do you know?"

"We have to." His tone was resolute, as if failure wasn't even a consideration.

"I feel like some whiny person who sits and cries over something instead of *doing* something about it."

He gave her a sideways glance, a smirk tugging at his lips. "Well, you are grieving. But if you want to take your frustrations out on someone, fighting is a great way to do it. How can that not be good?" He winked, and she rolled her eyes despite the smile creeping up on her face.

Gabriel stood and dusted the sand off his hands, then reached for hers, pulling her up. The warmth of his hand lingered even after he let go. They stood inches apart, the proximity making her heart beat faster. "If you don't want to sit around, we can learn to fight right now."

"What's the point of fighting someone who can make me go blind? Or put images in my head? Or set me on fire without my powers?"

"You gotta get rid of that defeatist attitude." His smile was easy, but his tone was firm. "If you're fast enough, you can take them down. Besides, when we do leave to find Havok, there are plenty of … things out there that don't have powers." He released her hand and stepped back, gesturing for her to follow him. "First, let's work on your stance. Keep your feet apart, knees bent. One foot slightly forward for balance. You want to be able to pivot fast."

Ava adjusted her position, planting her feet in the sand. The cool grains shifted beneath her toes, making it harder to stay grounded.

"Good. Now, keep your arms up. Elbows tight, fists guarding your face. You need to protect your head and keep your movements fluid. Don't block too much. Dodging is faster."

She nodded, raising her arms as instructed.

"Imagine I can shoot fire from my hands. You've got to be quick. Either dodge or block, but don't hesitate."

He mimicked shooting fire from his hands, and Ava ducked, rushing toward him. But he stopped her mid-move with a raised hand.

"Try again. Quicker this time."

She narrowed her eyes, her body tensing with focus. This time, when he pretended to shoot, she dodged and struck toward him. Gabriel seized her wrist, spinning her around, but she pulled away and jumped back.

"Better." His smile widened. "But once you've dodged, don't give them a chance to recover. The second they miss, that's your opening. Strike fast."

He moved toward her again, and this time Ava lunged forward, knocking him off balance. As Gabriel hit the ground, she jumped back, avoiding a potential counterattack.

"Perfect." He stood, brushing sand off his clothes. "You're fast, and that's your biggest advantage. Use it. Strike hard and get out of reach before they can react."

Her breath came in short gasps, but a smile tugged at her lips. The physical effort made her feel more centered, and for the first time in weeks, she felt strong.

Gabriel's expression grew more serious. "When it comes to mental abilities, though, it's a different game. You need to be able to shield your mind like you shield your body. Don't let them see your emotions. The second you feel someone trying to get in, like Savina did, push back. Your focus is your best defense."

Ava winced at the memory of Savina's mental intrusion, how invasive it felt, like someone gripping her thoughts and wrenching them free. She shuddered at the thought.

"It's okay. You're getting really good at hiding your emotions, so you have to do the same with your mind. Concentrate, because what happened on that field could happen again. But if someone takes your powers or negates them, you've got to catch them off guard. Once they're down, if you hit hard enough, you can choke them or take them out quickly."

They practiced for a while longer, the ocean a quiet rhythm beside them, the cool air bracing against their heated bodies. With every move, she gained more confidence, her progress slow but steady. By the end, she was breathless but exhilarated, a feeling of empowerment settling into her bones.

Perhaps it worked better having Gabriel teach her. He understood her in ways others didn't. Maybe she should have been training sooner, but right now, with him, it felt right.

He glanced at his phone. "It's getting late. We should head back."

"What time is it?"

"Almost nine."

Ava blinked in surprise. "We've been out here for five hours?"

"Guess we lost track of time."

Her stomach growled, and she laughed. "First time I've actually been hungry in a while."

"That's a good sign. Means you're getting better."

Ava's smile faded. "Maybe." The stress of Peter, the war, her missing friends threatened to settle back on her shoulders now that the quiet peace of the beach was ending.

Gabriel studied her for a moment. "Come on, let's get something to eat."

"I should go home. I'll eat with my dad."

"You sure? We could grab something on the way."

"I'm sure," she said, but she couldn't quite shake the sense that he was disappointed, even though he didn't push it. They walked back to the car in comfortable silence.

The drive to the Manor was filled with easy conversation, though Ava's mind wandered. The peace she had found at the beach faded with every mile closer to the Manor, replaced by a low hum of dread. She didn't know if she could handle seeing Peter again, seeing the distance between them grow wider every time they were together.

When they arrived, the Manor's firelight greeted her, but Ava's stomach tightened as she spotted Peter sitting in the lounge. He was surrounded by Katarina, Eric, Ilya, Konstantin, and Lance, his attention focused on the conversation. He didn't even look up when she entered.

Eric noticed them and headed over, grinning. "Glad you're back. If I had to listen to one more minute of their chemistry debate, I might've passed out."

Gabriel chuckled. "I'll change, then we can grab food."

Eric raised an eyebrow at Ava. "You joining, Grasshopper?"

She smiled at the nickname but shook her head. "Not tonight. Thanks."

With a shrug, Eric wandered off, leaving her alone with Gabriel.

"You good?" Gabriel asked.

"Yeah. Thanks for tonight."

"Anytime. See you tomorrow?"

"Definitely."

With a final smile, Gabriel disappeared upstairs, and Ava turned back to Peter. She took a seat beside him, but he never glanced at her, his attention still on Konstantin's thickly accented explanation of chemical reactions. The conversation was alien to her, filled with terms she didn't understand, and it made her feel even more disconnected.

"But the chemical equilibrium doesn't occur in irreversible reactions," Peter said.

Ava stared at him, feeling like she didn't know him at all. This was the boy who used to talk to her about everything. Who used to make her feel like she was the center of his world. Now, he seemed so distant, so wrapped up in things she couldn't reach.

Out of the corner of her eye, she caught Lance giving her a knowing look.

He shrugged, a small, tired smile on his face. "They've been at this for an hour," he whispered, rolling his eyes at the others. Exhaustion was etched into his angular features, making him look far older than his years.

Ava leaned closer. "How are you holding up?"

Lance's expression faltered, and he leaned back against the couch, his eyes staring at the floor. "Some days, it feels impossible. I wake up, and for a second, I forget what's happened. Then it all hits me again. I try to get out of bed, but … what's the point, you know?"

"I know what you mean. Every day feels like a battle just to keep going."

"I miss them," he whispered. "I miss Melissa, I miss Jeremy. Some days it feels like I'm drowning in it."

Ava squeezed his arm. "I miss them too. Every second."

"I don't know how you do it, Ava. You lost Colden too … how do you keep it together?"

"I don't. Not really. I've been blaming myself for everything. If I hadn't—" she paused, swallowing the lump in her throat. "I've spent so much time thinking about what I could've done differently. What I should've done. But it's just…" She trailed off, unsure how to put her guilt into words.

"I get that. I keep thinking I should've been stronger. Smarter. Something. Maybe if I'd done things differently, Melissa would still be here." His voice cracked at the mention of her name, and Ava's heart ached for him.

She didn't know what to say that would help, because the truth was, she didn't know how to ease the pain for herself either.

"Well, at least some of us are healing." He nodded toward Peter. "He's starting to open up again."

A pang of guilt hit her. Why hadn't *she* been the one to help Peter? "He seems to have made good friends with the Russians."

"Yeah, they're a tight group. I should get home." Lance stood with a groan. "Talk tomorrow?"

Ava nodded, and he walked away. Sleep sounded tempting, but she knew the nightmares would come. She moved closer to Peter, tapping him on the shoulder. "You're still coming over tonight, right?"

He glanced at her, his face neutral. "Actually, I'm gonna stay here. We'll hang out tomorrow, I promise."

The casual dismissal crushed her, but she masked her disappointment. "Okay."

He gave her a quick kiss on the cheek before turning back to the conversation, as if her presence didn't matter.

Ava stood there for a moment, feeling invisible. She hadn't been there all night, and Peter hadn't even noticed. He hadn't cared. The realization felt like tiny bugs gnawing at her insides.

What was so important there that he couldn't be with her anymore? His constant rejections, his growing distance exhausted her.

As Ava slipped her keys from her pocket, ready to head out the door, Ilya called from behind her. "Ava, wait up."

She turned to face him.

He caught up to her with a soft smile. "Mind if I walk with you?"

She nodded, appreciating the quiet company as they stepped outside, the cool night air brushing against her face.

They walked in silence for a few moments before Ilya glanced over at her, his gaze warm yet contemplative.

"Are you okay?" he asked.

Ava's shoulders slumped. "Honestly … I'm not. Everything just feels so off with Peter lately. I keep wondering if there's something I missed, if it's me."

"I know it hurts, seeing him drift like this," he said. "But sometimes … people change, especially after everything you both have been through."

"I just don't understand. It's like I don't even know him anymore."

"Maybe he's trying to make sense of everything in his own way. Sometimes the best thing you can do is let people find their own path." His voice was kind, but there was a note of finality, almost as if he was encouraging her to loosen her grip on Peter.

"But what if that path doesn't lead back to me?"

Ilya smiled, reaching out to squeeze her hand. "Then maybe it means there's something better waiting for you. Don't lose yourself waiting for him, Ava."

Maybe he was right. Maybe she needed to let go a little, to give Peter space, and, as Ilya had put it, stop losing herself trying to hold on to something that seemed to be slipping away.

As she approached her car, a fleeting moment of clarity pierced the fog of her thoughts.

"Thanks, Ilya." She gave him a small smile.

"Anytime, Ava. Just remember, you're not alone in this."

He gave her a reassuring nod before stepping back, and as Ava slipped into her car and started the engine, his words lingered. But on the drive home, her thoughts swirled with doubts. Was this the end of her and Peter? Had he already slipped away from her?

The night felt darker, colder, and Ava couldn't shake the unsettling sensation that someone—or something—was watching her. The wind blew through the bare branches, making them rattle like bones, and clouds crept in, blanketing the moon. She shivered and hugged herself tighter, her breath coming out in shaky puffs.

She scanned the quiet parking lot, her pulse quickening. Nothing appeared out of place, but the feeling of being watched lingered for a moment longer, then disappeared. A chill crawled up her spine. Had someone been inside her apartment?

Her heart hammered in her chest as she bolted across the lot and up the stairs. Her fingers fumbled with the keys, the door lock seeming to resist, but she got it open. "Dad?" She flicked on the light. Relief flooded her when she saw him sprawled on the couch under a blanket.

Her father groaned, squinting against the sudden brightness. "What is it?" He pushed himself up, revealing pillow marks pressed into his bearded face.

Ava moved closer, eyeing him. He looked pale, his eyes bleary. "You okay?"

He sneezed, pulling out a handkerchief from his flannel pajama pants pocket to blow his nose. A handkerchief.

Ava cringed. Why couldn't he use disposable tissues like everyone else?

"Not really," he rasped. "Think I've caught the flu."

Her alarm spiked. "Do you want me to call Savina?" She reached for her phone.

"No need." He waved her off. "I took some medicine. I'll be fine in a few days."

Ava rolled her eyes. "Dad, seriously? You always do this. You hate asking for help."

He grunted in response. "How was tonight?"

His attempt at distraction added to her frustration, but she let it go. "It was fine. I didn't watch tonight."

"Oh, you practiced?"

"Not exactly." She hesitated. "Gabriel and I went to the beach … we swam."

"Swimming? In December?" His eyebrows shot up, and a glimmer of alertness crossed his face. "Wait—are your powers coming back?"

"Sort of. I can change my temperature again, but nothing else."

"That's progress. I'm proud of you."

"I don't know what you're proud of. I haven't done anything."

"Don't start that again."

She raised her hands in surrender. "Fine. But I'm calling Savina tomorrow."

"You will not. Don't bother her with this flu nonsense."

"Dad—"

"Ava, I mean it."

"Okay," she sighed. He lay back down, exhausted. "Do you want to go to bed?"

"No." He pulled the blanket up to his chin. "I'll watch TV out here if I can't sleep."

"I'll stay with you. I haven't been sleeping much anyway."

He didn't argue as she fetched a blanket from the closet and dropped it onto the easy chair. Before sitting down, she leaned over to kiss his forehead. "I love you."

"I love you too," he muttered as he closed his eyes.

Ava turned off the light and sank into the chair. The TV's soft glow bathed the room in a faint blue light, flickering over her father's face as he drifted off to sleep. She pulled out her phone, the bright screen blinding her for a second. No messages. She hadn't heard from Peter all night. Anxiety twisted in her stomach as she dialed his number, needing to hear his voice.

"Hello?"

"Hey…" She hesitated. "I just wanted to make sure you got home okay." She cringed at the lie as soon as the words left her mouth.

"Yeah, I'm home." He sounded distant, as if he were already half-asleep.

"Oh." She paused, uncertain.

"I'm really tired, Ava. Can we talk tomorrow?"

"Yeah, of course. Goodnight."

"Night." The line went dead.

Ava hung up, her heart sinking as she clutched her necklace, trying to tune into Peter, feeling the low hum of his remorse. But why? She couldn't make sense of it. Everything felt so out of reach, so tangled.

As she was tumbling into her own spiral of thoughts, her phone buzzed. She opened the message and smiled to herself when she saw Gabriel's name on the screen.

Let your brain rest, Grasshopper. Get some sleep. We'll talk tomorrow.

Ava rolled her eyes, and a small warmth spreading through her. She took a deep breath, forcing her body to relax as she let Gabriel's words sink in. Maybe he was right. Maybe tonight, she could let herself rest.

8

WATER FALLS

The sun was setting, painting the sky in deep orange hues as Ava parked her car at the Manor. She unraveled her scarf, the cold air biting at her cheeks. Her breath formed soft clouds as she walked onto the field. She didn't know why she came. Maybe it was out of habit, or maybe it was the lingering hope that tonight might feel different.

As she scanned the field, the icy wind tugged at her hair. The others were scattered, their figures silhouetted against the fading light. Peter's laughter drifted over the cold night as he stood with Konstantin and Katarina, his smile so genuine. Thomas was showing off again, fire dancing across his palms, his grin wide with pride. Her chest tightened. Everyone was making progress. Everyone but her.

Her gaze shifted, catching sight of Lance standing apart from the group. His shoulders slumped, his hands shoved deep into his coat pockets. He looked as disconnected as she felt. Ava walked toward him. "Lance."

He turned, surprise flashing across his face. "Hey."

"How are you?"

He shrugged. "I never really know how to answer that."

"Yeah, me too." She followed his gaze to the group, where laughter and flickers of light punctuated the evening air. Though a pang of envy coursed through her, she suppressed it. "I take it things haven't gotten any easier."

He let out a dry chuckle. "You could say that. What about you? Have you tried anything?"

"No. It feels like I'm stuck."

"You can say that again."

"It's been the hardest six weeks of my life."

"No kidding." He paused, kicking at the dead grass. "It's funny, you know. We were always so unsure of our powers before, maybe even took them for granted. But once they're gone, you realize how much you miss them."

Ava titled her head, studying him. "When were you ever unsure?"

"When they first developed. It was terrifying. But talking to Melissa ... she helped a lot. She wasn't scared of anything."

"You're not scared of much either," Ava said.

He gave her a sad smile. "That's because I never shared that side with anyone but Mel. She kept me grounded. I'm surprised she never spilled the beans, honestly."

"Melissa the Gossip Queen? I'm shocked."

"She told me everything. Every little thing that happened at school. Didn't matter if it was some girl wearing a hideous orange skirt or a guy showing up with a cowlick."

Ava snickered. "A cowlick? Really?"

"I kid you not." He shook his head. "She even brought the poor guy some gel the next day."

She laughed harder, the tension in her chest easing for the first time all evening. "That sounds just like her."

"She once got a subscription to a fashion magazine for one of her teachers, just because she didn't like the outfits they wore," Lance continued. "God, I miss her."

Ava's laughter faded, replaced by a familiar ache. "Me too."

He wrapped his arm around her shoulders, pulling her into a tight hug. For a moment, neither of them said anything, both lost in the memories of the ones they had lost.

"How's Gillian?" she asked.

"She's still sick."

Ava nodded. "I should check on her, but ... she just lashes out. At everyone. Especially me."

"She doesn't mean half of what she says," Lance said. "She's hurting. We all are."

"I know, but I can't reach her. It's like she's put up this wall, and no matter what I do, I make it worse. Same with Peter. I miss when it wasn't so hard. When we were ... us."

"I know. I think she'll be better if you're there for her. Even if she doesn't say it, she needs you, Ava. Just like the rest of us do."

After a long pause, Lance pulled back, his hand dropping to his side. "I should probably get going. I'm not feeling so great myself."

"You're not getting sick too, are you?"

"Probably just tired. I don't know. Everyone seems to be getting it. Gillian, and Melissa's parents aren't doing too well either." Lance's brow furrowed. "Even your dad, right?"

She nodded. "Yeah, he's got the flu. Stubborn as always, though. Refuses to ask Savina for help."

"That doesn't sound familiar at all," he teased, a slight smirk. "I'll be fine. I just need to sleep it off."

"Make sure you rest. If you need anything, let me know."

"I will," Lance promised. He squeezed her hand one last time before stepping away. "Take care of yourself, okay?"

"You too."

Maybe I should go home, too.

But Ava didn't want to wallow in disappointment or stand on the sidelines watching the training while she felt useless. She needed something else. Something real.

Her eyes drifted over the field and settled on Gabriel, standing a little way off with his arms crossed, observing the group with his usual calm demeanor. Ava made her way toward him, her feet carrying her faster than her mind could process.

"Grasshopper." He turned to face her with a smile, his sharp blue eyes softening when they met hers. "What's up?"

She hesitated for a moment, and bit her lip. "Do you ... want to hang out?" The words felt clumsy. "I just ... I don't want to be here right now."

"Sure. I'll drive."

The relief that washed over Ava surprised her. She nodded, and together, they made their way to his car. The cold air stung her cheeks, but she welcomed it. It cleared her head a little.

They climbed into his car, and they pulled away from the Manor. The atmosphere between them was easy, though neither spoke for a while. Ava leaned back in her seat, gazing out the window as the darkened landscape rushed by.

After a few minutes, Gabriel glanced over at her. "So ... where do you want to go?"

Ava thought about it for a second, then shrugged. "The waterfall, maybe?"

His lips quirked into a small smile. "Good choice. Relaxing spot."

They drove in comfortable silence for a while, the only sounds were the hum of the engine and the occasional whisper of wind against the car.

The tension unraveled from her shoulders, as if leaving the Manor helped her breathe a little easier.

When they arrived at the waterfall, the familiar sound of rushing water filled the air, and a wave of calm washed over her. It felt like stepping into another world, one where everything else didn't matter.

They walked toward the edge of the pool, where the sound of the waterfall thundered in the background. Ava took a deep breath, letting the cool air fill her lungs as she gazed at the water cascading down the rocks.

Ava settled onto the damp rock beside Gabriel, the coolness of the stone seeping through her jeans. She hugged her knees to her chest, resting her chin on them as the roar of the waterfall filled the air. For a moment, she let herself exist in the silence, the crashing water acting as a buffer between her thoughts and reality.

"You've been quiet." He leaned back against the rock. His blue eyes flicked toward her, catching the faint glow of moonlight.

"I've been thinking. It's hard not to."

He tilted his head, studying her. "What's on your mind?"

"Same stuff. Guilt. Loss. Feeling stuck. You already know the Ava pity party playlist." She forced a weak smile.

"It's not a pity party. You're grieving. That's human."

"I don't feel very human. I feel ... hollow. Like there's nothing left but guilt and anger."

His gaze lingered on her. "You're not the only one who feels that way."

"What do you mean?"

He sighed, running a hand through his hair, his fingers lingering at the back of his neck. "I guess I'm scared of a lot of things. Losing people again. Losing myself in all of this. Everyone thinks I've got it together, but ... sometimes

I don't even know who I am without all of this—powers, responsibility. What if I'm just ... empty?"

With a hesitant touch, her fingers grazed his arm. "You're not empty, Gabriel. You're one of the strongest people I know. Powers or not."

He glanced at her, his eyes shadowed with something beneath the surface. "You don't know the whole story."

"Then tell me."

"It's been so many years ... decades. You'd think it still wouldn't haunt me."

"What haunts you?"

He looked away, his gaze fixed on the rushing water. "My sister. She was everything to me. She was two years younger than me. After our parents died, it was just the two of us. Our uncle took us in but he ... he wasn't kind. She was my anchor. Always smiling, always finding a way to make things bearable when things felt out of control." His voice faltered, and he let out a shaky breath. "I failed her."

Her throat tightened as she took his hand.

His eyes were fixed on her palm, scrutinizing every crease and line. "I was sixteen when my powers manifested. Teleportation. It was chaotic, uncontrollable. One minute I was there, the next ... I wasn't. I'd disappear for hours, lost in some random place, unable to find my way back. My uncle was terrified of me, thought I was dangerous. And he was right."

"You're not—"

"I took her with me once. We were arguing with my uncle. He wanted to send her away. I grabbed her hand, and suddenly we were somewhere else. By a lake, deep in the forest. She couldn't swim." His voice cracked.

Ava's breath hitched as tears welled in her eyes. "Gabriel…"

"I tried to get to her, but every time I teleported, it was to the wrong place. I couldn't control it. By the time I reached her … she was gone." He gritted his teeth, his hands forming fists as he stared at the ground. "It's my fault."

She moved closer, wrapping her arms around him. He tensed at first but let out a shuddering breath, leaning into her embrace. "You didn't kill her," she whispered. "You didn't mean for any of that to happen."

"I took her there," he rasped. "I was supposed to protect her."

"You were just a kid. You didn't know how to control your powers." She drew back, meeting his gaze. "It wasn't your fault."

He met her gaze, his eyes glassy with emotion. "It feels like it was. And no matter how much I control my powers now, I'll never forget what I did."

She held his gaze, her heart aching for him. "You've come so far, Gabriel. You've learned to control it. You protect people now. You're not that boy anymore."

A long silence followed, broken only by the waterfall's deafening roar.

With a nod, Gabriel squeezed her hand. "Thanks, sensei."

"I'm always here," she said.

WARNING SIGN

9

The small house rested beneath the tangled arms of dogwood trees, their bare branches swaying in the crisp winter breeze. Ava hadn't been there in months, but she decided it was time to visit and try to make amends. She was tired of the bitterness between them.

She hesitated as she reached the faded white door. The paint had chipped and peeled, exposing the worn wood underneath. The porch creaked beneath her feet, and she half-expected one of the old boards to give way under her weight. Leaves cluttered the corners of the porch, and a small wind chime hanging by the door tinkled a soft, lonely melody in the cold wind.

Am I really the right person to check on Gillian? I've lost so much. I can't lose her, too.

With a deep breath, Ava rang the doorbell. After a moment, the door opened to reveal Mrs. Madison. Her wide blue eyes lit up, a warmth in her expression that seemed misplaced, given the tension between Ava and Gillian. A baggy sweater swathed her plump figure, and strands of gray streaked her dark curls.

"Ava, honey! It's been ages." Mrs. Madison smiled, her voice as bright as ever. "Come on in. It's freezing out there."

Ava followed her inside, the familiar smell of vanilla candles and something floral filling her nose. The dim living room was cluttered with family photos and Mickey Mouse memorabilia. Figurines, pillows, clocks, and cups. It was like stepping into a whimsical, messy museum of childhood nostalgia. It was overwhelming.

"I came to see Gillian," Ava said, her hands tucked into her jacket pockets.

Mrs. Madison waved a hand toward the hallway. "Oh, she's fine. Just the flu. She hasn't been out of bed all week, though. Poor thing's been running a fever and barely eating. Stubborn as ever. I tried inviting Savina to come, but Gillian didn't want her to. Maybe you can get her to snap out of it."

"I'll see what I can do."

"Good luck, sweetheart. She's been more grumpy than usual. Can I get you some tea? I made some fresh ginger and honey. It's good for the throat."

"No, thanks. I'll check on her first."

Ava made her way down the narrow hallway, the soft carpet muffling her footsteps. When she reached Gillian's door, she knocked.

There was a muffled groan from inside, followed by a hoarse, "Go away."

Ava rolled her eyes and pushed the door open anyway. The air inside was stuffy and warm, the faint scent of menthol clinging to the blankets piled high on Gillian's bed.

A messy tangle of hair and the top of her flushed face peeked out from the covers. "Are you deaf?"

"Yep." Ava stepped further into the room. "How are you doing?"

"What's it look like? Why are you here?"

"I came to make sure you're okay."

"Well, as you can see, I'm not dead. You can leave now." Gillian pulled the blanket higher over her head, her irritation prickling Ava's necklace.

"Are we seriously going to be like this forever? I'm so tired of it. Melissa and Jeremy are gone, G. We need each other more than ever. So can you please, for once, stop pretending you're okay and actually talk to me?"

Peeking out from under the blanket, Gillian glared at her. "Talk? What, like you've been doing these past few weeks? Ignoring all of us and only being around Peter? You've got some nerve."

"I know, and I'm sorry. But you haven't made it easy for me to be around you either."

Gillian's expression softened. "I needed someone to blame. Peter was easy. Maybe because it wasn't really about him."

Ava sat down on the edge of the bed. "I don't hate you, Gillian."

"You should. I've been awful to you."

"Yeah, you have." She smiled. "But you're still my friend. And I need you. More than you know."

"You ... need me?"

"Yes. I know things have been messed up. You're angry about Peter, and I get it. But I need my friend."

Gillian stared at her for a long moment before pulling the blanket down to her shoulders. Her cheeks were flushed with fever, her hair sticking out in every direction, but her eyes carried a vulnerability Ava hadn't seen in weeks. "I thought you chose him over us. It felt like all you cared about was Peter. And I was pissed. I didn't know how to handle it."

"It was never like that. I never wanted to make you feel like I was choosing him over you."

Gillian's eyes welled up, but she blinked them away. "You really don't hate me?"

"No. I don't. We've all changed. We've all been through hell. But I'm still here for you. If you'll let me."

For the first time, Gillian's scowl faded. "I don't feel good enough to argue with you right now," she muttered. "I'm still mad, but … I'll think about it."

Ava smirked. "Good. You should. And when you're better, we'll go to the Manor to train. I'll see you later."

She turned to leave, and as her hand landed on the doorknob, she heard Gillian's voice, softer this time. "Ava?"

"Yeah?"

"Thanks. For not giving up on me."

Ava gave a small smile. "I'll see you soon."

As Ava stepped back into the cold evening air, her emotions churned—relief, sadness, and a flicker of hope. Things weren't perfect, but maybe they didn't need to be. For now, this small step forward was enough.

That night, Ava made her way to Blackhart, hoping the physical exertion would dull the emotional chaos swirling inside her. Each punch, each dodge, and every block felt heavier than it should have. It wasn't just the absence of her powers, it was something deeper. Something wrong.

Gabriel barked instructions, his voice steady and calm, but it felt distant. Lance sparred beside her, his movements sharp and precise, but Ava couldn't match his rhythm tonight. Her body felt sluggish, her limbs weighed down by exhaustion that went beyond the physical.

By the time they broke for dinner, Ava felt like she was running on fumes. Her throat was dry, and an ache had settled in her chest that no amount of water or rest seemed to soothe.

She noticed the absence of Thomas and Nicole as they headed inside, the unsettling thought taking root. Spotting Link near the entrance, she caught his arm. "Where's Nicole?"

"She's not feeling well," he said. "I told her to rest tonight and come back tomorrow."

She exchanged a look with Lance. "My dad's sick, too. And Gillian."

"Thomas has been sick for days," Lance added.

Link shrugged, his tone dismissive. "It is that time of year. People get the flu."

But Ava couldn't shake the unease growing in her chest. "I don't know," she muttered, half to herself. "It seems like a lot of people are getting sick all at once. Do you think it's because we're vulnerable right now, without our powers?"

Lance tilted his head. "Could be. Makes sense. Stress doesn't help either."

"Let's head inside," Link said with a playful grin. "It's starting to rain, and I can't have my hair getting frizzy."

Lance laughed, nudging him. "Priorities, right?"

Ava managed a smile, but her mind stayed focused on the growing sense of dread gnawing at her. As they entered the Manor, her gaze found Peter across the room. His shoulders slumped, his face blank, but she felt the storm inside him—sadness, frustration, and something else she couldn't quite name.

Steeling herself, she approached him. "Peter?"

His eyes flicked to hers, and he schooled his expression. "Hey."

"What's wrong?" she asked.

"Nothing." The word was flat, automatic, and unconvincing.

"You seem ... out of it."

"I'm just tired." His tone was both cold and dismissive.

Ava swallowed the sting of his words. She took a small step closer. "Are you sure? You can talk to me, Peter."

With a heavy sigh, he rubbed the back of his neck. "I'm fine, Ava. I'm going to train with Ilya and Gustav."

"Do you want to come over later?" she asked, desperation creeping into her tone. "We could just hang out, talk, watch something—"

"I can't. I told Ilya I'd help him with some drills. I'll be too exhausted afterward."

Her breath caught in her throat as she tried to maintain a blank face. "Right. Okay."

Peter turned and walked away, leaving her standing there, rooted in place. Her heart felt like it had been ripped out and left in the open for everyone to see. She swallowed hard, blinking back the tears that threatened to fall.

The room was suddenly too crowded, too loud. Anxiety coiled in her stomach, making her feel nauseous and dizzy. She hugged herself, her arms crossing tightly over her chest. Needing to escape, she fled the room, her gaze fixed on the floor. As she rounded the corner, she collided with someone, firm hands catching her before she could stumble. "Sorry," she mumbled, trying to pull free.

"Ava?" Gabriel's voice was gentle, tinged with concern. His hands lingered on her arms, steadying her. "Hey, are you okay?"

"I'm fine. It's late, I should—"

Gabriel's piercing blue eyes searched hers. "Are you? You look like you're about to collapse. Is it Peter?"

She bit her lip, trying to hold back the flood of emotions threatening to overwhelm her. "I'm sorry," she whispered. "I'll see you tomorrow."

Gabriel's hands didn't drop from her arms. "Ava, you don't have to do this. You don't have to pretend you're okay."

The sincerity in his tone nearly broke her. She shook her head, forcing herself to step away, but she could feel his gaze on her as she walked down the hall, her vision blurring with unshed tears.

10

PLAGUE

All Ava wanted when she got home was a hot shower and some sleep. She checked on her father first. He was still adamant about refusing Savina's help, a stubbornness that had begun to grate her nerves. She didn't have the energy to argue tonight, so she heated up some soup for him, the low hum of the microwave filling the silence.

She knew she needed to eat, too, but her stomach churned with anxiety. Opening the refrigerator, she grabbed the pot of leftover spaghetti. As she raised the lid, a putrid, sour odor slammed into her, causing her to gag.

Her body reacted before she could stop it. She barely made it to the bathroom in time, retching until her stomach was empty. Tears blurred her vision as she slumped against the cool tile, her forehead pressed against the cabinet. Her breath came in shallow bursts, each one reminding her of her fragility. Just when her powers were returning, something else knocked her down.

This wasn't just anxiety. It felt like her body was betraying her. Feverish, aching, dizzy. Was this how her father had been feeling? Had she gotten the flu, too? She needed to check on him, but getting to her feet felt like a monumental task. The room spun as she gripped the edge of the sink, waiting for the dizziness to pass.

Finally, she staggered out into the living room.

Her father's coughing echoed in the silence, harsher than before. "Dad?" she called, her heart already pounding. His coughing grew more violent, almost choking, and the sound sent a spike of panic through her chest. Flipping on the light, she rushed to his side.

"Dad!" Ava grabbed his shoulders and pulled him into a sitting position, but as she did, the blanket slipped away. Her eyes went wide as the sight hit her like a hammer to the chest—blood-soaked sleeves, dark stains seeping through the fabric. She pushed his pajama sleeve up and recoiled in horror.

His arm was rotting. Blackened, dry tissue clung to exposed bone, the sickening smell of gangrene filling her nostrils. Her stomach lurched again, bile rising in her throat, but she swallowed it down. She had to focus.

He coughed again, spraying blood across the blanket. Ava's heart pounded as adrenaline surged through her body. Her hands shook, and her mind raced. *Savina. I need Savina.*

She propped him up against the back of the couch and sprinted to her room, grabbing her phone off the nightstand with trembling fingers. She tapped Gabriel's name.

The phone barely rang before he answered. "Ava? What's wrong?"

"I need Savina! He's coughing up blood."

"We're on our way." Gabriel hung up.

The silence afterward felt deafening as Ava stood frozen, phone still clutched in her trembling hand. She returned to her father's side, her chest tight with fear. She prayed they'd get there in time.

Clinging to her father, Ava rocked him, her body trembling with fear. Nausea threatened to engulf her, but she held it back, refusing to give in. Her father's labored breathing filled the room, a constant reminder of how close she was to losing him.

The door swung open, and Savina and Gabriel rushed inside. Relief flooded her, but it wasn't enough to calm her racing heart.

"Oh, good heavens!" Savina knelt beside Ava's father.

Ava stood, her legs wobbling beneath her, and stumbled into Gabriel's arms. She couldn't hold back the sobs any longer.

"It's okay." He wrapped his arms around her, holding her as they stood together.

She nodded, burying her face against his chest, but the tears wouldn't stop. She felt like she might vomit again, but somehow managed to hold it back. Everything spun around her.

A few moments later, Savina touched her shoulder. "He is out of danger."

Pulling away from Gabriel, Ava turned to face her father, her legs trembling. "Thank you," she whispered. Her heavy head pounded, the world around her swam in a haze of exhaustion, and the room tilted, threatening to send her tumbling.

"Savina, I think she's ill, too." Gabriel's voice sounded distant, as if it were underwater.

As Ava's eyes fluttered shut, the last thing she saw was Gabriel's worried face.

When she blinked awake, she was lying on the floor, her cheek pressed against the cool wood.

Gabriel and Savina hovered over her.

She blinked, trying to gather her thoughts. "What happened?"

"You fainted," Gabriel said. "Savina healed both of you."

Relief washed over her as she sat up, taking a moment to steady herself. She glanced over at her father. His color had returned, and his arms, once marred by gangrene, were back to normal.

"Dad." She rushed to his side, clutching his hand. With the tension gone, tears streamed down her face.

"It's okay, sweetie," he murmured.

"He will be tired for a bit, but he is fine," Savina said.

Ava wiped her tears, her mind still racing. "How could I have missed the gangrene? I thought he had the flu."

Savina's expression turned grim. "The plague—Corbin's plague—starts out slowly, like any illness. But then it attacks with a vengeance. Once it reaches the bloodstream, it spreads rapidly."

Ava froze, her breath catching in her throat. "Corbin was here? How? Why didn't he—" She swallowed hard. "Why didn't he take me?"

Savina shook her head. "Corbin wasn't here. He doesn't need to be. He sends underlings to do his dirty work. He doesn't want you dead, Ava. He's testing you, like he did when you were younger."

"Testing me? Why? And ... he's testing all of us. Gillian, Thomas, Nicole, Melissa's parents. They're all sick! You have to help them!"

Savina's eyes widened in alarm. She pressed a hand to her mouth. "Oh dear." She turned to Gabriel. "We have to go. Now."

"Of course," Gabriel said, already taking her hand.

"Will you come back?" Ava's voice was small, almost afraid to ask.

He met her gaze, his expression firm. "I will," he promised, and in a blink, they were gone.

The room fell into silence, the faint hum of the heater the only sound. Ava turned back to her father, her heart still heavy with lingering fear. She took his hand again, squeezing it.

"Dad, why didn't you let me call Savina earlier?"

"I didn't realize it was so bad. I'm sorry I worried you."

She pulled him into a tight hug, her tears returning. "I thought I was going to lose you."

"I'm okay now." He rubbed her back. "I promise, next time I'll call Savina right away."

Ava buried her face against his chest, letting herself be comforted, though deep down, she couldn't shake the dread growing in the pit of her stomach about Corbin's plague, about Peter, about everything.

They stayed like that, huddled together, waiting for Gabriel's return. Ava chewed on the inside of her cheek, her leg bouncing as anxiety gripped her. She couldn't stay still not until she knew the others were safe.

"What's going to happen when I leave?" she asked. "Who's going to heal you then?"

He gave her a reassuring squeeze. "A few of us will stay at the Manor. It's protected."

"Why wasn't our apartment protected? Why didn't Savina place a charm over it?"

"She did. Ava, I could have gotten this from anywhere."

Her pulse pounded in her ears, a steady drumbeat that matched the rising panic in her chest. The room felt too small, the walls pressing in on her as her mind raced. Her vision blurred at the edges, and the air seemed to thin, as though all the oxygen had been sucked out, leaving her gasping.

"What are we going to do?" Her thoughts spiraled out of control. "This is turning into a pandemic, isn't it? He's spreading the disease to the Ephemerals. Savina can't save them all. What if—what if it's too late?"

"Ava, calm down. One thing at a time."

But she couldn't calm down. Her chest felt tight, like it was being crushed by an invisible weight, squeezing the air from her lungs. Her breathing grew shallow, quick, like she was drowning and couldn't find the surface. Her hands clutched at the couch cushion beneath her, the fabric rough under her fingers as she tried to ground herself, but the panic surged higher, making her body tremble.

Her heart pounded so hard it felt like it might burst through her ribs. "I can't breathe!"

"Ava!"

The roaring in her head drowned him out.

He shook her gently, but it did nothing to pull her back from the edge.

The room spun around her, colors and shapes melding together in a dizzying whirl. Her chest heaved, but no matter how hard she tried, she couldn't draw in a full breath. It was like the air had turned to smoke, thick and suffocating. Her vision tunneled, shrinking until all she could see was darkness creeping in at the edges.

Gabriel was in front of her, his warm hands cupped her face. "Ava." His blue eyes locked onto hers, calm and focused, cutting through the storm in her mind. "Look at me. Breathe with me."

Her heart was still racing, but focused on his face, the smooth cadence of his voice, his thumbs stroking her cheeks.

"Breathe in, Ava. Slowly. Just like that. Now let it out."

She followed his lead, pulling in a shaky breath, feeling the cool air rush into her lungs. It hurt at first, like her chest was still too tight to expand fully, but she managed to exhale, releasing a small fraction of the panic with it.

"There you go," Gabriel murmured, his hands still on her face, keeping her tethered to the moment. "Again. Another deep breath."

She loosened her death grip on the couch as she took another breath. Her chest still felt tight, but it wasn't crushing her anymore. The sharp edges of her panic began to dull, replaced by the steady rhythm of her breathing.

The room stopped spinning. Her pulse calmed, the ringing in her ears subsiding.

"Good," he said. "Keep breathing, Ava. You're okay."

She nodded, her eyes welled with tears as she focused on the feel of his hands on her face. She could feel her feet on the ground again, the solidness of the floor beneath her. "I thought I was going to die," she whispered.

"You're okay. I've got you."

She took a few more deep breaths, each one easier than the last. The panic had loosened its grip on her chest. The reality of what was happening clawed at her, but Gabriel's presence made it bearable. "Is everyone okay?"

"Yes," he said gently, dropping his hands. "Savina is already working on it. She's rushing to make potions for the Ephemerals as we speak."

"I want to help her," Ava said. "She can't do this alone."

Her father stood from the couch, his energy returning. "How is she going to administer the potions to all the Ephemerals?"

"We're going to add it to the drinking water," Gabriel explained. "It'll prevent anyone who isn't infected from contracting the illness."

Her father straightened, determination replacing his fatigue. "All right. Let's go help Savina."

Gabriel held out his hands, one for Ava and one for her father. Without hesitation, they took them. A second later, the familiar, disorienting tug of teleportation hit Ava, and they appeared at the Manor.

The kitchen buzzed with activity. Enchanters were moving around, gathering herbs and other ingredients for Savina's potions. The air was thick with the scent of simmering brews, the clinking of glass vials and the low murmur of voices creating an undercurrent of intensity.

Savina stood at the center of it all, mixing ingredients in large pots, her hands moving swiftly. Buckets lined the counters, already filled with the finished potion, sealed and ready for distribution. The urgency in the room was palpable, and Ava felt it settle into her bones.

She jumped in, grabbing herbs and mixing them as she had seen Savina do. It was a welcome distraction from the storm raging inside her.

"Ava," Aaron called. "I'm going to need your help. We're putting this in the town's drinking water. You'll administer it into the holding tanks. The water listens to you. Gillian will handle the guard at the plant."

She nodded, her pulse quickening. "Okay."

"I'll go with them," Gabriel said. "There will be alarms, and we'll probably have to do some fence hopping."

Aaron nodded. "Good. Take Lance. He can mimic your power."

The four of them set off in Lance's SUV, the hum of the engine the only sound in the otherwise quiet night. Ava sat in the backseat, hands gripping her knees. The air in the car felt thick with anticipation, the headlights cutting through the dark as they approached the water treatment plant.

Lance slowed to a stop beneath an orange streetlight. The locked fence loomed ahead like a silent sentinel. "Ready?" He cut the engine.

Ava exhaled. "Let's go."

They stepped out into the chilly night, the cold biting at their exposed skin. Lance and Gabriel hefted the heavy buckets of potion, their breaths coming out in white puffs. Gabriel grabbed two buckets and teleported inside the fence, the space where he'd been now empty. Lance followed suit, mimicking Gabriel's power until all the buckets were inside.

Gabriel reappeared and took Ava's hand, the world spinning for a brief moment as they teleported to the other side. Lance did the same with Gillian. An eerie silence hung in the air, broken only by the distant hum of machinery.

"So far, so good," Lance whispered.

Crouching low, they moved toward the towering holding tanks, the metal steps cold beneath Ava's hands as she climbed. Gabriel was right behind her. At the top, he twisted the wheel to open the tank's lid, and a rush of cool, metallic air hit her face. Ava hesitated for a moment, staring down into the dark water, unsure of how to proceed.

But she closed her eyes, raising her hands over the surface. The water pulsed, as if recognizing her, and began to respond. A tingling sensation spread through her arms as the water latched onto her, a connection forming that sent a surge of energy through her veins. She smiled.

"It's ready," she said.

Gabriel tipped the bucket, the thick potion splashing into the tank. They watched as the water absorbed it, the mixture swirling and disappearing into the depths. Without missing a beat, they raced to the next tank.

As they reached the top of the stairs, an ear-splitting alarm blared through the night.

Ava cursed under her breath. "We have to hurry!"

In the distance, a flashlight cut through the darkness, the beam bouncing off the metal tanks.

The dimness almost swallowed the security guard, a stocky man in an off-white uniform. "Who's out there?" His gruff voice echoed.

Her heart leapt into her throat. "We're going to get caught."

Gabriel's hand brushed hers. "Don't worry. Gillian's got this."

Ava swallowed hard, trusting Gabriel's words as she turned back to the water. She focused, ignoring the blaring alarm and the footsteps growing closer. The water responded to her call once again, and as it did, Gabriel poured the second bucket of potion in.

Distant sirens cut through the air, growing louder by the second. The police were coming.

"We've got to move faster," he said.

Panic clawed at Ava, but she forced herself to keep going. They dashed to the next tank, her heart pounding in her ears. She extended her hands over the water, her body trembling with urgency, willing it to obey her as the wailing sirens drew nearer.

Red and blue lights flooded the plant as the police arrived at the gate. The clatter of voices and the sound of the gate swinging open sent a jolt of fear through Ava. But she and Gabriel worked methodically, pouring the final dose of potion into the water as the police stepped inside.

Gabriel didn't waste a second. He grabbed Ava's hand while Lance and Gillian reached for them. With a flash, they teleported, reappearing at the front entrance of the Manor, all panting for breath.

"Talk about in the nick of time," Lance said between gasps. "I really liked that SUV, too."

"You mean the stolen one?" Gillian arched an eyebrow.

"Finder's keepers," he shot back with a grin.

Gillian rolled her eyes, and despite everything, they all laughed, an anxious, relieved kind of laugh.

Ava's chest still ached with worry, though. She hoped, with everything in her, that the potion was enough to save the town.

11

OVER

For the first time in weeks, Ava felt good. A sense of accomplishment simmered within her as she walked out of school, the last day of the semester finally over. It was one less thing to worry about. Her mind turned to training with Gabriel. She shouldn't have been so stubborn about it earlier, it was a distraction, a way to feel stronger, more in control. And Gabriel always knew how to take her mind off the chaos.

But issue number one, Peter, walked beside her, his eyes glued to his phone. Again. The drizzle resumed, droplets beading on their jackets. The rain had been relentless for days, turning the skies into a constant blanket of gray. Ava pulled her hood tighter, trying to keep the damp chill from seeping in.

When they reached her car, she turned to him. He still hadn't looked up from his phone. "Do you want to come over tonight after practice?"

He shoved his phone into his pocket. "I can't. I told Ilya and Katarina I'd hang out with them."

Ava pressed her lips together, the sting of rejection hitting her like a slap. It wasn't the first time. She tried to calm her breathing, but the pressure built inside her, like a dam about to burst. "No!" The word escaped before she could stop it. She exploded. "That's like the thirtieth time you've declined. I'm sick of it. You didn't even know my dad almost died. What's going on, Peter?" Her voice trembled as she crossed her arms, trying to hold herself together as passing students splashed through puddles, their laughter a distant echo in her ears.

Peter's shoulders tensed, but he avoided her gaze. "Ava—"

"And don't tell me it's stress. I'm stressed, too. We're all going through a lot. But you never come over anymore. You never touch me. You can't even look me in the eye. Why are you avoiding me?"

He adjusted his backpack, his eyes darting to the ground. "We … need to talk."

Her stomach dropped, the icy grip of dread tightening around her chest. "We are talking." Her voice had lost its edge.

"Somewhere more private." His gaze flicked around at the dwindling students, but Ava couldn't wait. She needed answers now.

"It's just us. No one's paying attention. What is it?"

He exhaled, rubbing the back of his neck. His hair was damp from the drizzle, sticking to his forehead. He looked so tired, so distant, and it made her want to scream. "Ava, I don't know how to say this."

Her body trembled, the fear creeping up her spine. She knew what was coming but prayed for anything else. Her hands balled into fists, her nails digging into her palms. "Spit it out!"

Peter finally he looked her in the eye. "This is hard for me, okay?"

"Then why are you doing it?" she whispered.

He reached for her hand, but she jerked away, taking a step back. Her pulse thundered in her ears, drowning out the soft rain around them.

"We should break up." The words slammed into her like a physical blow.

Her heart stuttered, and the world tilted around her. She stood frozen as the words sank in, her chest tight with disbelief. "Why?" The question had circled her mind for months, but she knew the answer.

"Ava, we haven't been on the same page for months." He shifted, guilt flickering across his face. "We argue all the time. You've been ... different. I don't know how to fix it."

"We can work on it," she pleaded, her throat thick with tears. "We've always worked through things before."

Peter shook his head. "It's not the same anymore. I'm sorry. I wish things were different."

Tears slid down her cheeks, hot against the cold drizzle. "You're just giving up on us? After everything?"

"Ava, I have feelings for someone else."

The words flew out of his mouth so fast it was like she'd been hit in the chest by a ninety mile-per-hour fastball. It took the breath right out of her.

She stared at him, numb with shock, the world spinning. Her vision blurred. "What? You're lying."

"I'm not. I'm so sorry." His eyes shone with guilt and ... relief?

Relief? He's actually relieved.

"You haven't been yourself for a while," he continued.

"I was grieving!" she cried, her voice raw. "I hid my feelings to protect you, so you wouldn't feel guilty. That drove you away? My grief made you like someone else?"

"No. I didn't mean it like that." He rubbed his temples. "It's hard to be around you when you're angry all the time. I tried to help you, but you didn't want my help."

"I did! I've been training. I've been getting stronger. I kept everything inside for *you*."

"I never asked you to do that."

"So, you've been stringing me along this whole time? You haven't loved me for a while, have you?"

"Ava, I do love you. But I'm lost. I don't know what to do anymore."

Anger flared through her, heating her skin. Water began swirling around her arms, dripping onto the wet pavement as if ready to strike. Her power surged with her emotions, threatening to lash out.

He took a step back. "Please calm down."

"You think I'd hurt you?"

He shook his head. "No, I just—"

"*Leave*," she said through clenched teeth, her heart pounding.

"Ava, please don't—"

"I said leave!"

Peter turned and walked away, his figure disappearing into the misty rain.

Ava stood frozen, chest heaving, her heart shattered into pieces. With trembling hands, she climbed into her car. The parking lot was nearly empty, making for an easy exit, but everything felt wrong. She gripped the steering wheel until her knuckles turned white, her breath coming in ragged bursts.

She felt Peter's remorse, anger, guilt. That was what he'd been feeling guilty about the whole time. He'd been too afraid to tell her the truth and let her become invisible.

Rain pummeled her car like angry fists, the noise a relentless assault. She forced herself to focus on the road ahead, parting the rain with her powers, creating an invisible shield over her car. The tears welled up in her eyes, but she swallowed them down, refusing to let them fall.

Not a single thought of Peter lingered in her mind. Only emptiness and a cold ache filled her.

When Ava got home, she bolted up the stairs, her heart racing faster with each step. Holding back the tears, the growing discomfort in her stomach begged for an outlet. Her hands shook as she fumbled with her key, forcing the door open before she slammed it shut behind her.

She made it to the bathroom in time, clutching the cold porcelain as her body convulsed, purging all the hurt she'd been swallowing down for weeks. She hated the sensation, the rawness it left in her throat, the way it made her feel exposed, emptied. When it was over, she ran a washcloth under cold water, pressing it to her flushed face, hoping the chill would numb everything.

The shower was next. She turned the heat up high, letting the steam fill the room, fogging up her reflection in the mirror until all she could see was a blurred outline. It was better that way. The necklace around her neck had become suffocating, the pulse of emotions from everyone else digging into her already raw nerves. She reached up, her fingers trembling as they unclasped the chain. An unfamiliar lightness filled her as it slipped from her fingers and landed on the counter with a small, final clink. It was almost like she'd shed a piece of herself, but it was freeing. For once, no one would sense her agony, not Gabriel, not Peter. She could keep this to herself.

Under the pounding water, Ava let her tears fall, her cries mingling with the powerful stream, muted and contained. The water wrapped around her, almost like it understood, its warmth cradling her as she leaned against the tile wall, letting out quiet, jagged sobs. She pressed her face into a towel, stifling the muffled screams that fought their way out. The pain, the loss all surfaced, wave after wave. What was the point of feeling nothing if it didn't stop the pain?

Later, curled under her blankets, she sank into her pillow, her grief pouring out. Memories and faces surfaced: Colden's laugh, her friends, her mother's betrayal, and now Peter. He had been her anchor, her first love, and now even he was gone. She clutched her pillow tighter as it all crashed down on her, squeezing her breath until only broken gasps came out. The tears wouldn't stop. She yearned for it all to be a dream, but as the night pressed on, the hollow ache in her chest grew sharper, a constant reminder that she was awake, that it was all real.

12

BLACK TANGLED HEART

This wasn't supposed to happen. Ava and Peter were invincible. They loved each other. They were meant for each other. Then why had he fallen for someone else? The words replayed in her mind like a song on repeat. Taunting her. Her heart felt like it was sinking, drowning in an ocean of pain. Her stomach knotted, and a wave of nausea hit.

Cursing, she stumbled out of bed, her legs weak and shaky, and rushed to the bathroom. The acid burned her throat as she heaved, leaving it raw. The cold tile floor pressed against her cheek as she slumped down, her breathing shallow and ragged. The faint scent of the soap on the sink mingled with the acrid tang of bile, made her want to puke again.

Everything hurt. Her heart, her chest, her stomach. The ache spread through her body like a sickness, sapping her strength. She wanted to disappear, to fade into the quiet, where no one could touch her.

The doorbell rang in the distance, followed by a frantic knock.

She didn't move. Couldn't move.

The knocking intensified. The door creaked open. "Ava?" Gabriel's voice was sharp, edged with panic.

Her heart sank, and she blinked back tears. Why was he here? She wanted to call out, to say something, but her throat was dry.

His footsteps grew louder, more urgent, until the bathroom door swung open.

She flinched at the sudden movement, her gaze slowly lifting to meet his.

Gabriel stood there, his blue eyes wide with alarm, his breath coming in uneven gasps. He looked like he'd just run a marathon. For a moment, neither of them spoke, and his gaze fell on the necklace she'd left on the counter. "You scared the hell out of me." He crouched down in front of her, his hands hovering near her shoulders but not quite touching. "Ava, what happened?"

She shook her head. "I'm fine."

"You're not fine. Why isn't your necklace on?"

"I didn't want anyone to feel this. I didn't want you to feel it."

He let out a shaky sigh, as if trying to rein in his emotions. "Ava, you can't just—" He stopped himself, his hands falling to his sides. "We all thought something happened to you. Savina, Link, everyone. I thought…" He trailed off. He was quiet for a moment, and his hand brushed against hers. "I'm already feeling it, Ava. Whether or not you wear that necklace. We care about you. I care about you. You don't have to shut us out."

The front door slamming open startled them both. Heavy footsteps pounded through the apartment. "Ava?" Her father's voice was frantic.

A fresh wave of guilt crashed over her. "In here," she croaked.

Gabriel stood, stepping back as her father appeared in the doorway. His face was pale, his eyes wide with fear as he took in the scene. Ava on the floor, her necklace missing, Gabriel standing nearby.

"What happened?" her father demanded, his gaze darting between them.

"She's okay," Gabriel said. "She needed some space."

Her father's gaze landed on her, his expression softening but still filled with worry. "Ava…" He knelt beside her, his hands trembling as he helped her to her feet. "You scared me. I've been getting calls all night. Why didn't you answer your phone?"

"I couldn't," she said. "I just needed one night. I didn't mean to—"

"You didn't mean to?" His voice rose, and she flinched. He softened, pulling her into a tight hug. "Ava, don't ever do that again. Promise me."

"I'm sorry," she whispered, her tears spilling onto his shoulder.

Her father guided her to the bed, tucking the blankets around her as he had when she was little. "Put your necklace back on," he said. "Promise me."

She nodded. "I will."

"What happened?"

She rolled onto her side, gripping the blanket. She didn't want to explain the reason. A tear escaped down her cheek, tracing a cold path she wiped away.

"Did Peter … did he do something?"

Her breath hitched, and fresh tears pricked her eyes. "Dad, please. Just … don't say his name."

Her father's eyes softened as he leaned forward, brushing her hair away from her face. "Sweetheart, I know you're hurting, but this isn't the way. Taking off that necklace doesn't make the pain go away. It cuts you off from the people who care about you."

"I know. I'm sorry."

Her father glanced at Gabriel, his expression a mix of gratitude and concern. "Thank you for being here."

Gabriel gave a small nod, his gaze lingering on Ava. "I'll check on her tomorrow."

As her father walked Gabriel out, Ava curled into herself. She hadn't wanted to scare anyone or hurt them. But now, sitting in the silence of her room, the guilt was almost unbearable.

Gabriel's hushed and unwavering voice drifted from the hallway, stirring the faintest flicker of solace within her. "She's stronger than she thinks," he said. "Just remind her of that."

Her father's response was lost as the door closed behind them.

As soon as they were gone, the floodgates opened. Ava lay on her side, staring into the dim room, her chest heaving with silent sobs. Memories surged through her mind, each one sharper than the last. She tried to imagine what Colden would tell her if he were here. Or Melissa. Or Joss. They'd tell her to be strong, to fight through it. But she couldn't summon their voices to drown out her own doubts.

How could Peter do this? How long had he lied about loving her? Was it her fault? Had she pushed him away? Her eyes fell to her wrist, where a silver bracelet shimmered in the low light. *Without you, I'm nothing.* He'd given it to her for her eighteenth birthday, swearing it was true.

But it wasn't. It was all a lie.

Her hand trembled as she tore the bracelet from her wrist and hurled it across the room. It hit the wall with a metallic clink before landing somewhere out of sight. She gripped her pillow, wishing she could rid herself of every memory, every trace of him. The photos, the gifts. Thank God they had all burned in the fire. But the guilt clawed at her, relentless and suffocating.

She buried her face, muffling the sobs that wracked her body. The tears spilled out, hot and unstoppable, as the ache in her chest grew heavier. She pressed her face deeper into the covers, surrendering to the tide of pain.

She didn't know how long she cried, but when the tears finally subsided, she was left with a hollow, aching silence. She clung to the blankets, her breath shuddering as she closed her eyes. *Tomorrow. I'll put the necklace back on tomorrow.*

But even as she made the promise, she felt herself slipping further into the void.

— 15 —

EVERYTHING'S GONNA BE FINE ONE DAY

Ava woke to the sound of pebbles against her window, or so she thought. Annoyed, she squinted in the dim room, her mind hazy with sleep, and realized it was the rain tapping against the glass, relentless. Daylight oozed through the clouds, dull and gray, signaling the start of another day. She felt like she'd slept for ages but with no real rest, her body aching and her head foggy. Reaching over to her phone, she braced herself as the screen lit up with notifications.

Missed messages flashed on her screen: Lance, Thomas, Nicole, Link… her stomach clenched as she saw Peter's name. And then Gabriel's messages. Her fingers hovered before she tapped his name.

Ava, are you okay? What happened?

Please talk to me. I can't feel you. No one can.

I hope you find your way through the darkness, but I'm here if you need help.

The last message left a bitter sting of guilt, burning like a sharp, icy shard in her chest. She could picture the sadness in Gabriel's eyes, remembering how crushed he'd been when she'd seen the Necromancer without warning. Shutting everyone out was just another reckless decision. Taking a breath, she reached for her necklace, feeling its weight before clasping it around her neck. A familiar hum surged through her, connecting her to the coven once more.

Her phone beeped.

There you are. I missed you.

A small smile tugged at her lips at Gabriel's message, and she threw back the blankets. It was time to shake off her misery. When she stepped into the living room, her dad looked up from his recliner, his eyes flicking to her with a mix of relief and concern.

"How are you feeling?" His gaze followed her as she slumped onto the couch across from him. The faint sounds of a football game buzzed from the TV, red and yellow uniforms blurring as players clashed on the field.

"Okay, I guess." She hugged her knees to her chest.

"You need to eat something. You haven't had anything since Thursday. I'll heat up some soup." He got up, shuffling into the kitchen, and returned a few minutes later with a bowl of hot soup, the steam swirling in the air between them. "And some water," he added placing a bottle next to her on the end table.

She held the bowl close, letting the heat seep into her palms. "Thanks, Dad." She managed a few bites, but each one felt heavy in her stomach. "I'll eat more later," she promised, though he didn't press her. The game continued, each whistle and cheer prodding at her nerves. It reminded her of the battle they'd all been training for, how everyone had waited on edge, and how stagnant everything had felt since.

"Why can't we leave already?" she asked.

He muted the TV. "Because you still need to heal. All of you do. You have to be patient, Ava."

"Patient? I've been patient! We're just sitting here, doing nothing." She bolted up from the couch, batting away the tears forming at the corners of her eyes. She couldn't stay in the apartment another minute. She darted into her room, pulling on jeans, a sweater, and boots. She stormed toward the door and down the flight of stairs.

"Ava!" Her father's voice echoed through the breezeway. Stopped and turned, her eyes meeting his worried gaze.

"Where are you going?" he asked.

"For a walk. I just need some air."

He nodded, a small sigh escaping him. "Be careful."

"I will."

Trudging through the woods, Ava's breath was visible in the cold air. The branches clawed at her as she pushed through, their sharp edges scraping her skin. The biting wind stung her face, and her fingers, already numb, stung with each step. She ignored it, forcing herself forward until the cabin came into view.

She didn't expect anyone to be there. When she climbed the creaky wooden steps and pushed the door open, she froze at the sight of Lance sitting by the fireplace. The flames crackled, casting a warm glow, and he was staring into them, lost in thought.

"Sorry," Ava said. "I needed to go somewhere."

Lance's head snapped up, and his face flooded with relief. He jumped to his feet and crossed the room in a few strides, wrapping her in a tight, almost desperate embrace. "Ava! What happened? I couldn't feel you anymore. I called, but your dad said you were sick." His dark eyes searched hers, pleading for an explanation.

Drawing back, she sat by the fire, its warmth soothing her chilled skin. "I'm sorry."

"Please don't do that again. I can't feel Melissa and Jeremy... I can't lose you, too."

She swallowed hard, her guilt deepening. "I won't. I promise.

Lance sat next to her, his gaze heavy with concern. "What happened?"

Ava stared into the fire, the flames dancing in front of her, reflecting her swirling emotions. "I don't want to talk about it."

"It's Peter, isn't it?"

She exhaled, avoiding his eyes. "I can't talk about it with you. You're dealing with so much already."

"We all are, Ava." He took her hand. "Don't shut me out. You need to talk. Please."

The sincerity in his voice almost broke her. She didn't know how to talk about Peter, not when Lance was grieving Melissa. The burden of it all became too much, and she blurted out the words before she could think.

"He ... has feelings for someone else." The words burned in the back of her throat.

"What? Who?" Shock contorted his features.

"I don't know. He didn't say. I didn't give him the chance. I just ... made him leave. He said it started because I stayed away from everyone, locked in my room, and that we haven't been on the same page for months." Her breath hitched as tears welled up. "I thought he needed time. I didn't think he was falling out of love with me."

"That's ridiculous," Lance said, his voice tight with anger. "We're all grieving. We need each other more than ever now."

"I risked everything for him. I made all of you believe we were in love. That he loved me. How could he just...?" She choked on the words, unable to finish as nausea rolled in her stomach. She trembled.

Lance pulled her close, his strong arms wrapping around her as she buried her face in his chest and sobbed.

"How could he protect me through everything? The pain with Thomas, the war, all of it, only to cause the worst pain of all? How could he tell me he loved me and then ... betray me like this? It's my fault. If I hadn't been so stubborn, if I'd listened to everyone, maybe ... maybe none of this would have happened."

"Stop. It's not your fault, Ava. You didn't know he'd do this. None of us did."

She shuddered, tears flowing. "He lied to me. After everything he promised, he just ... lied. I've never felt so weak."

"You're not weak. Peter ... he made a mistake. But that doesn't mean you're weak."

She wiped her tears with the back of her hand, her fingers trembling. "I shouldn't be crying on your shoulder. You should be the one leaning on me."

"We can cry together." He gave a pained smile.

Ava let out a shaky laugh through her tears. "Even in my darkest moments, Thomas was there for me. But Peter just ... abandoned me."

"I'm so sorry, Ava."

"Me too."

They sat in silence for a while, the only sound the crackling of the fire and the occasional gust of wind rattling the windows.

Lance nudged her. "We should probably head to the Manor."

Ava stiffened at the thought of returning. "Do we have to? I don't want to see him."

"I know it's going to be hard. But I won't let him near you. I won't let him hurt you again. Just concentrate on your strength and practicing. You're stronger than this."

"Thank you."

"You don't have to thank me. I'd do anything for you."

"And I would for you." She rested her head on his shoulder for a brief moment, grateful for the solace he offered.

Once they reached the Manor, Ava and Lance walked down the hallway toward the conservatory, but she slowed to a stop, gripping his hand.

"You okay?" he asked.

She swallowed hard. "I'll be fine. If anyone asks, I'll smile and tell them I'm fine."

"You got this."

She took a breath, determined to face the others.

"Ava!" Gillian's voice rang out down the hall. Ava turned and Gillian sprinted toward her. "I'm so glad you're safe." She flung her arms around Ava, pulling her into a tight embrace. "When I couldn't feel you ... I was so scared."

She shifted, feeling the awkwardness rise within her, unsure of this unexpected kindness. Even though they'd reconciled, she hadn't thought they were quite back to being friends again. "I'm okay."

Gillian's chin quivered, and tears rolled down her cheeks. "I'm so sorry for being so awful. None of that stupid drama matters anymore. I just wanted to know you're okay."

Ava found herself comforting Gillian, despite the strangeness of it. She rubbed her back in gentle circles, unsure of what to say. Out of the corner of her eye, she saw Thomas and Natalia approaching, their expressions a mix of worry and relief.

"Thank God you're okay," Thomas said, his relieved smile making his blue eyes shine. "You had us worried."

Natalia fixed Ava with a hard stare. "You gave us quite a scare the other night. Satisfied with your little stunt?"

Lance stepped forward. "That's a bit harsh, don't you think?"

Natalia's eyes flicked to him. "Removing the necklace was reckless, especially now." Her gaze returned to Ava. "Haven't you done that before?"

"I'm sorry, Natalia. It won't happen again," Ava said, a pang of regret hitting her chest.

"Aaron and Savina want to see you in the parlor." Natalia brushed past them.

Gillian pulled back and wiped her tears. "I'll come with you."

Ava faked a smile. "I'll be fine." With one last look at Lance, she turned and made her way to Savina's parlor with Gillian by her side.

"What happened, Ava?" Sadness and worry tugged at the corners of Gillian's eyes and left bags underneath them.

Ava hesitated, the words caught in her throat. She wasn't ready to share everything, not yet. "Let's go see Savina, first."

She kept her mind clear, focusing on staying composed, just as Gabriel had taught her. Entering the dim parlor, she took in the familiar warmth of the L-shaped red couch, the crackling marble fireplace, and the soft, ambient light that bathed the room in a soothing glow. Savina and Aaron appeared from the shadows, relief plain on their faces. Before Ava could react, they embraced her.

"Gillian, let's give them a moment," Aaron suggested. With a nod, Gillian followed him out, leaving Ava alone with Savina.

Savina settled into a high-backed chair and motioned for Ava to sit. As Ava sank onto the couch, her gaze fell on the crystal vase holding white chrysanthemums. She stared at the flowers until they became a blurred image. She'd been reckless and worried everyone. Again.

"Ava, remember, you can trust me." Savina's tone was inviting rather than scolding.

Her head jerked up, guilt flooding her cheeks. "I know."

"What's troubling you?" Savina's eyes softened with concern. "There is a deep sadness within you. I realize you may not wish to share it, but I'm concerned after you removed your necklace. We've spoken of its importance, especially now."

"I'm sorry. It's nothing important."

"You don't always have to be so strong."

The words lingered in the air, and Ava's defenses cracked. "Peter likes someone else." She still didn't want to admit they'd broken up. It made it all too final. A part of her clung to the faint hope it wasn't over.

Savina's face fell, her expression one of empathy rather than pity, and for that, Ava was grateful.

"I'm so sorry, Ava. I know it hurts deeply. You are not weak, though I know you feel that way. Love can be fickle, a force that changes people. Perhaps there was something else in the cosmic forces that brought you two together."

Ava knew Savina meant George. Her first love, taken so cruelly by Corbin. But Peter wasn't dead. He had simply ... chosen someone else. After promising to love her forever, he had found someone new.

"I know what it feels like to lose someone you love deeply," Savina continued, her voice heavy with sorrow. "My father ... it still pains me to see him as he is now. To know he's become a man consumed by hate, no longer the father I once adored."

Ava tried to imagine that kind of loss but couldn't. Her own father, despite everything, was still her rock. Savina's words made her pain over Peter feel both small and yet valid. She tried to push down her feelings, but the ache was there, raw and pulsing.

"I know you're hurting, and it's natural to feel some anger. But try not to let this turn into resentment. Don't let him become your enemy. You're strong, Ava. Promise me you'll talk to someone rather than keeping it all inside."

"I promise ... I just want to know what I did wrong."

Savina met her gaze, her eyes filled with understanding. "Only one person knows the answer to that, and it's not you."

"I'm not talking to him. I'll be fine. Really." She shifted in her seat, needing to move past this topic. "Do you know when we'll leave for Caprington?"

Savina considered her words. "When everyone's at full strength. It may feel like we're stalling, but we need to be prepared. Havok has more Enchanters than I could have imagined."

"Do we have a plan?"

"Only a tentative one. You Elementals are crucial. We may have to split the group to increase our chances."

Ava's stomach dropped. "Split us up? We're barely managing as it is. Losing Melissa and Jeremy was hard enough. I can't lose anyone else."

"I understand, and I know it's difficult. But our goal is to ambush Havok where he's weakest. If we separate into two forces, we can cover more ground. It's not final, so don't worry just yet."

"Do you think they're okay? Tell me honestly."

"Yes." Savina locked eyes with Ava. "Havok would not hurt them. He knows what he wants. They're alive."

Ava released a breath she hadn't realized she was holding. "How can you be so certain?"

"I know Havok well enough to predict his moves. He's waiting. This is a test, nothing more."

"Savina … can I ask you something else?"

"Of course."

"When we found out my mom promised my soul to Havok … what does that really mean? I know it's why I've felt so … different, but what happens if he actually reaps the Elementals' souls? What happens to us?"

The question hung in the air, heavy and laced with fear.

Savina looked at her for a long moment, her lips pressed together before she spoke. "Ava, when a soul is promised to Havok, it means that you are bound to him in a way that is not easily broken. If Havok reaps your soul, or any of the Elementals' souls, it's not death you face. It's enslavement. He would control every part of you, even after death."

"Enslavement?"

"Yes. He wants your power. If he reaps your soul, he will not just claim your life, but everything that makes you, *you*. He will harness the Elementals' powers, use them to further his cause. That's why he's so relentless. To Havok, you're not people. You're weapons. And with each soul he reaps, his strength grows. The Elementals are key to his plans."

Ava swallowed hard, the truth heavy on her heart. "So, if he gets to us, we lose our powers and ourselves?"

"Yes. But he's not invincible. There are ways to protect your soul. That's why your amulets are so important. They are part of what protects you from Havok's direct influence, but you must always be on guard."

"So, my mom, she basically handed me over to him?"

"I don't believe your mother knew exactly what would happen. But the promise she made is real, and it binds you to Havok. We will find a way to break that promise before it's too late."

Ava stared at the ground, her mind spinning. The familiar sensation of dread crawled over her, but also a burning resolve. "We can't let him take any of us. We have to stop him."

Savina placed a comforting hand on Ava's shoulder. "We will. And I believe you, Ava. You're stronger than you think. Havok knows that too, which is why he's trying so hard to break you. But you're not alone in this fight."

Ava nodded, the fear still present but tempered by determination. She squared her shoulders. "Let's go train."

The bitter cold bit Ava's cheeks as Savina opened the door to the field. The leafless trees swayed against the wind, their skeletal branches offering no protection from the biting chill. Ava shivered but warmed herself with a flicker of effort, grateful that she still could. Savina squeezed her hand and walked out to join Aaron and Gustav.

As Ava lingered in the doorway, her gaze swept across the training grounds. The usual buzz of activity should have comforted her, but instead, it emphasized the ache inside her. Her eyes landed on Peter almost instinctively. He stood with Katarina, his laughter carrying through the air, striking her like a physical blow. The ache resurfaced, raw and heavy, and she looked away, willing herself to focus.

"Ava," Gabriel called as he approached. His voice held a note of concern that tugged at her, and the sadness in his eyes made her feel even worse. She had been careless, reckless. She hated that she had hurt the people who cared about her.

"Are you okay?" he asked.

"I'm fine." The lie slipped out too easily, and she forced a smile to make it convincing.

But Gabriel wasn't convinced. His gaze lingered for a beat too long before he nodded. "All right. Let's get started, then."

Ava followed him onto the training field, her steps sluggish. Her attention flicked to Gillian, who stood with Anastasya.

A dark cloud of smoke swirled around them, lashing at Gillian's hair before she waved her hand, dissipating the cloud.

Anastasya collapsed to her knees, breathless.

With a triumphant smirk, Gillian crossed her arms.

A wave of longing washed over Ava. Gillian had regained her powers. Everyone else was moving forward. Why couldn't she?

"Let's work on summoning water today," Gabriel said, his tone shifting to something more professional. "After that, we'll move to—"

Ava's attention drifted again. Peter and Katarina were laughing together, standing close. Too close. Her stomach churned as Peter brushed a finger across Katarina's nose, eliciting a playful giggle.

"Ava!" Gabriel yelled.

Her head snapped toward him. "What?"

"Are you even listening?" His frustration was evident.

"I'm sorry."

"Focus," he said, his jaw tight. "Let's try again."

Ava nodded, but her heart wasn't in it. She tried to concentrate, tried to channel her energy, but her eyes betrayed her once more. Peter's dimples appeared as he smiled at Katarina, his hand brushing hers. Ava's chest tightened, her breath coming in shallow gasps. She could feel the water forming along her arms, dripping down to her fingertips as her emotions spiraled out of control. The necklace against her skin grew hot, warning her to calm down, but she couldn't.

A powerful force slammed into her, knocking her to the ground. "You're distracted. Again."

"I'm trying," Ava snapped.

"No, you're not. You're letting yourself get pulled under by everything else, and it's not helping. You need to focus."

"I can't just turn it off! Do you think I *want* to feel this way? I'm trying, Gabriel. I'm trying, and it's not enough!"

The frustration faded from his eyes, replaced by something gentler. "Ava…" He helped her to her feet. "Let's try again."

But Ava couldn't. Her gaze flickered to Peter once more, and her heart shattered all over again as Katarina's fingers grazed his cheek. He leaned into her touch, and his smile, the one that used to be hers, cut deeper than any wound. The nausea rolled through her like a tidal wave, and her legs wobbled.

"I can't do this," she whispered as she met Gabriel's eyes.

"What are you—" His brow furrowed in confusion.

"I'm sorry." She turned and fled.

The emotions crashed down on her, drowning her. Ava sprinted through the Manor, past the conservatory and into the entryway. She reached the front door, gripping the handle. Her breath came in ragged gasps as she fought to steady herself. She couldn't let anyone see her like this—weak, broken, humiliated.

"Ava." Gabriel rested a hand on her shoulder. "What did he do?"

Her body stiffened. She couldn't turn around, couldn't face him. "Please," she choked out. "Just let me go."

"No. Not like this."

The door creaked open under her hand, and the cold air stung her skin as she stepped outside. She needed to escape, to breathe, to be anywhere but there.

Peter's voice cut through the air like a knife. "Ava!"

She froze, and her stomach flipped. The sound of her name from his lips was like a wound being torn open again. Her chest constricted, and the heat of her necklace spiked against her skin.

"Ava, please wait." He thudded down the hallway to them.

Gabriel stepped between them, his posture tense. "I think you've done enough harm."

"I need to talk to her," Peter insisted.

"No," Gabriel insisted.

Ava didn't wait to hear more. She turned and walked away, her steps quickening as she passed the garden and disappeared into the woods. Tears blurred her vision, and the emotions she'd been holding back surged forward.

The grief, the anger, the betrayal clawed at her insides, threatening to consume her. But as she pushed deeper into the woods, she realized something else. The anger wasn't just at Peter. It was at herself. How could she have been so blind, so foolish to trust him with her heart?

Her legs gave out, and she sank to the ground, the cold earth pressing against her knees. The sobs came then, raw and unrelenting, spilling out of her as she clutched her arms around herself.

Peter was gone. He had moved on. And now, she had to find a way to do the same.

14

ELASTIC HEART

The roar of the waterfall grew louder as Ava neared, its power vibrating through the air. With a deep breath, the fresh, misty scent of water filled her lungs as the cool spray kissed her skin. The wind whipped through the trees, bending their branches as though they, too, were bowing to the cascade's force. She paused at the edge of the rocks, her eyes on the water that plunged into the pool below.

Focus, she thought to herself. *Lift the water.*

Shutting her eyes, she willed the water to rise at her command. But after a few frustrating moments, the water remained still, unyielding.

With a frustrated sigh, she climbed over the rocks, stepping closer to the pool. The dark, deep water swirled below her, beckoning her with its mystery. She wondered what it would be like to let go, to be swept away by the current, allowing the water to control her instead of the other way around. She brought her feet closer to the edge, and dove in.

The cold water enveloped her as she sank deeper, the world above disappearing in a muted blur. But then, air filled her lungs. She could breathe underwater again. A sense of peace settled over her as she floated there, watching fish dart around her in the bubbling depths. Lying on the bottom, the sound of the waterfall's thunder muffled, she gazed up through the black water, the surface distorted and unreachable.

Three days of wasted tears, crying over someone who no longer cared. She was relieved in a way. At least now she knew the truth. Grief replaced shame, and she wished she could be as fierce as Melissa.

Something disturbed the water. Her eyes snapped open, startled as she felt hands grabbing her waist. She twisted, kicking hard, and her attacker let go. Ava bolted toward the surface, gasping as she pulled herself onto the rocks.

"Ava!"

She whipped around, breathless. "Gabriel?"

"I came to check on you!" He treaded water below her.

"What were you doing? I could've killed you!"

"I didn't know what you were doing." He hauled himself out of the water. "And when you didn't come up, I thought you needed help."

Ava sighed, wrapping her arms around herself. "I just wanted to be underwater. I'm sorry." She stilled, remembering his story about his sister and his panic over not being able to save her. "I'm so sorry. Your sister... I didn't think—"

"It's okay." He sat beside her on the rock, his white shirt soaked and clinging to his frame. His hair dripped, and water trickled down his pale face, but his expression was calm. "I know you can swim."

Ava shivered, though not from the cold. "Sorry for kicking you."

He laughed. "No worries. You've got a solid defense kick. At least I know you can handle yourself."

They sat together in silence, the waterfall pounding behind them, filling the empty spaces where words didn't need to be. Gabriel gave her the space she needed, offering comfort without demands. Ava let her mind wander to Peter, and the image of him laughing with Katarina played in her mind again. It stabbed at her like a sharp blade. She buried her face in her hands, trying to hold back the tears, but they came anyway.

"I'm sorry." He rubbed her back in slow circles.

She wiped away the tears that seemed never-ending. "No, I'm sorry. I shouldn't have run off like that."

Gabriel moved closer, pulling her into a tight embrace.

Ava let herself cry, sinking into the moment of vulnerability she had been avoiding for days.

After what felt like an eternity, he tensed. "Oh, no."

"What?" Ava blinked, sitting up. Blinded by the sun's glare, she froze. They were no longer by the waterfall. Instead, they sat on the edge of a high cliff, the endless expanse of ocean stretching out before them.

She gasped, clutching Gabriel. "Wh-what happened? Where are we?"

He rubbed the back of his neck, looking sheepish. "The Cliffs of Dover, apparently."

"You teleported us? To England?"

"Yeah... about that. I might've gotten a little carried away."

Ava's shock gave way to a small smile as she took in the beauty around her. The white cliffs stretched for miles, and the calm water of the Strait of Dover shimmered under the winter sun. The air was crisp, the grass beneath their feet was the greenest she'd ever seen, and for the first time in weeks, she felt the warmth of sunlight on her skin.

"This is amazing. What made you think of this place?"

Gabriel hesitated before answering. "Uh ... It's a good place to clear my head."

She glanced over at him with a soft smile. "You didn't mean to bring me here, did you?"

He shook his head, a hint of amusement flickering in his eyes. "No, but I don't mind sharing."

They both stood there, the wind whipping through their hair, staring out at the sun-drenched strait. Ava could just make out the shoreline of France in the distance. After days of gray skies and suffocating emotion, this felt like a reprieve, a small moment of peace she hadn't realized she needed. Closing her eyes, she basked in the sun's warm rays.

"This is exhilarating." She moved closer to the edge of the cliff. Below, the waves washed over the pebbles, carrying some of them away with the tide. She watched the water, feeling the steady rhythm echo inside her.

Gabriel stood beside her, his presence grounding her even as her mind wandered. The vastness of the ocean mirrored the emptiness she felt, but here, on the cliffs, the emptiness didn't seem so overwhelming. It was just ... there. A part of her, but not all of her.

And that was okay.

Ava took a deep breath, gazing out at the ocean stretching beneath the cliffs. The wind tugged at her hair, carrying the scent of salt and sun-warmed earth. "I wish I could do this. Travel all the time. Just escape whenever I wanted."

"Maybe one day." Gabriel gave a slight smile, more at ease than she'd ever seen him. "I used to go wherever I wanted. Now it's just a few places, ones that feel like home."

"Can't you teleport us to Caprington?"

He glanced at her with a knowing look. She knew it would be too dangerous.

"I guess that would be too easy," she said.

"Besides, I wouldn't know how to get there."

The waves crashed far below. "If he knows where we are and waits to attack, why don't we leave? Find a better place to hide?"

His gaze drifted out to the horizon, his tone even but carrying an edge. "Havok's not going to attack here. He's biding his time, waiting for us to move first. I'd bet he's placed Cimmerian ambushes on the way to Caprington. He wants us on his terms, at his mercy."

"He's already gotten inside our heads once. What's stopping him from doing it again?"

"We'll have … protection." He hesitated. "And when we finally do leave, you'll have to hide what you're feeling. Havok's people are trained to exploit any weakness, especially emotional ones, like Trudy did."

Ava shuddered, recalling Trudy's mind games. As if sensing her tension, Gabriel's hand slid over hers. A single tear slipped down her cheek. "How do you do it? How do you hide everything so well? I thought I was managing, but instead, I pushed people away until it was too much. That's why I took off my necklace. I didn't want you feeling all that, but I also didn't want to hurt anyone."

His eyes softened. "Burying it isn't the same as cutting yourself off. You learn to turn off the hurt." He held her gaze a little longer. "It takes practice, but I understand how difficult it is. When they took Joss, Maggie, and Kira, you never felt my grief, did you?"

"No. I never felt anything from you."

For a brief moment, his eyes seemed to reveal a sadness he kept buried. "You turn it off, so it doesn't swallow you whole. Keep busy. Lose yourself in something else. It's the only way I know how."

She squeezed his hand, feeling the weight he carried in his silence. "Just when I think I have a handle on things, something else happens. Another loss, another blow."

"Unfortunately, that's life. But you're stronger than you realize, Ava."

Her gaze shifted back to the horizon, where the sun cast a golden glow across the waves. *He's right.* She needed to face the pain head-on, not run from it. The words slipped from her before she could stop them. "Peter broke up with me because he's … fallen for someone else."

He tightened his grip on her hand. "I'm sorry, Ava."

Her eyes stung, but she willed herself not to cry. "Maybe it's my fault. We haven't been on the same page for months. Ever since he became an Enchanter, he changed, and I pushed him away." Her voice faltered. "I thought he was the one. I was so sure of it. How could I be so wrong?"

"That's your doubt talking. Maybe Peter was an escape when your life shifted, someone who seemed constant. But there was something real there. I saw it, too. Unfortunately … maybe it wasn't meant to last." He winced. "Sorry, that was blunt."

"It's fine. He abandoned me when I needed him most. He told me he forgave me, but he never really did."

"Are you talking about what happened with Drew and Jonah?"

"Yeah. And the Necromancer. I thought he'd moved past it, but deep down, I don't think he could. He sided with Valerie, who told him he'd wind up dead because of me."

Gabriel set his jaw. "It still baffles me that he took her side. Becoming an Enchanter changed him. Maybe that's why the universe brought you together. To prepare him for this role. To protect us."

"What about now? Am I ... unprotected?"

The question lingered between them. Gabriel's eyes softened as he searched for words.

"I can handle it," she pressed. "I already know."

"He still cares about you, but ... his protection is shifting. Katarina is teaching him to spread his power to protect all of us, not just one person."

Ava groaned, pressing her palms against her eyes as if to stop the flood of emotions. The knots in her stomach grew tighter. She took a few deep breaths, willing herself to stay strong. "Thank you. For being here, and for being honest." She managed a small smile. "I know it can't be easy having to listen to all of this."

"Of course. I'm always here."

His gaze softened, and Ava felt a quiet tenderness she hadn't known she longed for.

"We should probably head back. They'll wonder where we disappeared to."

"Right." With one last glance at the cliffs and the ocean stretching out before her, she inhaled the invigorating air.

He gently squeezed her hand, pulling her close. "You can see it again," he murmured, so softly it was almost lost in the wind.

They were back by the waterfall, the gray sky heavy above.

Ava stepped back, still feeling the lingering warmth from the cliffs. Within her, something loosened, allowing a glimmer of peace. She turned to him. "How did you know where I was tonight?"

"Just knew." A faint smile tugged at his lips, his gaze meeting hers.

Her own lips lifted in a half-smile. "I don't want to go back yet."

"Then we should practice here, while you're surrounded by water."

"Are you getting enough practice yourself?"

He grinned, eyes twinkling with a familiar playfulness. In an instant, he was behind her, his arms around her.

She elbowed him, catching his arm, and threw him to the damp ground with a soft thud.

"Hmm," he mused. "Guess I'll need to step up my game."

"Maybe."

Gabriel chuckled as he dusted himself off. "See? Not everything knocks you down."

$$15$$

JUST TONIGHT

Shrouded in darkness, Ava tore through the woods, branches clawing at her arms. Shadows pursued her. Black-masked figures who somehow kept up by merely walking, their slow strides matching her frantic speed. How? She was fast, always had been, but now her lungs burned from the bitter air as her heart thundered.

"Peter, help me!" she screamed.

Lightning cracked beside her, illuminating shadows and casting harsh, fleeting light on the figures. She stumbled, crashing to the ground. Rough hands yanked her up, pressing her back into a chest she didn't recognize. One hand clamped around her throat, squeezing, suffocating. She lashed out with a kick, but her sight was hazy.

The masked figures closed in, surrounding her in a tight, sinister circle. One stepped forward, removing his mask to reveal a face that turned her blood to ice. Thick brown hair she'd once run her fingers through, familiar eyes that had looked at her with tenderness now cold and indifferent.

"Peter?" she choked out, gasping as the hand on her throat loosened.

"Who else?" He gave a sinister grin. With a flick of his fingers, the grip on her throat tightened, and a dark laugh echoed through the circle of onlookers.

"What are you doing?" she asked.

"Taking you to Havok, of course. Did you really think I loved you?" His laugh was low, taunting, echoed by the others.

"What? You ... you're one of them?"

"Surprise." He smirked.

"No. This isn't possible."

He leaned closer, his voice dripping with disdain. "You were just a way in. An easy target to get closer to Savina. You were good for a time," he mocked, "but you're too weak for me. Too ... pathetic."

Ava gasped, feeling the hot sting of betrayal. Desperate, she slammed her elbow into the gut of the man behind her. She broke free, swinging her fist at Peter only to feel softness. Her eyes shot open as her hand met the pillow. She lay in her bed, breathing hard, the shadows of her room filling the space where the dream had been. Her necklace warmed, glowing in the dark. Tears welled in her eyes as she rubbed them, willing the lingering dread away.

It wasn't the first time she'd dreamed of Peter since he'd broken her heart, but each one left her feeling heavier, the scenes darker. In each dream, Peter was cold, his eyes empty, his voice harsh. Sometimes, he started with sweet words, leaning in to kiss her, only to pull away laughing, pointing. Her dreams were vivid, the kind that lingered even after waking. She'd been trying to ignore them for the past two weeks, and though she'd managed to train with Gabriel without letting Peter and Katarina get to her, the dreams always pulled her back into the ache.

Everyone was growing stronger in training, but one worry lingered: she still couldn't heal. She wondered if that part of her was lost forever, broken along with her heart. Savina had assured her it would return, that healing came from within and needed time. But Ava wondered if she was too damaged to be a healer anymore. She shook her head, pushing down the pessimism.

It was Christmas day. Gone were the days when Christmas was magical, a time to look forward to. Her mom's death had dimmed the holiday's joy. Now it felt emptier than ever. But this year, Ava was determined to have a good day. She wouldn't dwell on Peter, or her lost friends, or even on Colden.

The early morning sun broke the horizon, painting the sky pink and orange. Ava peeked through the blinds, watching the colors deepen across a cold, clear sky. It was a peaceful winter morning, though snow hadn't fallen. She waited until the sun was up, then dressed in a thick black sweater and jeans and padded out to the living room, where her father was watching TV in his armchair.

"Good morning. Merry Christmas." He smiled.

"Merry Christmas."

They'd bought a fake tree and decorated it for the apartment, sticking to the tradition. It was simple and new, but it felt like a piece of home. Her eyes moved over the green and red garland hanging on the white mantel, the two red candles on either end. A small fire crackled, casting a cozy glow. She hadn't expected the setup to make her feel so nostalgic. A few ornaments dotted the tree, and among them was a pewter one with three ravens on a red ribbon, a nod to her love of Edgar Allan Poe. Her dad had managed to find it for her.

And under the tree, a single gift.

"What's that?" she asked.

"I got you a little something."

"Dad, we said no gifts this year."

"Neither of us kept that promise." He gestured to the new art supplies on the coffee table, and she smiled. "I haven't painted since…" He trailed off. Since her mom died.

Ava reached for the small, thick box, wrapped in goofy snowman paper, and pulled back the wrapping. She lifted the lid and froze. Underneath layers of tissue paper was a framed photograph. Luci, her dad, and a younger version of herself smiling back at her. Tears filled her eyes. It was the same picture that had always sat on her nightstand. She thought everything had been destroyed in the fire.

"Where did you get this?" she asked.

"I had a copy at work and saved it after … everything."

"Dad…"

He took her hand, his face calm yet sad. "I know, given the circumstances, you may feel differently toward your mom now. I know I do. But I know she loved us, no matter what. She cherished you. Thought you were her greatest joy."

Ava lowered her gaze. "But … why? Why would she do what she did?"

"I can't answer that. But I don't want to give up on her, not yet. Maybe there's something we don't understand, something she couldn't share."

She wasn't ready to forgive Luci, not yet. Not after all she'd learned. But her dad looked at her with a hope she didn't want to crush. She thought back to something Mr. McNabb had said to Peter once. "May you never forget what is worth remembering, nor ever remember what is best forgotten."

Her dad looked thoughtful, nodding. "I like that. Where'd you hear that?"

"Peter's dad."

"Wise words. Do you believe them?"

"I'm trying." She managed a small smile.

He hugged her, and she wrapped her arms around him. Ava couldn't imagine saying goodbye to him, especially with everything coming. She took a deep breath, finding some strength in the quiet moment. She released him and gave him a nod.

"Come on," he said. "Let's make breakfast."

Before she joined him, she took the picture to her room, placing it on her nightstand. She studied Luci's face, the warm smile, the familiar gray eyes. She always looked at Ava with love, protected her. *Maybe Dad's right. Maybe Mom did love us.* But there were still questions she wasn't ready to answer.

Her phone buzzed and she checked the message. It was from Gabriel.

Merry Christmas! Are you awake or did Santa kidnap you?

She typed a response.

Merry Christmas. Nope, Santa didn't visit. Guess I wasn't a good girl this year.

Ha. His loss. Hurry up and get here. Things are getting crazy.

Crazy?

Yes. Reindeer games. And elves took over and it's out of control.

Now I really can't wait.

Good. See you soon.

She laughed and realized she was excited to see him. Gabriel had become one of her favorite people, and she looked forward to spending time with him. *Today is going to be a good day.*

While they ate breakfast, Ava and her dad reminisced about the good times, as if an unspoken rule forbade any mention of sadness.

"Are you coming to the Manor for the Christmas party?" she asked. She didn't want her dad to spend the day alone nor did want to go alone risk seeing Peter and Katarina together.

"Yeah. They said the Irish Aureole will be there."

Her eyes lit up. "I didn't know that."

"They're great, a lively bunch. It'll be fun."

So that's what Gabriel meant by crazy, she thought with a grin.

The Manor had transformed into a winter wonderland. The soft glow of low lights filled the air, casting a warm and cozy ambiance. Silver and blue magic danced along the walls, shimmering and twinkling like stars, enveloping the room in an ethereal, enchanting glow. Ava paused in the dining room doorway, taking in the energetic scene. She smelled roasted turkey, honey-glazed ham, and duck in the center of the table, surrounded by casseroles bubbling with melted cheese and trays of fresh vegetables. On a sideboard nearby, decadent cheesecakes, cobblers, pies, and delicate brownie bites were laid out like something from a holiday spread in a magazine.

Ava's stomach grumbled at the mingling sweet and savory scents. She managed a polite nod to the unfamiliar faces scattered around the table.

"Oh, would you look there." A tall, burly man with thick curls and a broad Irish accent set down his mug, rising to shake her dad's hand. "Connor Hannigan, as I live and breathe!"

Her father grinned. "Sean! It's been too long." He gestured to Ava. "This is my daughter, Ava. Ava, meet Sean. We go way back."

Sean's calloused hand swallowed hers in a hearty shake. "A pleasure, lass."

"Just like her mother," a woman with long brown curls said, a kind smile lighting up her face. "I'm Shannon, love. Your mother was one of my dearest friends."

Ava shifted under Shannon's intense, affectionate gaze. "Thanks," she murmured, a little awkward in the midst of strangers.

Shannon turned, introducing her family: two sons, Aidan and Ronan, a niece named Moira, and a nephew, Nathan, whose expressive green eyes met Ava's in an amused smile. Despite their warm greetings, Ava's stomach knotted, especially at any mention of her mother. She cast her dad a quick look, the signal that she needed to step away.

"Nice meeting you all," Ava said, edging toward the door. "I'm going to find my friends."

She slipped down the hall to the conservatory, letting out a breath as she took in the sight before her. A delicate snowfall filled the air, vanishing before it touched the ground, while blue and silver ribbons draped the walls, casting a wintry charm over the entire room. Crowds of Enchanters mingled, dancing and chatting as if the recent threats were a distant memory. This was her first Christmas at the Manor. Last year, she had stayed home, focused on protecting her father.

Spotting Lance with Gillian, Thomas, and Eric near the edge of the dance floor, she made her way over. "Merry Christmas," she greeted them, receiving hugs and grins in return.

"Merry Christmas," Eric said, eyeing the punch bowl. "I vote we see who can spike it first."

"I'm in," Thomas said with a grin, his attempt at holiday cheer tempered by a distant look in his eyes.

"Savina really went all out," Ava said, marveling at the decorations. "I didn't realize how festive the Manor could get."

"That's what the Elders want you to think," Eric interjected. "In reality, Thomas, Gabriel, and I were the ones on ladder duty for hours. No credit, as usual."

Thomas smirked. "You're just mad because you dropped an ornament and shattered it."

"It was one ornament!" Eric protested. "And it was a defective hook."

Ava let out a small laugh, the banter easing some of the tension in her chest. But her momentary relief faded when her gaze flicked toward the dance floor. Peter was there, dancing close to Katarina, their heads tilted together as they laughed.

"It's amazing, really," Gillian said with a wistful look. "Jeremy would have loved this."

Lance took her hand. "Would you dance with me?"

Gillian hesitated but allowed herself to be led away.

"And that's my cue before I get pulled into a dance." Eric left Ava and Thomas standing together. She scanned the room for any sign of Gabriel but didn't see him.

Thomas nudged her. "How's your dad?"

"He's good. He really liked his present. It's been nice, just the two of us." She paused, feeling a pang of sadness. "How about you?"

He shrugged. "First Christmas without my dad."

"I'm so sorry. How's your mom holding up?"

Thomas's expression shifted, conflicted. "She's hanging in. It's complicated … he was a Cimmerian, you know?"

"It's hard to know how to feel."

After a pause, he gestured toward the punch bowl. "Want a drink?"

"No, thanks."

He cracked a half-smile. "Dance?"

She chuckled. "Not tonight."

They moved toward the terrace, but someone grabbed Ava's hand. She turned around.

"Can we talk?" Peter asked.

She hesitated. She didn't want to talk not here, not now, but they needed to. "Fine."

Peter motioned for her to follow him to a quieter corner of the conservatory, away from the crowd. The distance from the others made her heart pound harder. She crossed her arms, bracing herself for whatever he had to say.

"I'm sorry. For everything."

"What exactly are you sorry for, Peter? Breaking up with me? Falling for someone else? Or lying about it for weeks?" Her tone was sharp, the anger she'd been holding back bubbling to the surface.

"I didn't mean for any of this to happen. I never wanted to hurt you."

"Right. Because the second things got difficult, you left. I stayed by your side when you needed me most. But I wasn't worth the effort to you, was I?"

"You wouldn't let me help you."

She shook her head. "Maybe I didn't want to throw myself into the Manor every day. But that doesn't mean I didn't try. You didn't care enough to try for me."

"You gave up on us long before I did."

How could he say that? Water trickled from her fingertips, forming small puddles on the ground as she tried to keep her emotions contained. Her necklace grew warm.

He shook his head, then turned and walked away.

Ava exhaled, willing herself to let go. *I'm here to have a good night.*

A few minutes later, she made her way back inside and joined Gillian and Lance. She looked up to see Eric, Natalia, and Gabriel walking into the conservatory.

A hint of pink colored Gabriel's cheeks as he smiled. Dressed in comfortable jeans and a fitted black sweater, he appeared relaxed and at ease. His sharp jawline and clear blue eyes caught the low light, making him look like someone out of an old, glamorous painting. As soon as he met her gaze, his eyes lit up. "Ava!" He sounded a little more exuberant than usual. "There you are!" He pulled her into a one-armed hug. The faint scent of juniper clung to him, wrapping her in an odd sense of comfort. "I'm glad you came. No one else here tolerates my terrible jokes and questionable dancing."

"Questionable dancing?" Eric chimed in as he walked by with a cup of punch. "Don't undersell yourself, Gabe. You're a disaster on the dance floor."

"Disaster is a strong word. I prefer 'chaotic genius.'"

Ava laughed, the sound surprising even herself. Gabriel's playful energy was infectious.

As they chatted, her gaze drifted back to the terrace, where Peter and Katarina were now dancing. A sharp ache gripped her stomach, and she glanced down.

Gabriel leaned in. "Don't let him ruin this for you. Just tonight … don't think. Be here with us. Enjoy it while you can."

"I'm fine."

"Liar," he teased. "Come on. One dance. Just one."

"Oh, no," Ava started, but he was already pulling her toward the floor. Her heart raced, every instinct telling her to refuse, but his genuine smile relaxed her.

"See? Not so bad," he said as they moved, his steps surprisingly stable for someone who'd had a few drinks. "Now, the key to a successful dance is confidence. Doesn't matter if you're good, as long as you believe you are. Confidence is everything. Also, wine. But mostly confidence."

She laughed again, the sound freer this time. Dancing eased the heaviness she felt in her heart.

His hands were firm, and his crooked smile gave her a sense of calm she hadn't felt in ages. "Just let go," he whispered, his breath hot against her ear, sending a shiver down her spine. "Don't think about anything else."

A dreamy, upbeat song with a vibrant rhythm filled the room, its notes weaving through the room. The singer's voice, strong and soulful, resonated in Ava's chest, blending with the beat that matched her own heartbeat. With every step, her mind let go, surrendering to the spell of the music. The stress she'd carried for months lifted, piece by piece, dissolving into the melody.

With effortless ease, Gabriel steered her, his touch light but reassuring. His smile radiated warmth that seemed to brighten even the dim corners of the room. The sparkle in his eyes drew her in, lighting a spark within her that had felt dormant. In that moment, there was nothing but the music, the dance, and his loyal, reassuring presence.

Each time his hand brushed her skin, a thrill shot through her, like ripples on still water. It was a sensation both gentle and exhilarating, and she let go entirely. The room around them blurred as they spun together, each step carrying her further from her worries, into a world where only the music and their shared rhythm mattered.

16

JUST WATCH THE FIREWORKS

Thomas shot a fireball into the fireplace, igniting the wood. Ava recognized the spark in his eyes as he glanced at Moira. Definitely showing off.

Once the music turned to slow songs back at the Manor, the group decided to retreat to the cabin, where the energy was cozier, quieter.

"We need more wood." Gillian dropped down on the couch beside Ava.

"I've got it." Gabriel flashed a cocky grin before vanishing, only to reappear moments later with his arms full of wood.

"Whoa, that was cool," Thomas said.

Eric rolled his eyes. "Yeah, but he does that all the time."

"It's a lot more amazing when he takes us with him," Moira chimed in, settling onto the rocky hearth.

"I bet you did that a lot growing up. I know I would have." Gillian twisted a curl around her finger. "Especially when my parents were mad. See ya! Gone to Paris."

"I didn't do it too much then." Gabriel settled on the floor next to Eric. "I didn't have much control over it." He grew quiet, and Ava knew his past was difficult to talk about.

"But you must've seen so much," Thomas said.

"Oh, he's seen a lot!" Moira grinned, nudging him playfully. "He's been my own personal travel guide." She tousled his hair, and Ava felt a pang of nostalgia as she remembered when he'd taken her to the Enoch library and the Cliffs of Dover.

"Where are you from, Gabriel?" Ava asked, realizing she'd never known.

"Originally? Puxley, a little village in England."

Gillian's nose wrinkled. "Really? Where's your accent?"

"Long gone. I've been here too long to keep it."

"Ah, but he's a frequent flyer to Ireland to see us." Moira's eyes sparkled as she spoke. "I was born in Dublin, into a coven unlike these two." She pointed at Eric and Gabriel.

Ava leaned forward. "How did you two meet?"

"London," Eric answered with a grin. "Met him at a bar and dragged him to meet the Elders."

"And before that?" Gillian asked.

"I ... wandered a lot."

Eric glanced at him and gave his shoulder a reassuring squeeze.

Gillian's jaw dropped. "By yourself? How long were you alone?"

He hesitated. "A while."

"Have you ever been back to your hometown?" Thomas asked.

"Not much," Gabriel said. "We traveled a lot when we thought Corbin died."

"We lived in several different places before settling here with Savina and Aaron," Eric said.

"So, do you live in the Manor?" Gillian asked. "Don't you have a place to yourselves?"

"We do," Eric paused. "Just ... doesn't seem right to live there without Joss."

Gillian frowned. "I'm sorry. Where were your favorite places you've been?"

"Hands down, Italy," Eric said, a wistful smile on his face.

"I've always wanted to go there. I bet it's gorgeous."

"It is," Eric said. "Especially this time of year."

Moira gasped and covered her gaping mouth. "We get to go!"

"Are you thinking what I'm thinking?" Eric turned to Gabriel.

Gabriel sighed, though his eyes betrayed a hint of mischief. "I don't know if it's a good idea..."

"We'll be fine." Moira tapped her head.

"How do you know?" Thomas asked her.

"I'm a Seer. I can see bits of the future."

"Where are we going?" Gillian asked.

"I'm sure it'll be fine," Eric said. "Come on, everyone needs this."

Gabriel hesitated but gave in. "Alright. Who wants to go?"

Gillian and Lance eagerly volunteered.

Ava fidgeted on the couch. "I think ... I'll just head home."

The energy in the room deflated.

"What? You can't miss this!" Gillian looked crestfallen.

Ava glanced toward the dark windows. "I ... I think I'd like some time to myself."

She wasn't sure why she felt like that. She craved quiet, even for a moment.

The group clasped hands, and they disappeared.

Gabriel reappeared before her with a small, hopeful grin. "Do you like Christmas trees?"

She blinked. "I … yeah?"

"Good enough for me." He reached out, taking her hand, and in a blink, they were on a snowy hillside.

As Ava's gaze lifted, her breath caught. Before her stood the largest Christmas tree she had ever seen stretched across the dark slopes of a mountain, towering like a living beacon against the night sky. Rows of emerald lights outlined the enormous tree, their glow casting a surreal, shimmering reflection against the cool winter landscape. The mountainside sparkled, a thousand points of colored light nestled into the deep evergreen of the forest.

At the top, a radiant white star blazed, its light piercing through the crisp, cold air, illuminating the surrounding hillsides with a soft, gentle glow. Each tiny light on the tree pulsed in harmony with the quiet hum of the town below, as if the tree were breathing, alive with holiday spirit. The tranquility of the place, the calm drifted down like the faint mist that hovered above the nearby village.

The air was tinged with the fresh, earthy scent of pine and frost, a scent that mingled with a faint smokiness from distant hearths below. Cold nipped at her cheeks and nose, and she pulled her coat tighter, the crispness of the air like a gentle reminder of the season's magic. Around her, the group murmured in awe, each entranced by the beauty and magnitude of the sight before them.

"Wow," she breathed. "Where are we?"

"Gubbio, Italy," Gabriel whispered. His face caught the glow from the lights, a quiet smile illuminating his features.

"It's so gorgeous," Gillian whispered, wiping a tear. "Jeremy would love this."

"Mel would love it," Lance said.

"This is one of Joss's favorite places," Eric added.

Ava gazed up at the stunning display, lost in its beauty. For the first time in weeks, her tension seemed to fade, replaced by a calm she couldn't explain. She squeezed Gabriel's hand. "You keep taking me to these amazing places. I'm going to get hooked."

He opened his mouth, as if to say something more, but nodded with a gentle smile.

Ava extended her arms, summoning a stream of water that sliced through the cold air, striking a tree branch with a forceful crack. The branch snapped, tumbling to the ground with a dull thud.

"Show off," Lance teased, raising an eyebrow.

"It's easy if you think of it like how Thomas makes his fireballs." She shrugged.

After Christmas's fleeting peace, her worries crept back in. She wished that night had lasted longer. Another week of nothing but training passed, with Aaron pushing them all toward peak condition. The Elders kept a close watch as New Year's Eve approached, but Ava, restless and tense, decided to stay outside, away from the noisy party Savina threw. Eric, Lance, Gillian, and a few others joined her. Inside, Thomas seemed to be enjoying himself with the

Irish Aureole, particularly Moira. She assumed Natalia had Gabriel under close watch inside, away from her.

"Yeah, yeah, you make it sound easy," Lance muttered, trying to gather water in his own hands. "But it's a lot harder than creating fire."

She gave him a half-smile. "Maybe the water just prefers females."

"Jerk." He rolled his eyes but couldn't hold back a grin.

"Just remember, I didn't learn all of this in one night."

"True enough." He paused, glancing at her with concern. "Are you sleeping any better?"

"Not really." The dreams of Peter hadn't faded. If anything, they'd grown more disturbing. In them, he was always cruel, a different person. And yet she still felt a strange pull toward him, an ache that lingered when she woke. She couldn't shake the feeling that the dreams were trapping her in some strange, painful cycle.

"Have you tried talking to him?" Lance's dark eyes softened, a quiet apology in his gaze.

She shook her head, swallowing back the bitterness. "I don't want to."

"Guys are idiots," Eric chimed in.

Ava looked up, and he met her gaze.

"No, really," Eric continued. "If Joss had brought me into a coven the way you did for Peter, and I turned around and ditched her like that, she'd have electrocuted me on the spot."

Ava laughed.

"Seriously though. I'm impressed with how well you're keeping it together. I know it's not easy."

She aimed another burst of water at a nearby branch, and it splintered with a satisfying crack. "It helps having all of you around," she murmured. But inside, a gnawing doubt persisted: *Had it all been a lie?*

Gillian let out a frustrated sigh. "Ava, he's not worth all this. You should move on."

Ava tensed. She willed herself to stay composed, hating that her vulnerability was so clear. With a flash of anger, she sent another shot of water at a thicker branch, the limb landing with a thud a few feet from Gillian.

Eric laughed, nudging her. "Good one."

"Sorry," she mumbled, offering Gillian a sheepish look.

The sound of laughter and loud voices drifted from the house as a few people spilled outside, carrying drinks, their faces flushed and eyes bright with holiday cheer.

"Oh great," Eric muttered. "It's almost midnight."

As more people poured out of the Manor, their laughter and cheers grew louder, echoing in the crisp night air. Ava hugged herself, feeling the dread from Lance and Gillian, but her own heart raced, betraying her.

The countdown surged, each number sharp in her ears, until finally, "Three… two… one!" Everyone broke into a collective cheer, and colorful explosions erupted in the sky, painting the winter night in vivid reds, greens, and silvers. The cheers and laughter of the crowd faded into a dull hum as her gaze locked onto Peter and Katarina, illuminated in the glow of the fireworks.

She wished she hadn't seen it, wished she hadn't looked, but her eyes betrayed her. Peter's hand brushed along Katarina's cheek with a gentleness Ava once thought was meant for her. Then, as if the world hadn't already turned against her, he leaned in, and their lips met.

A sudden ache gripped her chest, as if an iron hand had clenched around her heart, squeezing the air from her lungs. Nausea seized her as the fireworks' sharp light, magnified by her tears, blurred their features. She tried to breathe, but her chest felt hollow, every heartbeat echoing with a sharp, hollow pain that left her dizzy.

Her fingers clutched her necklace, and in an instant, Peter's emotions surged into her senses, pure thrill, joy, yearning, the ones he only had for her. The intensity of his happiness burned through her, leaving a bitter chill in its wake. She blinked hard, but the tears threatened to spill over as she staggered back a step, feeling the ache coil tighter, suffocating her.

She couldn't breathe.

With each new burst of color in the sky, she felt like she was breaking further, pieces of her heart splintering away. The finality of it was undeniable. Peter had moved on, found happiness without her, and in that devastating realization, Ava felt herself collapse inside, the echo of the fireworks drowning out her silent heartbreak.

<h1 style="text-align:center">17</h1>

ESCAPE ARTIST

Explosions lit up the night sky, vivid streaks of reds, greens, pinks, and blues bursting above the forest. Each firework seemed to echo the turmoil in Ava's chest, hot and sharp. The chill of the winter air bit her face as she sprinted through the woods, her breath coming in ragged gasps. Tears blurred her vision, and water dripped from her fingertips, her powers spiraling out of her control like her emotions.

"Ava!" Eric called out, but she pressed forward, weaving between thick pine trunks, ignoring the sting of the freezing air against her lungs. The forest was dark and quiet, yet felt alive, whispering around her as she crashed through brittle branches, too focused on her own pain to care about anything else.

Her body slammed into something solid, and she stumbled backward, crashing into the ground with a thud. Strong arms caught her before she could hit harder. She blinked, and there was Gabriel.

He'd taken the brunt of the fall, his arms still wrapped around her as they hit the forest floor together.

She struggled against him, twisting in his grip. "Let me go!"

"Not until you calm down." Gabriel's voice was serene, his gaze locking onto hers. His hold loosened, giving her enough space to scramble to her feet, but he didn't step back.

"What are you doing here?" She glared at him, rubbing her aching head.

"I could ask you the same thing. But for now, I'm here to stop you from doing something you'll regret."

She turned away, trudging deeper into the woods, but he was faster. His hands grasped her shoulders, firm but not forceful, turning her back to face him. "Where are you going?"

"I need to get away." She brushed away her tears with a trembling hand.

"You can't run from this, Ava. Not like this."

A rustling sound made her glance back. Eric appeared through the trees, his breath clouding in the freezing air as he bent over, hands on his knees, panting. "What the hell, Ava?" he wheezed. "Are you trying to give me a heart attack?"

Her lips trembled, and she turned away, sliding down to the ground against the rough bark of a tree. "I can't do this anymore. None of this would've happened if I'd just left him alone."

"So, he wouldn't have had the chance to break your heart?"

"I didn't say that."

Gabriel crouched down in front of her, his movements slow, deliberate. His eyes met hers. "So, what's the plan here? Run until you can't anymore? Then what?"

Ava shook her head, tears brimming. "I just needed some time. I can't … I can't stand there and pretend I'm okay. Not with him. Not with her."

"I'm no expert at this." Eric dropped down beside her. "But I do know that if you keep holding onto that anger, it'll only weigh you down. It'll make everything hurt more."

She scoffed. "Easy for you to say. I just felt Peter's happiness with someone else. I'm sorry if my anger bothers you." She rubbed her eyes, but the tears wouldn't stop.

Gabriel tilted his head, studying her. "And running's supposed to make it hurt less?"

She flinched at his words. "What do you want me to say, Gabriel? That I'm fine? That it doesn't hurt watching him laugh with her like I never mattered? Because I can't." Her fists tightened against her thighs. "I don't know how to make it stop."

"You don't have to pretend with me, Ava. Not ever. But you can't keep running from it, either. You're only hurting yourself more."

"Why does it even matter to you? I'm a disaster. You don't have to stay and clean up my broken pieces."

"Because you matter to me, Ava. Broken pieces and all."

Her breath hitched at the sincerity in his tone, her gaze dropping to her trembling hands. She felt raw, exposed, but there was a calmness in him that kept her from retreating completely. "I don't know how to fix this."

"You don't have to figure it all out tonight. Stop punishing yourself for feeling. It's okay to hurt, Ava."

The tears she'd been holding back spilled over, and she turned her face into her knees, her body trembling with quiet sobs.

Gabriel didn't move closer but stayed rooted in place.

Time passed, the cold wrapping around them in silence. Despite her frustration, she sensed their patience, a steady, unspoken concern beside her. The anger and resentment were still there, but so was something else, a feeling she hadn't expected: gratitude.

She knew they didn't want to spend New Year's sitting out in the woods, waiting for her to let her pain settle, but somehow, they were.

"I'm sorry for that," she whispered.

"It's all good," Eric said. "Gave me time to calm down from my near heart attack."

Ava let out a small laugh and she met Gabriel's gaze.

He got to his feet and helped her to her feet.

"I'm not one to complain," Eric said. "But do we really have to walk all the way back?"

"Are you that lazy?" she asked.

"Yes," he admitted, and Gabriel chuckled.

"We're miles away. You *really* wanted to get away. Gabe can get us back sooner. I'm sure people are worried about us."

Ava shrugged. "I'm content to walk back." The longer it took to return, the better.

"Come on, he's right." Gabriel extended his hands, and Ava and Eric each took one.

When Ava opened her eyes, a shiver went down her spine. She clutched Gabriel's hand.

"Um, Gabe?" Eric said. "This is not the Manor."

Half-burned buildings surrounded them on the cracked, empty street. The windows of deserted storefronts were shattered, and crumbling debris from caved-in roofs littered the ground. A thick, ashy smell hung heavy in the air, mingling with the metallic tang of charred metal. The only movement was a soft drift of ash falling like snow. It was hauntingly still. A strange, unsettling feeling permeated the air.

Ava took a cautious step forward, the crunch of glass beneath her feet echoing. The sky beyond the buildings glowed with an unnatural red light, an odd, almost pulsating hue that highlighted the jagged mountains in the distance.

"This is wrong." Gabriel scanned the decaying ruins.

She dropped his hand and wandered closer to a store window. "Where are we?" She leaned forward, her own reflection barely visible in the soot-smeared oval mirror inside. She could see her red hair, tangled and matted, her gray eyes looking hollow with exhaustion. Even her reflection seemed lost here, haunting and unfamiliar.

"I don't know," Gabriel said.

"We need to get back—Ava, get away!" Eric's shout made her whirl around.

Hands shot out of the darkness, grabbing her waist and yanking her toward the empty store. She seized the broken frame of the window, gasping as sharp glass bit into her hands. Two cloaked figures tackled Gabriel and Eric to the ground. In a flash of moonlight, she caught a glimpse of white hair beneath one of the hoods, like Kira's.

The figure dragging Ava into the shadows tightened their grip. She kicked out, fighting to break free. Desperation surged through her, triggering her power. She focused, willing water to come, her palms tingling with energy. But it didn't come. She glanced up at the pipes and focused.

With a deafening crack, pipes beneath the building burst, sending a flood of water roaring out onto the street. The wave surged around them, the force like stones pounding against her skin. The cloaked figure struggled to keep hold of her, choking as water rushed over them.

As the street filled, debris floated in the rushing currents, and the cloaked figures released Gabriel and Eric. Ava jabbed her elbow into her captor's neck, breaking free. She kicked against the current, swimming toward Gabriel and Eric.

Gabriel's hand closed around hers. In an instant, they were gone.

They landed hard near the Manor, Ava tumbling to the ground as she released Gabriel's hand. She lay there, drenched and trembling, her hair clinging to her face. Around her, dry leaves stuck to her clothes, mingling with pine straw.

"Ava," Eric gasped, bent over with his hands on his knees. "Was that you?"

She nodded, wringing water from her soaked hair, her breathing shaky.

Gabriel leaned against a nearby tree, his face pale. "Where the hell were we?" he whispered, still rattled.

She stared at him, a new fear creeping up her spine. "Gabriel, the Cimmerians did this to you before. Did they … get into your mind again?"

He cursed, running a hand through his hair. "I was thinking of the Manor. I don't even know that place." His usual confidence was gone, replaced by a hint of fear. His confusion radiated.

"Could someone be … watching us?" she asked.

Eric glanced toward the Manor, then back at them, his face tense. "I don't know, but Aaron's upset. We need to go back now. Everyone's worried."

They arrived at the practice field of the Manor and halted.

Ava's gaze fell on Peter and Katarina, their intertwined hands sending a jolt of discomfort through her. Lance and Gillian had worry written on their faces. Thomas stood with his arm around Moira's shoulder. Savina's mouth was pressed into a hard line, and both she and Aaron looked furious. Ava looked away, shame rising within her.

Natalia marched toward them, her hazel eyes blazing. "Gabriel."

"Natalia, don't," he warned, his tone guarded.

"What the hell happened?" she demanded. "You know Aaron forbade you to teleport outside the Manor's protection. There are Cimmerians out there. Were you trying to impress *her*? How reckless can you be?"

"Calm down," Gustav said, though his expression was grim.

Gabriel took a breath. "I was bringing us back here, but we ended up … somewhere else." He cast an uncertain glance at Aaron.

A muscle in Aaron's jaw twitched, and he met Gabriel's gaze with a hard, unyielding stare. "Come with me."

They followed the Elders into the Manor, each step feeling heavier than the last. Ava's shame grew as she replayed what had happened. She hadn't known Gabriel wasn't allowed to teleport, and she realized how reckless it was to run past Savina's protection charm. She'd put them all in danger, and her selfishness nearly cost them everything.

In the parlor, Aaron shut the door with a thud. "Tell me what happened."

"I-I—" Ava stammered.

"Ava needed to get away," Eric said. "She didn't realize she went past the charm. I suggested Gabe teleport us, but I had no idea he wasn't allowed."

Aaron's brow furrowed. "You should have known better," he told Gabriel, his voice brimming with quiet fury. "All of you know the dangers. Have I taught you nothing?"

Gabriel's face fell. "You have. I'm sorry, Aaron."

"It was my fault," Ava said, her voice small. "I shouldn't have run off."

Aaron's gaze shifted to her, cold and piercing. "No, you shouldn't have. What were you thinking?"

"I wasn't."

"Where did you end up?" Aaron asked.

Gabriel's face darkened. "A desolate town. Burned-out buildings, deserted streets. A figure grabbed Ava from a mirror, and others ambushed us. Ava flooded the area, and I teleported us back."

"A mirror?" Gustav repeated, his tone sharp. "Did it pull you in?"

Gabriel nodded, his expression unsettled. "It tried."

"The Cimmerians could have been using it to lure us in. But we didn't feel you, or sense anything," Gustav said. "Wherever you were, Havok's charm masked you from us."

Aaron's gaze sharpened on Ava. "You ran past our protection, letting them get inside Gabriel's head. This could have ended much worse. Next time, think." His words stung, and he turned, dismissing them.

She'd been reckless. When would she ever learn not to be selfish and risk everyone's lives?

"Ava, come with me," Savina said.

Ava followed Savina down the corridor, past Colden's old room, swallowing the sadness that tried to rise within her.

Inside a small room lined with red curtains and filled with cabinets of mysterious liquids and powders, candles flickered to life. Savina took Ava's hands, which were covered in small cuts. "How did you hurt yourself?"

"Glass," Ava mumbled, now noticing the stinging. "I cut myself trying to hold onto the window frame."

Savina's touch was warm as she healed the wounds.

She didn't miss the strain in Savina's eyes, the fine lines that marked the Elder's worry.

"You must stop being reckless, Ava. I'll move you to a room on the third floor where I can keep a closer eye on you."

Ava's heart sank. "But what about my dad?"

"He'll join you." Savina released her hands. Her voice softened. "I know this is hard, but you need to consider the people relying on you. No more impulsive decisions."

Ava managed a small nod. She thanked Savina and walked away, feeling the crushing burden of her mistakes.

Back in the hallway, Gillian and Lance were waiting for her. "Why do you keep doing this?" Gillian asked, exasperated. "That's the second time I thought you'd died."

Lance's voice was softer. "Are you okay?"

Ava nodded, grateful for his concern. "I'm fine. Do you know where Gabriel and Eric are?"

"They're in the library," Lance said.

Approaching the library door, Ava paused when she heard Natalia's voice, her words sharp and biting.

"I expect this from her, but not from you two," she said. "Running after her recklessly. Do you have any idea how dangerous that was?"

"It wasn't even her!" Eric shot back. "It was me. Ava helped us escape."

"You're always throwing yourself into danger for her, Gabriel. Do you really think she'd risk herself like that for you?"

"Enough." Gabriel's voice was calm but firm. "This isn't about taking risks for no reason. Ava needed help. I'm not going to turn my back on her."

"It's going to get you killed," Natalia said.

A wave of heated shame poured over Ava. Taking a deep breath, she stepped into the room. "Please stop fighting. I'm sorry. This was my fault, not theirs."

Natalia's glare shifted to her, disdain clear in her eyes. "They should banish you."

"Back off, Natalia," Eric snapped.

Irritation flashed in Gabriel's eyes, but when he saw Ava, his expression softened. "Are you alright? Were you hurt?"

"I'm fine. What about you and Eric?"

Eric grinned. "Almost drowned, but at least I looked cool doing it."

Gillian leaned forward. "What exactly happened out there?"

Ava shifted, averting her eyes as she explained the night's events. She avoided meeting anyone's gaze, feeling a wave of guilt settle on her like a heavy cloak.

Ilya gasped, his face paling. "The Liquid Mirror."

"The what?" Thomas asked.

Eric leaned forward. "It's a device linked to Havok's castle, made of liquid gas. It looks like a mirror, but they can watch you from the other side, even reach through it if they want. It's a trap … and sometimes a portal. You're not supposed to go near it."

"So … someone tried to grab me?" Ava asked. "To pull me through?"

"Yes." Eric sounded more serious than usual.

She sank back into her chair. She'd been seconds away from being taken. She'd been so stupid to get that close. And almost got Gabriel and Eric hurt or worse.

Her pulse spiked as Aaron and Gustav entered.

Aaron's gaze settled on Gabriel. "We need you. Now."

A chill settled over her. "What's going on?"

Aaron exchanged a glance with Gustav, who stepped forward. "We need to return to that village. Sean can show us exactly what happened there. And we need to destroy the Mirror."

"But ... it's connected to Havok's castle," Ava said, dread coiling in her gut.

"Yes," Aaron said. "The Cimmerians wanted Gabriel to teleport there. We think they're using the Mirror to monitor us."

Gabriel ran a hand through his hair, his posture tense. "Great. Nothing like a deathtrap to start the new year. Can't wait to hear Sean's take on it. 'Gabriel, hold this volatile shard of glass while I poke at it with a stick.'"

Eric smirked. "Sounds foolproof."

"Don't encourage him." Gabriel narrowed his eyes at Eric. "I'm already regretting this."

Fear gripped Ava's heart, squeezing it until it felt like it might burst. "What if it's a trap? What if they're waiting for you?"

"It probably is a trap," Gabriel said. "But that's why we're going in prepared."

Aaron nodded. "We need to make sure they can't use the Mirror again. If we don't, they'll have a way to reach us or worse, pull someone through."

Fear rose inside her as she looked at Gabriel. "But what if they try to control you again?" Ava asked. "Or Katarina? Or—"

Gabriel stepped closer, placing a hand on her shoulder. "Hey, no spiraling. We've got this."

"But what if something happens to you?" She hated the vulnerability in her words.

He smiled. "Sean will be there. He's invincible, remember? Or so he keeps telling everyone. Something about whiskey immunity."

A faint, strained laugh escaped her. "Be serious."

"I am serious. That's his tagline: Sean the Invincible, Slayer of Mirrors and Whiskey." He paused, his humor giving way to sincerity. "Look, Ava, I'm not saying I'm not scared. I'd be an idiot if I wasn't. But we have a plan, and we'll come back."

"I don't want you to go."

"And I don't want to either. But someone's got to make sure Aaron doesn't accidentally punch the Mirror."

Aaron shot him a glare.

Gabriel took Ava's hands in his. "Promise me something."

"What?"

"No more running. And no more blaming yourself for everything. Deal?"

She swallowed the building lump in her throat. "Deal." She wrapped her arms around his neck, holding him. His warmth enveloped her, a soothing heat that felt like a safe haven. For a moment, she allowed herself to let go of her fears, clinging to him as if he were her lifeline.

Gabriel stiffened slightly, but his arms came around her. His hand rested gently on her back, and the tension within her eased a little.

"I'm sorry," she whispered. "I keep putting you in danger. If something happened to you—"

Gabriel pulled back enough to meet her gaze, his hands resting on her shoulders. His blue eyes softened, but there was a seriousness in them that made her pause. "Ava, listen to me. You don't control me, and you don't control my choices. I decided to teleport us. That was *my* decision."

"But—"

"No buts. You didn't force me to do anything. I know the risks, and I accept them. This isn't on you."

Her lips quivered as she nodded, unable to shake the guilt. "Okay."

"Good." His lips quirked into a small smile. "Rest now, sensei." With a final, reassuring nod, he stepped back, giving her one last, lingering glance before joining the others.

And then, he was gone.

Her heart plummeted, leaving an empty ache behind as silence fell over the room. She stood there, numb, coldness seeping into her bones as if darkness had swallowed her whole. She drew a shaky breath.

"I won't be able to sleep until they're back," Eric said.

"Nor will I," Moira said, her gaze distant. "It's like they're … gone. The charm on that place blocks me from sensing them. I can't even feel if they're alive."

Natalia crossed her arms, her sharp glare cutting through the room. "They wouldn't have to do this if people stopped acting recklessly." Her eyes snapped to Ava, filled with a sharp, cutting disdain.

"Enough, Natalia," Eric snapped. "This isn't helping."

Ava barely heard them, too lost in the storm of her own thoughts. Guilt overwhelmed her, bearing down on her with suffocating force. She touched her necklace, her breath uneven as she struggled to hold herself together.

If something happened to Gabriel, Aaron, Sean, or Katarina because of her actions, she'd never forgive herself. Her mind raced with worst-case scenarios: the Cimmerians lying in wait, the Mirror pulling them through to Havok's castle, or Sorcha weaving another spell to control them.

Ava stared at the fireplace, its light flickering over the room, casting long shadows. The crackling embers mirrored the quiet turmoil in her chest.

"They'll be okay, you know," Eric said. "Gabriel's got a knack for getting out of trouble."

Her fists tightened, her nails biting into her palms. *You can't lose him, too.* But fear wouldn't bring him back. Only strength would.

18

WAITING

Not even the lyrical, comedic words of *A Midsummer Night's Dream* could distract Ava from the worry over Aaron, Gabriel, and the others venturing back to that cursed town. Hours had slipped by since they'd left, and the fire had burned down to smoldering embers. Exhaustion clung to her like wet, heavy clothes and her eyes stung from sleeplessness.

She leaned back, casting her gaze around the room. Moira lay on the floor nearby, one arm tucked under her head, the other wrapped around herself. Ava wondered where Thomas had gone. She'd overheard him and Moira talking for hours before. Eric snored beside her, head stuck to the table in a way that looked uncomfortable. And behind her, Peter sat slumped forward, his head resting on folded arms. His brown eyes, red-rimmed and staring into space, were framed by his tousled hair.

An ache stirred inside her. She wanted to comfort him, but at the same time, she didn't. All night she was aware of his presence, a heavy tension filling the silence between them. She didn't know why, but his anxiety weighed her down even more than her own.

Setting her book face down on the table, she stood and stretched, a yawn breaking through. She wandered out into the hallway, where a cold, gray morning light filtered through the high foyer windows. The rich aroma of coffee drifted from the dining room. Following it, she found Thomas already there, sipping from a mug while Savina refilled hers.

"Good morning, Ava," Savina greeted her with a gentle smile.

"Good morning."

"Mornin'," Thomas said, his tone warmer than usual. "Did you sleep at all? You look like crap."

"So do you." Ava smirked, crossing to the chair beside him. "I didn't even see you leave the room."

"I was quiet."

"I can't believe you all stayed in the library." Savina shook her head. "Coffee?"

"No thanks. So, you haven't heard from them?"

Savina's brows creased, worry shadowing her expression. "No, nothing yet."

Silence fell as they sat, sipping their coffee. Others began trickling in, rousing from sleep with slow, stiff movements. Ronan and Aidan shuffled in, heading straight for the coffee pot. Shannon followed Cara, who balanced little Lucas in her arms, cooing at him as he babbled in response. Ava rested her head against the table, trying to find comfort in the rhythm of life around her, even as her heart beat with dread.

Thomas leaned in. "What really happened last night?"

"You already know."

"No, I mean … why did you run?"

Ava tensed. "I think everyone knows."

"Because of Peter and Katarina?"

"Are you trying to get a rise out of me?"

He sighed, running a hand over his face. "No. I … suck at this. What I'm trying to say is … I know how it feels."

The vulnerability in his voice caught her off guard. She'd never expected to hear this from Thomas. She swallowed, emotions swirling. "I'm sorry."

"Don't." He shook his head, his eyes earnest. "I just need to know … what was it about him that made you lose interest in me?"

"It wasn't just him. You and I grew apart. We're different, Thomas. You became so … intense. I thought I had to stay with you because of the coven, but it wasn't right."

"You're right. We're different." His gaze dropped to his hands, his fingers fidgeting against the coffee cup. "But for what it's worth, I'm sorry for how I treated you. I'll never forgive myself. Aaron helped me see that."

Her brows furrowed in confusion. "How did he?"

Thomas hesitated. "You didn't know they thought about banishing me, did you?"

"What? No."

"Yeah … Aaron worked with me on my anger. He helped me realize that you and Peter were right for each other, in a way we never were. I think it drove me mad. Seeing how you looked at him, how different it was." He paused, his broad shoulders lifting in a slow, resigned shrug. "I couldn't compete with that."

Ava felt a lump in her throat as she watched him. His words were so unlike the egotistical Thomas she'd known, the one who used to call her "babe" and hold onto her like a possession.

"Why are you saying all this now?" she asked.

He rubbed his thumb over his knuckles, his gaze soft. "Because I know the pain you're feeling, and it didn't hurt this bad for me. No offense."

Ava's lips quirked in a bittersweet smile. "Aren't you lucky?"

With a soft chuckle, he shook his head. "That's not what I mean. What I'm saying is … it got better, even if it took time. Aaron reminded me we'd always be in the same coven, so there was no point in holding grudges. I'm not saying this to make amends right now, just … take it one day at a time. Maybe even try to understand his feelings for her. I know it's hard. Believe me."

She took a breath, feeling a sliver of gratitude. "Thanks."

"You're welcome," he said. "I just … really do understand now."

"I'm sorry I put you through that," she whispered.

He gave a dismissive wave. "It was for the best. And you don't owe me an apology. I know I didn't treat you well toward the end. Power or no power, I knew better."

She nodded. "I didn't see this coming with Peter. And knowing how he feels about her … it hurts in ways I wasn't prepared for."

"It does. But it will pass. And maybe the trip will help keep your mind off things."

At that moment, Moira and Eric stumbled in, both looking half-asleep. Eric's eyelids drooped, and he looked seconds away from slumping onto the table.

"Morning." Thomas gave Moira a small smile.

She huffed, folding her arms. "You left me alone on the floor."

"Sorry," he said.

Ava noticed the way he looked at Moira, his pale blue eyes lighting up even in his sleep-deprived state. She could tell he loved her wild, tangled hair and the way she didn't mind the messiness. Moira's brown eyes sparkled despite her own exhaustion, though there was a shadow of sadness there, perhaps missing Gabriel.

More of the coven trickled in, voices filling the quiet space. No one looked like they'd slept, and as Ava glanced around, she realized that, in spite of everything, they were all there for each other. The night may have left them weary and worn, but a quiet strength ran through the room, binding them together in ways she was beginning to understand.

A shriek pierced the room, drawing everyone's attention toward the wide entrance. Shannon sprinted across the floor, throwing herself into Sean's arms. Aaron approached Savina with a soft kiss on her forehead, and a wave of relief rippled through the room as the returning group was welcomed with embraces.

Anastasya, Ilya, and Konstantin surrounded Gustav, each pulling him into a heartfelt hug. Katarina rushed toward Peter, and he caught her. The tender kiss, verging on intimate, caused a sharp pang in Ava's chest. She lowered herself into the nearest chair, her knees weak and unsteady as her mind spiraled. *You and I are invincible. I will never let you go.* Peter's words echoed in her mind, a ghost she couldn't shake. Her hand drifted to her necklace, now warm against her skin, but it offered little comfort.

"Gabriel!" Moira cried, breaking through Ava's haze. She launched herself into Gabriel's arms, his body tensing before he caught her with a tired but steady grip.

At the sound of his name, Ava's breath hitched. Relief surged through her chest, hot and overwhelming, releasing the knot of fear. Her hands trembled as she gripped the chair, blinking back tears of gratitude. *He's okay. He's safe.* But as her gaze lingered on him, she noticed the lines of exhaustion etched into his face, the shadow in his eyes. The sight stirred another emotion, hesitation. Would he see how shaken she was? Did she even have the courage to face him now?

"What happened?" Moira clung to Gabriel's arm.

"Let them rest," Savina said.

Aaron shook his head. "They should hear it." The room silenced as everyone gathered around the table, leaning in to catch every word. "We returned to the town. Sean let us see that it was once a village of Ephemerals before the Cimmerians destroyed it. They killed many and kidnapped others, mostly children, to turn them into Enchanters."

Gasps and murmurs filled the room.

"The Cimmerians left behind a trap," he continued. "Mirrors, enchanted by Havok, allowing them to watch us and move through them. Gabriel, Eric, and Ava encountered one. They tried to pull Ava through it." Aaron's sharp gaze swept across the room, lingering on Ava. "They almost succeeded."

She shrank back into her chair, the memory of the Mirror's pull fresh and raw. Her stomach churned with guilt. *If something had happened to him because of me…*

Aaron's voice hardened. "Someone tampered with Gabriel's mind, guiding him to that Mirror. We believe it was an attempt to capture him."

"How would they know he could teleport?" Link asked, his tone sharp with suspicion. "Are Cimmerians spying on us?"

"Not here," Savina assured him. "The Manor's charm protects us from their reach."

"Either way," Aaron said, "Gabriel is no longer teleporting unless he's accompanied by a protector." His gaze swept the room, landing on Ava, then moving to the others. "We leave for Caprington in five days."

Excitement swept through them. Some cheered, while others exchanged tense glances, eager and nervous all at once. Relief rose in Ava's chest like a tide. They were moving forward, preparing to reclaim their Aureole instead of waiting and wondering. She scanned the faces around her, sensing a mixture of determination and worry.

"We have to be careful and strategic," Gustav cautioned. "There are countless threats, both known and unknown. Anyone who wishes to stay behind will remain safe under the charm here at the Manor."

But no one stepped back. Instead, each person seemed to plant themselves, as if drawing strength from the ground beneath them.

"We must train as much as we can," Sean added. "Our Aureole's power holds more potential than we realize, and we want every advantage on our side."

Aaron's gaze turned somber. "Understand, we're walking into danger. If any of you have doubts, voice them now."

But Ava felt a newfound clarity, ready to face whatever was ahead if it meant moving on from the constant waiting.

She barely registered Aaron's final instructions about keeping the protectors nearby, her mind already drifting to what lay ahead. Of course, the irony wasn't lost in her: the two people she most wanted to avoid were now the ones tasked with protecting her.

"We will rescue them," Aaron declared. "And we will prevail."

Excited murmurs rippled through the crowd, some eager, others nervous. But Ava stayed seated, her relief at Gabriel's safe return tempered by a weight that wouldn't lift.

As the group began to disperse, Gabriel moved toward the door. Ava's breath caught. She wanted to call out to him, to say something, anything, but the words stuck in her throat. Before she could muster the courage, he was surrounded by others, their voices overlapping as they pulled him into brief conversations.

She rose, her legs shaky, and made her way to the third floor, her feet dragging as she neared her new room. Her hand rested on the door handle, but she paused, her attention drawn to the tall arched window at the end of the hall. She drifted toward it, captivated by the frost-covered flowers outside, glittering in the early morning sun like delicate shards of crystal.

The thought that they would be leaving in a few days made her heart pound. They were close to reuniting with Melissa, Jeremy, Joss, Kira, and Maggie. She wished they could somehow send a message ahead, to let them know they were coming, that they were ready. But a dark cloud lingered in her mind. The image of that ruined town and all the lives the Cimmerians had destroyed, children snatched from their families, homes reduced to ash. How close had they come to encountering Havok himself? Had he been there hours before?

"If you're planning to water the flowers, maybe open the window. Or, you know, go outside."

Ava jumped, spinning around.

Gabriel leaned against the wall, a small, tired smile tugging at his lips, his dark eyebrows raised.

"What?" she asked, still caught off guard.

He nodded toward her hands. "They're watering."

She looked down, startled to see water streaming from her fingertips, pooling on the carpet beside her boots. Concentrating, she willed it to stop. "Sorry, I didn't even notice."

"What were you thinking?" As Gabriel approached, his voice was soft, his eyes never leaving her.

"It's nothing."

"You were worried and angry. Your hands always do that when you're upset. Like they're bracing for a fight."

"Actually … yeah. I guess they do."

"It's nothing to worry about." His faint smile returned, though his usual spark was dimmed. His bloodshot eyes and tense posture betrayed his exhaustion. Yet there was something more. Something unspoken in the way he held himself. A restrained sadness that made Ava want to reach out, to pull him back from whatever haunted him.

"I was thinking about what you all saw."

Gabriel's expression darkened. "Havok's getting impatient. He knows we're coming, and he's going to make it hell for us. There will be more ambushes." He paused, his eyes softening as he looked at her. "But you have a gift for keeping calm under pressure. You've saved my life more than once."

"Was the town … still flooded?"

"Oh yeah." He winked. "Why aren't you out there practicing with the others?"

"I stayed up all night waiting for you—all of you to come back," she admitted, correcting herself.

"You didn't sleep?"

"No. I couldn't." She hesitated, self-conscious under his gaze. "I was worried. And I keep having nightmares."

"I'm sorry, Ava. For now, try taking a few deep breaths. Clear your mind, as hard as it is. It helps."

She realized how much she'd missed him. Through everything, he'd always been there, so loyal. "Gabriel?"

"Yeah?"

"I'm so sorry you had to go through all of that again. I'm so glad you're back … in one piece. I don't know what I would do without you."

His expression shifted, and in two strides, he closed the distance between them, wrapping his arms around her.

Ava's heart raced as he held onto her like she was his anchor in a raging sea. The faint smell of smoke clung to him, a stark reminder of the horror he'd endured. Through her necklace, she felt glimpses of his pain, his sadness. It was as if he was holding himself together by sheer willpower. She pulled back, searching his face.

His hands lingered on her waist as their gazes locked, his eyes filled with something new, a deep, tortured vulnerability.

"Gabe … are you okay?"

He averted his gaze, and his jaw muscle twitched. "They burned everything, including people. That's what Havok did to my home … to my family." He took a ragged breath. "Sean showed us what happened, how they invaded. We saw children ripped from their parents, running for safety…" His voice broke. "We were only watching, but it felt like we were there, reliving it. The Cimmerians wanted us to see it. I'll never forget those images."

A sharp pain gripped Ava's chest. "I'm so sorry, Gabriel."

"They left everything in ruin—fire and death. Just like they did to my family." Shaking his head as if to rid himself of the memories, he gazed at her with such intensity that she was left breathless. "But in all that chaos, all I could think about was getting back to—"

"Gabe!" Natalia's voice rang out as she crested the stairs, her eyes widening with concern. She strode toward him, pulling him into a tight embrace, breaking his connection with Ava. "What's wrong? I felt you."

Even as he hugged Natalia, his gaze lingered on Ava, something unspoken hanging between them. He looked utterly drained, his vulnerability clear even through his usual composure.

"Come on." Natalia guided him toward his room. "You need rest."

As they disappeared down the hall, her hand pressed against her chest, where her heart still raced. The wounded look in his eyes troubled her. She hoped, more than anything, that he wouldn't be haunted by the memories. A pang of jealousy prickled through her as Natalia led him away, wishing she were the one comforting him.

With a heavy sigh, she made her way to her room, closing the door behind her. Leaning back against it, she slid down to the floor, her hands trembling. Her phone felt heavy as she stared at it, debating whether to reach out. Would he even want to hear from her now?

She wanted to do something, anything, to let him know she cared, that he wasn't alone.

Taking a deep breath, she opened their message thread and typed.

You're not alone. I'm here for you. Always.

Her finger lingered over the send button, nerves threatening to stop her. But she pressed it, the message sending with a quiet whoosh.

Seconds felt like hours as she waited, her heart pounding in her chest. When her phone vibrated with his reply, she exhaled a shaky breath and opened it.

Thank you, sensei. That means more than you know. Now go to bed before I have to teleport over there to make you.

She couldn't help but smile at his response, a mix of humor and sincerity that was so typically Gabriel. Setting her phone aside, she pulled the blankets closer, her heart calming as she settled in. Even though there was still so much uncertainty ahead, his words brought her a small sense of peace.

For the first time in what felt like forever, she closed her eyes and drifted off with a faint, genuine smile on her lips.

19

GOODBYE

The frigid night air made each breath a fleeting wisp of mist that vanished. The leafless oaks crouched around the Manor, shadows sprawling across the clearing, while tall pines stood as silent, watchful sentries. Overhead, the remnants of the blue moon cast a faint glow, bathing the scene in eerie light. An electric energy charged the air, buzzing with the anticipation of battle.

The Enchanters were locked in focus, bodies tense, every move precise. Elders stood at the edges of the training ground, murmuring praise or calling out adjustments. For days, the group had sparred, each session more intense than the last.

Gabriel leapt backward, dodging the searing fireball that erupted from Thomas's hand, leaving a trail of burning smoke in the cold air. He shifted toward Gillian, who greeted him with a crooked smile, her eyes glinting with mischief.

"Stop," she commanded, voice slicing through the noise.

Gabriel's eyes glazed over, his muscles freezing as she tightened her grip on his mind.

"Attack Eric," she ordered, her tone smooth and unwavering.

Gabriel lunged forward, eyes unfocused. But his hands clutched empty air as several versions of Eric scattered in every direction, taunting him with echoes. The real Eric darted behind Gabriel, his form blurring as he knocked him to the ground.

Thunder rolled overhead, dark clouds gathering as lightning split the sky, each flash casting eerie, staccato shadows across their faces. A sharp wind whipped through, sending loose leaves spiraling into the air, and with a sudden gust, Gillian stumbled, breaking her hold over Gabriel.

Ava summoned water, the cold liquid spiraling upward in a sleek, powerful jet aimed at Aidan, who had conjured the storm. Katarina countered with a burst of radiant energy, the glow from her hands bright enough to pierce the gathering darkness. She launched it toward Ava, who raised a shimmering shield of water in time. The impact rippled through her shield, sending frigid droplets spraying across her face.

Undeterred, Katarina raised her hands for another strike, but Lance intercepted, absorbing the pulsing energy before redirecting it back at her with a fierce thrust.

A shrill, high-pitched sound tore through the air. Ava's hands flew to her ears, pain lancing through her as she fell to her knees. The ground beneath her felt cold and unyielding, but she forced herself up as Thomas flung another fireball toward Natalia. She dodged it with a dancer's grace, her eyes locking onto Thomas. A faint shimmer crossed his face, his expression softening under her charm.

A small bomb detonated and knocked Natalia backward, sending her sprawling against a tree. Thomas shook his head as if emerging from a trance, glancing at Link, who gave him a curt nod before refocusing.

Nearby, Moira grappled with Konstantin, every movement fluid as though she anticipated his next strike. She ducked, evading his punch, and countered with a swift, calculated sweep of her leg.

Each Enchanter pushed their powers to the limit, their breaths visible in the chilled air, and by the end, muscles quivered with exhaustion as the Elders called an end to practice.

The Enchanters gathered in the Manor's dining room, where the familiar warmth of food and chatter enveloped them. Ava's father and several other parents had come to join them for one last meal. Mr. and Mrs. Rollins arrived, their faces tight with concern despite their smiles. Sean, ever the storyteller, held court, recounting humorous tales that left Aidan, Ronan, and Moira blushing.

"Ah, my boys are the best," Sean said, a grin stretching across his face. "Once, Shannon asked Ronan to kill a spider for her. He was about seven and flat-out refused. Then little Moira, just five, hopped off her chair, hand on her hip, and said, 'Fine, I'll do it.'" Sean burst into laughter, and soon everyone joined him.

Shannon rolled her eyes, though she smiled. "She's always been like that. Takes after her father." She winked at Moira.

Cailin, Melissa's mother, sighed, a sad smile crossing her face as a few tears spilled over. "Moira and Melissa would have gotten along so well." She looked at Lance, her voice barely a whisper. "I hope you find her. Bring her home."

"I promise, I will," Lance said.

"We'll save them all," Sean added, then turned to Ava's father. "Connor, it's a shame you're not coming along."

"Yeah, I know," he said, a hint of regret in his voice.

Sean looked at Ava, his eyes warm. "Your father's a fighter, you know. He saved so many of us, including your mother. She was a firecracker herself."

Shannon nodded. "You remind me of her, Ava. Brave and determined."

Ava shifted, discomfort lodging her chest. She hadn't wanted to discuss her mother tonight, especially with what she'd discovered. But no one else knew what her mother had done.

"Ava's always had that bravery in her," her father said. "I remember when she was about five, she saw a car coming toward a neighbor's kid and ran out to push him out of the way. Luckily, the driver swerved just in time."

"Goodness!" Shannon gasped. "How extraordinary."

Moira's jaw dropped. "Wow."

Ava glanced down, a bit embarrassed by the attention.

"I'm not surprised," Gabriel said, his eyes warm as he looked at her. "That sounds exactly like you."

Her cheeks heated, but Gabriel's words settled in her heart.

Her father glanced at her, concern flickering in his eyes. "It's getting late."

"You're not leaving, are you?"

He smiled. "No, I'm staying here tonight." He stood, exchanging goodnights with those around him. Ava walked with him to the bottom of the stairs, where he paused, studying her.

"Don't be nervous," he said.

"I'm trying not to be." She bit her lip. A hesitant thought surfaced. "Can we … can we visit Mom's grave in the morning?"

Her father's brow furrowed, a flicker of surprise crossing his face. "Are you sure?"

"I'm not ready to forgive her. I just need…" She trailed off, unsure of what exactly she needed. A sense of closure, perhaps, or a final goodbye.

He nodded. "I'll talk to Savina. You should get some rest." He pulled her into a tight embrace, and she held on, burying her face in his shoulder. His hand stroked her hair.

"Don't get all emotional on me now. We'll see each other in the morning."

Ava fought back tears as she let him go, managing a shaky smile. "I'll be fine."

He cupped her face for a moment, pride shining in his eyes. "Yes, you will. Goodnight, sweetie."

"Goodnight, Dad." As he ascended the stairs, a sense of heaviness settled over her. She shut her eyes as she forced herself to take slow, steady breaths. What if it was the last time she'd ever say goodnight to him?

Laughter echoed from the dining room, pulling her from her thoughts. Aidan, Ronan, and Moira emerged, still chuckling.

"Do they always have to tell that story?" Ronan sighed, shaking his head.

"I swear, they get crazier every time they visit," Aidan muttered with a smile.

Ava followed them into the library, where most of the Enchanters had retreated. She sank into the seat Gabriel pulled out for her, stretching her legs, trying to push aside her anxieties about tomorrow.

Gillian turned to Aidan, Ronan, and Moira, her curiosity evident. "I've got a question for you three."

Moira raised her brows. "Alright, shoot."

Gillian leaned forward. "How is it that your parents still have powers even though you have yours? I thought the magic was supposed to transfer."

Ronan's smile widened. "It's different for every family line. Our powers don't replace our parents.' They're shared. Some families lose their powers as they pass them on to their kids, but for others, like ours, the magic bonds grow stronger with each generation. Our parents just learned to balance their abilities with ours."

Aidan shrugged. "Some families say it depends on the strength of the lineage. The power divides differently depending on how many Enchanters are in one family. For us, everyone keeps a bit of their original magic."

"Interesting," Gillian mused. "Is it weird to have your parents so involved in all this?"

"Not really," Ronan said. "We've all been preparing for this together since we were kids. It's just … part of our lives."

"How old are you all?" Gillian continued.

"Aidan and I are nineteen, and Moira's seventeen," Ronan answered.

Gillian's gaze grew more intense. "Have you encountered any Cimmerians before?"

Ronan's face darkened. "Not directly. But we've heard plenty of stories, and we know what they're capable of." He gave her a sympathetic look. "I'm sorry for what they've done to you all."

She looked away, her fingers twisting around a loose curl. "Yeah. We've all lost people to them." Lance wrapped a comforting arm around her shoulders.

"Alright, enough gloom." Ronan grinned. "You want to hear about the time Aidan tried to 'cool off' an exam room with a light breeze and ended up starting a full-on thunderstorm inside?"

Moira burst out laughing. "It was like being in a tropical storm but in a classroom!"

Gabriel raised his eyebrows. "A thunderstorm? Indoors?"

"Oh yeah." Aidan laughed. "I'd just started working on my weather manipulation, and it was this super hot day. I thought I'd make things more 'comfortable' by bringing in a little cool breeze for the class. Next thing I know, everyone's papers are blowing everywhere, and then somehow, I still don't know how, it escalates into actual rain."

Ronan picked up, laughing at the memory. "One poor kid got drenched because he was sitting right under the 'cloud.' And when Aidan tried to stop it, he ended up making it worse. Lightning crackled, and the teacher was yelling for everyone to take cover."

With a sheepish grin, Aidan shrugged. "Let's just say they weren't thrilled. I spent a month in 'training' afterward to control my powers. So, lesson learned: there's a time and place for indoor weather."

Gabriel chuckled, shaking his head. "Noted. We'll keep you away from any small, enclosed spaces if there's a risk of a weather system forming."

Laughter filled the room as they exchanged amused glances.

Aidan shook his head, still laughing. "Hey, at least I didn't accidentally read a librarian's memories." He shot Ronan a teasing look.

Ronan groaned, covering his face. "Look, I touched a book, got a little distracted, and … well, I might've said something out loud. It was super embarrassing."

"Turns out," Aidan added, grinning, "he tuned into the librarian's memories of a one-night stand. Right there in the middle of the library!"

The room exploded with laughter, and even Ronan couldn't keep from smiling, though his face flushed. "Yeah, lesson learned. Don't get distracted in the library, or you'll end up blurting out someone's dirty secrets."

Eric's grin widened. "Oh, here's a good one. So, Gabe likes to act all tough, right? But there was this one time we were out in the woods, and a tiny garter snake slithers by. And I mean tiny, like barely a foot long."

Gabriel narrowed his eyes. "It was *bigger* than that…"

Eric laughed. "Sure, buddy. Anyway, he sees this snake and lets out this yell. Like a full-on, high-pitched scream, and jumps back like he's seen a dragon."

Ava raised an eyebrow, grinning. "Afraid of snakes, are we?"

"It surprised me, okay? I was just … being cautious."

The group dissolved into laughter again. Gabriel's embarrassed smile showed he was taking it all in stride, though he shot Eric a look that promised a payback story someday.

Moira leaned back with a smirk, glancing between Ava and Gabriel. "So, let me get this straight. We've got a girl who pushed a kid out of the way of a car when she was five…" She turned to Gabriel, eyebrow raised. "…and a grown man who's afraid of tiny snakes?"

Gabriel rolled his eyes, a smile tugging at his lips. "I prefer to call it a healthy respect for nature."

Ava snickered. "Sure, we'll call it that."

Savina and Aaron entered. "Tomorrow marks the beginning of a long journey," Savina said. "Tonight, you need to rest and prepare yourselves."

Chairs scraped back as the group stood, preparing to leave. Savina raised a hand, her warm smile softening her gaze. "Before you go, remember no matter what happens, our priority is survival. We will do whatever it takes to end this conflict. You are an incredibly talented, resilient group, and I am confident in each of you. The enemy expects us to leave, but they do not know when. Be ready."

She hugged each of them as they departed, her embrace was a silent pledge of protection and trust. When she reached Ava, she held her a moment longer. *You are strong. Never forget that,* she spoke into Ava's mind, filling her with a surge of quiet courage.

As the others filed out of the library, Gabriel lingered by the door as though waiting for Ava to catch up.

They walked together down the quiet hallway, the echoes of laughter fading as the idea of tomorrow settled back in. Gabriel glanced sideways at her, a soft smile playing on his lips. "So, our resident hero and fearless snake-slayer, all in one group. We make quite the team, don't we?"

Ava chuckled, nudging him. "Guess we balance each other out. You handle the big threats, and I'll take care of any tiny snakes."

Gabriel laughed, but this time it was softer, more reflective.

As they reached her door, Ava paused, looking up at him. "Are you scared?"

He nodded, his gaze turning serious. "Yeah. But knowing I've got a hero watching my back … it makes it a little less scary."

"Hero? That was just another one of my famous reckless moments."

"No, it was brave. You might be a little too brave sometimes. But for what it's worth, I've got your back, too."

Their eyes locked, and a wave of warmth washed over her, melting the tension in her chest. "Thanks, Gabriel. I know you do."

They stood in comfortable silence, an unspoken understanding passing between them.

Gabriel gave her a gentle nod before turning to head down the hall. Each of them carried a small comfort as they went to their rooms, readying themselves for whatever the next day might bring.

Black clouds hovered above like an omen. The morning was silent and cold, and a thick fog clung to the cemetery grounds, blurring the path ahead. Ava paused under the arched entrance, as her father moved toward her mother's grave. Her feet wouldn't budge. She'd been there too many times over the past year, and if she ever made a New Year's resolution list, "no more funerals" would top it. But they were headed to war, and she knew the reality. Some of them wouldn't return, and those who did would be forever changed. She wondered if any of them might surrender to Havok's influence rather than endure the fight.

"Are you okay?" Gabriel asked from behind her. He'd teleported her, her father, Aaron, and Katarina for the special trip.

"Yeah. I was just giving my dad some time alone," she said, her voice steadier than she felt. She wasn't sure if she even wanted to approach her mother's grave.

"If it helps, I visited my uncle's grave once. Thought it might … bring some closure."

"You did? What happened?"

He shifted, looking away for a second. "At first, I was angry. He'd given up on me. Left me alone to figure everything out. I was young, and it almost broke me. But after I got through the anger, I said my piece. More for myself than for him. And I left. Haven't gone back since."

"Did you ever forgive him?"

"Forgiveness is tricky. But no, I never did. And that's … okay."

"So … maybe I don't have to forgive my mom," Ava whispered, more to herself.

"I can't decide that for you. But if you don't forgive her, it doesn't make you a bad person."

She exhaled, her gaze on the fog-laden headstones. "I feel like I should understand why she did it, like I need to know her reasons. But even then, would that excuse her?"

"Maybe not. But you're here. Soul intact. Havok doesn't own you. He never will, unless you let him."

She considered his words, a chill running through her. "Maybe it was all an empty promise."

"Maybe."

Ava looked at her father standing alone, his head bowed as he wiped his eyes. "I'm the only one he has left. I have to come back."

"You will."

Swallowing her tears, she gritted her teeth and took a deep breath. "I'll be back."

"I'll be here."

Ava met his eyes, feeling a surge of gratitude. She moved toward the arched entrance under the bare oaks and slumping magnolias. She passed a weathered angel statue atop a headstone, its gaze fixed on the fog beyond, and a stone dog guarding its master's grave. The silent witnesses to years of unspoken goodbyes.

She reached her father. He took her hand, giving it a gentle squeeze. Her mother's name, carved into the stone, caused a strange numbness to wash over her. She thought of her father beside her, the only person she'd ever relied on. "I don't want to leave you."

He gave a bittersweet smile. "I know, but you have to."

"Who'll protect you?"

"Savina's putting extra charms over the Manor. We'll be fine."

"Still … what if there's another outbreak or something happens while you're out?" She bit her lip. "What if—"

"Ava." Her father turned to face her, his eyes kind but firm. "You can't live by what-ifs. Savina's left us with healing potions, and we're still Enchanters, even if our powers are fading. We can manage." He gave her a reassuring wink.

"I'm scared." Her chin quivered as tears welled in her eyes.

He drew her into a hug, and she held on, breathing in his woodsy scent, memorizing the way his arms felt around her. She clung to him, not wanting to let go, feeling her tears spill over despite her effort to stay strong. Her father's hand rubbed her back, comforting her like always.

After a few moments, he pulled back and kissed her forehead, his green eyes filled with a mix of sadness and pride. "We'll see each other again, Ava. Listen to the Elders. Follow their guidance. Don't get tangled up with Peter, and for heaven's sake, no more running off. You've got this. I'm so proud of you."

Nodding, she wiped her cheeks. She could do this. She had to.

"Come on. It's time," her father said, glancing toward Gabriel, Aaron, and Katarina, who waited by the entrance. As they made their way back, Ava cast one last look at her mother's grave, a cold determination settling in her chest. Havok wouldn't win. Not this time.

Back at the Manor, Thomas embraced his mother in a bear hug that lifted her off the ground. Nathan held Lucas high in the air, both father and son laughing as Cara wrapped her arms around them, her eyes brimming with tears. Ava looked away, unable to imagine saying goodbye to a husband, hoping he'd return. She wanted Lucas to have his father back safely.

"Thank you," she whispered to Gabriel, glancing up at him. "For bringing us there. It meant a lot."

"You're more than welcome." His eyes lingered on hers for a moment.

"Let's leave them," Aaron told Gabriel. "We'll be waiting in the conservatory."

Ava nodded, turning to her father, her pulse quickening as she fought back another wave of emotion. She didn't want to say goodbye.

"Remember the task at hand," her father said. "You're brave, Ava. I know you'll do well. I love you. Never forget that."

"I love you too, Dad." She swallowed the lump in her throat. He hugged her one last time, and she fell into the embrace.

When they pulled apart, she forced herself to turn away, her vision blurring as she made her way toward the conservatory, refusing to look back.

There would be no goodbye. Only her determination to return.

20

THE BEGINNING

All the Enchanters gathered around the glowing circle on the velvet rug, and the powerful, shared energy seeped through her skin, warming her like sunlight from within. The collective energy pulsed, uniting them all with a strength she hadn't felt in weeks.

"We are one," Savina said. "May our energies and protections guide us on this journey. May our strengths fulfill the task. By all the power within us, we cast this charm, so may it be."

As they released hands, a slight hum of energy lingered in the air, and they filed out of the conservatory. When Ava stepped outside, her breath caught as her eyes landed on Peter, his head tilted toward Katarina's, their lips meeting in an easy, intimate kiss. The scene struck her like a cold wind, making her draw in a shaky breath. She forced herself to look away and let the others stream past as she hung back.

"I'm sorry," Gabriel said as he matched her stride. "I wish there was more I could do."

"You've already done enough. I just think too much."

"Nothing new there," he chuckled.

"It's hard having to see him all the time. But I can handle it."

Eric caught up to them. "I'm pumped. How 'bout you two?"

"Think you'll survive the walk?" Ava teased.

Eric lifted a brow. "Oh, we've got a jokester now!"

"I'm working on it." She surprised herself with how natural it felt to joke with them.

"You've been hanging around Gabe too much."

Gabriel chuckled. "You know, I'm flattered to be such an influence."

"Still ... all this walking feels a little archaic," Ava said.

"Gabriel's practically our speed dial, but there are protocols." Eric smirked. "Tunnels, portals. It's been a while since we've traveled like this."

"Great, more chances for Cimmerians to pop out," Ava said, half-serious.

"If anything happens, you know you'll be safe," Gabriel said.

"Yeah, yeah. Peter and Katarina."

"I wasn't talking about them." His eyes held hers with an intensity that made her heart race. "I meant me."

She swallowed, heat rising within her. "Thanks."

They joined the others, who had arranged themselves strategically: Savina and Aaron led up front with Moira and Gustav, the protectors stayed near the center, and the Elementals formed the core.

"Think of all this time we get to spend together," Gabriel said.

Ava found herself liking the idea more than she expected.

They trudged for miles through the forest, passing the now-empty field where they had fought the Cimmerians. The ground was soggy from recent rains, and a fine mist hung in the air. Soon, a steady drizzle turned into a heavy downpour.

Ava raised an invisible umbrella over herself and quickened her pace, eager to escape the memories of the battle.

"Whoa. Did you just—how are you not getting wet?" Gabriel asked, his eyes widening.

She gave a knowing shrug.

"That's the coolest trick. Can you do it for others, too?"

"Let's find out." She expanded her shield to cover him.

He grinned, looking up as the rain stopped hitting him. "This is awesome."

His admiration for her skills filled her with a warm feeling. Taking a deep breath, Ava extended the cover over the whole group. Though she considered leaving Peter and Katarina out, she knew she couldn't bring herself to do that. Soon, the rain poured around them but left them untouched.

Thomas and a few others glanced up, dumbfounded.

Ava laughed at their surprise.

"Ava, pet, are you doin' this?" Shannon asked, bewildered.

"Yep." She grinned.

"You've been able to do this the whole time?" Gillian asked, incredulous.

She rolled her eyes. "I just figured it out. Calm down."

They walked for what felt like miles, but the cold, damp forest was alive with the soft rustle of leaves and the muted rhythm of footsteps. Her heart ached each time she caught a glimpse of Peter and Katarina ahead, leaning into each other and whispering with easy laughter. Each touch, each glance was like a small thorn, prickling her resolve, but she took a deep breath, brushing the feeling aside.

I won't let this hold me back. She'd come this far. She wouldn't let a broken heart define her any longer. It was time to focus on the journey, to fight for something beyond herself, and she could feel something strong and constant guiding her forward.

Night descended faster than Ava had realized, the early dusk of winter closing in around them. When Aaron stopped near a small log cabin, announcing they'd stay there for the night, her heart dropped.

"What do you mean we're stopping?" she asked.

"We can't wear ourselves out completely," Gabriel said. "There's still a long way to go."

"I'm not even tired." She crossed her arms, feeling the chill prickling her skin as the night deepened.

Gabriel gave a slight smile. "Trust me, as soon as your head hits the pillow, you'll be out."

She rolled her eyes but couldn't stop a small grin as he winked. "So, we're all cramming into this little cabin?"

Gabriel bit his lip, trying not to laugh. "Yeah, right. You'd think so from the outside."

"It's called magic," Eric chimed in, smirking at her skepticism. At their puzzled looks, he continued, "It's an *Invisibili Aula,* 'invisible palace.' Only Enchanters can see the inside. There are several palaces hidden in forests, but you need the right charm to enter."

Once the Elders led them through the door, Ava's breath caught in her throat. The cabin's quaint exterior vanished, replaced by an opulent interior that looked like a five-star hotel. Towering crystal chandeliers glittered overhead, illuminating high ceilings draped in royal blue curtains. Massive floor-to-ceiling windows framed the room, casting reflections on plush rugs spread across gleaming hardwood floors. Cozy seating areas were tucked into corners, and on either side lay grand dining and parlor rooms, each brimming with luxurious detail.

The centerpiece was a winding white marble staircase carpeted in deep maroon, bordered by a wrought iron railing decorated with intricately spiraled flowers and leaves. Ava couldn't help but stare at the ornate craftsmanship, feeling a strange sense of calm in the lavish surroundings. Maybe this is what the Elders intended. A temporary reprieve from the tense journey.

"It's like something out of a dream," she murmured, following the others up the wide staircase. The splendor didn't sit quite right with her; it felt too indulgent, a little too distracting from their real purpose.

As her friends picked out rooms, Gabriel trailed behind her, his eyes scanning the intricate designs of the staircase and halls. "Too bad there's no library."

"That would be nice." She glanced at him. "I could use a distraction."

"Me too," he whispered with a look that lingered a moment too long before he pulled away.

Gillian linked arms with Ava and Nicole, pulling them down the hall, and they chose a room.

Ava walked inside and marveled at the spaciousness. "This place would be way too empty on my own," she admitted, grateful for the company.

"Isn't this amazing?" Gillian ran her hand over the sleek mahogany furniture and touched the blue quilted comforters with admiration. "Feels like staying at the Ritz-Carlton or something."

Ava chuckled, letting Gillian's enthusiasm ease her tension.

"When all of this is over," Gillian continued. "I'm going to marry Jeremy, and we'll stay somewhere like this."

"Already thinking about marriage?" Nicole raised her eyebrows and lay stomach down on the bed.

"Why not? We're soulmates."

Ava shifted. "I think I'll take a shower."

Nicole's teasing grin softened into a look of sympathy. "Oh, Ava…"

"Wait a minute," Gillian interrupted, hands on her hips. "What's going on with Gabriel?"

Ava blinked. "What do you mean?"

Gillian gave her a look. "He's always around you. He's always looking at you."

"We're just friends." Her cheeks grew warm.

"The way he looks at you, though," Gillian pressed, "seems friendlier to me."

Ava rolled her eyes. "I know you're trying to help me get over Peter, but trust me, Gabriel and I are just friends. He doesn't look at me *that* way."

"Whatever you say." Gillian raised an eyebrow and turned to Nicole. "What about you and Link?"

Nicole's face reddened. "I don't know. We're … we hold hands, but he hasn't kissed me yet. I thought maybe he would on New Year's."

"Sometimes you have to draw people a map." Gillian grinned. "I bet he thinks you don't feel the same way. I can set something up, if you want."

Ava laughed as she listened to them. It was a relief to hear about something normal, a welcome break from the pressures of their task. For a few moments, she felt like an ordinary girl in a fancy hotel room, gossiping with her friends.

She excused herself for a quick shower, leaving Gillian and Nicole giggling over their matchmaking plans. It was a nice break from the fear and anticipation that waited for them. For now, she'd let herself enjoy it.

As night settled in, the rain outside turned heavy, drumming a steady rhythm against the windows, the sound a low, monotonous thrum. Ava's footsteps echoed in the polished hall as she made her way down to the dining hall, where the others were gathering. Inside, the room glowed with warm golden light that bounced off silverware and glass goblets, arranged at each setting on the royal blue velvet chairs surrounding the long table. She slid into her seat between Nicole and Gillian, her gaze drifting toward the grand window where the rain sheeted down in misty waves, streaking like faint tears across the glass.

Gustav, Katarina, and Anastasya entered, each carrying an assortment of dishes that filled the air with the savory scents of spices and broth. Katarina ladled out steaming bowls of golden broth, tiny onions and sprigs of dill swirling in each serving.

Gillian eyed her bowl with suspicion. "Um, what is this?"

Katarina's face softened with a nostalgic smile. "It's *rassolnik*—a pickled cucumber soup with beef. My mother used to make it." Her gaze held a faraway look for a moment before she returned to her seat beside Peter. As she did, Peter leaned over, his dimpled smile brightening as he kissed her cheek.

Ava looked away and sipped her soup, surprised at the rich, salty-bitter flavor mingling with the tender beef and earthy onions.

"These are amazing," Ilya said, passing a plate of pastry-like rolls to Gillian, who nudged it toward Ava.

"What is it?" Ava asked.

"*Pirozhki,*" Ilya explained with pride. "Like a calzone but filled with sautéed onions, mushrooms, or cabbage."

"These are my favorites," Katarina said.

Ava took one and passed the plate to Nicole, catching Gabriel's amused glance from across the table. She bit her lip to hide a grin, a shared look passing between them as if he'd read her thoughts on Katarina's excitement. She turned to her pirozhki, savoring the flaky crust and hearty filling, pleased by the homestyle comfort it offered.

When the meal ended, Ava helped Anastasya and Katarina clear plates. In the expansive kitchen, stainless steel counters gleamed under fluorescent lights, casting a faint, sterile shine on Anastasya's short, dark hair and the scar above her eye. She rinsed the dishes with a measured patience that Ava admired.

"This is the last of them." Katarina set another stack near the sink. Her vibrant blue hair shone under the lights, and she leaned against the counter. "Did you enjoy dinner?" she asked Ava with a soft, tentative smile.

Ava forced a polite nod. "It was very good, thank you."

Katarina beamed. "Maybe someday you can all come to Russia. When this is over, I'd love for Peter to come back with us."

Ava's hand slipped as she placed a plate in the dishwasher, her pulse quickening. The thought of Peter leaving brought an unfamiliar heaviness to her heart. She forced herself to keep her focus on stacking the dishes, pretending her heart wasn't stinging from Katarina's words.

Anastasya lowered her voice at Katarina, a wry smile quirking at her lips. "Slow down with the boy," she warned. "Take your time. And mind what you say."

Swallowing the tightness in her throat, Ava muttered a quick, "Thanks for dinner. I'll head up now." She slipped out of the kitchen, past the few who lingered in the dining hall, their laughter and conversation fading as she made her way up the grand staircase. When she reached the bedroom, she found it empty and changed into the soft, flannel pajamas folded on the bed. The hotel felt foreign and cold, despite the warmth of the lavish room. She wanted to cry but resisted, tired of burdening the others with her pain.

As Ava sank onto the bed, wrapping her arms around her knees, Gillian's words from earlier flashed in her mind: *"The way he looks at you seems friendlier to me."*

She scoffed, dismissing it as wishful thinking on Gillian's part. There was no way Gabriel would feel anything beyond friendship. But as she closed her eyes, his face flashed in her mind. The way he'd grinned when she'd shielded him from the rain, or the quiet concern in his voice every time he asked if she was okay.

He was unlike Peter. Calm and steadfast, offering the quiet reassurance of solid ground beneath her feet.

A soft knock startled her. "Yes?"

Gabriel peeked his head in, his expression soft. "You left the dining room kind of fast."

She managed a small smile. "I just … needed to get away for a minute."

He nodded. "If you need anything or want to talk, you know I'm here, right?"

His words wrapped around her like a comforting embrace. "Thanks. I'm here, too."

With a tender smile, he closed the door, leaving her to the gentle rhythm of the rain on the window. For the first time in a while, her thoughts drifted to something other than Peter and Katarina. She found herself focusing on the steady presence Gabriel brought, leaving her feeling a little lighter as she drifted off.

THE SHADOW KINGDOM

Ava gripped the straps of her backpack, her fingers digging in as she trudged through the forest ahead of Peter and Katarina. The chill of the morning air crept into her skin, and she kept her head down, her eyes on the muddy path. If she didn't have to look back, maybe she could ignore the fact that Peter's eyes had followed her all through breakfast. His gaze had seemed worried, almost apologetic, yet she hadn't felt any of that concern in her necklace.

Gillian and Lance flanked her on one side, with Eric keeping pace on the other. Gabriel and Natalia walked behind, while Thomas lingered near Moira, both quiet but alert. The whole group had fallen into a kind of wary silence. Ava guessed the night's unfamiliar setting had left them restless, but maybe it was something else, an unspoken dread hanging in the air.

The path wound through thick patches of mud, and every time they encountered a new puddle, Gillian would hesitate, looking around for a way to avoid it, a quiet groan escaping her each time her boots sank into the sludge.

"You kinda remind me of Kira," Eric said.

Both Ava and Gillian glanced his way, surprised. "Who does?" Gillian asked.

"You. Kira hates the rain, too. She's tough, got a hard edge, but she's as fussy about getting wet as you are." Eric chuckled.

Gillian scrunched her nose. "I hate getting wet. Even showers sometimes."

"Oh, Kira would get along with you just fine," Natalia said from behind them, and Eric laughed, shaking his head.

Gillian slid in beside Eric. "You think they're okay?"

"They're fine," he assured her.

Their voices faded as Ava's attention drifted to the rustle of branches. She felt a tap on her shoulder and tensed, glancing back at Peter's familiar face. She rolled her eyes and turned forward again, refusing to let herself feel anything at his touch.

"Ava, please," Peter pleaded, matching her stride. "Can we talk?"

She gritted her teeth. "There's nothing to talk about."

"She doesn't want to talk to you," Gillian chimed in, shooting Peter a sharp look.

Peter sighed. "Ava, please. I want things to be okay between us."

Her pulse quickened as a swell of conflicted emotions grew, but she clamped down on it, shaking her head to clear it away. She took a step forward, misjudging the uneven ground, and her foot caught on a root. The earth seemed to rise up toward her, but Peter's hand shot out, steadying her before she fell. Her arm burned where he touched her, but she yanked it away, shrugging off the encounter as she strode ahead, chin high.

"Ava, I'm sorry. I feel what you're going through, and it kills me. I feel it every day."

"Stop. We have a mission to accomplish, and that's all I'm here for." She kept her voice low, but each word felt like a razor's edge.

A distant hum of conversation drifted through the group, but Ava kept her focus straight ahead.

Aidan called out, "Heads up, everyone! We're about to go through a portal."

The tension in the air shifted as the group stood before the shadowed opening. Ava quickened her steps, catching up with Gillian as they followed Aidan, who was parting a curtain of thick, brown vines draped over a large boulder with a gaping, shadowed hole at its base.

"It's just an opening in the rock," Aidan explained, grinning as they approached. "To Ephemerals, it's nothing but an old cave. But to us, it's a portal to *Regnum Umbra*, the Shadow Kingdom. Stick close when we go through. It's pitch-black in there."

Ava glanced at Gillian, sensing her friend's unease. The portal exuded a musty aroma of damp earth, and its shadows flickered with an eerie, unnatural movement.

"I don't like this," Gillian muttered under her breath, clutching Ava's arm.

"It'll be fine," Ava whispered, trying to reassure herself as much as Gillian.

The group filed into the cold, dark mouth of the tunnel. The air thickened, heavy and oppressive, wrapping around them like a smothering blanket. The walls felt too close, pressing in on all sides, and every step forward seemed to stretch the tunnel endlessly.

"I can't see a thing," Gillian said.

"Keep walking forward," Aidan told them.

"Couldn't we have lit a torch?" Peter grumbled, his frustration cutting through the silence.

Ava focused on the sound of their footsteps. A faint, damp chill brushed over her skin, but the deeper they went, the sharper the air became, as though the tunnel itself was alive. She reached for her necklace, the slight heat offering a small anchor in the darkness.

Then, she heard a faint hiss.

A pang of unease shot through her and she froze. The sound was sharp, menacing, and far too close. *No, it's nothing. Just the wind. Or my imagination.*

Another hiss, louder this time. A long, low hiss, like scales sliding over stone. She grabbed Gillian's arm, her breath quickening. "Did you hear that?"

Peter bumped into her from behind. "Hear what?"

"I—" Another hiss interrupted her, this time unmistakably real. Her pulse thundered as she whipped her head around, but the darkness swallowed everything.

A slick, cold coil brushed against her ankle. She gasped, stumbling backward.

"They're everywhere," Gillian whimpered. "Ava, they're wrapping around my legs—"

"What are you two talking about?" Aidan asked.

"Snakes!" Ava cried as another slithering creature coiled around her wrist. The sensation was vivid. Smooth scales, the subtle tightening of a body constricting. She tried to move, but panic paralyzed her.

"There's nothing here," Peter said, his tone sharp with worry. "Ava, Gillian, you're imagining things!"

The hissing intensified, coming from every direction. Shadows seemed to shift and ripple around them, like countless serpents weaving through the air. Something heavy and cold dropped onto Ava's shoulder. She screamed, batting at it, but her hands hit nothing.

"Ava, get rid of them!" Gillian yelled.

She willed water to her hands, the cold energy surging through her trembling limbs. With a sharp motion, she sent a powerful jet into the darkness. The hissing recoiled, the sensation of the snakes lifting, but the shadows still pressed close.

"What are you doing?" Peter demanded.

"Saving us!" She fired another blast of water, her hands shaking as she tried to push the unseen threat away.

The hissing faded, leaving the sound of water dripping onto the stone floor.

Ava's chest heaved as she clutched Gillian's arm. "Are they gone?"

"I think so." Gillian's voice shook.

Moments later, a faint light began to glow at the end of the tunnel. Aidan helped them climb out, the crisp forest air hitting Ava like a slap, sharp and cleansing. She stumbled forward, her knees threatening to buckle.

"What happened in there?" Savina demanded, rushing to their side. Her piercing gaze darted between Ava and Gillian.

"Snakes," Gillian muttered, her face pale. "They were everywhere."

"Snakes?" Peter repeated, his brow furrowed. "There was nothing in that tunnel but darkness."

Gillian shook her head. "No. We felt them. I swear, they were real."

Ava stayed silent, gripping her necklace as she tried to steady her breathing. She could still feel the cold, constricting touch of the scales on her skin.

"It must be a manifestation spell," Savina said. She exchanged a tense glance with Aaron. "The Cimmerians enchanted the portal to attack their minds, playing on their fears."

"Are you okay?" Gabriel came to Ava's side, resting his hand on her shoulder.

She gave a shaky laugh, still catching her breath. "Oh, just battling snakes. Had to make sure they were all dead before they got to you."

"Aww, my hero." He placed his hand over his heart. "Snakes, though?"

"Yeah, I can see why you'd shriek at the sight of one." She inhaled. "It felt so real."

"Because it was, for you. Don't second-guess yourself. Whatever it was, you fought it, and you won."

"Well, someone had to. Couldn't run away screaming."

"Excuse me, I don't scream. I strategically retreat with enthusiasm."

She laughed and her nerves calmed.

"We need to assume every portal we encounter is trapped," Savina said. "The Cimmerians are trying to weaken us before we even reach them. Stay vigilant."

Ava exchanged a glance with Gillian, her expression mirroring her own unease. Whatever lay ahead, they had to be ready for the Cimmerians, for Havok, and for the shadows still lurking in their minds.

Thick clouds churned overhead, their brooding shadows draping the trail in an oppressive gloom. The forest around them remained still, but Ava couldn't shake the growing unease pressing against her chest, as though the very air had thickened, charged with unseen tension. In the distance, the smoky outline of mountains loomed like ghostly sentinels, their jagged peaks cutting into the horizon. A shiver ran through her veins, a primal instinct whispering that this place was wrong, dangerous. Nothing about it felt safe.

She tightened her grip on the straps of her backpack. But just ahead, Peter and Katarina walked side by side, their quiet laughs carrying back to her, and her stomach twisted. Her pace slowed as she tried to push away the pang of resentment, to let go.

Lance moved up beside her.

She sighed. "I'm sorry. I'm trying so hard. Every day, I see him with her, and all I can think about is what it was like … and how much I want it back." Her voice cracked, surprising even herself. "I miss him."

"Why?" Gillian asked. "He's a jerk. I know you loved him, but you're better off without him. You shouldn't have been with him anyway."

"Gillian, don't," Lance warned.

Ava's face flushed with irritation, heat rising in her cheeks. "Why don't you mind your own business?" she snapped, hating the bitterness in her voice, but the sight of Peter was a fresh wound, one she didn't know how to close.

"It's the truth, Ava, and you know it," Gillian insisted.

Ava stopped in her tracks. The pain simmered into something sharp. "And why do you say that?"

Gillian hesitated. "Because. You should have never fallen in love with Peter. He wasn't right for you. He's better off with Katarina."

Her jaw dropped, her hands shaking. "What is wrong with you?" A rush of heat prickled along her skin as water began to gather in her palms, trickling to the ground. "How can you say that?"

"Don't yell," Gillian whispered, her eyes flicking to the others as they began to turn, curious.

Water poured from Ava's fingers, like the emotions she struggled to hold back. "You can't mean that."

"Ava, calm down," Gabriel said.

She took a shaky breath and willed the water to stop.

"I just … don't want you to hurt anymore," Gillian said. "I know you're holding onto it, but he's not worth all this."

"Everyone, hush!" Aaron's booming voice soared through the group.

A heavy silence descended. No one dared move, each face drawn tight with sudden fear. A low, deep growl rattled her bones. The growl intensified, vibrating through her chest as her pulse quickened.

Hot breath brushed the back of her neck, sending icy chills down her spine. Ava held her breath, every muscle frozen. The terror in Lance and Gillian's eyes forced her to resist turning around. Every instinct warned her to stay still. Meeting Gabriel's eyes, she clung to the only grounding point she could find.

Her heart pounded like a drumbeat in her ears, each beat echoing with a raw, primal fear.

22

BETRAYAL

The beast yelped as a sharp crack split the air, as if lightning had struck nearby. The ground shuddered under them, scattering leaves and sending everyone's tense expressions into shock as they moved to assess the scene.

Ava remained frozen, her gaze searching the space where Gabriel had been moments ago. Then she felt a gentle tug on her hand.

"It's okay now," Gabriel said. "You can breathe again."

She let out a shaky exhale. "What … what was it? A wolf?"

"Not exactly. A saberwolf."

Ava glanced over to the creature sprawled on its side against a broken tree. Its massive white body lay still, its long saber teeth glinting beneath a wolf-like snout, but its paws were as wide and furred as a polar bear's. The sight of it made her shudder.

"The Cimmerians are watching us closely," Aaron mused, studying the beast with a hardened gaze.

"How do you know it's them?" Gillian asked. "Couldn't it just be a wild animal?"

Aaron shook his head. "The way it targeted us, and what happened in the tunnel, suggests we're being tracked. They could be manipulating what we see."

Ava cast a nervous glance around her surroundings. Her hand drifted to the warm stone of her necklace, but a sense of unease remained. Could Trudy McVaine have cast illusions to control what they saw? She remembered something Havok had once said about how she, Gillian, and Thomas had the weakest minds. She remembered how he sauntered toward her in Colden's body. Wearing Colden's necklace. The realization dawned with a sudden clarity. "We need to take off our necklaces."

Savina turned, startled. "What?"

"If Havok can track us, it's because he still wears Colden's necklace. He'll know exactly where we are and when we're vulnerable. If we take them off, he might think we were killed by … this thing." She nodded at the saberwolf.

"It would at least buy us some time," Eric said, "assuming they aren't actually watching us."

Savina hesitated. "I don't like the idea of not sensing you all."

Aaron placed a hand on her shoulder. "Ava's right. We have to try it. It's our only advantage."

Savina nodded, though her expression was tense. "It'll feel as if you're all gone. As if you … died."

"We'll be fine. We're all here."

One by one, everyone removed their necklaces, the atmosphere shifting with a strange sense of freedom but also vulnerability. A weight lifted from her chest. Her pain and frustration were now her own, shielded from everyone else.

"Why did that thing target Ava, though?" Gillian asked, looking at the saberwolf. "It went straight for her."

Gabriel's brow furrowed. "Saberwolves are drawn to intense emotions. Anger, especially."

Ava swallowed hard, glancing away. Her cheeks flushed as she remembered her irritation moments before the attack.

"Yeah … that was probably my fault," Gillian mumbled, guilt spreading over her face. "I don't know why I said those things."

"Protectors," Aaron called, "we need to remain vigilant. Let's keep moving."

The group resumed their march, the forest seeming darker and denser as they left the saberwolf's body behind. Ava exhaled, letting go of the tension in her shoulders. "I've had enough excitement for one day," she muttered, stealing one last look at the strange creature. "What's next? Vampires?"

Gabriel chuckled. "Not quite. But hey, if Edgar Allan Poe can be a vampire…"

"Oh, right." She gave a small laugh, though her mind lingered on the saberwolf. "Did you … did you kill it?"

"Yes."

"Just like that?"

He hesitated. "I stopped its heart."

She looked at him, shocked, and Gillian darted ahead to avoid any more gory details.

They walked in silence for a while until Gabriel turned to her, his expression gentle but serious. "You all right? About what Gillian said?"

Ava sighed, trying to hide the sting she still felt. "I'm fine."

"You don't have to brush it off. You're allowed to feel things. Even the hard stuff."

"I don't think Gillian understands. Sometimes I wonder if it would've been better if she'd cursed Peter instead of me. I don't get how he could just … move on."

"Gillian's scared and wants things to go back to normal. She cares more than she shows."

She nodded. "I know. Thanks, by the way."

"For what?"

"Saving my life."

He smiled. "You've saved mine a few times yourself."

"Only because I got you into trouble."

Her gaze drifted ahead to Peter and Katarina holding hands. She stifled a pang of jealousy, reminding herself to let go.

"Does it bother you that I talk about all this?" she asked.

"No."

"Have you ever been in love?" She didn't know what prompted the question.

He looked ahead, his voice thoughtful. "I've had girlfriends … but never anything that felt … lasting."

A flicker of jealousy surprised her. "Were they not your type?"

"You could say that. I never felt strongly enough to stay."

"Yeah, well, even if you find someone, chances are it'll end sooner or later. People just move on."

"Maybe … but not everyone moves on so easily, Ava," he said, but she could have sworn there was a hint of frustration. Glancing at her, his intense blue eyes locked onto hers. "You can't think everyone will walk away. Some people stick around, even when it's hard." As he stared at her, his brows knitted together in a slight frown. "But you have to let them."

With every step they took, the awkwardness between them grew, leaving Ava with the lingering feeling that she had somehow angered him.

Night settled over the camp, casting shadows through the trees as clouds rolled in, thick and heavy. The small, rugged cabins stood in a circle, a stark contrast to the luxurious lodging they'd left behind. Ava took in the simple structures with a mix of relief and unease. She didn't mind the humble accommodations, but something about their exposure made her feel vulnerable. It was quiet, save for the rustling of leaves and the soft, whistling wind winding its way through the trees. Ever since they entered the Shadow Kingdom, an unsettling chill consumed the air, and Ava couldn't shake the feeling that they were being watched.

"I'll see you at dinner," Gabriel said, a hint of aggravation shadowing his face.

She opened her mouth to say something, an apology perhaps, but he was already walking toward his cabin. Her heart sank, guilt prickling as she wondered if he was upset with her.

She walked into one of the cabins, its creaking wooden floorboards amplifying every step. Each bed was made, their thin frames lining the walls with spare sheets folded at the foot. It reminded her of a camp from childhood stories, except with a haunting silence rather than cheerful chatter. She dropped her pack onto the floor, the dust swirling under the dim light as it caught the settling night outside.

When dinner arrived, they all gathered around a fire, a thick slab of deer roasting and crackling. The scent filled the air, a smoky warmth that almost masked the gnawing tension in the camp. Ava watched the flames, her mind drifting. Across the fire, Peter's arm was around Katarina, his fingers tracing familiar patterns on her shoulder. He leaned close, pressing a gentle kiss to her forehead, the same way he used to with her. She blinked hard against the blur of oncoming tears, but when her gaze drifted back, she saw Peter watching her, a flicker of something in his eyes. She looked away, swallowing hard.

"Hey." Moira's quiet voice brought her back. She sat beside Ava, a nervous smile on her face. "I know this might be … awkward, but I wanted to ask you something."

Ava shifted, bracing herself. "Sure. What is it?"

Moira hesitated. "I think I like Thomas … a lot. And I know you dated him. I didn't want to … overstep."

Ava sighed, a bittersweet smile tugging at her lips. "Thomas and I—it was complicated. We weren't really right for each other, even back then. I loved him once, but we both changed, especially after all of this." She paused. "Things ended badly. I hurt him when I fell for Peter."

"He mentioned that he … hurt you, too."

The image flashed in Ava's mind. Thomas's rage, the fire scalding her arms. She swallowed, feeling the echo of that pain. "Yeah, he did. But he's changed since then. He regrets it. And he's a good person now."

"Thank you for telling me. I just needed to know … if it's okay."

"You two would be good together, Moira. Really."

They sat for a moment, Moira squeezing her hand in thanks. It was comforting to have someone else there. But her gaze wandered again across the fire, catching Peter's hand intertwined with Katarina's. She fought the urge to leave the campfire altogether.

"What about you?" Moira asked. "Are you … moving on?"

"I don't know. It's hard when it's all still so raw." She thought of her conversation with Gabriel earlier, his words still lingering in her mind. She liked him, she realized. Really liked him. But there was still so much she couldn't let go of with Peter.

As the fire crackled, Moira reached out to touch her shoulder. "You remind me of Joss. Strong and fierce, no matter what. It'll get easier, I promise." Her tone was soft, but her eyes held a knowing look.

"Promise, huh? Is that from experience or … one of your visions?"

Moira gave a small smile, her gaze distant for a moment. "Let's just say I get glimpses sometimes. And I get this sense that your heart won't feel so heavy forever." She bit her lip, as if holding back more.

Ava wasn't sure what to make of that, but there was something comforting in Moira's confidence, and she let herself relax a little. "I hope you're right."

"I am. Even if I don't know exactly how it happens."

"Thanks, Moira."

"You're welcome." She hesitated, glancing toward the darkened cabins. "And for the record, I see you smiling again someday, and not because of anything, or anyone, you left behind."

Her heart gave a strange flutter. She wasn't sure if she could believe it, but as she turned her gaze back to the fire, she held onto Moira's words, letting them soothe her a little.

"Tell me about Melissa and Jeremy," Moira said.

"Melissa … Mel's like this force of nature. She speaks her mind, doesn't care who she challenges. She saw Peter and me together before anyone else did, and she was my biggest supporter." She paused, her heart clenching. "And Jeremy … he's the kindest person I've ever known. We could talk about anything. He's wise in ways I can't explain."

"He sounds like someone Gabriel would get along with." Moira smiled.

Ava felt a blush warm her cheeks as her thoughts lingered on Gabriel. She scanned the campsite but couldn't find him.

"He's reading," Moira said with a teasing smile.

"I wasn't—no, I wasn't looking for him."

"Sure, sure." Moira winked, her laugh lightening the mood.

"So, do you live with Shannon and Sean?" Ava asked.

"Yeah. They're my aunt and uncle, but honestly, they're the only parents I've ever known." Moira's eyes drifted to the firelight. "My mom … she turned to the dark side, decided the Cimmerians were right. It sounds like some dramatic story, I know, but that's what happened. She tried to take me with her, but my dad wouldn't let her. He stepped in, and she…" Moira hesitated, a glimmer of pain crossing her face. "She killed him and fled before Sean or Shannon could reach her."

She frowned. "Oh, Moira, that's … that's awful."

"Thanks. But I don't remember him. I was too young. It's just … hard, you know? Growing up without him."

"There are so many of us like that. We have to end this."
A rush of heat surged through her veins.

Moira laid a gentle hand on Ava's arm. "Whoa, deep breaths."

Ava glanced down to see droplets of water dripping from her hands, her powers responding to her emotions. She closed her eyes, taking a breath. "Sorry."

"It's okay. Trust me, we'll take them down."

"Do you ever see it?"

Moira frowned. "Not like that. I don't see the future in long, drawn-out scenes. It's more like … fragments. Glimpses that sometimes connect, sometimes don't. And my mind gets boggled by it all." She paused, a slight grin breaking through. "I am getting better at predicting things, though. Takes time."

"Do you ever get annoyed when something happens just like you imagined? Doesn't that leave, like … no surprises?"

Moira shrugged, her thick, dark hair falling around her shoulders. "Sometimes. But like I said, the precognition isn't always right. Just because I get a glimpse doesn't mean that's the only way things can turn out."

"Do you ever see something and try to change it?"

"Sometimes. But I learned early on that it's tricky. Trying to interfere rarely works the way you hope. I think things happen for a reason, even the really awful stuff."

"I don't know about that." It was hard to accept that her breakup with Peter, her mother's betrayal, and Havok's brutal actions could all have a purpose. As far as she could tell, they were senseless acts of pain.

They were quiet for a while, each lost in thought, until Thomas joined them. The soft look in his eyes told Ava all she needed to know. She didn't need to stay and witness the budding connection between her friends, nor see Peter and Katarina again.

"I'll see you all in the morning." Ava forced a smile and retreated to her cabin. She lay on the small, rough bed, curling into herself as the firelight flickered through the window. She wondered if Gabriel was still upset with her. Missing him and worrying about his silence felt odd. But as exhaustion pulled her under, she held onto the memory of his words, his gentle reminder that not everyone would leave.

Like the night before, sleep was elusive, slipping through her grasp whenever she thought she might fall into it. A cold dread squeezed her heart, chilling her to the bone. Seeing Peter every day wasn't helping her heal. It felt more like she was constantly picking at an open wound. And earlier he wanted to talk? What more could he possibly have to say? She couldn't believe how hurt she still felt or why she wasted so much time replaying what might have been.

After hours of tossing and turning, Ava slipped out of the cabin, careful not to let the creaky door slam shut behind her. The fire from earlier had faded to a faint glow, the dying embers giving off enough light to outline the trees and make shadows dance. She shivered against the bite of the night air but warmed herself with a touch of magic. Her fingers found a half-burned stick, and she began poking the embers, each jab sending up tiny sparks and making the embers pulse with a brighter orange. Holding the glowing end close to her face, she blew softly, watching the small flame stretch and grow, feeling the heat brush her skin.

"Do you ever sleep?" Gabriel startled her as he came up behind her.

Her heart gave an unexpected flutter. She turned, unable to hide her surprise. "Sorry, did I wake you?"

"No." A hint of a smile played on his lips. "And yes."

"Okay?"

He sat beside her, close enough that heat from his body comforted her from the chill. "Not directly. I … I guess I was thinking about you."

Her heart skipped a beat. "What about me?"

"I can see how much you're struggling."

She bit her lip. "I don't want to be. I thought I was doing better for a while, but seeing him every day…" She poked the embers harder, watching the sparks flare up. "It feels like I'll never move on."

Gabriel took her empty hand in his.

Startled, she dropped the stick into the fire, and it crackled as flames licked up around it. "Did I upset you earlier today?"

He hesitated, his eyes searching hers. "Sometimes your … outlook gets a little dark. But I know it's coming from a place of hurt. You don't have to change for me, though."

She let out a small laugh. "I appreciate that." Gabriel was unbelievably patient with her. She glanced at him, grateful for his quiet strength. "It's funny how things shift. I used to feel closer to Gillian, I guess. Melissa would just call things as she saw them, and it used to drive me crazy. But now, I miss that. Talking to Gillian doesn't help much."

"What about Lance?"

"Lance has been great, really. But … I can't keep unloading on him. I don't think guys want to hear this stuff."

"You've been talking to me."

"That's different. You listen, and you never judge me. I'm sure everyone's tired of the Peter drama by now."

"What do you think Melissa would say to you if she were here?"

"She'd probably tell me to cut the nonsense and move on already." Ava gave a hollow laugh, staring into the fire. "But then she'd hug me. I feel like I should be over this by now. It's been … it feels like forever."

"It's only been a few weeks. You're dealing with heartbreak from someone you risked a lot for. That doesn't go away quickly."

"But he loved me, Gabriel. I know he did."

"I'm not saying he didn't—" he started, but another voice broke in.

"I still do."

Ava turned, heart pounding.

Peter stood there, his face shadowed in sorrow.

As she and Gabriel stood up, he released her hand. "I'll give you two a moment," he murmured, stepping away.

Ava wished he would stay, but she nodded.

Peter's face weary and lined with regret. "Ava, I never wanted to hurt you. I still love you, but … Katarina …" He rubbed his face, his words trailing off. "I don't know what happened. I'll never forgive myself for hurting you, and I don't expect you to, either."

Tears blurred her vision, and she felt a surge of anger and sadness swell in her chest. "I can't pretend I'm okay. Or that I'm not furious with you. After everything I did for you…"

He moved toward her. "I'm sorry, Ava."

She stepped back, swallowing hard. "It's too late for that. I should be focusing on finding Melissa and Jeremy, not wasting time crying over you."

Peter's face fell, and she caught a glimpse of his hurt. Part of her wanted to comfort him, but her own heartache held her back.

"You're right," he said. "I'm sorry for dragging you through this. I wanted to be there for you, but it felt like I didn't know you anymore. You kept shutting me out."

Her anger flared up again, hot and raw. "Relationships are hard, Peter. But it was you who stopped letting me in, not the other way around. I held on as tightly as I could, and you just let go."

"I know, and I hate myself for it."

She wanted to look away, to not let him see how broken she felt. "Seeing you with her … it hurts. I don't know how long it'll take me to get over this." Her voice cracked. "But I don't want to keep thinking about you, Peter. I don't want to keep crying over you."

"I know it's too late. But I still care about you, and I'll always protect you, Ava. Even if you can't forgive me."

"Don't say that. We can be civil, for the sake of the mission, but don't think we'll be friends."

She turned and walked back to the cabin, the pain swelling up inside her like a storm. She could still feel the ache, but she knew she had to find a way to let go. As she lay down, clutching her pillow, she thought of Moira's words. *One day, you'll smile again, and it won't be because of anything, or anyone, you left behind.* She wiped her eyes, praying that day would come soon.

The faint light of early morning leached through the small cabin window, casting a cool, pale glow across the room. Ava shivered, pulling the thin blanket tighter around her. Last night's tears left their mark – raw eyelids, a sore throat, and a dull headache pulsating behind her eyes.

Pushing aside the covers, she sat up, blinking at the sight beyond the window. A thick layer of snow blanketed everything outside. She wrapped her arms around herself, dreading the icy reminder of her own loneliness and unresolved heartache.

Ava slipped outside, the cabin door creaking as she closed it. She took a step into the snow, which crunched beneath her boots, and crisp air stung her cheeks. The sight was beautiful. Soft layers of snow weighing down branches, the ground stretching out pure and untouched. Snowflakes fell, drifting lazily in the air, catching in her hair and on her coat.

Others moved around the camp, bundled in their coats and laughing, voices muffled by the snowfall. Aidan, Ronan, Moira, Link, and Nicole were in a full snowball war, their laughter carrying over the gentle morning quiet. Lance laughed as he pelted Gillian with snow, while she squealed and ducked, muttering about her hair frizzing in the cold. She smiled, feeling the nostalgia of childhood winters when everything seemed simpler and carefree.

She caught sight of Peter and Katarina throwing snow at each other, their laughter mingling with everyone else's. Her heart twinged, but she forced herself to breathe through it, determined not to let it ruin the moment.

A snowball splatted against the side of her face, cold wetness slipping down her neck. She brushed it off, searching for the culprit.

Gabriel stood a few feet away, arms crossed with a mischievous grin spreading across his face.

"Nice aim," she deadpanned, though a smile tugged at her lips.

"Couldn't help myself." His eyes twinkled. "You looked way too serious out here."

"Funny." She scooped up a handful of snow. "You look too clean." She tossed the snowball, hitting him square in the chest.

"Oh, so that's how it is?" he teased, grabbing his own snowball.

They broke into a back-and-forth snowball fight, their laughter and quick steps echoing in the morning air. Ava ducked behind a tree. She peeked out, and threw another, catching him off-guard.

"Not bad," Gabriel called, brushing snow from his shoulder. "Though I have to say, you missed a few shots."

"Oh, really?" she challenged, crouching low. "Let's see you do better."

They kept at it until her hair was dusted with snow and her cheeks flushed. Gabriel moved closer, snowball in hand, but he paused, a playful glint in his eye. "I guess I should warn you. I never lose."

"Oh yeah? Prove it."

But she slipped on an icy patch, tumbling down into the snow.

He strolled over, chuckling, his step exuding a casual confidence that she found sexy. When he reached her, he extended a hand to help her up. "Guess we'll call it a draw," he said, his smile softening as he met her eyes.

Her heart did a small flip as she took his hand, letting him pull her to her feet. "Fine. But only because you caught me off guard."

His gaze lingered on her, his tone gentler now. "You should let yourself laugh more. You look good when you're happy."

Blood rushed to Ava's cheeks, causing her to avert her gaze and brush off the snow from her coat. The feeling in her chest was unfamiliar, but it had a strange pleasantness.

"Ava!" Gillian's figure emerged from behind them, her face contorted with anger and distress.

Ava turned. "What's wrong?"

"How could you?"

"What are you talking about?"

Moira trailed after Gillian, her face pale as she wrung her hands. "It's … it's not true. It was just a vision."

A chill prickled over Ava's skin from the look in Moira's eyes. "What did you see?"

"I'm sorry, Ava. I dreamed you joined Havok. That you … became a Cimmerian."

Ava's heart plummeted. "No … no, that can't be right. I would never."

"Then why did she see it?" Gillian demanded.

"She hasn't done anything," Lance said. "This is just a vision."

Moira nodded, her eyes pleading. "Most of my visions come true … but not all of them. And this one, it doesn't feel right. I don't believe it."

"What else did you see?" Gabriel asked.

"Nothing," she refused to look at him.

"Moira, what else did you see?" he demanded, and Ava wasn't sure she wanted to know.

Sighing, she looked up as tears rolled down her cheek. "Thomas was there, too."

Gillian gasped and brought her hand up to her mouth. "What would make you two join him? Why would you do it?"

Ava's mind raced. "Why would I join him? That makes no sense. I could never do that."

A few others looked at her with worry, as if she already wore Havok's mark. Shame crept up her spine, her cheeks flushed. "You know me. You all know me," she said. "I would never betray you."

"What's going on?" Aaron asked as he and the Elders approached.

"Moira had a vision," Gabriel said. "It … showed Ava and Thomas standing with Havok." His words hung in the air like the snowflakes drifting down around them, heavy with implication.

Savina's sharp gaze landed on Ava, her face unreadable, but after a pause, she stepped closer and touched Ava's shoulder. "I know what's in your heart. You are not evil. You're stronger than whatever dark fate was imagined for you."

Ava looked into Savina's eyes, finding a flicker of belief that warmed her. But the words lingered. Would she ever give in to that darkness? Was it possible? She couldn't even fathom being a Cimmerian. Was that what they meant a few months ago when they said it was her destiny? Her mother told her to join them in her dreams. She couldn't become a Cimmerian. Terrorize towns and kill people. Or kidnap children. She could never give in.

23

FALLING FAST

The fierce wind howled, whipping through the air, its icy tendrils cutting into Ava's exposed skin like a swarm of angry bees. The blizzard raged on, a chaotic dance of swirling white that swallowed up everything in its path. Every step Ava took was accompanied by the sharp crunch of compacted snow under her boots, a sound that echoed in the stillness of the frozen landscape. With each breath, a visible cloud escaped her lips, quickly dissolving into the frigid air. Above her, branches groaned under the weight of the thick icicles that clung to them, bending under the burden. The sky, once a calm blue, was now a foreboding smoky gray, casting an eerie shadow over the desolate scene. Ava couldn't escape the bone-chilling cold, despite warming herself.

She squinted against the snowflakes catching on her lashes, each one melting into cold pinpricks on her cheeks. Keeping her head down helped shield her from the wind and kept Peter and Katarina out of her line of sight. But thoughts of them were just a distraction, something smaller to focus on as her mind circled back to Moira's vision. It haunted her. How could she be strong enough to resist the pull of Havok? And what in her heart could make her betray everyone? *He can't take your soul,* Gabriel once said. His words replayed in her mind, his faith in her offering a flicker of hope.

The silence of the group grew heavier with each labored step, mirroring the relentless snowfall. Finally, they arrived at another cluster of cabins as the day came to an end. The cabins were a strange comfort against the wildness of the woods, each huddled against the storm, scattered around a clearing like they were from another world. She thought of her father and the calm of their living room, the TV casting warm light as he fell asleep in his recliner. She ached to be home, safe and free from all the darkness that now wrapped around her life.

Dinner passed quietly, the only sounds their forks scraping against plates, and afterward, everyone drifted toward their cabins. Ava knew sleep wouldn't come. Moira's vision tormented her, and the caution in her friends' eyes lingered. She crossed to the window, leaning against the icy frame, and watched the snow piling higher outside. The silence was broken by Thomas's loud snoring and Gillian's quiet murmurs as she tossed in her sleep.

"Aren't you going to sleep?" Nicole whispered as she leaned on the other side of the window.

Ava shook her head. "I can't."

"I'm sorry about what happened. But I believe you can change it." Her tone held quiet strength. Ava studied Nicole's face, feeling a surge of sadness. This world wasn't supposed to belong to Nicole, and yet she seemed to have grown into it, even carrying a small smile with her determination.

"I hope so. How are things with Link?"

Nicole's smile grew. "We're good. No kisses yet, though."

"Why not?" Ava asked, feeling a glimmer of interest at the familiar teenage problem amidst their chaotic lives.

Nicole shrugged, her gaze dropping to her hands. "Feels strange, falling in love when so much is at stake."

"Yeah. But maybe we have to take those chances when we can."

"You're right. My life changed so fast. I had it planned out. College, UMass, all of it." She paused, gazing into the swirling snow outside.

"You can still go."

"Maybe." She took a deep breath. "But I wouldn't trade meeting all of you for anything. I think I was made for this."

"I believe it." Her gaze drifted to the distant light in Moira's cabin, curiosity nudging her. "I'll be back in a bit. Need to check on something."

She crossed through the snow toward the glow, her boots sinking into the powder with each step. When she knocked on the cabin door, it creaked open to reveal Gabriel, standing in a white t-shirt and dark jeans, his hair tousled from rest.

He blinked at her in surprise before a gentle smile curved his lips. "Ava?"

"I didn't mean to bother you. I thought Moira might be awake." She hesitated in the doorway.

"She's out like a light. You're not bothering me. Come in." He stepped aside to let her in. The space was quiet, cozy, with a faint glow from the lamp on the nightstand beside Gabriel's unmade bed. He sat back on the edge of the mattress, motioning for her to join him. "I was just reading. Helps me keep my mind off things."

She perched on the bed beside him, fidgeting with the hem of her sweater.

"What's keeping you up?"

Her shoulders sagged, and she leaned forward, resting her elbows on her knees. "Moira's vision. I can't stop thinking about it. What if she's right? What if I do betray everyone?"

His arm moved around her shoulders, pulling her to his side, warming her. "You're not going to betray anyone, Ava. We're not scared of you. We're scared for you because we don't want to lose you."

She tilted her head up to meet his gaze. "What about you? Are you scared of me?"

A shadow crossed his face, and he looked away for a moment. "If you only knew..." The words came out so softly, she almost didn't catch them. He squeezed her shoulder. "You don't need to rely on anyone's belief in you. I know you wouldn't join Havok. Not willingly."

Tears pricked her eyes, as his conviction both soothed and overwhelmed. "But what if I don't have a choice? What if he forces me?"

Gabriel lifted her chin gently, his gaze meeting hers. The intensity in his eyes made her heartbeat quicken, chasing away the doubts. "If that happens, we'll fight him together. You're stronger than you think. Even Havok can't take that from you." His thumb brushed away her tears, and his touch lingered, warm against her cheek.

She took a shaky breath, feeling her pulse calm. "Thank you." But her mind flashed with an image of herself standing beside Havok. A version of her that looked as if she had given up, as if she'd lost everything that made her who she was. The thought burrowed deep into her, leaving her breathless and her chest constricted. "You mentioned before about hiding your feelings."

Gabriel tensed. "Yeah?"

"Can you teach me?"

His brows furrowed. "Why do you want to do that?"

"Because if Havok tries to get inside my head, I need to be ready. I can't let him see my fears, my weaknesses. If I do, I'll lose."

His jaw tightened, and for a long moment, he didn't say anything. He sighed, rubbing the back of his neck. "Ava, this isn't some party trick. What you're asking for, it's dangerous."

"I can handle it." Her voice held steady, but she felt a flicker of doubt under his intense gaze.

"All right. But you need to understand what you're asking for. The heart of stone isn't just hiding your emotions. It's severing them. Completely. You stop reacting. Stop feeling. It works, but it's not without consequences."

"What kind of consequences?"

"Turning them off is easy," he said. "Turning them back on is the hard part. If you go too far, you risk becoming someone else. Someone cold, detached. That's why the Cimmerians are so ruthless. Many of them never come back from it."

She swallowed hard. "Have you done it before?"

Gabriel's shoulders tensed, and his blue eyes flickered with a hint of something darker. Pain, perhaps, or regret. "Let's just say I wasn't myself for a while."

"What do you mean?"

With a sharp exhale, he leaned forward, his elbows resting on his knees. "There was a time when I thought shutting everything off was the only way to survive. And maybe it was. But when you live in that state for too long, it's easy to lose sight of who you are. I lost sight of who I was."

"How did you come back from that?"

He hesitated, his fingers running through his dark hair as he searched for the right words. "It wasn't one moment. It was a fight. Every day, every second. Someone reminded me of who I was, but I had to want to feel again. To let the pain in. I had to remind myself why I started caring in the first place. It's not easy, Ava. Turning it off is a trap. It feels safe, but it's not living. It's existing. And existing … isn't enough."

"Someone?"

"It doesn't matter, Ava. What matters is that it wasn't easy. And it wasn't immediate. I was stuck in that state for years, and it nearly destroyed me. It made me do things I can never undo." The shadows in his eyes deepened.

"What if it's the only way to keep Havok out of my head?"

"That's why I'm teaching you," he said. "But you have to understand, this isn't just a skill. It's a risk. If you're not careful, you could lose yourself in it. You'll feel nothing. No anger, no fear … but no love, either. No joy. I almost didn't make it back, Ava. And if you go too far, you'll need someone to pull you out."

The vulnerability in his voice struck her, and she placed her hand on his arm. "You don't think I can handle it."

"I think you're stronger than I ever was. But strength can also make you reckless. You need to promise me that if it ever feels like you're losing yourself, you'll stop. You'll let someone in before it's too late."

"I promise."

He straightened. "Alright. Let's begin. But know this: I'll stop you if I think you're going too far. No questions, no arguments."

"Okay," she whispered. "I'll be careful. Let's try it."

His blue eyes locked onto hers with a seriousness that made her pulse quicken. "Focus on my words. Don't let them sink in. Don't let them affect you. Ready?"

"Ready."

"You're beautiful."

Heat surged through her face, climbing her neck with the speed of a wildfire. "What?"

"Failed." He smirked, though his eyes still carried a hint of caution. "You can't react. Not to anything."

"Don't start with things like that!"

"You're going to have to be ready for anything, Ava. The Cimmerians kidnapped Melissa and Jeremy."

A sharp pang clutched her chest as the memory rushed back. She took a shaky breath, trying to force it out, but it clung to her like a shadow. She focused on his words as if they were just sounds, nothing more. Gradually, the ache began to fade, the images in her mind dulling.

"Turn it off," he reminded her. "Let it go."

She closed her eyes, imagining the emotions like water slipping through her fingers, leaving nothing behind. When she opened them, the weight in her chest had lessened.

He studied her, his eyebrow lifting. "Quick learner."

"But it feels so … empty."

"It does," he said, his tone tinged with a quiet regret. "Like cutting off a part of yourself. That's why you have to be careful not to rely on it too much."

A heavy silence settled between them. Ava leaned against him, her head resting on his shoulder as exhaustion crept in. "Thank you."

"You're welcome. Promise you'll be careful. Losing your humanity isn't worth it. You don't need to be that strong."

She shifted, meeting his gaze. There was something raw in his eyes. "You don't regret teaching me, do you?"

"No," he said. "But I know how stubborn you are." He gave her a teasing smile, but something in his gaze held, lingering a bit longer than usual. "Just … don't let it consume you."

"It won't," she murmured, matching his smile.

For a moment, neither of them spoke. The stillness between them was heavy, almost suffocating. Ava shifted, and her eyes darted to the book lying on the nightstand. "What's it about?"

"An FBI agent chasing a terrorist."

She yawned. "Sounds like riveting bedtime reading."

His smirk deepened "Clearly, you're captivated. But it's better than listening to Eric snore all night."

"Is he really that bad?"

"You have no idea. Sometimes I think he's trying to start a new rhythm every night."

"So, what about you? Do you snore?"

He flashed her a mischievous grin. "Only one way to find out."

Her jaw dropped, and she shoved him playfully. "Gabe."

"Hey, I don't know! I'm asleep!" He raised his hands in mock surrender.

She rolled her eyes and jabbed him in the side. A playful glint appeared in his eyes, and his hands darted to her sides, his touch featherlight but relentless. He tickled her mercilessly.

She squealed as his fingers danced across her ribs, twisting and laughing. "Gabriel! Stop!" she gasped, trying to push his hands away.

"Oh, no." His grin widened. "You started this."

Her attempt to escape sent her tumbling back onto the bed, tangled in the covers.

Gabriel followed, his arms braced on either side of her as he leaned over her. His laughter softened, giving way to something quieter, something unspoken.

Her laughter faded as the moment shifted. He hovered above her, his blue eyes meeting hers with an intensity that made her breath hitch. The flickering lamp cast warm shadows over his face, tracing the sharp lines of his jaw and catching the faint stubble along his chin.

Her chest heaved, the sound of her racing heart echoing in the silence. She could feel the heat radiating from him, his breath brushing her cheek. The air between them grew charged, every second stretching endlessly. For a moment, the world narrowed to his closeness, his warmth, the unspoken tension that crackled between them.

Ava swallowed hard, her throat dry as she struggled to find her voice. "You're—" she began, but the words faltered, her cheeks flushing under his piercing gaze.

The corners of his mouth tugged into a faint smile. He eased back, giving her space to sit up. "You okay there, sensei?" he teased, his voice low and smooth, breaking the spell.

She brushed her hair out of her face, her hands trembling. "Yeah, but you're terrible at letting someone win."

"Lesson number one," he said with mock seriousness. "Never start something you can't finish."

Ava's lips twitched into a nervous smile, though her pulse still raced. She shoved his shoulder, but the moment lingered.

A comfortable silence fell between them as they both leaned against the headboard.

Ava's pulse quickened as the thought crept in. This could be more than friendship. The thought made her cheeks warm, a sudden realization mingling with the safety and comfort he gave her. He met her gaze again, and for a moment, neither of them looked away. She felt her own smile falter, unsure, but still drawn to the depth she saw in his eyes.

She closed her eyes, letting herself sink into the feeling of him beside her, her heart calm, mirroring his.

Ava blinked awake, momentarily disoriented by the dim light filtering through the small window. The room was filled with a warm silence, broken by the soft rhythm of breathing beside her. She glanced to her left and froze. Gabriel was still beside her, his face relaxed in sleep.

She'd fallen asleep with Gabriel. In his bed.

The usual sharpness in his expression had softened, and for a moment, she was captivated, noticing little things she hadn't before. The slight curl of his lashes, the way his hair fell over his forehead. An unexplainable heat bloomed in her chest, and she couldn't look away.

He stirred, his eyes fluttering open. Their gazes met, and heat filled her face. She scrambled to sit up, nearly tripping over the covers as she tried to make herself look casual.

His eyes were still heavy with sleep as he gave her a lazy, bemused smile. "Morning, Ava."

"Uh, morning." She glanced down, fiddling with the hem of her sweater. She hoped he didn't notice the pounding of her heart. "Didn't, um, didn't mean to wake you."

He smirked. "I'm a light sleeper. Plus, I think I could feel you staring."

Ava's eyes widened, and she let out a nervous laugh, feeling her cheeks flush even deeper. "I—uh, I wasn't staring!" she said, a little too quickly, and regretted it as he chuckled.

Gabriel rubbed his hand over his face, a faint blush coloring his cheeks. "Sure. It's fine. I wouldn't blame you if you did."

She laughed, a mix of embarrassment and amusement rising in her chest. "Sorry. I didn't mean to fall asleep here."

"I'm not exactly complaining. But next time, remind me to wear shin guards."

"Right. Well," she mumbled, trying to play it off as she tucked her hair behind her ear. "Guess it's time to start the day."

As she turned away, she could still feel his gaze on her, making her heart beat a little faster. The comfortable quiet lingered between them, leaving her both flustered and strangely happy as they got ready to join the others.

They trudged through the snow again, but this time, the path was easier without a storm raging around them. The quiet crunch of snow underfoot seemed louder in the stillness. They walked for miles, their eyes darting across the trees and shadows, alert for anything unusual. Thomas and Moira exchanged flirty glances, while Gillian, never missing a beat, nudged Ava with a sly grin.

"So, are you going to tell me what happened last night?" Gillian whispered, her breath visible in the cold air.

Ava shrugged. "I talked to Gabriel."

She raised an eyebrow, her curly hair now a frizzed halo from the damp cold. "All night?"

"We just talked for a couple of hours. It's not the first time."

"Mhm." Gillian studied her face, ready to pry further, but a harsh squawk from above interrupted them.

Ava's head snapped up to the darkening sky, where a cluster of black-winged creatures circled ominously, their movements deliberate, almost like they were waiting. The air grew colder as their shadows passed over the snow, casting a chill even deeper than the icy wind.

"What are those?" Gillian's voice wavered.

The ground trembled beneath them. It started as a low rumble, like distant thunder, and then grew into a powerful shaking that made her heart race. Icicles shattered from the tree branches above, raining down like shards of glass. Snow clumps fell in heavy thuds as the earth continued to groan beneath them.

The group huddled, forming a tight circle, their backs pressed against one another, every sense on high alert. Ava held her breath, her pulse hammering in her ears. The vibrations grew stronger, each one closer than the last.

"Saberwolves," Aaron muttered.

Ava's blood ran cold.

From the east, a massive shadow burst through the trees, and then another, barreling forward like unstoppable forces. Trees snapped like twigs in their path, sending ice and snow cascading down. The saberwolves, larger than any she'd seen, with fur as thick and wild as their feral eyes, charged toward them. The air filled with the low, menacing growls of the creatures as they closed in.

She thrust her hands forward to send a torrent of water toward the approaching wolves. Around her, fireballs lit up the darkened forest, casting brief glows on her friends' determined faces. Waves of energy and explosions echoed across the snow. The group fought back with everything they had, but the saberwolves kept coming. Ava braced herself to create a larger wave, but the chaos made it hard to concentrate.

A force slammed into her side, sending her sprawling into the snow. Her chest throbbed with pain as she scrambled to her feet, her vision swimming. Gabriel was by her side in an instant, an arm outstretched to guard her as he glared at the wolves, his body tense.

The saberwolves stopped, their massive bodies heaving with restrained energy, eyes gleaming with hunger. Mounted atop each wolf were figures cloaked in black, faces obscured but watching them. Ava's heart sank. The same people she, Gabriel, and Eric had encountered in the deserted town.

One of the riders, a burly man with an unmistakable air of authority, looked down at them with a smirk, his voice roaring through the woods, clear and mocking. "I knew it was only a matter of time before you showed up."

Ava caught Gabriel's eyes, saw the fierceness there, the resolve shared by Thomas, Gillian, and the others around her.

Aaron stepped forward, his stance unyielding. "We have no problem defeating you."

The man laughed, deep and ominous. "Sir, we have fifty saberwolves and our own powers. Give us the Elementals, and we will not kill you."

Aaron didn't flinch. "We will never surrender."

The man shrugged, his expression cold. "Your funeral." With a flick of his hand, he signaled, and ten saberwolves advanced, their riders barely visible atop the massive beasts.

Ava's heart pounded as the wolves crept closer, the snapping of their powerful jaws echoing in the icy air. She stood her ground, water already forming at her fingertips. They were ready to fight, but she could feel the tension, the quiet, pressing fear. This was only the beginning.

FEARLESS

A cluster of saberwolves charged toward the group, their pounding steps sending vibrations through the ground. Some of the hooded figures held back, watching with ominous interest.

"Follow my lead!" Gabriel shouted, running forward.

The group scattered, moving in all directions. Shouts, screams, yips, and growls reverberated off nearby boulders. Ava followed Gabriel's lead as he darted toward one of the beasts, slamming into it with surprising force. She gasped as the saberwolf staggered, injured from the impact.

The ground shook beneath her as another saberwolf barreled her way, its eyes gleaming with animal rage. It lunged, swiping a giant paw with claws that flashed in the dim light. She dodged to the side, her heart pounding, and it roared, the sound nearly deafening as it rattled through her bones. Bracing herself, she punched toward the creature's chest with a burst of energy. Pain shot through her arm from the impact. The saberwolf crumpled in front of her, its body crashing into the snow, leaving her breathless.

A hooded figure leapt from the wolf's back, landing with a sinister grin. Scars crisscrossed his face, his dark eyes alight with malice. He lunged at her, pinning her in a chokehold. Ava's pulse pounded as she gripped his arm, summoning water from her hands that surged toward his face. The flow was weaker than usual, but she had to concentrate, feeling herself start to tire. The water trickled over his skin, finally strong enough to smother his breath. He choked and stumbled back.

But before she could regain her stance, he seized her neck with an icy grip. The man lifted her effortlessly and threw her against a nearby tree. She hit the trunk with a force that knocked the air from her lungs, and snow rained down around her. Chest heaving, she lay still in the snow, pretending to be lifeless as pain radiated through her body.

The man turned, but she kept her eyes fixed on him. She envisioned him drowning, engulfed in relentless waves. The man gasped, clutching his throat as if caught in a whirlpool. He staggered, sinking to his knees, and collapsed, the life draining from him. Ava remained still, her chest heaving, taking a few moments to regain her breath before forcing herself to stand. Her head throbbed, and every muscle in her body protested, but she pressed on.

Thomas hurled a giant fireball at another attacker. The impact threw the man backward with a bloodcurdling scream, his form vanishing into the snow. Gillian was besieged by three hooded figures, but with a wave of her hand, their faces went blank. The men turned on each other, their powers clashing with brutal force under Gillian's control. Link's bombs detonated, shaking the ground. A violent tornado of snow erupted around a saberwolf, swirling with icy fury.

A crackling jolt hit Ava in the back, making her muscles seize. She collapsed backward, her body rigid, unable to move.

"Ooh, did that hurt?" A woman's voice purred above her.

Ava gritted her teeth, her entire body tingling as she regained movement. "No, but this might hurt you." She summoned the snow around them, forcing it to melt into puddles that pooled at the woman's feet. The woman snickered, raising her hand for another strike, but Ava acted first, using the water to grip the woman's ankles. The woman staggered, losing her balance and falling forward as Ava sent a surge through the puddles. The woman's eyes widened as her own electricity arced through the water. She spasmed, her body convulsing, then went still as smoke curled from her clothes.

Ava wiped her brow, fatigue clawing at her as she stumbled back. She turned, catching sight of another hooded figure sneaking up on her, and struck him in the back, feeling the sickening crunch of bones breaking beneath her fist. His scream pierced the air as he fell forward, staining the snow dark red.

A sudden weight crashed into her, pinning her to the ground. Her face pressed into the snow, and her muscles screamed in protest as a burning sensation spread across her body, pricking her skin like a thousand needles.

"You should give up," her assailant hissed.

"Never," Ava snarled, fighting to focus. She forced the snow around them to melt, flooding the ground. They both sank into the cold water, and with a final burst of energy, she sent water crashing over his face. It clung to him, wrapping around his head like a living mask. As his grip on her loosened, she wriggled free, gasping as he choked and thrashed before he went limp.

An unseen force slammed into Ava, sending her sprawling into the snow. The icy chill bit into her skin. She grappled against the invisible attacker, her heart pounding in her ears. Her mind swirled with disjointed flashes, fragments of memories that didn't belong to her.

Her mother's voice echoed. *Ava, let go. Join them. This is your destiny.*

"No!" Ava shook her head as the vision took hold. Her surroundings warped and dissolved until she wasn't in the snow anymore. She was standing in her old kitchen, her mother's gentle face smiling at her across the table. But something was wrong. Her mother's eyes were hollow, her smile too sharp.

"Ava," her mother urged. "Let go. You don't have to fight this."

A piercing pain snapped Ava out of the vision. She blinked and realized she was being dragged backward through the snowy woods, her boots leaving deep grooves in the frost-covered earth. Trees rushed past her in a dizzying blur, their skeletal branches looming overhead like claws.

Trudy.

Gritting her teeth, fury ignited inside Ava. She focused, her hand reaching out, blindly searching until her fingers latched onto something icy and solid. Trudy's wrist. Though invisible, Ava could feel the wicked energy radiating from her captor like a noxious fog.

Summoning the water around her, Ava concentrated, her power surging through her veins like liquid fire. The snow beneath her undulated, transforming into glistening, liquid tendrils. The water coiled around Trudy's unseen form, her figure shimmering into view as the frost clung to her.

"Let. Me. Go!" Ava growled.

The water turned to ice in an instant, its frigid temperature snaking up Trudy's arms and locking her in place. A sharp gasp escaped Trudy as the frost spread, creeping over her shoulders and chest. Her lips turned a sickly shade of blue, her eyes wide with shock and fury.

Ava staggered to her feet, yanking herself free from Trudy's grip. Her breath came in ragged bursts as the water surged again, wrapping around Trudy's entire body like a frozen cocoon. The crackling sound of ice echoed through the silent woods as the frost encased her from head to toe.

Trudy struggled, her body jerking against the encroaching ice, but it was futile. Her movements slowed, her breaths visible in short, desperate bursts.

Ava clenched her fists, her power thrumming with raw intensity. The ice thickened, spreading deeper, until Trudy's movements ceased. A sickening stillness filled the air punctuated by the faint whisper of wind through the trees.

Ava staggered back, her legs threatening to give out beneath her. Her chest heaved as she fought to catch her breath, the adrenaline still coursing through her. The vision of her mother lingered at the edges of her mind, but she shoved it away.

She turned away from Trudy's frozen form, the cold seeping into her bones as she forced herself to move, heading back toward her group with shaky steps.

A suffocating silence fell over the battlefield, pierced by the agonized moans of those who lay injured. Ava trudged back toward the group, her breath clouding in the icy air as her gaze swept over the carnage. Saberwolves and fallen Enchanters lay sprawled across the snow, their lifeless bodies staining the pristine white with streaks of crimson.

In the clearing, familiar faces came into focus. Savina knelt beside the injured, her hands glowing with healing energy. A few feet away, Moira clung to Thomas, relief etched across her face. Link cradled Nicole, pressing comforting kisses to her forehead. Aaron, Gustav, and Peter gathered with the Irish and the Russians. Despite the overwhelming grief and exhaustion in the air, a flicker of hope began to kindle among them.

"Ava!" Gillian called. She released Lance and sprinted toward her, throwing her arms around Ava's neck.

Lance joined them. "I saw Trudy dragging you. I couldn't get to you—"

"She's dead," Ava said.

Gillian drew back, Ava's mind remained restless as she scanned the group for someone missing. The embrace ended as a new wave of worry surged through her. Her heart quickened. "Where's Gabriel?" Her voice cracked as panic clawed at her throat. She whirled around, her boots crunching through the snow as she scanned the battlefield. "Gabriel!" The name tore from her throat like a plea. *He has to be okay.*

Movement at the edge of her vision drew her attention. A figure hunched over in the snow, rocking. Her breath hitched. She darted toward him, her heart in her throat. When she reached him, the sight made her stomach drop. "Gabe…" she whispered.

He was kneeling, his body taut with pain. Patches of his clothing had melted away, exposing raw, blistered skin eaten away by acid. His arms, neck, and face bore bubbling burns, the flesh angry and red. The sharp, acrid smell clung to him, mingling with the iron tang of blood in the air. Shallow gasps escaped his lips as his trembling body convulsed with each breath. He looked up at her, his crystal-blue eyes dull with pain, yet still soft as they focused on her. He gritted his teeth, struggling to speak. "The damn Enchanter … poured acid on me," he rasped, each word sounding like it cost him.

Her hands hovered helplessly for a moment, unsure where to touch without causing him more pain. "Savina!" she screamed. Tears blurred her vision as her gaze swept his injuries. "Oh my God…"

Despite his agony, his gaze flicked up to meet hers, and a faint trace of concern softened his features. "You're bleeding."

"I'm fine," she choked out, blinking back tears. "You're the one—just hold on, okay? Don't move." She knelt beside him, willing herself to stay calm.

"Omigod, Gabe…" Natalia's voice quivered as she, Lance, Eric, and Gillian approached, their faces contorted in shock.

A rustle in the woods drew her attention. Ilya stumbled into view, clutching his stomach, his hands slick with blood from a deep gash. The sight made her breath hitch, and her chest tightened. Her vision blurred as panic surged, the walls of the forest closing in around her.

She breathed in short, ragged gasps. *Just breathe.* Gabriel's voice echoed in her mind. She squeezed her eyes shut, forcing a deep breath. *I can't lose him.*

Trembling, she took his arm. Desperation surged within her as she focused on the water deep within her being, willing it to her fingertips. It trickled out, cool and clear, before surging with purpose. The water cascaded over Gabriel's burns, shimmering as it touched his skin. She held her breath, praying it would work.

At first, he groaned, his body tensing. But the blisters began to fade, the redness receding. The angry burns smoothed, his skin repairing itself as the water worked its way over each injury. Her own breath steadied as she poured every ounce of her strength into the flow, not daring to stop until his wounds were gone.

The group released a collective sigh, the tension melting into quiet relief.

Gabriel slumped forward, his head resting against her shoulder as he exhaled. "Thank God," he murmured. "That was … excruciating."

"You're okay now," Ava said. She steadied him before turning her attention to Ilya. Rushing to his side, she knelt beside him as he let out a strained groan. "It's going to be okay." She guided the water to his wound. It moved like a living thing, weaving across his torn flesh, sealing the gash as his ragged breathing slowed.

Ilya took a deep breath. "Thank you. I owe you."

"You don't." She sank back on her knees. A wave of exhaustion washed over her, her limbs trembling from the effort.

Gabriel appeared behind her, kneeling. "You have to heal yourself."

"I'm fine. Just got electrocuted."

"You're bleeding, Ava. Heal yourself."

She glanced down, noticing for the first time the blood stains darkening her front. The cuts stung now that she'd registered them. "I've never healed myself before."

"Pull the water from within," he urged. "It'll work."

She closed her eyes, focusing inward. Her power stirred within her, rippling through her veins like a steady current. Slowly, she drew it to the surface, the water rising through her pores and spreading over her injuries. A cooling sensation washed over her, soothing the pain and sealing her wounds. When she opened her eyes, the discomfort had vanished, leaving her feeling renewed.

"Better?" Gabriel asked.

She nodded, offering him a tired smile. "Better."

Behind him, Ilya watched her with an intent gaze, his expression unreadable. "That's impressive. Your abilities are more advanced than I thought."

Ava shifted, brushing off his words. "Just instincts kicking in."

Ilya tilted his head, his lips curving into a slow smile. "Not everyone can heal like that. It's … rare. You know, there are people out there who would give anything to have that kind of power."

A chill pricked over her skin as her power ebbed. "I guess I'm lucky, then."

"Ilya's right," Gabriel said. "We should keep this a secret from Havok."

"He already knows … when I healed Colden."

"But he doesn't know it's back now," Ilya added. "If he thinks your healing's gone, that could be to our advantage."

Gabriel stood, and helped Ava to her feet. His gaze met hers, his blue eyes warm despite the exhaustion etched into his features. Turning to the group, he asked, "Everyone okay?"

"We all made it," Aaron said, his voice calm but resolute as he surveyed the group.

"Does anyone need healing?" Savina asked.

Gabriel glanced at Ava, a faint pride lighting his face. "Ava already took care of us."

With a soft sigh, Savina clasped her hands together. "Good."

Aaron's gaze shifted to the battlefield, his expression somber. "The scavengers will have a good meal here for a few days."

Ava followed his gaze, her stomach churning as vultures began to descend, their dark forms silhouetted against the gray sky. With hungry glints in their beady eyes, they swooped down on the fallen, their sharp beaks tearing into the corpses. She turned away, nausea rising in her throat. The grotesque sight made her steps falter, but she pressed forward.

"Do they always know when death is coming?" Gillian asked.

Aaron nodded. "They can sense it. So, yes, anytime you see a vulture, it's a warning."

Natalia grimaced, her face paling as she shut her eyes. "Can we leave? I'd rather not watch them devour what's left."

Gabriel smirked. "She's always had a weak stomach."

"Gillian too," Lance added, winking as he steadied her when she wobbled, unsettled by the vultures.

"Oh, please," Gillian groaned, swatting at him. "Who actually wants to see that?" She glanced once more at the carnage before cringing. "I'm definitely going to be sick."

"Any minute now, Natalia's going to faint, too," Eric joked, earning him a roll of her eyes.

Natalia turned to Ava, her tone soft. "Thank you for healing Gabriel."

Ava opened her mouth to respond, but Gabriel cut in, a playful grin tugging at his lips. "Oh, actually, she missed a spot on my arm."

Ava gasped, scanning his arm only to realize there wasn't a single mark left. "Really?"

"Careful, or next time, she might not heal you at all." Natalia snickered.

Gabriel winked at Ava, giving her a light nudge on the arm. "Thank you, sensei. That was … agonizing." He looked down at his arm. "Can't believe there's not even a scratch."

"You're welcome. Though, I'm sure Savina would've handled it if I hadn't."

"Maybe. But somehow, it's not quite the same."

Ava met his gaze, and her cheeks warmed.

The group began to move, the crunch of boots on snow breaking the momentary quiet. As Ava fell into step, she caught a glimpse of Peter in the distance, his gaze locked on her. Something unreadable flickered in his brown eyes, a mixture of emotion she couldn't decipher. She forced herself to look away, fixing her attention instead on Gabriel's hand, still intertwined with hers. Despite the chilling cold and the vultures circling overhead, his touch brought a comforting sense of ease.

After a grueling day, Aaron called for them to set up camp, leading them several miles away from the battleground. The trees thinned enough to give them space, and they worked in silence, pitching their tents under the cover of Savina's protective charm.

They gathered around a small, flickering fire that crackled, its orange embers struggling to push back the biting night chill. Cold air pricked at Ava's skin, slipping through layers of clothing and making her huddle closer to the warmth. The firelight danced over their weary faces, casting long shadows across the snow-dusted ground, which seemed to swallow up any noise they made. The scent of damp earth and pine needles mingled with a hint of smoke.

As the wind rustled through the trees, a whisper of leaves and brittle branches, it felt like even the forest was holding its breath, aware of their vulnerability.

Ava crouched beside Gabriel, lifting his arm to examine it again in the firelight. Dark hair dusted his forearm, and while his skin was unmarked, she couldn't shake the worry that lingered. "How's your arm?"

"It's fine," Gabriel assured her. "You healed it. Unless you think it's going to start boiling again?" His playful smirk faded to a soft smile.

"It's just ... all of this is still kind of new for me," she admitted, letting her fingers hover near his skin.

He met her gaze, a hint of gratitude in his eyes.

They fell silent for a few moments, letting the crackling fire fill the space between them.

"I wasn't expecting any of that today." Gillian drew her knees up to her chest as she rocked, eyes glossy with tears.

"None of us were," Thomas said.

Gillian's chin trembled as she looked around the group. "Any one of us could have died," she whispered as a tear slipped down her cheek.

Eric moved closer, resting a hand on her shoulder. "Look at it this way: none of us did. We're still here."

Her shoulders began to shake as her emotions spilled over. "I just ... I need Jeremy," she sobbed, clutching her knees. "I don't know how much more I can take. Today was terrifying, and I don't want to think about what's coming next."

Ava scooted beside her, wrapping an arm around her.

Gillian clung to her, her quiet sobs blending into the sounds of the forest.

"We'll find them. We have to."

"What if … what if it's already too late? What if he's used their souls? What if they're gone?" She pulled back, her tear-streaked face mirroring the fears they all shared.

Thomas sat forward. "Don't go down that road, Gillian. You need to hold on a little longer."

"It's hard right now," she said.

"I know it is," he whispered.

She sniffed, running a hand under her nose. "I can't help it. I keep thinking … what if we get there, and they're all dead? That everything we're doing is meaningless?"

"They aren't dead, Gillian," Natalia said with confidence.

Thomas nodded. "And when we get there, we'll destroy Havok and the Cimmerians. We finish this, for good."

"Until someone else decides to start up another army," Gillian muttered.

"It won't happen," Thomas said. "You really think any one of us would start another war?"

Gillian's eyes darted to Ava, her gaze clouded with fear. "I don't know what any of us will do anymore. Apparently, you and Ava are supposed to become Cimmerians. Who knows what will happen?"

The accusation permeated the air, constricting Ava's chest as she met their worried gazes. "I won't," she said, her voice unwavering as she forced herself to meet their eyes. "I swear to you all, I won't." She rose, taking Gillian's hand

and helping her up. "Come on, let's get some rest. Today's taken enough out of us."

"Will you stay with me until I fall asleep?" Gillian asked.

"Of course." Ava led her into the tent and sat beside her as she slid into her sleeping bag.

Gillian sniffled, wiping her damp cheeks. "I don't want that vision to come true. I want to believe you're strong enough to fight it. But Havok…" She trailed off, her fear heavy in the air.

"We're strong together, remember? That's how we beat him." Ava squeezed her hand. "You don't need to worry about me."

"I'm glad you're here. I know I haven't made it easy for you these past months. Always doubting, distrusting… I'm sorry. Can you forgive me?"

Ava brushed a piece of hair from her friend's face. "There's nothing to forgive."

"Please, just say it."

"Okay, I forgive you."

They sat in silence for a moment, letting the quiet settle over them.

"I think I've been seeing Jeremy," Gillian whispered.

"In your dreams?"

"No, it feels … real. Every night this week, he's been there, talking to me."

"What do you mean?" Ava's pulse quickened as she searched her friend's face. She hoped Gillian hadn't lost her grip on reality.

"He visits me, tells me to join the Cimmerians … says we're fighting for the wrong side."

Ava froze. "Do you think the Cimmerians are getting inside your head again?"

"It doesn't feel the same as before. You never see him?"

"No. I don't."

Gillian's shoulders slumped. "Maybe I'm going crazy. I miss him so much."

"We'll find him, I promise."

"Were you scared today, Ava?"

"Terrified. At one point, a Cimmerian threw me into a tree. I'm still amazed my head is in one piece."

A faint smile tugged at Gillian's lips. "You were incredible today, though. I saw you take down three of them by yourself."

"I just kept thinking of everyone. What they mean to me. What Jeremy would want us to do. We have to believe he's still out there."

"Thank you."

Ava stayed beside her until her breathing slowed, then slipped out of the tent and zipped it. The night air nipped at her cheeks, and she found Thomas and Lance waiting nearby, both looking worried.

"How's she doing?" Thomas asked.

Ava sighed. "She's okay for now. She said she's been seeing Jeremy … like he's really there."

Lance raised an eyebrow. "Yeah, she told me. I've been seeing Melissa."

Thomas and Ava exchanged a glance. "What?"

"Maybe it's dreams, or … I don't know. I've been so exhausted I can't tell." Lance ran a hand over his face.

"Maybe Trudy was in your heads," Ava said. "She's finally dead. And Gabriel can teach us how to strengthen our minds tomorrow. We could all use it."

Lance nodded. "I need that. Get some rest."

Ava slowed as she approached her tent, spotting Gabriel standing beside it.

He glanced up and smirked.

"Come to tuck me in?" she teased, crossing her arms but unable to hide the soft smile tugging at her lips.

He chuckled, standing up. "Only if you need it."

A blush rose to her cheeks as the memory of the previous night flashed in her mind. How they'd stayed up talking, leaning against each other, and how, somewhere in that quiet moment, she'd drifted off with him beside her without a single nightmare. It hadn't felt strange, only … comforting. And now, standing there with him, that same feeling washed over her again, leaving her heart unexpectedly full.

"I think ... I'm good, but thanks," she said with a half-laugh, trying to brush off the moment.

He grinned, but his gaze softened, lingering on her with something that felt deeper. "Good. Just know, the offer's always there. I think you could use a little peace."

She gave a shy smile. "Maybe a bit."

"Thanks again for what you did back there." He rubbed his arm.

"Of course. I'd do anything for you," she added quickly, "and the group."

He smiled. "Well, goodnight, Ava. Sleep well."

"Goodnight," she whispered as he turned and walked away. She took a deep breath, her heartbeat slowing as she ducked into her tent, feeling a little lighter.

After slipping into her sleeping bag, she closed her eyes, the exhaustion taking hold.

As the wind howled and battered Ava's tent, she pulled her blanket tighter around her shoulders. She wished she'd taken Gabriel's offer to share his tent. It would have been warmer, safer, less isolating.

The faint crunch of footsteps in the snow shattered the quiet, sending a jolt through her. Her breath caught in her throat, and she froze. Someone, or something, was out there. The wind whipped against the tent walls, drowning out any further sounds, but her heart pounded in her chest. She strained to listen, every nerve on edge.

"Ava?" Peter whispered from outside.

She sat up, the chill of the night slipping under her blankets. "Peter?"

"Can we talk?"

She groaned, rolling her eyes, frustration mixing with something else she couldn't name. "What about?"

"Please let me in. I really need to talk to you."

Reluctantly, she shifted aside, muttering, "Fine."

The tent's zipper hummed as he slipped inside. She shuffled to make room, though they were so close she could feel his body heat radiating through the cold night air. She reached for the small lantern, lighting it, its flame casting a dim orange glow that flickered shadows across his face. His eyes looked lost, almost haunted, and Ava felt a pang of confusion, her heart tripping over itself as he held her gaze.

"What's wrong?" She was cautious, unsure of what was coming.

He swallowed, eyes searching hers. "I think … I think I made a mistake." He hesitated. "I miss you, Ava. I … I still love you."

She tensed. "What?"

"I know, I know." He ran a hand through his hair. "I deserve worse than this. But I've been miserable, Ava. Being away from you—it's all I can think about."

Her heart hammered, each beat sharp and frantic as the words filled the small space between them. "Why are you doing this?"

"I don't know how to stay away from you. Every time I see Gabriel with you, it tears me apart. Letting you go was the biggest mistake I've ever made."

"Peter, stop," she demanded. Her body betrayed her, inching closer to him even as her mind warned her to stay away.

"I know you still love me, Ava." His eyes held a familiar tenderness as his hand reached out to graze hers.

She pulled her hand back, her breaths shallow as she fought to stay grounded, but her resolve was slipping. "Don't do this," she whispered, and she wasn't sure if she was begging him to stop or begging herself to resist.

He leaned closer, his face inches from hers, and she felt his breath against her skin. "I can't help it. I need you, Ava." His voice was a rough whisper, and for a moment, her heart betrayed her, longing overpowering caution. She wanted to believe him, to feel the comfort of his embrace again.

But something in the back of her mind flared up, like a red flag in the dark, warning her to pull away. "Peter, are you sure this isn't someone else's influence?"

His sincere look made her stomach churn. "No one's controlling me. This is all me." His words hung heavy between them. He cupped her face, pulling her toward him, and pressed his lips to hers.

The kiss was urgent, filled with a desperation that shattered the walls she'd tried to build. She fought herself to resist, but her hands slipped into his hair, her body melting against his. She had missed him, missed this, and it was like her heart remembered all too well how to fit with his. Ava's senses were overwhelmed, her heart pounding in her chest. His lips trailed along her neck, leaving a trail of tingling sensations in their wake, evoking a soft moan that escaped her lips, a delicate echo in the night. A mixture of anger and frustration welled up within her, resenting the ease with which he awakened dormant emotions and desires.

But as his touch grew bolder, her mind fought back, like a flickering caution light, its bright flashes warning her not to lose herself again. She tried to pull back, but he held her close, his murmurs against her neck sending shivers down her spine. "I love you, Ava. I never stopped."

The words hit her hard, and for a moment, she let herself believe them, let herself imagine this was real. But logic clawed its way through, and she managed to push him back, panting, her mind screaming at her to stop before she lost herself.

"I can't do this, Peter." Her hands trembled as she kept him at arm's length.

"Why not? I could've lost you today, and that thought alone..." His words faltered, and he pulled her close again, lips grazing her neck as she shivered against him.

She forced herself to pull back, hating the ache in her chest as she did. "This isn't fair. Not to me, not to Katarina." Her heart screamed to give in, but her mind pushed her to resist. "Go back to her, Peter. You need to figure this out."

"I know." His gaze lingered, his fingers trailing down her arm before he pulled away. "Just … don't say anything yet. I need time to make things right."

He kissed her one last time, a slow, lingering kiss that left her reeling, then he slipped out of the tent, leaving her alone with her racing heart and a tangled mess of emotions.

As the silence closed in, Ava leaned back against her sleeping bag. Peter's words, his touch, lingered like an echo, each one stirring up emotions she thought she'd managed to bury. She pressed a hand to her lips, feeling the warmth left behind by his kiss, but already it was fading, replaced by a hollow ache.

Why did it still feel like this with Peter? Even after everything he'd put her through, she could still feel herself wanting to believe him, wanting to lose herself in his arms again.

But it couldn't be real. Maybe Peter needed closure.

25

THE LAST GOODBYE

The snow crunched beneath their boots, muffling their steps as they trekked deeper into the woods. Ava had once found beauty in the snow, but now she was sick of it. Sick of the cold seeping through every crack and seam, no matter how much she tried to warm herself. Her magic could fight the chill, but it drained her energy, and she knew she had to conserve what little strength she had left.

The sky stretched above them, a pale, oppressive gray. The gaunt, leafless trees clawed at the horizon, their long shadows coiling and dancing as the wind whispered through the branches. The scene felt endless, a desolate mirror to her own tangled thoughts.

"You're awfully quiet today." Gabriel said.

Ava glanced sideways, caught off guard. The night before dragged her thoughts into an endless spiral. "Sorry." She adjusted her scarf to hide her face.

Gabriel slowed his pace, his sharp gaze fixed on her. "Did you sleep okay?"

She hadn't. Her dreams had been haunted by saberwolves, Trudy's mocking laughter, and Peter's voice. A voice that shouldn't have been there but had felt so real. She shifted her gaze.

"What's on your mind?" he pressed.

Everything. Peter's late-night confession played on a loop in her mind, tangling with her memories of his laughter with Katarina earlier. Could it really have happened? Or had the Cimmerians planted the moment in her head to unnerve her? Doubt and hope wrestled for control, each tearing her apart.

"Nothing." She knew her evasiveness would annoy him, but she couldn't bring herself to explain. Not when she was fighting to keep the shame and confusion from overwhelming her.

Gabriel didn't push, but the silence that followed felt heavier than the snow beneath their feet.

The day dragged on, each hour blurring into the next as the group pressed forward. By the time they set up camp beneath a canopy of empty branches, Ava's mind was spinning, caught in a web of questions and fears. The glow of the evening fire felt remote, its warmth failing to touch the chill that clung to her chest.

Across the fire, Peter and Katarina sat close, their heads tilted together in easy conversation. Laughter sparked between them, bright and careless, as if the worry of the war didn't touch them. The pain in Ava's stomach intensified, becoming unbearable.

Gabriel slid closer to her. "Are you okay?"

She forced a nod, tearing her gaze from Peter. "Actually, I was thinking maybe you could help Thomas, Lance, and Gillian with the heart of stone. They could use some practice."

He frowned, studying her for a beat before nodding. "Sure." His concern lingered in his eyes, but he turned to the others.

As Gabriel guided the group through the technique, Ava tried to focus, but her mind refused to settle. The flickering firelight cast strange, shifting shadows that seemed to reflect her restless thoughts. Every laugh, every glance between Peter and Katarina felt like a knife, slicing deeper into her fragile composure.

She caught Ilya watching her from the other side of the flames, his face half-shadowed, a strange intensity in his gaze. For a moment, she thought he was looking at her, but his focus seemed distant, lost in the depths of the firelight. The flicker of shadows cast a harshness over his expression, a tension she hadn't noticed before.

Ilya shook his head. "Does it even matter? This heart of stone … it's just not enough. Havok's too strong. He'll see right through it."

Ava tensed, a ripple of unease washing over her as Ilya's words settled in. The fire crackled between them, but the others were silent, exchanging uncertain glances, discomfort etched into their faces. His defeatism hovered over her fragile resolve like a dark cloud.

Gabriel's face hardened. "We're doing what we can, Ilya. It may not seem like much, but it's a defense. A way to prepare."

Ilya let out a hollow chuckle, his lips twisting into a cynical smile as he shook his head. "If you say so. Feels like we're fooling ourselves. You can't trick someone like Havok. Not for long."

Frustration knotted in Ava's chest, mingling with a pang of sympathy. She understood his fear. Havok was powerful, relentless. "But we have to try."

Ilya's eyes flashed, a bitter edge darkening his gaze. "Alena tried and look where that got her."

"Ilya…" Katarina reached out, taking his hand in hers, her face soft with understanding.

But Ilya pulled away with an annoyed sigh as he rose and walked off into the shadows.

A heavy sigh escaped Katarina's lips. "He's … just having a bad night."

They all were, but as Gabriel continued the training session, dread coiled in Ava's stomach, like Ilya's words had seeded a darkness that wouldn't leave her. What if the heart of stone really wasn't enough? What if Havok's control was inevitable?

The questions hammered away at her mind. A pulsing headache forced her to her tent, where she lay in the dark, exhaustion dulling her senses but unable to quiet the confusion churning inside her.

The thin fabric of the tent did nothing against the powerful winds. Ava's breath misted in the lantern's dim light. She couldn't stop replaying last night in her mind. Peter's words, the feel of his hand on hers. It felt surreal, as if it had been a half-remembered dream. She brushed it off, tried to tell herself it was nothing. Just one night. Just one mistake.

But the crunch of footsteps in the snow sent a jolt through her. The footsteps stopped outside, and her pulse quickened.

"Ava?" Peter's whisper slipped through the night, low and almost pleading.

She gripped her blanket, willing herself to stay strong. "Go away."

"Please, Ava."

Against her better judgment, she unzipped the tent. He slipped inside, the small space was stifling as his gaze met hers. Desperation flickered in his eyes, and her heart betrayed her, stirring with an ache she couldn't suppress.

He leaned in, but she turned her head away. "What do you want?"

"I needed to see you. Last night … it felt like I finally understood how much you mean to me." His eyes held hers, full of a longing she had almost forgotten.

She swallowed, pulling her blanket tighter, trying to keep some distance between them. "Peter … no."

He reached for her hand, his touch warm against her cold fingers. "But I feel like I'm just going through the motions with Katarina. It's *you* I want."

A soft ache pulsed in her chest as she felt her resolve slipping. His gaze was intense, and she hated how her heart responded to it, stirring up hope she had tried to bury. But a small, persistent voice in the back of her mind whispered of Gabriel, of his kindness, his faithful support, sparking a twinge of guilt inside her.

"Peter, you have to make a choice. You can't keep doing this."

"I know. I promise, I'll talk to her tomorrow." He inched closer, his hand moving to her cheek. "But tonight, I needed to be near you."

She closed her eyes, feeling his hand against her face, letting herself lean into it for a moment. But as his lips brushed against hers, guilt surged, a warning flashing in her mind.

She pushed him back. "I can't do this, Peter." She forced herself to look away, shame burning in her chest like a hot coal.

His face fell. "Why? I'll make it right, Ava. I promise."

As he slipped out of the tent, Ava sat back, her heart pounding. The guilt surged stronger now, not only for Katarina but for Gabriel, who had stood by her without expectation. She knew she was letting herself fall for Peter's words again, letting herself be pulled back into the past when she should be focusing on the present. But Gabriel … he was so calm, so safe, and yet, she wasn't sure she deserved that kind of devotion.

The next morning dawned bleak and gray, the air thick with an oppressive stillness that mirrored Ava's exhaustion. Her limbs felt leaden as she trudged along with the group, her gaze fixed on the ground to avoid catching sight of Peter and Katarina. Yet, her eyes betrayed her, flickering to where they walked close, speaking in hushed tones that sent a sharp pang through her chest.

They laughed together, their voices soft but intimate, as if nothing had changed, as if Peter's whispered words in her tent the night before had been nothing but a cruel fantasy. Frustration and anger bubbled beneath her surface, but doubt and confusion held her back, tangling her emotions into a suffocating knot. She clenched her fists, fighting the urge to confront him right then and there. Not here. Not now.

By the time dinner ended and the others retreated to their tents, Ava couldn't hold it in any longer. She approached Peter, her steps heavy, and gestured for him to follow her into the woods.

He hesitated but complied, his brow furrowed with confusion. The crunch of their boots on the snow was the only sound as they moved farther from camp. Once they were far enough that the glow of the campfire disappeared behind the trees, Ava stopped, crossing her arms.

"You wanted to talk?" Peter asked. The confusion in his tone fueled her anger, her emotions teetering on the edge of control.

Ava's fingers dug into her arms as she took a deep breath. "Why are you doing this?"

"Doing what?" He looked bewildered.

"You came to me the past two nights. You said you missed me, that you wanted to be with me." Her voice trembled, a mixture of hurt and anger spilling over. "And then you go back to her as if nothing happened."

Confusion etched his face as his hands lifted in a defensive gesture. "Ava … I don't know what you're talking about. I haven't come to your tent."

The words struck her like a physical blow, her breath catching in her throat. "You're lying." But even as she said it, the truth clawed at the edges of her mind, sharp and unrelenting. What if it hadn't been real? What if the Cimmerians had planted the memory to torment her, to shatter her focus?

"I'm not lying," he said. "Ava, what's going on? What are you talking about?"

She turned away, her vision blurring with tears. The betrayal, whether real or imagined, stung, scraping against the already raw wound in her heart. She couldn't stand to look at him any longer, couldn't bear the thought of being vulnerable again. Her steps quickened, the snow crunching louder beneath her boots as Peter's voice trailed after her.

"Ava, wait! What are you—"

She didn't stop, her shoulders stiff as tears slipped down her cheeks. The forest stretched ahead, vast and dark, as the night closed in around her. The icy air burned her lungs with every ragged breath, and the snow's endless expanse seemed to swallow her whole. She dropped to her knees, her body trembling as she pressed her hands into the frozen ground. Her sobs broke free, raw and unrestrained, each one heavy with confusion, anger, and heartbreak.

She'd let her guard down. She'd let herself hope. And for what? To be shattered all over again?

Through the blur of her tears, a faint light appeared ahead, soft and beckoning. It floated like a distant star, casting a warm glow that cut through the darkness. Her legs wobbled as she struggled to rise, but her curiosity pushed her toward the light.

But as she neared, it dissolved like mist, fading into nothingness. A thick, shadowy fog swirled in its place, cold and suffocating, wrapping around her like a vice. The air grew heavy, pressing against her chest, and her vision blurred as the darkness closed in.

Ava tried to fight it, but her body betrayed her, collapsing into the snow. The icy cold, so intense it pierced through her clothes, left her skin tingling as her heart slowed to a crawl, each beat a faint echo in her ears. The world tilted, slipping further and further away, until only the shadowy fog remained, pulling her into its depths.

26

DROWNING

When Ava opened her eyes, snowflakes fell around her as she lay sprawled on her back in the dense, snow-covered forest. The air was sharp and biting, stinging her exposed skin as her breath came in short bursts. Shadows stretched long and jagged between the gaunt trees, their bony forms casting eerie patterns on the pristine snow. She tried to summon warmth to her fingertips, but nothing happened. The comforting heat of her powers, the energy that usually wrapped around her like a shield, was gone. Panic prickled up her spine as she struggled to sit up, glancing around wildly.

The campsite was gone. No tents, no firelight, no voices. Just an endless expanse of snow-covered trees stretching into the gray void.

How far did I walk? Did I run away again?

"P-Peter?" she stammered, her voice shaky from the cold. She cursed herself. Why did she always think of him first? "Gabriel?" Her words echoed, swallowed by the unyielding stillness of the woods. The quiet was heavy, the only sound the muffled crunch of snow under her boots as she trudged onward. Her breath misted in the frigid air.

She stumbled, her legs heavy and unsteady, each step piercing the dead quiet like a warning. The gray sky above shifted as clouds parted, revealing a star-strewn canvas. Moonlight spilled across the landscape, turning the snow into a shimmering expanse of silver. The light offered a faint reprieve, guiding her to the edge of a frozen lake. The surface sparkled like a million tiny diamonds, smooth and flawless, extending out to the horizon. She clutched a nearby tree for balance, her breaths ragged and shallow.

"Beautiful, isn't it?"

The voice slithered through the air, low and taunting, freezing her in place. Her stomach dropped as she spun around, her heart pounding. There, emerging from the shadows, stood the figure she had feared most.

Havok.

His ghostly pale face gleamed under the moonlight, his black eyes glittering with a predatory gleam. His long, dark hair framed his face like a shadowed veil, draping over his shoulders in sharp contrast to the snow around him. Every inch of him exuded cold malice, an aura so oppressive it seemed to chill the air further.

Her instincts screamed for her to run, but her legs refused to move. Her fists clenched, shaking with fury, but no power answered her call. She was entirely exposed.

"The way the moon shines across the lake," he murmured, "the snow sparkling like liquid diamonds ... it's all so breathtaking, isn't it? Just like you." He took a step forward, his gaze gleaming with something darker. "You'd make such a strong Enchanter ... if you chose to join us."

She forced herself to stand straighter, though her body trembled with equal parts anger and fear. "I'll never join you. I'll fight you until the end."

A flicker of annoyance crossed his face, but it smoothed back into a cool, condescending smile. "Perhaps. But you will join me, Ava. In time. Even Moira knows it."

A knot of dread tightened in her stomach as his words sank in. *He had been there*. Watching, hidden, observing their every move. "You seem to know a lot. Spying on us?"

He chuckled, a low, hollow sound that sent shivers racing down her spine. "An excellent job you've done so far. Taking out Trudy, battling saberwolves, healing your comrades … impressive. Truly." His slow, mocking applause echoed over the frozen lake. "But Trudy was one of my best. And your Aureole? They talk about you like you're already a lost cause."

She stiffened, his words digging into her like claws. "You don't know anything about them."

"Oh, but I do," Havok purred. "I see how they watch you. Wondering. Waiting for the day you turn on them. Wouldn't it be easier to give in? To join the ones who *truly* understand you? Ones who wouldn't abandon you to die in the snow?"

"You can't scare me," she said.

"Can't I?" He inched closer. "Look around you, Ava. No powers, no allies. Just ice and darkness. How long can you keep this up?" His tone dropped, smooth and venomous. "Perhaps you simply need a little persuasion."

An invisible force gripped her throat, cutting off her air. Her hands clawed at her neck as panic surged, her lungs burning. Havok's expression remained calm, his hand twitching as she rose from the ground, her boots dangling above the ice.

"Such a shame," he mused. "I thought you had potential. But you're nothing without me."

With a flick of his wrist, the force released her, and she plummeted, crashing onto the frozen lake. The ice splintered beneath her, the impact jarring her to the core. Her legs buckled with a sickening crunch. White-hot agony flared through her legs. She gripped her knees, fingers slipping as blood trickled onto the fractured ice.

Havok's laughter rang out, hollow and cruel, as she lay gasping for air.

"Join me, Ava," he murmured, stepping closer, his shadow looming over her broken form. "No more pain. No more betrayal. Just power."

Her vision blurred with tears, but she met his gaze. "I'd rather die than stand by you."

"Brave words," he sneered, "for someone who's barely standing."

The ice groaned, splintering beneath her, and in a final, jarring moment, it gave way. She plunged into the freezing water, the cold stabbing into her like a thousand knives. The current pulled her under, her limbs sluggish and numb as she fought to the surface.

Havok's mocking voice slipped into her mind like a shadow. *How long can you keep fighting, Ava?*

Her vision darkened, the moonlight above fading into the void. But even as the cold consumed her, fragments of faces flickered in her mind—Gabriel, Gillian, Lance. Promises she had made, a purpose she couldn't abandon. *Not like this.*

27

BLACKOUT

Kick! A voice erupted in her mind, as clear and forceful as her own heartbeat. Ava jolted, blinking through the freezing darkness, the shock giving her a jolt of focus.

You can do this! The voice urged. For a brief, surreal moment, Ava thought it was her mother. But it wasn't. *Savina.* She could almost feel her presence. *Come on, Ava! Be strong! Kick!*

Gritting her teeth, Ava forced her legs to kick, though each movement felt like fighting through quicksand. Her legs were stiff, numb, almost beyond feeling except for the intense, bone-deep cold that had swallowed her. Every cell in her body ached to give in to the freezing depths, but Savina's voice rang out again, sharp as a whip.

You've got to get out of this!

She pushed harder, her arms cutting through the icy water, her mind clinging to each small command. Her feet kicked with whatever strength they could muster. Her chest felt like it was burning and collapsing all at once, but then a flicker of light danced above her, shifting through the cracks in the ice.

You're almost there!

With a final burst of desperate energy, Ava surged upward. Her head broke through the surface, the air slicing into her lungs like knives. She gasped, the raw, dry winter air tearing at her throat. Shaking, she dragged her arms onto the ice, the chill of it pressing into her skin like needles.

Pull yourself out! Get out of the water!

Her frantic gaze swept the vast, silent lake. Still shaking, she heaved herself onto the ice, collapsing on her back. Her body convulsed with shivers as she lay staring up at the stars, each breath clouding above her like tiny ghosts. Her hair was already stiffening in the cold, tiny crystals forming along the wet strands.

Get off the ice!

Groaning, Ava crawled, each movement a raw struggle, pulling herself across the ice. She reached the snow-covered bank, fingers digging into the soft powder until she felt the solid grip of a nearby tree. She clung to it, gasping, her mind dazed and foggy.

Had she wandered off again? She couldn't remember. All she knew was Havok had found her … and left her for dead.

The soft, cold snow around her offered a strange sense of comfort. She let her head sink down, closing her eyes to the stars.

"She's freezing cold!" A familiar voice, raw and shaken, cut through the fog that had consumed Ava. The words felt distant, like they were traveling through water to reach her.

Her eyelids fluttered open with immense effort, revealing a blur of faces above her. Warm orange light flickered from a lantern nearby, casting shaky shadows across the worried expressions hovering over her. Yet the warmth didn't touch her. Not the light, not their concern. Ice still clung to her, gnawing at her limbs. Her legs were heavy and lifeless, as though they were still submerged in the frozen water. A shudder of fear rippled through her, weak but insistent, making her chest ache with the effort.

She tried to move her arms, but they didn't respond. Her entire body seemed caught in the clutches of the cold, the numbness crawling higher, wrapping her stomach in a vice-like grip. A strangled noise escaped her throat, more instinct than conscious effort.

"Ava, can you hear me?" Gabriel's voice cut through her haze, rough and urgent. "Talk to me!" Warm hands cradled her head, the contrast against her frozen skin startling enough to make her blink. The intensity in his gaze, so close, his eyes burning into hers. For a fleeting moment, her mind scrambled for clarity. Was this real? Had the encounter with Havok been a nightmare? If so, why couldn't she feel her body?

The cold surged higher, choking her breath, squeezing her chest until it felt like she was drowning in the frozen lake all over again. She tried to speak. "I-I…"

"Stay with me, Ava! Keep watching me!" His crystal-blue eyes locked onto hers, unwavering, filled with a fear that mirrored her own. He wasn't just trying to reach her. He was *anchoring* her, holding her tethered as the numbness pulled her further into the void.

"She's slipping into a coma," Savina said, panic lacing each word.

"Then do something! Heal her!"

The voices around her started to warp, stretching into echoes as the edges of her awareness blurred. Her vision darkened at the corners, the flickering lantern light fading until only the glow in Gabriel's eyes remained, a piercing beacon in the encroaching blackness.

The darkness swallowed her whole.

Heat draped over Ava as she opened her eyes, adjusting to the dim light filtering through a narrow window. Her body felt unnaturally stiff, and as her senses sharpened, she took in her surroundings: three single beds lined the walls, each adorned with identical, neatly made covers. Beside the beds stood small tables cluttered with glass bottles, cotton balls, and gleaming medical tools. She flexed her fingers and toes, then froze. *Where am I?*

Sitting up slowly, Ava swung her legs over the edge of the bed, surprised by the steadiness beneath her. There was no pain. No frostbitten skin. No fractured bones. The memory of the icy lake rushed back, chilling her all over again. Her heart raced as she scanned the room, searching for clues.

Was it a dream?

She crossed to the window, pressing a hand to the cold glass. The breathtaking scene outside unfolded before her: rolling green hills stretched endlessly under a cerulean sky, while snowcapped mountains pierced the horizon, their peaks glistening with the morning sun. Tulips of every color blanketed the landscape below, their vibrance at odds with the cold still clinging to her bones. A weak sun hung low in the sky, casting a soft glow. The air seemed impossibly serene. Too serene.

This can't be real.

A soft creak caught her attention. She spun around, her back pressing to the window.

Melissa.

Relief and disbelief flooded her chest as Melissa barreled toward her, arms outstretched. Ava bolted forward, meeting her halfway. The hug was firm, almost overwhelming, but its sincerity grounded her, tethering her to the present.

"Melissa…" Ava whispered.

"I was so scared we'd lost you," Melissa whispered, pulling back with a trembling smile. Tears welled in her eyes. "Havok pulled you from the lake. He found you in time. I thought …"

Havok?

Ava's relief soured into confusion. "He … saved me?"

Melissa nodded. "It's unbelievable, isn't it?" She hugged Ava again, her grip almost crushing. "You're here. You're safe. We're safe."

Safe? Ava's stomach churned. None of this made sense. "No … Havok dropped me. He's the one who—"

Melissa furrowed her brows. "No. Peter chased after you, and you fell in the lake. Peter just … left you there. But it's fine. He's dead now. It was so satisfying to kill him."

Ava recoiled, her blood running cold. "What?" Melissa's words were so casual, so jarring, that she couldn't process them.

"Yes! We finally defeated them, Ava. We can all live free, now. You, me, Lance, Gillian, Thomas, and Jeremy."

"What do you mean 'defeated' them?"

"Savina, Aaron, Gustav … all of them." Melissa's expression shifted into something colder. "Well, except Gabriel."

Her heart slammed against her ribs. "Gabriel?"

"Oh, he's good," Melissa sneered, her tone mocking. "He's got you wrapped around his finger, doesn't he? Did you really think he cared about you?"

Tears pricked Ava's eyes as a painful knot grew in her stomach. "Stop. You're lying."

A predatory look took over her face, distorting her smile. "You got me." Her blonde hair darkened as her features sharpened into something cruel and unfamiliar. Her voice deepened, morphing into a chilling purr. "I'm Eve. You really are easy to fool, aren't you?"

Ava backed toward the bed, her chest tightening as panic took hold.

"Gabriel doesn't care about you. He's one of us, Ava. Always has been. He loves me."

"No. You're lying."

Eve's laughter sent shivers down her spine. Images flooded Ava's mind. Gabriel walked through the ruined village, his face grim, his eyes vacant. He gave cold orders, ignoring the pleas of villagers as fires consumed everything around him.

"What-what was that?" Ava clutched her head.

"The truth. He used you. And now he's back where he belongs. With me."

"No," Ava hissed, fury rising despite the fear clawing at her.

Eve tilted her head. "You're more like him than you realize. It's in your blood. You've killed for power, haven't you? Doesn't it feel good?"

"I'm nothing like you."

Eve stepped closer, her smile predatory. "You are. You feel it, too. The darkness inside you begging for freedom. It's only a matter of time. Join us, Ava. Embrace who you are."

Her gaze darted to the table beside her. A glint of metal caught her eye. A scalpel. Her fingers twitched, inching toward it as Eve drew nearer.

"I'll never join you," Ava growled, gripping the scalpel.

"You will." Eve laughed, the sound echoing through the small room.

Ava lunged, the scalpel plunging into Eve's abdomen.

Eve gasped, her eyes wide with shock. Blood bloomed against her dark clothing as she stumbled back, clutching the wound.

Ava darted for the door, her vision swimming. Each step grew heavier, her strength draining. Her breaths came in shallow gasps as the world around her rippled and distorted.

"You can't run, Ava," Eve called, her laughter cold and sharp. "You'll never escape."

The darkness closed in, swallowing Ava whole.

28

TEMPEST

The cold crept over Ava, locking her limbs in icy chains until she felt like a statue, entombed in frost. Movement was impossible. Even the sensation of her own body was slipping away, drowned under the relentless chill sinking deep into her bones. She was blind. Whether her eyes were closed or frozen shut, she couldn't tell. Her awareness was fading.

A faint, pleading whisper broke through the darkness. *Please wake up. Please. Ava, wake up.* The voice sounded urgent, the words like a lifeline anchoring her to consciousness.

With a start, Ava's eyes flew open. Snowflakes brushed her cheeks, dissolving as they touched her skin. She blinked up at snowy branches dusted in pale blue moonlight, casting shadows over a frozen lake below. The scene was serene, almost beautiful, yet a deep unease stirred within her. This place was tainted. *Havok's been here.* But how did she get here?

As she sat up, a cold realization sank into her mind: *What if the others are truly gone? What if I'm alone?* Eve's words echoed, whispering of Gabriel as a Cimmerian. Could it be true? Could he have deceived her all along? The idea sliced through her, leaving a wound that ached in the silence. And if he had betrayed her … did that mean everyone else was already lost?

Gritting her teeth, Ava pushed herself to her feet, snow crunching beneath her boots as she began to run. Each breath stung, the air burning cold against her skin. Time felt meaningless as the frigid air gnawed at her strength. She stumbled, legs shaking from exhaustion, and leaned against a tree to catch her breath. *What did Havok do to me?* She pressed a hand to her chest, feeling the rapid, desperate beat of her heart.

The quiet of the woods shattered. A faint crunch of snow nearby. She stiffened, scanning the shadows as another crunch sounded, closer this time.

"Ava?" A familiar voice pierced the silence.

Her breath hitched as she turned, her heart both hopeful and wary. "Jeremy?"

He stepped forward, his sandy blond hair falling over his collar, his topaz eyes catching the moonlight. Relief warmed her chest, yet a cold prickle remained. His expression was strangely blank, devoid of the usual warmth.

"Are you okay?" he asked.

"Jeremy … why are you here?"

"I came looking for you. They said you'd be here," His eyes met hers, but something was off.

They? Her gut twisted.

"Why are you shivering?" Jeremy moved even closer. "Can't you make yourself warm? You'll die out here if you don't. Here, let me help." He reached for her hand, his smile disarmingly gentle.

Hesitating, she extended her shaking hand, but his touch felt wrong, like a fire that burned instead of comforted, needles of heat prickling up her arm.

"Why are you out here?" he asked again, impatience creeping into his tone. His grip tightened. "You don't belong in the cold. Why aren't you with us? Let me take you back. It's safe there."

"No." She tried to pull her hand free, her heart hammering with the sudden dread. "This … this isn't you."

"You're confused, Ava. This is no place for you." He tugged her forward, his fingers clamped like a vise around hers.

"What happened to Caprington? How did you escape?" She dug her heels into the snow.

"I didn't escape. You don't understand, Ava. Savina and Colden. They were in the wrong. Havok made me see that." His face hardened, a strange light in his eyes. "We've been deceived, all of us. Ephemerals—*they're* the true enemy."

Her stomach dropped as he looked at her, his eyes glinting with a malice she had never seen in Jeremy before. "Jeremy … you don't believe that. You know Ephemerals aren't the enemy."

His face darkened, his voice filling with anger. "You're so naïve, Ava. All those years, and you still don't understand." He released her hand, glaring. "Pathetic. You never trusted me."

This wasn't Jeremy. Her heart stopped as his eyes shifted, a bottomless, inky blackness replaced the topaz hue she knew. Panic clawed at her as her breath quickened. "You're not Jeremy."

His face morphed into a cruel grin, his gaze cold and lifeless. "Took you long enough to figure that out. I have his powers now."

The snow rose around them, whirling into a violent storm, jagged ice slicing past her skin. She shielded her face, her breaths shallow. "Stop!"

A dark laugh rumbled from within the storm, like a voice in her ear. "Join me, Ava." His face contorted, Jeremy's features melting into Havok's cruel smile. "It's in your blood. I know you *feel* it."

She clung to a nearby tree as the blizzard intensified, wind ripping branches and ice into the maelstrom. Her hands burned as she gripped the rough bark, blood seeping from her scraped knuckles. "Please!" she choked out.

"You could end this," Havok taunted. "Join me, and all of this pain, this suffering will end."

"I'd rather die!"

He let out a disappointed sigh. "So be it."

The storm intensified, uprooting the tree she clung to. She was thrown, her body slamming into the ground, her vision blurring as she hit the frozen earth. Havok loomed above her, his dark cloak casting a shadow across her battered form.

"You're strong, Ava, but this resistance is meaningless."

She pushed herself up, her body shaking as blood trickled from cuts on her face and hands. "We don't need you. We're powerful without you."

A cold smile spread across his face. "And yet, here you are. Alone. Weak. Without anyone left to lead you." His gaze was piercing, like ice settling over her.

"Savina's not gone." *This has to be a trick.*

Havok's expression darkened. "She is. Soon, you'll see that you have no choice but to join me, or waste away in suffering." His eyes glinted with satisfaction. "Your mother knew it would come to this. She knew I would own you."

"You will never own my soul." Her body shook from the cold, but she held her ground, her teeth clenched to stop their chattering.

He shrugged, his smile widening. "Believe what you will. You'll come to see the truth." With a final dark laugh, he vanished, leaving her alone in the stillness of the forest.

The icy wind surged again, hurling sharp pellets of hail against her skin like knives. She shielded herself, curling up against the onslaught, until a searing blow to her head sent her reeling back into darkness.

I'm right here, a voice murmured, somehow calm amidst her pain. It sounded desperate, almost pleading. *Come back to me, Ava.*

29

THE THREE ACTS

Stay strong, Ava. Don't give up. A soft, pleading voice echoed in her mind, reaching through the heavy darkness surrounding her. Ava clung to it, savoring its calm, desperate tones. She couldn't place the voice, yet something about it felt safe, like a forgotten memory surfacing from deep within. It filled her with a flicker of hope, a gentle warmth against the cold emptiness that threatened to swallow her whole.

Please. I need you to hold on.

Ava found herself kneeling in a snow-covered forest, utterly alone. Above, thick clouds raced across the sky, parting to reveal slivers of midnight. The faint moonlight cast an eerie glow through the branches, illuminating the desolation around her. She tried to sit up, wincing as sharp pain stabbed through her scraped palms and blistered face. Her fists throbbed, the raw skin stretched tight and raw. She exhaled, watching her breath cloud in the frigid air, yet her body felt warm. Reaching out, she tried to summon water or heal herself. But still nothing happened. No power. The biting cold chilled her to the core, stealing her strength with every ragged inhale.

Get up. Run toward the daylight, another voice, sharp and insistent, demanded.

Ava's head jerked up, recognizing Savina. *Savina's still alive … she's reaching me.* Hope flickered. Gripping the tree beside her, she pulled herself to her feet, her heartbeat erratic, almost sluggish.

Run! Savina urged.

Ava lurched forward, clutching at branches as she staggered through the snow. Her legs wobbled, almost collapsing beneath her, and her lungs burned with each shallow breath. Every step felt heavier, her heart pounding a dull, relentless beat in her ears. Dizziness crashed over her, and she stumbled, slumping against a tree for support.

Squinting through the branches, her heart froze as she saw the forest open up into a cliff. The blazing fire cast ominous shadows on the snow as cloaked figures gathered around it in a circle. A tall stake loomed at the center, stark in the pale light. A faint glow illuminated the horizon, as the sky shifted to a deep, foreboding orange.

Ava pressed herself against the tree as the Cimmerians laughed and danced around the fire. Panic gripped her chest as she scanned her surroundings. There was no escape without alerting them. She glanced behind, considering retreat, but Savina's voice pushed her forward. *Is it really Savina? Or is this a trap?*

A hand seized her shoulder, and she jerked around, eyes wide.

"We're waiting for you." Xavier's low voice curled through the frigid air, his crooked smile as cold as his grip. He leaned in, his breath hot on her cheek.

Ava wrenched herself back, but he tightened his hold, his fingers digging into her arm. "You'll be waiting forever."

Xavier chuckled, his fingers pressing into her jaw, forcing her to meet his gaze. "We know how this ends, Ava. You belong with us." His hand lifted, brushing away a strand of hair from her face, his gaze burning with a twisted desire. "I thought I preferred your blonde friend, but you … you might change my mind."

Her disgust flared, and she kneed him hard. He stumbled back, a growl escaping his lips.

Ava bolted along the edge of the cliff, ducking between trees. Branches whipped her face, and her lungs seared, but she pushed on, her heart pounding as she heard him closing in. Suddenly, darkness swallowed her, thick as ink. She couldn't see, but Xavier's hands clamped down on her shoulders, dragging her down into the snow. She struggled, her muffled scream lodged in her throat, desperate to stay hidden from the Cimmerians below. The darkness lifted, and he pinned her beneath him with a cruel smile.

"You should watch this," he hissed, hauling her to her knees and holding her in place, forcing her to look down at the fire below. Two towering Cimmerians dragged a slender, blonde woman toward the stake, her face pale and terrified.

"Melissa…" Her voice cracked, dread flooding her veins. *No, this can't be real.*

She struggled against Xavier's grip, but his hand clamped over her mouth, silencing her. "This is the best part," he murmured, his breath warm against her ear, a sick grin stretching across his face.

Below, Melissa's pleas echoed through the clearing as the men bound her to the stake. Flames began to lick at the wood, casting jagged shadows across her face. Her eyes met Ava's, wide with terror, before the fire consumed her feet. Her piercing scream filled the still dawn, raw and unrelenting, tearing into Ava's mind like a knife.

"Where's the fearless Ava we all know and love?" Xavier mocked.

The scream faded, and Ava's eyes snapped open. Melissa's limp, charred body hung against the stake, thin wisps of smoke curling around her. Ava's chest heaved with a strangled sob, but Xavier's hand silenced her once more.

"Oh, don't worry. It's almost your turn."

Desperation surged within her, fierce and wild. She slammed her feet into the ground, jerking backward with all her strength, forcing him against a tree. Snow rained down as the branches shook, but he trapped her between his legs.

His breath brushed her neck, his voice a venomous whisper. "Relax." His lips brushed her shoulder as his hand slid along her arm.

Her skin crawled. Rage bubbled up inside her, and she clamped her jaw shut.

"I said relax." With a brutal yank, he ripped her arm, sending a wave of pain through her shoulder and a sickening pop. White-hot agony filled her vision, and he chuckled, his mouth close to her ear. "Keep struggling, and I'll take your other arm too."

Her fury ignited, a burning need to retaliate, to hurt him. She wanted to drown him in the icy lake, rip his head from his body, anything to make him suffer.

"Oh look, act two is about to start."

She wriggled enough to see below, where two Cimmerians were dragging Jeremy toward the fire. *Not Jeremy…* Her mind reeled, her heart hammering. Was this real or another one of Havok's tricks? She bit her lip, bracing herself for the screams.

When the silence settled again, she opened her eyes. Jeremy's charred, lifeless form slumped against the stake, smoke coiling around him. Ava shuddered, bile rising as tears pricked her eyes. She couldn't break. Not now. Not here.

"Time for act three," Xavier whispered. He jerked her to her feet, his fingers biting into her wrist. "Shame you won't join us. You and I … we could have had some fun. Like Melissa and I did."

Revulsion twisted her stomach, and she choked back her rage. "You're a sick bastard."

He smirked, shoving her toward two towering men who yanked her to the stake. With her back against the frigid wood, they tied her up. Her gaze fell on the charred remains at her feet. Burnt hair, brittle and blackened, caught her eye. Nausea rolled over her, threatening to pull her under.

"Here are the others," someone announced, as they dragged Gillian, Lance, and Thomas forward.

Gillian sobbed as they secured her to the stake beside Ava, her eyes wide and panicked. "Don't do this," she cried.

"Don't give in, Gillian," Ava urged. "Hold on. This isn't real."

"But what if it is?" Thomas murmured, his gaze hollow and distant.

Sorcha stepped into view, her hood pulled back to reveal a cascade of red hair and a cold, calculating smile. She leaned close, her eyes narrowing. "Just say the word, Ava, and this all ends. I see us becoming … good friends," she purred.

Ava glared. "Not a chance."

Sorcha's smile widened as she motioned to a nearby Cimmerian. He held a torch, flame flickering in his hand as he touched it to the base of the stake. Fire crept up, licking at the wood. Ava felt its first bite, searing against her legs. She refused to scream. The heat spread, scorching her skin, crawling up her body in painful waves.

Stay strong, the voice in her mind urged. But as the flames reached her chest, her strength faltered, her head growing heavy, and her body fell limp, overcome by the searing pain and darkness.

30

DECISIONS

I know you're still in there. Come back to us.

The voice, a gentle whisper in the howling storm of her pain, resonated through the fog of her mind, each word a beacon of hope. Ava clung to it, the voice pulling her, fragile but persistent, toward something beyond this darkness. She fought to focus, feeling it capture her, giving her a direction in the vast, spinning emptiness.

Come back, Ava. We need you … I need you.

Long after the fire had faded to ash, Ava drifted in and out of consciousness, the agony pinning her to the frozen ground. Her skin, raw and seared, welcomed the biting chill of the snow. It was the only relief she had as it numbed the worst of the agony. When the first rays of dawn pierced through the trees, she squinted, half-blinded by the light that felt too bright, too harsh against the lingering darkness around her.

Afraid to look, she forced herself to remain still. She didn't dare turn and see the bodies she feared would be left charred and crumpled behind her. *How am I even alive?* Havok's torment, a persistent ache that pulsed in time with her heartbeat, invaded every inch of her being. Each shallow breath was painful, and her dislocated arm sent bolts of agony up her shoulder as she shifted, forcing herself up enough to see her surroundings.

Just a little further. You can do it. Do it for Melissa and Jeremy. And your Aureole, the voice whispered in her mind, coaxing her back to life.

But they're all dead, she thought. *Everyone is gone.*

She tried to summon even the faintest flicker of her powers, a drop of water, anything to soothe her wounds. But nothing came. All she managed was a shallow melt in the snow beneath her fingers, the water trickling down, cold but useless, mocking her helplessness. *Home.* The thought filled her with longing. *I want home.* She thought of her father's comforting presence. She thought of Gabriel, and the unexpected ache surprised her with its force, how much she missed him. But as reality sank back in, the thought echoed: *He's my enemy now, and everyone else is gone. Everyone is gone.*

The crunch of footsteps approached, slow and deliberate. Her heart thudded as a shadow fell over her. She barely had the strength to roll onto her back before a rough hand seized her, flipping her with a sharp jerk that sent pain lancing through her entire body. She gritted her teeth, but a small whimper escaped as she looked up and saw a familiar, ice-cold gaze fixed on her.

Sorcha stood above her, her green eyes glinting with cruel satisfaction, her red hair a sharp contrast against the white snow. Ava's heart sank as she realized they weren't alone. Dark shapes gathered around them, Cimmerians surrounding her in a silent circle.

"Please," Ava choked out. "If you're going to kill me … just do it quickly."

Sorcha threw her head back with a laugh, sharp and cruel. "Kill you? Oh, Ava." She knelt until her face was level with Ava's. "We wouldn't waste such potential. I'll give you one last chance to accept our offer." She tilted her head, her smile widening. "Will you join us?"

"I'll never be one of you."

Sorcha's grin didn't falter. "Never say never." She straightened, giving a small nod, and two hooded Cimmerians stepped forward, dragging a figure toward them, their face hidden beneath a dark cloth.

They ripped the cloth from the mystery person, and her stomach churned.

Her father looked at her, his face ashen with terror.

"Dad?" Her voice cracked, her pulse hammering as panic surged through her. *No. They can't have him too.*

"Ava, I'm sorry," he gasped. "They caught me … they've kept me here, waiting for you."

A sharp slap from Sorcha sent him to his knees, and Ava's body tensed as Sorcha's fingers pressed into his shoulder, making him wince. "It's simple," Sorcha sneered. "Say the word, Ava, and he lives." She leaned down, her breath warm against Ava's ear. "Just one word."

Ava's mind raced, her pulse pounding with frantic desperation as her father writhed in pain. "No… please!"

She struggled against the Cimmerians holding her down. "I'll do it. Just don't hurt him!"

Sorcha raised an eyebrow, her face a mask of mock pity. "Is that a yes, then?" She leaned closer, her whisper felt like poison seeping into Ava's soul. "All it takes is one word."

The sight of her father, bound and suffering, tore through her, unraveling her resolve. *I'd do it,* she realized with horror. *I'd do anything to save him.* She opened her mouth, the word forming on her lips, ready to surrender herself if it meant saving him. And she had nothing left. Everyone was gone.

But as she was about to speak, a familiar voice broke through her thoughts, urgent and pleading. *Don't give yourself to them! This is a test!*

Ava hesitated. *Could this all be a trick?*

Her father cried out again, the sound of his pain a visceral, raw wound in her mind.

Sorcha tilted her head, a knowing smile on her face. "What's it going to be, Ava?"

The voice echoed once more, firmer now, like a hand reaching out to pull her from the edge. *Don't! This isn't real!*

She closed her mouth, the answer dying on her lips. Her breath hitched as the figures before her began to fade, their shapes blurring and softening, dissolving like smoke in the wind. The Cimmerians, her father, Sorcha—all of them melted into mist. The snow around her seemed to vanish, leaving silence.

She slumped back, her entire body weak and trembling. Relief washed over her, mingling with bone-deep exhaustion. She had been so close to breaking, to surrendering, but the voice, the voice had saved her.

31

WAKING UP

Awareness crept back, like daylight breaking through heavy storm clouds. The world returned to Ava in fragments, sharp and blinding. Sunlight streamed through a nearby window, slanting across her bed in golden beams that seemed too bright, too warm, for the cold numbness spreading through her body. She blinked, wincing as the light sent a sharp stab of pain through her skull. Turning away, her surroundings blurred into shifting shapes and colors before settling into clarity. She was in a simple, rustic cabin with a fire in the hearth crackling.

Her fingers twitched. They moved with ease, a stark contrast to the searing pain she remembered. A strange calmness settled over her. No pain, just a deep, aching fatigue that rooted her to the mattress. Her body felt stiff and foreign, as though she'd been frozen for days. Even breathing felt strange, shallow and disconnected, like her lungs weren't quite hers.

She turned her head, the motion straining muscles that protested the movement. Beside her, a familiar figure sat hunched over a worn, weathered book. Natalia. Her olive skin glowed in the soft light, her hazel eyes scanning the pages. One leg was pulled to her chest, the other tucked beneath her on the chair.

As if sensing her gaze, Natalia froze. Her head shot up, her wide eyes locking with Ava's. "Ava!" Natalia cried as her face broke into a radiant smile as the book slipped from her grasp. "You're awake. It's so good to see those eyes of yours."

Ava stared at her, the sight sending a sharp ache through her chest. Relief and joy were etched into Natalia's face, but Ava couldn't bring herself to believe it. *No. This is another of Havok's tricks.* She turned her head away, her throat tightening. Natalia wouldn't look at her like that. Not with tenderness. Not with care.

"I'll get Savina. I'll be back soon, I promise."

"Don't bother." Ava's words were brittle, her voice raspy and weak. "Whatever you're trying to make me believe, I'm not playing along. You know my answer."

Natalia hesitated, her brows knitting in confusion. "Ava, it really is me." But before Ava could respond, Natalia hurried out the door.

Panic bubbled in Ava's chest. She had to get out. Forcing her arms to move, she pushed herself upright, ignoring the screaming protest of her stiff muscles. Her legs swung off the bed, hitting the icy floor, but when she tried to stand, they buckled beneath her. Her knees hit the ground hard, sending a jolt of pain through her, but the rest of her body felt disconnected, as though she were moving through someone else's skin.

The door burst open, a rush of familiar voices flooding the room. Savina. Gabriel. Eric. Peter. Lance. Sean. Natalia. They crowded the space, their faces etched with a mixture of concern and relief. Ava froze, her pulse racing. *How do I know if any of this is real?*

She raised a trembling hand to stop them, but her arm gave out, and she crumpled to the floor once more. Before she could process the humiliation, strong arms lifted her, enveloping her in warmth. She stiffened, bracing herself for the illusion to shatter.

"It's me, Ava," a voice murmured, low and steady. Juniper and fresh air filled her senses. Gabriel.

Her gaze lifted, locking with his. His eyes were like the Caribbean Sea, endless and unshakable, but exhaustion lingered in the lines of his face. His hair was slightly disheveled, his beard thicker than usual, his entire being worn thin with worry. Something about him looked fragile, vulnerable in a way she'd never seen before.

"Place her back onto the bed," Savina instructed.

Gabriel carried her with careful ease, setting her down on the mattress as though she might break.

Ava flinched under his touch. "No!" She pushed against him, but her strength was laughable. "This isn't real. None of you are real."

Gabriel froze, pain flashing in his eyes. He stepped back as Savina approached, taking Ava's trembling hand in hers.

"How do you feel?" Savina asked.

"What … happened?" Her voice was hoarse, each word a painful rasp that felt like sandpaper on her throat.

"You were in a coma," Savina explained. "Peter and Gabriel found you in the forest, hypothermic and unconscious. I healed the cold's effects, but something repelled any further healing, and you didn't wake. For almost two weeks, we watched over you, hoping you'd return."

"Two … weeks?" Ava's breath caught as she scanned the room, her gaze darting between the familiar faces. *Is this real?* Her fingers curled into the blanket. "None of it happened?"

Savina exchanged looks with Sean. "None of what, dear?"

"My father. Xavier. The fire."

"Havok was tormenting you," Sean said. "It was all in your mind."

Ava swallowed hard, the memories clawing their way back. "They tortured me … broke my legs, burned me alive."

Gabriel flinched as though her words were sharp, cutting into him.

"How could he do that?" she whispered, more to herself than anyone else. "I thought he only spread disease."

"Havok has learned many things over the years," Savina said.

"They wanted me to join them." Her mind sifted through the memories, struggling to separate nightmare from reality. "They even had my father." She shot up, ignoring the searing pain in her limbs. "They're torturing him. We have to—"

"Ava." Savina's hands caught hers. "Your father is safe. Havok made you think otherwise. The Manor's charms are impenetrable."

"But it felt so real."

Gabriel fixed his gaze on hers. "It's over now. You're safe."

Safe. The word reverberated in her mind, empty and hollow. Havok had warped her reality so deeply that even now, staring into the familiar faces around her, she wasn't sure who she could trust. Shadows of doubt crept in. *What if it's another trick? What if this is still Havok's doing?*

Sean stepped forward, his expression calm but serious. "Ava, we'd like to see what you experienced. It will help us understand how he manipulated you."

"She just woke up," Gabriel said. "We can wait."

Ava's gaze flicked to him, startled by the intensity in his tone. His blue eyes burned with quiet anger, though it wasn't directed at her. She felt a flicker of something, gratitude, maybe, but it was drowned by the unease swirling in her chest. "Will it hurt?"

Sean shook his head. "You'll only be an observer. You won't feel the pain."

Gabriel set his jaw. "We can wait until she's stronger."

"I don't want her in pain after all this," Lance said, his dark brown eyes filled with worry as he moved closer to the bed.

Sean's gaze softened, and he nodded. "Of course. Only when you're ready, Ava."

Ava scanned the room. "Where is everyone else? Please tell me—"

"They're safe," Savina assured, her gaze gentle but firm. "Aaron led the others to Lighthollow Village to wait for us. He felt they could push forward, get closer to Havok, maybe stop the torture we suspected you were enduring. We stayed behind to watch over you. As soon as you woke, I let him know."

She looked at Savina. "I heard you. Through everything. I was certain I heard you urging me on, telling me to stay strong. Were you inside my mind?" Her hands trembled, her heartbeat quickening. "Did you … did you see any of it?"

Savina's eyes softened. "I wish I could have. Your mind was closed off, Ava, like a wall was shielding you. I tried, and I did my best to keep reaching for you, to remind you to hold on. But it wasn't my voice that broke through."

"But … I heard two voices. One was pleading, telling me to wake up. The other kept encouraging me, helping me fight."

Savina exchanged a glance with Sean. "The voice pushing you forward could have been yours, Ava. Sometimes, our inner strength takes its own form when we're in darkness."

Ava thought about that, letting her mind drift back to the blur of voices in her dreams. Perhaps it had been her own inner fight for survival.

Savina studied her. "How are you feeling?"

"Exhausted. And … displaced. It felt so real. Everything. I didn't know what was true and what was…" she trailed off, trying to articulate the confusion still clouding her mind.

"Let's get you moving. If you stay still for too long, your muscles will weaken further. You need to move a little, to wake your body up again," Savina suggested.

"What do I do?"

Savina gestured to Gabriel. "Start by sitting up. Gabriel will help you stand. Just a few steps. Nothing more for now."

"Here." He offered his arm.

Ava hesitated before gripping his forearm. He steadied her as she shifted to sit upright, her breath hitching at the sharp ache in her back and shoulders. The simple motion left her lightheaded, her vision swimming.

"Take it slow," Gabriel said. "You've got this."

With his help, she swung her legs over the edge of the bed, her bare feet brushing the cold stone floor. Her legs felt foreign, heavy and unresponsive, as though they didn't belong to her. As she attempted to stand, her knees gave way, but Gabriel was there to catch her.

Lance was at her side in an instant, wrapping her in a fierce hug that felt like a lifeline. She clung to him, breathing in his familiar scent.

Eric approached with a soft grin. "Glad you're back with us, Sleeping Beauty."

"Thanks," she murmured, a weak smile surfacing as she leaned back into Gabriel. "I want to go outside."

Savina shook her head. "Ava, it's too much."

"I'll take her," Gabriel said. "Just for a moment."

After she added layers and Gabriel laced up her boots, he led her out of the cabin.

The frigid air slammed into her. The snowy landscape stretched out before her, the brightness of the sun almost blinding after the dim confines of the cave. She squinted, her hand gripping Gabriel's arm as her knees wobbled.

"Breathe," he said, his hand at her back. "You're doing fine."

Her breaths came shallow at first, the cold air burning her lungs. But as the sun warmed her face, a faint sense of clarity broke through the haze. She leaned against Gabriel more than she intended, her legs trembling with every step. "I was so sure that it was Savina's voice. I thought … maybe it was her telling me to keep going."

He hesitated, his gaze shifting to the ground. "One of those voices was me."

The words hit her like a jolt. A lump rose in her throat, and her vision blurred as her breath caught. "What?" she managed to whisper over the rush of blood in her ears.

"I stayed by you." His eyes caught hers, laden with something unspoken, something raw and unflinching, pressing against her chest like a hand she couldn't escape.

"I stayed, hoping you'd wake up."

Her pulse quickened. "I … they told me everyone died," she whispered. "But you—"

Memories surged, unbidden and vivid. Eve's taunts slithered back into her mind, cold and venomous: *You'll see it one day. Gabriel will betray you. He's one of us.*

Flashes of his face, twisted into something unrecognizable, something ruthless and cold, sent a shiver up her spine. His hands stained with blood, his eyes void of light. The images mingled with the sight of him now, gentle, concerned, holding her as if she might break.

Her breath came in short, ragged bursts as her heart hammered against her ribs. *What if he's lying? What if it's all true?* She pulled away, her legs nearly giving out beneath her.

Gabriel's hands shot out, catching her before she collapsed. "What's wrong?"

Her pulse thundered in her throat, her gaze darting between his face and the snowy ground as the unease took root, spiraling into something she couldn't control. "Get away from me."

His eyebrows furrowed, hurt flickering across his features. "It's me, Ava."

She sucked in a shaky breath, supporting herself against the tree behind her. "I … I want to go back. I can't…" The words tangled in her throat, refusing to take shape. How could she tell him that she wasn't sure who he was anymore?

He hesitated, his hands loosening their hold as he took a small step back. "Okay." His tone was steady, but the tension in his jaw betrayed him. "Let me help you inside."

He guided her back into the cabin, his touch light and careful, as though sensing how fragile her trust had become. Once inside, he eased her down onto her bed, his movements deliberate and slow, giving her space.

"Are you okay?" He crouched beside her. His voice was softer now, edged with something that sounded almost like worry. "Do you need anything?"

Ava shook her head, unable to meet his gaze. She gripped the blanket as guilt and suspicion warred within her. "Lance."

He stilled for a moment, then nodded. "I'll get him."

"Please. Don't … don't touch me."

The words hung in the air like a blade. His hand, halfway to hers, froze before withdrawing. The flicker of hurt in his eyes was brief, but it struck her all the same, carving a hollow ache in her chest.

"Of course." His voice was devoid of anger or accusation. He stood, his movements measured as though he feared startling her further. Without another word, he left the room, his footsteps soft but heavy, the door creaking shut behind him.

The silence that followed was suffocating. Ava's chest heaved as she fought to calm her breathing, her hands trembling against the blanket.

Moments later, Lance appeared, his broad frame filling the doorway. His eyes softened as they landed on her. "Ava." He crossed the room and sat beside her, slipping an arm around her shoulders. "I'm so glad you're finally awake. You have no idea … none of us knew when or if you'd come back to us. I know I might not show it, but it's been tearing me to pieces. Sean and Eric … they've helped me hold it together."

Ava glanced at the others gathered around the fire, faces illuminated by the flickering orange glow, their eyes shadowed with fatigue and worry. "Why wasn't anyone else affected? I mean, if it was Havok … why just me?" The question was as much for herself as anyone else.

He scratched his beard, brow furrowed. "We've been asking ourselves the same thing. Havok's been targeting all of us Elementals, but it was only you who fell into his grip like this. Though …" His gaze grew distant. "Gillian's still been having dreams about Jeremy. And … I haven't seen Melissa since you … fell into the coma."

Ava swallowed. "It's like Havok is weaving nightmares into our minds, turning our memories against us. But how could he have broken through? I've been trying so hard to keep him out. Strengthening my mind. I thought it would be enough."

"Havok is powerful, and he's desperate. Whatever it is, he's found ways into our minds, our weaknesses. It's like he's feeding off our fears, making them feel as real as he can."

"Maybe because my mom was Cimmerian." She shivered. "It's in my blood." She clutched her arms, the fire's warmth suddenly feeling faint against the memory of what she'd seen. She felt as if she were still surrounded by ice, Havok's taunts echoing in her mind. "It was so real. I watched all of you, Melissa, Jeremy, Thomas, Gillian, you, burn alive…" Tears blurred her vision as she pressed her face onto Lance's shoulder. "And they kept coming back, pushing me to join him, showing me my father … tortured."

"Ava, you're here now. Whatever Havok did, it wasn't real. You survived it."

The tension shifted in her chest as her thoughts flickered to Gabriel. She hesitated, wondering if she should share her doubt, but the words spilled out before she could stop herself. "They told me … Gabriel … that he was a Cimmerian, that he'd joined Savina just to use her. And what if … what if it's true?" Her breath hitched. "What if he's the reason I'm like this?"

He pulled back, searching her face, his expression grave. "Ava, have you seen the way he looks at you? He was a wreck the entire time you were out."

She looked away, her brow knitting as conflicting memories tangled in her mind. "Eve … she said he's good at manipulating. She showed me a memory. His eyes … they were so cold. So callous. And Peter came to me before, telling me he loved me, saying he'd made a mistake. And when I finally confronted him, he acted like he didn't know what I was talking about." Her voice grew shaky, eyes distant with the confusion still heavy inside her. "How could he do that?"

"Are you sure that wasn't Havok too? It sounds like his kind of game, messing with your emotions, twisting them until you doubt yourself."

"I don't know how long he's been in my head, but it felt real, Lance. Every part of it did." She looked up at him. "I don't know who to trust anymore."

Lance's hand covered hers. "You can trust me. And I really think you can trust Gabriel."

"Ava?" Peter's voice broke through her thoughts as he stepped closer, his face pale and etched with concern. "I'm … I'm so sorry. I should've been there to protect you. I don't know why it happened to you, but I should have done more." Frustration flashed in his brown eyes, and he looked down, ashamed.

"It wasn't your fault."

His gaze softened, filled with a sorrow that seemed to weigh on his every word. "I know I hurt you before, but I'd never play with you like that. Whatever's happening to you … I won't let it touch you again. I'll protect you."

She nodded, and he joined Eric by the fire. Her attention was drawn to Gabriel, standing a short distance away, his eyes focused on her, an expression she couldn't decipher that set her heart racing. Every look felt like another question, the doubt Eve had sown returning to her thoughts. What if this was all still part of Havok's torture, her mind playing out its own fears? Or was it possible that Havok had woven this web around her to make her distrust her closest allies?

Lance squeezed her shoulder. "Hey, loosen up."

"Please, don't let Havok into my mind again. I'm not sure I could survive it a second time."

"He won't. Not while we're here."

The silence was heavy, but for the first time, it felt breathable. For now, she would hold onto that.

After dinner, everyone gathered close under Savina's protective charm. Every sound, like the creaking wood beneath her feet, and every smell, like the faint wisp of pine smoke, stabbed at Ava's heightened senses, leaving her feeling raw and exposed. Gabriel's absence beside her registered as both a relief and a hollow ache, each stolen glance in his direction pulling her deeper into a storm of suspicion and hurt.

She couldn't shake the feeling that his gaze lingered, shadowed with secrets, and the thought festered like an open wound. Her conversation with Lance flashed through her mind, and a pang of guilt followed. Had Gabriel overheard them? She wasn't ready to face him, not when her emotions felt so raw, her thoughts tangled in fear and mistrust.

Savina moved to her side, taking her hand. "This won't hurt physically. It will feel like you are watching it live. If you need time to prepare, we can wait."

Ava forced a nod as the room's warm, candlelit glow grew dim in her vision. "No," she said, her voice steadier than her heart. "They need to see what happened."

Sean extended his hand toward her, waiting with patient eyes. Ava's hand hovered over his, her fingers trembling. Each second felt heavy, every heartbeat reminding her of what she was about to revisit. Finally, she placed her hand in his, and darkness swallowed her vision.

Moments later, she was back in the icy forest where shadows twisted, and snow stretched before her. She stumbled forward, calling out for Peter and Gabriel, her voice swallowed by the silence. The visions played like nightmares made real, each moment sharp, cutting through her with relentless clarity. She flinched as Havok's cruel grin filled her view, his mocking words slicing through her.

Gabriel froze when Eve appeared, his betrayal laid bare, the sickening truth of his deception exposed.

Ava's gaze flickered to him, catching the way he tensed, his expression etched in silent pain.

Eric's hand rested on Gabriel's shoulder, a gesture of support, and Natalia looked up at him, pity softening her gaze. Gabriel's throat moved, a subtle, tight swallow, his jaw clenching so hard she swore she could feel it. His hands curled into fists at his sides, the knuckles white with the strain of restraint. And he never looked at Ava.

Her pulse quickened, her breath shallow as she fought against the rising swell of anger, suspicion intertwining with the bitter pang of betrayal.

As the vision faded and the soft candlelight of the cabin returned, she wiped her face, only realizing then that she had been crying. Lance drew her into his arms, murmuring words of comfort, her gaze fixed on Gabriel. His face was blank, his eyes downcast, but pain and frustration flickered beneath the surface.

Across the room, Savina's brow was furrowed in thought, her lips tight. "How could Havok have reached you?"

"I've been doing everything I can to protect her," Peter said.

Savina nodded, though her eyes were clouded. "Something broke through the charm. Ava, do you remember anything before you fell under?"

She hesitated, the memory hazy but vivid enough to leave a trace of dread. "Peter and I were talking … he left to go to his tent. I needed a moment alone. Then I saw these strange orbs, like in my dreams about my mom. I … I followed them. That's all I remember."

Peter looked down, frustration darkening his eyes. "I tried to follow—"

Savina cut him off. "It's not your fault." She began pacing, her hands clasped in front of her, a gesture Ava recognized from Colden. Lost in thought, Savina's gaze drifted to Ava, her eyes glinting with concern. "None of this makes sense."

Ava looked at Gabriel, a pang of suspicion slipping out before she could hold it back. "Maybe there's a traitor here."

"You don't know what you're talking about," Natalia hissed.

After a pause, Savina drew a deep breath, regaining her composure. "We all need rest. We'll talk more tomorrow."

"What if he comes back in my dreams? Or if he starts … torturing someone else?"

"We'll keep watch." Sean said. "We'll take shifts through the night. No one's facing this alone." He and Peter volunteered to stand guard for the first few hours, and everyone dispersed to their own beds.

Lance sat close to Ava, his arm like a protective shield around her shoulders. She clung to him, unable to let anyone else near her.

Gabriel approached her, his eyes a deep well of sorrow. "Ava…" The tenderness in his voice nearly weakened her.

"Are you a Cimmerian?"

He closed his eyes as if bracing against the blow. When he looked back at her, his gaze held a sadness that almost broke through her defenses. "Ava … it's not what you think."

But his reluctance was answer enough, and she pulled back, crossing her arms over herself, as if she could shield her heart from the sting of betrayal. "Then tell me. Tell me the truth."

He opened his mouth, words hovering on the edge, but whatever explanation he had died in his throat. The way he looked at her, his eyes pained and pleading, tore at her resolve, but her mind churned with Eve's memories, with the fragments of lies and visions were too real to ignore.

"Stay away from me." The words came out colder than she intended, and another tear slipped down her cheek, betraying her need to maintain control. She turned away, unwilling to let him see the hurt that threatened to overwhelm her. Still, his silence lingered, his gaze heavy on her, and she fought the urge to look back.

"Ava, please." He inched forward, his eyes filled with desperation. "Let me explain—"

"I said stay away."

Hurt flashed across his face. As he turned and walked away, his heavy footsteps seemed to carry the heat with them, leaving her feeling chilled.

How could she have been so wrong? She wanted to hear his side, but distrust gnawed at her, leaving her raw and hollow. How could she trust him now? The ache of loss weighed down her chest.

"We'll figure this out, Ava," Lance whispered, pulling her into a gentle embrace.

She buried her face in his shoulder, allowing herself to break, her tears a release of all the confusion, grief, and betrayal that had weighed her down. "We have to tell Savina."

"Tell her what?"

"That he's the spy. It makes too much sense. Think about it. He's constantly around me. He teleported me to the place my mom died, and we got ambushed. And again, he teleported us to that deserted town … another ambush. He's telling Havok where we are."

"Don't let the paranoia take over. Look, try to get some rest. It'll help."

"I can't sleep. Don't you see? If I close my eyes, he'll be there, waiting."

"Stay right here. I'll tell Savina what you told me." He got up and walked over to Savina, exchanging hushed words.

Ava's eyes fell on Gabriel, his head in his hands as he sat slumped on the edge of his bed, looking utterly defeated. Natalia was by his side, her hand on his back, and Ava looked away, the image of his pain embedding itself in her mind.

When Lance returned, he handed her a cup of water. "Here, drink. Savina knows everything. We'll sort this out."

Ava took a sip, the cool water easing her parched throat. Exhaustion pulled at her, and she leaned onto Lance's shoulder, seeking some solace. Her eyes closed as sleep took hold, but even in the quiet, her heart ached with doubt and loss.

32

DELIRIUM

Daylight glistened across the snow, the warmth a startling relief against Ava's cold skin. How long had it been since she'd felt the sun? Weeks? Months? She rolled over, blinking away the fog in her mind, only to feel something wet and icy against her cheek. Snow.

Her pulse spiked as she sat up, taking in the endless stretch of white. Just inches away, the ground dropped into nothingness. A gasp escaped her, and she scrambled back from the edge, her fingers digging into the frost-slicked earth until her back hit the rough bark of a tree. She clung to it, her breaths shallow and frantic. Where was she? How had she ended up there?

The icy silence pressed in, but a faint wind whispered against the cliff.

"Ava!"

She jolted at the shout, her head snapping around. Peter sprinted toward her, eyes wide with horror. She lifted a

370

trembling hand toward him, but before he reached her, the ground gave way beneath her.

The scream caught in her throat as she plunged, the air tearing past her in a cold rush. The valley below stretched out like a snowy grave, waiting to swallow her whole. *No, this can't be happening.* Panic surged, her mind flashing to the faces she'd failed. Her father, her friends, Gabriel. She was going to die, and it would mean nothing.

As she braced for impact, an image burned through the panic. Gabriel's warm blue eyes, watching her with a quiet resolve that cut through her fear.

Strong arms caught her. She blinked up into familiar brown eyes, her heart skipping. "Peter?" She clutched him, relief flooding in, but it evaporated in an instant.

"Yes, Ava, it's me." His smile was wrong, distorted, and his gaze darkened as he held her too tightly. "I'm here, just like I always have been."

She stumbled back, a cold dread forming in her chest. "How did you...?" Her voice broke, glancing to where the cliff should be. "And where is everyone else?"

His face morphed into a smirk. "Everyone else? I killed them, Ava." The words hit her like a slap, and he leaned in close. "Why didn't you see this coming? I've always been one of them. A Cimmerian. Havok's follower."

Her breath hitched. *No. This isn't real. It can't be.*

He seized her arms, his grip like iron. "I'm in your mind, Ava. And I'll stay here, torturing you, until you say the word. So say it."

She wrenched free, a surge of fury burning through the fear. "No! I'll never give in to you!"

"Then wake up!" His face contorted, his voice a harsh, echoing whisper. "Wake up!"

Her eyes flew open, her heart pounding. She shot up in bed, gasping for breath.

"Ava?" Lance's worried face loomed beside her. The others stood a few feet back, eyes filled with fear and uncertainty.

She drew a shuddering breath, her mind still spinning as she looked from face to face. *It was just a dream. Just a dream.* The horror was so real, it coursed through her veins like a venomous, icy grip.

"Ava, what did you dream?" Savina asked, breaking through the haze, her green eyes soft with concern.

She described the dream, the cliff, Peter's haunting words, the revelation of betrayal. As she spoke, her voice wavered, unable to shake the feeling that part of it was more than a nightmare.

Savina's face hardened, her lips pressed into a grim line. "We need to keep moving."

Gabriel's brow furrowed in concern. "Are you sure that's wise? She's barely rested." His gaze lingered on Ava, intense and searching. "She's not in shape to travel yet."

"If we don't get to Lighthollow Village, Havok's influence will spread," Sean said.

"And if we push her like this, she won't make it," Gabriel said. "Look at her, Savina. She can barely stay upright."

Ava glared at him. "I'm fine. Stop talking about me like I'm not here."

Eric sighed. "You're not fine, Ava, and you know it. Havok's curse is draining you. If we keep this pace, you're going to collapse, and then what?"

"I said I'm fine. I don't need to be carried, or coddled, or—" She glanced at Gabriel. "—babied by anyone."

His eyes held firm, but his tone was laced with frustration. "This isn't about pride, Ava. It's about survival. If Havok takes over your mind or your body gives out, you're not putting yourself at risk. You're putting *all* of us at risk."

"Maybe I wouldn't be in this mess if someone wasn't feeding him information!"

"That's enough," Savina said. "No one here is working with Havok, Ava. You're exhausted, and exhaustion breeds paranoia. We don't have time for this."

"We're wasting daylight," Sean said. "If she can't keep up, what do we do?"

Savina turned to Ava. "You've been through enough. Let someone help you. Gabriel can carry you. It's the fastest way to get us all to safety."

"No. I don't need *his* help. I'll walk on my own."

"Enough, Ava," Savina said. "If you want to walk, fine. But the moment you start to falter, someone *will* help you, whether you like it or not."

"Fine. But I won't slow us down. I promise."

"Then listen to me," Savina said. "Havok is strong, but this is *your* mind. He can only twist what you let him. Focus on what's real. Our faces, our voices. Imagine a wall of light, bright and unyielding, around your thoughts. Peter will protect you, and I'll work on strengthening your aura. If you feel his pull again, ground yourself, press your hands into the earth, feel the cold snow. Stay in the now."

Ava nodded.

"Then let's move. Sean, Lance, Eric scout ahead. Peter, stay close to Ava and keep shielding her mind. Gabriel,

Natalia, take the rear." Her eyes flicked to Ava with a hint of warning. "And Ava, don't be reckless."

She tensed, discomfort swirling at the thought of Peter's proximity. But there was no time to argue. They gathered their things and moved into formation, each person stepping with a wary vigilance. The mountains loomed ahead, their snow-covered peaks stark against the sky, a vision hauntingly familiar.

Does Havok know our path? Ava glanced at Gabriel again. *Is he leading me into a trap? And if he's a Cimmerian, why has no one else seen it?* Dread crept in as she took in the narrow ascent. "Are we actually climbing those?"

"Yes," Gabriel said, his voice flat, dismissive.

Ava bristled, anger simmering beneath the doubt. *Was he a spy? Were they all spies?*

Her legs wobbled as they climbed, the rocky path narrowing until there was barely a foothold between them and the sheer drop. Ava's breaths came faster, sharper, tearing through her chest. Each step felt heavier than the last, her muscles trembling as exhaustion clawed at her. The snow was blinding under the sunlight, and the wind nipped at her face, making her shiver despite the heat she tried to summon.

Behind her, Gabriel loomed like a shadow, his hand darting out every time she stumbled. *Does he think I'll fall? Does he want me to?*

When the trail leveled out, Ava dropped to her knees, her hands sinking into the snow. "What's wrong with me?" she whispered.

Gabriel crouched beside her. "Are you in pain?"

She didn't look at him. "Just tired." She hit the snow, scattering frost. "I can't keep holding everyone back."

His hand hovered near her arm. "It's not your fault. Let me help you."

"What are you doing to her?" Peter shouted. He stormed over, his glare fixed on Gabriel. "She doesn't need your help." He lunged, shoving Gabriel backward into the snow.

The fight was a brutal clash of fists and bodies. Gabriel shoved Peter off, his muscles straining with the effort, before swinging his fist with a resounding thud against Peter's jaw. The impact sent shockwaves through the air, the sound reverberating and echoing across the frozen trail. Peter retaliated with a forceful punch aimed at Gabriel's side, the sound of their blows resonating through the crisp winter air.

Blood trickled down Gabriel's split lip, his eyes burning with determination. He ducked under Peter's wild swing, and drove his knee into Peter's gut, the impact stealing his breath. "Finally. You've been a thorn in my side for too long." Gabriel's voice dripped with malice. He stood over Peter's crumpled form. "You've always trusted the wrong people, Ava. I was never your ally."

Peter groaned, blood dripping from his temple. "Ava, he's working for Havok. I tried to tell you. I tried—"

"Enough." His gaze burned into Ava. "You're all so predictable. So easy to lead. Do you really think I've been protecting you? I've been delivering you straight to Havok. And now you'll give him exactly what he wants."

Ava stumbled back, her breath hitching. "No ... you're lying. This isn't real."

He sauntered closer. "Isn't it? Who else would Havok trust with a task this important? I've been playing this game far longer than you, Ava. And now it's over."

Her heart pounded as his words echoed in her mind. A faint, mocking laugh seemed to ripple through her thoughts, sending a shiver down her spine. *He's closer than you think,* a voice whispered, cruel and familiar.

Strong hands gripped her shoulders, pulling her back. "Ava, wake up!" Gabriel's urgent voice snapped her from the vision.

She blinked, her eyes darting around. "Where … where's Peter?"

Peter knelt nearby, his face pale, bloodless. "I'm right here." He reached for her. "It's okay."

Ava recoiled, scrambling away from him and faced Gabriel. "You—you attacked Peter. You're leading me to Havok."

Gabriel's expression darkened. "She's hallucinating. Again. Peter, you need to protect her better."

"I'm doing my best!" he snapped.

"Clearly not enough."

"Enough," Savina cut in, eyes fierce. Kneeling beside Ava, she placed her hands on Ava's shoulders. "You need to block him from your mind. Havok's influence is only going to grow."

She gritted her teeth. "I'm trying…" But the faint echoes of the vision still lingered, making her doubt her own strength.

The ground trembled beneath them, the rumble growing louder until it seemed to echo through the mountain itself. A chorus of deep, menacing growls broke the silence as a pack of saberwolves appeared, prowling down the slope, white snow billowing around them.

Ava clutched Savina's arm. "Am I … am I hallucinating again?"

"No. They're real."

33

NEVER LET GO

Ava's heart pounded so hard like it might burst from her chest. The saberwolf's amber eyes locked onto hers, freezing her in place as the cold air burned her lungs. The world around her blurred, muffled by the deafening rush of her own shallow breaths. The others' shouts felt miles away, drowned out by the low, guttural growl emanating from the massive creature in front of her.

The wolf lunged. Its massive frame slammed into her, knocking her into the frigid snow. Pain shot through her side, sharp and immediate. The beast's growls reverberated through her chest like a thunderclap, its hot, putrid breath mingling with the icy sting of snow against her skin. With a violent struggle, she thrashed, her foot connecting with its body in a desperate kick. The impact seemed to enrage the wolf, its snarls growing louder as saliva dripped onto her face, sickening and warm.

Every fiber of her being screamed in terror, but she refused to give in. She clawed at the beast, her fingers tangling in its coarse, matted fur, slick with melted snow. Her muscles burned as she fought against its crushing weight, her vision swimming. Its fangs glinted, razor-sharp and inches from her throat.

Summoning every ounce of strength left in her battered body, Ava swung her fist. Time seemed to slow as her knuckles collided with the wolf's chest. The impact sent a jarring pain up her arm, but it was enough. The wolf let out a deafening yelp and staggered, its body collapsing onto the snow with a heavy thud.

For a moment, she couldn't move. Her chest heaved as she stared at the fallen creature, its amber eyes now dull and lifeless. Relief flooded her, followed by an overwhelming wave of exhaustion that left her trembling. She rolled onto her side, the icy snow biting into her skin. As the world faded around her, the shouts of her companions became a distant, indistinct murmur. Her eyelids grew heavy, and she let them close, surrendering to the pull of weariness. For now, it was over.

"Ava!" Lance shouted.

Her eyes fluttered open. "I'm … I'm losing strength. It took so much to fight that one."

He lifted her to her feet, his face tight with worry. "It's okay. We'll keep going. We're almost there." He guided her up the path, her legs trembling with each step. The air felt thin, her lungs burning with every breath, but she pressed on, focusing on the crunch of snow underfoot.

A flicker of movement caught her eye, and she turned her head toward the trees on the right. "Did you see that?" Her gaze fixed on a shifting shadow.

Lance glanced over. "No, there's nothing there."

Another rustling sound made her stop short, her heart pounding. "There it is again." She squinted as a light flickered in the distance. "There's a fire … someone's out here."

"Ava, stop shouting." Peter reached for her hand. His grip felt too solid, too real. "It's just our campfire. Come on, there's a storm coming."

She blinked, confusion swirling in her mind. The snow was gone, replaced by dead leaves and broken branches. Her heart sank. *No.* She knew this place, near the cabin at home. "How did we get here?"

Peter gave her a puzzled look. "We live here, Ava."

"No, we were going to save Melissa and Jeremy. What happened?"

A cruel smile curled his lips. "They're gone. Don't you remember? They burned alive."

"No, that was Havok's doing…" She yanked her hand away. "This isn't real."

"You wish it was, though, don't you? You want me to hold you, to love you, to hurt you again."

"Stop!" Ava clapped her hands over her ears, but his voice grew colder, harsher.

"They all died because of you, Ava. Your father. Melissa. Jeremy. Because you won't join me. Think of how much stronger you'd be."

"Get out of my head!"

The darkness lifted, and Ava gasped, her surroundings snapping back into focus. Snow fell around her, and the group stared, their faces etched with worry.

"Another hallucination." She clutched her chest as shame burned her cheeks.

Peter's face darkened with frustration. "I'm failing at protecting you. I don't know what else to do."

"I do not know if this will help, but it's all I have." Savina pulled a vial from her robes and handed it to Ava. "Drink this. It may help you block him from your mind."

She hesitated, then tilted her head back and drank. The liquid was bitter, tasting like milky lemon coated blackberries.

Savina exchanged a look with Sean. "If this continues, Havok could break through entirely. We need to take precautions."

Lance pulled Ava close. "Come on. Let's rest. Tomorrow will be better."

Ava nodded, too drained to argue, but the cold dread clawed at her. As the sun began to dip behind the mountains, a strange resolve stirred within her. Her mind wavered, torn between the alluring promise of an end to all the suffering and the horror of what Havok's victory would mean. If she surrendered, she could stop the pain ... but at what cost?

She took a step forward, but Gabriel caught her wrist "Don't go running off, not in the state you're in." His tone was intense, and something in his blue eyes softened as he held her gaze.

"I don't need you telling me what to do." She glared at him. But even as the words left her lips, they felt wrong, too sharp. His hand lingered on her wrist for a moment too long, his fingers warm against her chilled skin. She hated the steadiness of it, hated how it made her want to believe him.

He didn't flinch, but his jaw tightened, and the faintest flicker of hurt passed through his eyes. "I'm trying to help you, Ava."

"Help me? Or control me?"

His shoulders dropped a little, the tension draining from them, but his eyes darkened. "Is that what you think?" His voice was soft, almost quiet enough to be lost in the wind. "That I'd try to control you? Or is that Havok talking?"

The question hit her like a slap, and anger flared as a desperate attempt to mask the guilt. "Maybe it is," she bit out. "Or maybe you're giving me reasons to wonder. You're always holding back. Always watching. What aren't you telling me, Gabriel?"

He froze, her words cutting through the space between them. For the first time, his expression cracked, not the usual stoic mask she'd come to expect, but something raw, exposed. "I'm not the enemy, Ava." He shook his head, his breath uneven. "But you've already decided I am. Because it's easier that way, isn't it?"

The hushed pain in his voice made her chest hurt, but she forced herself to look away. *Why does he have to sound like that? Like he cares?* "Trusting anyone right now is dangerous. You should know that better than anyone."

"I know what it's like to doubt everyone around you. To doubt yourself. But if you think I'd ever hurt you—" His voice cracked. "You don't know me at all."

"Stop," she said, cutting him off. Her throat felt tight, her chest too heavy. "I can't—I can't do this right now." She turned away, blinking hard against the sting of tears. "We should keep moving."

Gabriel didn't respond immediately, but she felt his gaze on her, heavy and unrelenting. "Fine. Let's keep moving."

Lance squeezed her hand. "Come on, Ava. Let's focus on getting to a shelter. You two can sort this out later."

She nodded, grateful for the distraction. Following behind, Ava couldn't shake the memory of Gabriel's voice, the way it had softened when he spoke her name. *Why does he have to look at me like that? Like I matter more than I want to believe?*

As they climbed higher, they came upon a natural overhang jutting out from the mountainside, its dark, rocky ceiling extending over a small, shallow cave beneath. The stone seemed weathered, worn by wind and centuries of harsh winter storms, jagged in places but rounded in others where water had smoothed the edges. Icicles hung like sharpened teeth from the rock above, catching the dying light and glinting, reminding Ava of the saberwolf's fangs from earlier.

The opening of the cave was narrow, with rocks spilling out onto a ledge that left room to sit without teetering near the edge of the steep mountain slope. Inside, shadows clung to every corner, giving the small cavern an oppressive, almost haunted feel. The cave walls were cold and damp to the touch, slick from melting snow trickling through cracks in the rock. A lingering scent of earth and ancient moss filled the space, heavy and stifling.

The ground was uneven and covered in loose stones, scattered with patches of frost, making every step uncertain. Ava shivered as she stepped into the shadowed entrance, the chill seeping up from the stone, wrapping her like an icy shroud. The wind howled outside, muffled by the rock, and sent echoes through the cavern, creating the illusion that something was breathing just out of sight. She couldn't shake the feeling that they were trespassing in a place not meant for them, a hidden refuge for those who truly belonged to these mountains.

As they huddled under the overhang, the biting wind still found its way inside, sweeping through the narrow gaps and cutting through their layers. Ava hugged her knees, pressing her back against the rock, willing herself to ignore the ominous depths of the cave. She forced herself to breathe, steadying her racing heart as she tried to find rest in the cold, unwelcoming shelter that would protect them.

As darkness fell, Ava's mind churned with questions and half-formed doubts. The boundaries of trust and deception had blurred to the point where she no longer knew who she was fighting, or who was fighting alongside her.

Inside the dim cave, shadows flickered along the uneven stone walls as the lanterns cast a warm, dancing glow. The others were busy catching fish from the nearby river, their muffled voices blending with the crackle of the small fire. For the first time in days, Ava's mind felt clear. The potion Savina had given her worked. The haunting hallucinations were gone, leaving behind a stillness that felt foreign.

Ava rested against the cool rock, exhaustion pressing down on her. She wanted to ask why Savina hadn't given her the remedy sooner but reasoned that Savina had hoped Ava was strong enough without it. But she wasn't.

Their sleeping bags were lined against the cave walls, neatly spaced, while outside, the moon hung high, its silvery glow illuminating the snowy landscape with a cold brilliance. The beauty of the night felt distant, detached. Even with her body begging for sleep, Ava hesitated to close her eyes, terrified that the reprieve from the dreams wouldn't last.

Lance kept watch beside her for a time before Gabriel took over, settling near her. He opened the well-worn thriller she recalled from the cabin, its dog-eared pages and faded cover a comforting reminder of normalcy amidst their chaotic lives.

Ava studied him in the dim light. His face, worn by fatigue and shadowed with days of sleeplessness, seemed both familiar and achingly different. His beard was thicker now, his expression more guarded, but the gentle determination in his eyes was the same. Lance had been right. Gabriel hadn't slept while she was out. He had been the other voice calling her to wake up from her coma. He'd been by her side through everything: when she lashed out at the Cruciari guard, when she killed Drew and Jonah, when she sought a Necromancer, when Peter broke her heart, when she fell into depression.

How could I have doubted him? He's not the enemy. He's my ally. My friend. He … he's more than that.

Her heart ached at the thought, and for a moment, it almost shattered the wall of doubt. But the vision came roaring back, vivid and cruel. Gabriel's face hardened, devoid of emotion, his hands covered in blood. The betrayal in his eyes seared into her mind, impossible to ignore. *Or maybe I've been a fool this whole time, letting him in, trusting him, when he was just waiting to destroy us all.*

Finally, she gathered the courage. "Was any of it real? You and me. Any of it?"

Gabriel lowered his book, his gaze meeting hers with quiet intensity. "Yes."

"How? You—you're a Cimmerian. Tell me what happened. Did you make a deal with them?"

A shadow crossed his face, the muscle in his jaw twitched. "I was never a true Cimmerian, Ava. Not in the way you think. I was lost, desperate, and young. I had no idea who they were … or what they were."

Ava narrowed her eyes. "You said you met Eric first."

"No." He let out a troubled sigh, running a hand through his dark hair. "I met Eve first. I was barely more than a kid. After my sister died … everything I knew fell apart. My uncle kicked me out." His words laden with years of pain wrenched Ava's heart. "I was alone for the first time in my life. I'd lost my family, my home, and I had this … power I couldn't control." He swallowed hard. "I teleported randomly. Sometimes just thinking of something or someone was enough to move me across the city. I'd never felt more like an outsider, even among friends. Then … I met Eve."

Bitterness crept into his tone. "She made me feel like I belonged somewhere. She talked about people like us, promised I'd find a home, and I wanted so badly to believe her. To believe that I wasn't broken. It was enough to get me to Corbin's side. For the first time, I wasn't alone. I had people who accepted me. We were all alike. Corbin taught me to fight, to block my thoughts, to channel my anger. And for a while, I thought they were my people."

"But you knew about the killings."

"Not at first." He shook his head. "They sold me on a story. That Ephemerals hunted us, feared us. They warned me that if people knew what I was, they'd betray me. And for a time, I believed them. Because of my uncle." His gaze darkened, lost in the memory. "But I came to realize Corbin thrived on hatred and revenge. There was no freedom, only duty to him. We were forced to recruit Enchanters, to kill

Ephemerals. We were just ... killing machines..." He trailed off, regret evident in his gaze. "I was never happy there."

"Then why stay?" she asked.

"I turned off my emotions because it was the only way I could survive," he whispered. "I was ruthless. I was evil. I didn't care about anything or anyone. I lost myself."

"It was her. Eve was the one who brought you back from shutting off your emotions."

He nodded. "She brought me out of it, but knowing all I did." He shook his head. "I fell into depression. The panic attacks alone almost crippled me."

Jealousy flared. "Did you stay for her?"

"At first. Eve was fiery, ambitious, and sure of her power. But she was possessive. There was a darkness in her that I could never love."

Relief washed over Ava. She looked down, hiding her face. "The vision Eve showed me ... was that real?"

His expression darkened, sadness and anger flickering in his eyes. "Yes."

She swallowed hard. "She said you'd betray me. That you were using me."

He leaned closer. "Ava, I would never betray you."

The certainty in his tone unraveled something inside her. Her breath hitched as she met his gaze, the connection between them suddenly too close to ignore. Her heart raced, a warmth building in her chest that she couldn't suppress.

"How did you get out?"

"I was on a recruiting mission, but I would go to bars and sit alone. One night, Eric came up to me. He knew I was an Enchanter, but he could tell something was off. I wanted to be a good person. I wanted a fresh start. But I didn't deserve any of that. He and I became friends, and he helped drag me from that darkness."

"How long were you with them?"

Gabriel hesitated, gripping the book. "Thirty years." His voice was heavy with regret.

She couldn't fathom it. Thirty years of living among the Cimmerians, thirty years of turning off his emotions, of becoming someone else entirely.

"Why didn't you tell me sooner?"

Pain flickered across his face. "Because I was terrified. Terrified of how you'd look at me. I didn't want to lose the way you saw me. I've wanted to tell you everything. But I was afraid of this. Of losing you."

Guilt twisted inside her. "Gabriel..."

"I didn't tell you because I didn't think I deserved you. Not after what I'd done. Not after the things I couldn't undo. I've spent so long trying to bury that part of me. I never wanted you to see it."

Her heart ached at his words. *He thinks he doesn't deserve me? How could someone like* me *deserve someone as good as* him?

"But I thought we trusted each other. I thought ... we shared everything."

"Do we?" He raised an eyebrow. "What about the days before your coma? Why were you so distant?"

Her cheeks warmed and she inhaled a shaky breath. "Peter came to me for two nights ... or so I thought ... confessing his love and wanting me back."

"That doesn't really explain your distance."

"Because ... he kissed me, but I stopped him. It meant nothing. I'm sorry."

"Are you apologizing to me for kissing him back?"

Yes. But she kept her mouth shut.

"Why did you stop him?"

"Because I—" A flush crept up her neck, and she dropped her gaze, confusion swirling within her. "I need some air." Rising to her feet, she stepped out of the cave, the cold air stinging her cheeks in a refreshing wave. Leaning against the rocky wall, she struggled to pacify her racing heart. She didn't understand the storm of emotions inside her, but she couldn't ignore the truth anymore. *I love him.*

"And here you are, accusing me of hiding behind walls," Gabriel said from behind her.

She exhaled, her breath curling in the cold. "It was because of you." The words slipped out before she could stop them

When she turned to face him, their eyes locked. His expression softened, and she saw the same yearning mirrored in his gaze.

"Ava." The way he said her name awakened something deep and unspoken, the quiet ache and longing threading through his voice.

Unable to resist any longer, Ava stepped toward him, her heart pounding as she threw her arms around his neck and pressed her mouth to his. His lips met hers, dissolving her fears, a silent promise woven into every touch. A rush of emotions flooded her being. With every soft press of her lips against his, a gentle tremor coursed through her body, causing her muscles to quiver in anticipation. Her heart, like a wild stallion, galloped against her chest, its powerful beats reverberating throughout her.

His hand slid to the small of her back, pulling her closer, and a shiver soared down her spine. Their lips moved in perfect rhythm, each kiss deeper, more urgent, a seamless dance of longing and surrender.

She gasped as his fingers threaded through her hair. Every nerve in her body came alive, her senses overwhelmed by the strength of his hold. She had always felt a pull toward Gabriel, a connection she'd tried to ignore. But now, in this moment, she knew it was deeper than anything she'd ever known.

When their kiss finally broke, she leaned her forehead against his, her breath mingling with his in soft, white clouds against the chilled air.

His eyes burned with a quiet intensity, his voice rough with emotion. "I've wanted to kiss you for so long."

An intense, primal desire awakened within her, coursing through her veins like a current of electricity.

The soft touch of his thumb brushed against her cheek, leaving a trail of fire and tenderness in its wake.

"Please tell me this is real," she pleaded.

He cradled her face in his hands, the roughness of his fingertips grazing her skin. "It's real. This is real."

Ava kissed him again, softer this time, her lips lingering as she poured every unspoken word into the touch. "I denied my feelings for so long because I didn't think *I* deserved *you*," she whispered. "But with you, I feel fearless. You give me hope."

Gabriel's hand skimmed over her waist as he pulled her closer, his warmth banishing the remaining cold. Their kiss deepened once more, slower now, more tender, as though savoring every moment. The strength of his body pressed against hers, igniting a wave of dizzying sensations that left her breathless. The rest of the world faded into nothing. There was only him. Steadfast, fierce, and utterly hers.

34

FATED FLAME

Ava's eyes fluttered open to the faint glow of early light filtering into the rocky shelter. The air was crisp, brushing against her cheeks, and she shivered beneath her blanket. The rugged ceiling above her stretched with rough edges and grooves, casting faint shadows that danced in the soft dawn light. She reached up, absently touching her lips as the memories of Gabriel's kiss sent a thrill through her. A smile crept onto her face, filling her with a quiet, swelling joy.

The sleeping bag next to her was empty, and she sat up, her eyes scanning the shelter.

"He's out catching fish with the others," Natalia said from her spot near the cave wall. She sat cross-legged, her gaze focused on the faint embers of the dying fire. "Did you have any nightmares?"

"No."

"That's good." Natalia hesitated, glancing at her. "I need to talk to you … about him. He told you the truth, didn't he?"

"Yes. Everything."

A trace of relief flickered across Natalia's face, but she didn't relax. Instead, her hazel eyes lingered on Ava, sharp and searching. "I've seen how close you two have gotten. And I'm happy for him. Really, I am. But I care about Gabriel … like family. I've watched him rebuild his life after so much loss. He's strong, but … but he's also—" She paused, searching for the right word. "Fragile in ways he doesn't show."

Ava's brow furrowed, unease prickling at the edges of her happiness. "You think I'll hurt him?"

Natalia met her gaze, her expression composed yet gentle. "I think he's waited for you. Hoped for you. Even when your heart was still with Peter."

"That's not fair," she said. "I … I didn't ask for that."

"I know. And I don't blame you for it. But Gabriel—he's given so much of himself already. If you're not sure, Ava, you need to be honest. He won't recover easily if you break him."

Ava looked away, her fingers tightening around the edge of her blanket. "What makes you think I'm not sure? What I feel for him … it's real. I love him, Natalia."

For a moment, Natalia's expression softened, but her voice remained cautious. "I don't doubt that you care for him. But love? Ava, love isn't just about what you feel. It's about what you'll do when things get hard. When Havok comes for you, because he will, what will you do then?"

The question hit Ava like a blow, and she stiffened, her heart racing. "I don't know."

"I don't mean to be harsh." Natalia reached out and squeezed Ava's hand. "But Havok is ruthless. And Gabriel already lived through so much darkness. If you give in, if you let Havok manipulate you … Gabriel won't survive it."

"I won't let that happen. I promise."

Natalia nodded, but her gaze lingered on Ava for a moment longer, searching. "Just remember, Ava, if you choose him, you have to give him all of you. Because that's what he'll give you."

Before Ava could respond, the entrance to the cave darkened as Eric walked in, his grin wide as he held up several fish. "Good morning! What's going on here?"

"Just a little chat." Natalia straightened, her warm smile returning as she joined Eric near the fire.

A wave of anxiety washed over Ava. Her earlier joy felt distant now, tangled with guilt and doubt. *Do they all doubt me? Does Gabriel doubt me, too?*

She sagged back against the wall, her hands trembling. The cold rock pressed against her back as her thoughts spiraled. *Would he survive if I failed him? Would I?*

With a deep, shaky breath, Ava walked outside, the crisp air chilling her cheeks. The sharpness of it was strangely welcome, easing the ache that churned in her chest. She lifted her hand to shield her eyes from the blinding reflection of light off the snow, blinking as her vision adjusted. Leaning back against the rocky wall of the cave, she breathed deeply, letting the brisk air sweep through her hair and clear her mind.

The landscape stretched before her, vast and silent. The snow-covered peaks glistened under the pale morning light, their beauty stark and untouchable. *Where is everyone?* The isolation pressed around her, both soothing and unsettling. Then curiosity drew her steps forward, closer to the ledge.

She stopped, peering down. The stubborn mist clung to the mountainside, hiding the depths below. A faint rush of water echoed up to her, tantalizing and distant. The sound filled her with an unexpected longing, sharp and undeniable. *If I could just touch it … maybe I'd feel whole again.*

Her hand gripped a nearby tree as she leaned forward, trying to glimpse the source of the rushing sound. The rough bark bit into her fingers, but her footing felt uncertain. A strong arm wrapped around her waist, pulling her back in one smooth motion.

Her breath hitched, and she whirled, panic flashing through her until her gaze met Gabriel's.

"Who did you think it was?" he murmured, amusement sparking in his eyes.

"I—I don't know."

"I didn't mean to startle you. But you were too close to the edge."

He softened his grip but didn't let go. His arm remained around her, his warmth bleeding through the cold as his hand found her hip.

Drawn to him like a magnet, she felt the steady beat of his heart against her skin. Her cheeks heated as his fingers touched her shoulder, lingering near her neck. The moment stretched, charged with unspoken emotions.

His gaze locked onto hers, his intensity both comforting and disarming. He leaned down, brushing his lips against hers. It was tentative at first, gentle and seeking. But as her arms reached for him, resting against his chest, the kiss deepened. He trailed a line of kisses down her jaw, his lips grazing her neck, sending a wave of heat that made her shiver. Her thoughts dissolved, replaced by a rush of sensation, each touch igniting something deep within her.

"We should go back," she whispered, though her voice lacked conviction.

He paused, drawing back a little. His gaze searched hers, concern shadowing his features. "Did I overstep?"

"No." She shook her head, but Natalia's warning flashed in her mind. She looked down. "I … I don't want to hurt you."

Understanding dawned in his expression, mixed with a flicker of frustration. "Natalia. She spoke to you."

"Gabe … she's just worried. She cares about you."

"She's protective." He tucked a strand of hair behind her ear. "But don't let her fears become yours."

"What if she's right? What if I become like them? What if Havok gets inside my head again?"

"You won't. You've survived everything he's thrown at you. You're stronger than you know."

"But I almost gave in," she said. "When they showed me my father … I almost said yes. Just to save him."

"But you didn't. "And that's what matters. He's only doing this because he wants you to *want* to join. He wants to break you before you realize your own strength. Don't let him."

Tears stung her eyes as she looked up at him. "If I ever do become a Cimmerian…" She took a shaky breath. "Please remember what's in my heart."

"Stop." His hand cupped her cheek, his thumb sweeping against her skin. "That won't happen. But even if it did, I would never forget who you are. What's in your heart."

"How can you be so sure?"

"Because even without the necklaces, I feel you," he said. "When you kissed me … I knew."

Her breath caught, and she felt something break open inside her. A fragile, hopeful part of her that had been locked away for too long. "I've felt this connection with you for so long."

Gabriel leaned in, his fingers tracing the curve of her neck, his touch igniting a fire that spread through her. Unable to hold back any longer, she pulled him closer, her hand threading through his hair as their lips met again. His kiss grew urgent, his arms encircling her as she melted into him, her body pressing closer to his.

Every touch sent sparks spiraling through her, a heady mix of comfort and awakening. As his hands slid to her lower back, Ava felt the last of her doubts melt away. In his arms, she felt unbreakable, as though no darkness could touch her here. As though she were entirely safe.

The final stretch up the mountain felt like an impossible challenge to Ava. Each step grew heavier, her legs trembling as though they were made of lead. The narrow ledge forced them into a single-file line, and Gabriel stayed close behind.

She stumbled, her knees hitting the icy ground hard. Pain shot through her, and Gabriel's hand was there, gripping her arm and pulling her upright with ease.

"Do you want me to carry you?"

"I can walk," she insisted. Her fingers tightened on her bag's strap, numb from the cold.

He sighed. "Ava, if you fall off this ledge…" He shook his head. "Why are you so stubborn? Do you have a rule against letting anyone help you?"

"Ha!" Lance, walking ahead, let out a short laugh. "Good luck winning that one, Gabe."

"It's called independence," she said.

Gabriel smirked. "Oh, is that what it's called? I thought it was a mountain-climbing death wish."

"Very funny," she muttered but couldn't stop the faint twitch of a smile at his words.

Her chest burned as the thin mountain air seared her lungs. She paused, doubling over to catch her breath, the icy wind cutting through her coat. The others moved ahead, their silhouettes blurred by swirling snow. She cast a glance back at Gabriel. "If Havok is taking away my strength, what will I have left for the battle?"

Without hesitation, he swept her up into his arms.

The world tilted as she gasped, the cold air rushing from her lungs. "Gabriel! What are you doing?"

"I know you can walk," he said, his tone matter of fact. "But this way, you'll have something left when it actually counts. Don't argue."

She opened her mouth to object, but he raised an eyebrow, silencing her. "You're impossible."

"And you're stubborn," he countered, his grin widening. "Guess we make a good team."

The playful exchange melted some of the tension in her mind. She rested her head against his shoulder. "Fine," she mumbled, though her body sagged in relief.

His warmth radiated like a beacon, chasing away the bone-deep chill that had settled in her frozen limbs. She had been holding on for so long, trying to keep herself warm, but it had drained her with every step. Now, wrapped in his strength, her eyelids grew heavy, and her body ached with fatigue.

"I can't keep myself warm anymore," she murmured, almost ashamed of her weakness.

His arms tightened around her. "Then let me handle it for now."

The gentle sound of his breathing calmed her. The mountain's icy winds still howled, but they felt distant now.

"Get some rest," he murmured, his breath warm against her forehead. "I've got you."

She wanted to argue, to insist she was fine, but her body betrayed her. Her eyelids drooped, and her breath slowed as her exhaustion overtook her. Trusting him to carry her the rest of the way, she let herself drift into a light, peaceful sleep, safe in his arms.

Ava's boot sank into the snow, the crunch loud and sharp. She glanced around, her breath hanging in the air.

"You know, you could've warned me about the snoring," Gabriel said.

Ava turned, narrowing her eyes. "What?"

Eric grinned as he caught up, brushing snow from his jacket. "Oh, he's right. I thought a bear was following us."

"I do *not* snore."

The mountain slopes loomed around them, towering and indifferent. Her steps faltered as her eyes caught something unusual to the left of the trail. A set of dark, heavy tracks pressed deep into the powder. Each print was enormous, far too large to be a normal wolf. Its edges sharp and crisp against the untouched snow. The claw marks fanned out, brutal and unforgiving, each claw embedding itself with ruthless intent.

"Wait." She halted, holding out her arm to signal the others

Gabriel's sharp gaze followed her line of sight, his expression hardening. "Saberwolves. And they're recent."

Ava's stomach churned as her eyes swept over the tracks again, noticing a second set beside them, lighter, more controlled, distinctly human. The clawed prints and human steps moved together, weaving a path through the snow. "And Cimmerians."

Sean, who had been a few paces ahead, retraced his steps to join them. His breath came in quick, shallow puffs, visible in the frigid air as he scanned the tracks. "They're close," he said. "We need to get off this mountain. Fast."

Ava's eyes followed the path of the prints as they disappeared downhill, winding through the trees. A sharp stab of worry shot through her chest. "Are they heading the same way as Aaron and the others? What if they reach the village before we do?"

Savina shook her head. "Aaron would've taken them a different route. He knows how to avoid being tracked."

Snowflakes began to fall, light at first, then thick and blinding as a sudden gust of wind swept down the slope. The air shifted, colder and sharper, stealing her breath. The tracks blurred, vanishing under the fresh layer of snow.

"Come on," Sean urged. "We need to keep moving."

The group resumed their descent, each step careful and deliberate. The usual sounds of the mountain, the whistle of the wind, the soft crunch of snow, seemed muffled, swallowed by the oppressive silence. The cold crept through Ava's clothes, leaving her feeling stiff and slow.

Her thoughts spiraled as they walked, her focus slipping in and out. A creeping haze dulled her senses, and a strange detachment settled over her. The snow swirling in the wind seemed to form shapes, shadows shifting and coalescing in the corner of her eye. One shape solidified, darker than the rest, looming like smoke curling through the air.

Havok.

His voice slithered into her mind, soft yet razor-sharp. *You thought you could silence me, little Enchanter?* His mocking laughter reverberated, curling through her thoughts like a storm. Her steps faltered, and her hand flew to her head as she tried to block him out.

Gabriel's hand on her shoulder pulled her back. She turned to him, her breath catching in her throat as his features shifted before her eyes. His familiar blue eyes darkened, his jaw elongating, and it wasn't Gabriel standing before her. It was Havok, his gaze dripping with malice.

Do you really think they'll protect you when they know the truth? Havok's voice was insidious, pulling at the deepest corners of her mind. Her mother's voice, like a wisp of smoke in the wind, joined his, whispering words of betrayal and despair, their faint, ethereal tones haunting the air. The mountain blurred around her, her senses spiraling into chaos.

"Ava?" Gabriel asked. "Stay with me." He squeezed her arm.

She blinked, forcing herself to focus on his face, but Havok's presence clung to her thoughts like an iron grip. *You're stronger alone. These ... companions of yours? They only make you weak.* His voice curled into her mind, showing her visions of destruction, of shadows stretching long and cold over her friends' broken bodies.

"Stop it," she whispered. "You're not real."

Aren't I? Havok pressed, a chill settling over her as she felt the brush of an icy hand on her shoulder. She jerked back, her foot slipping on a patch of ice, but Gabriel caught her.

"You're seeing him, aren't you?"

She hesitated, shame clawing at her chest. "It's … Havok. He's in my head. He's making me see things."

"He wants you to feel alone, but you're not. Trust me."

"Would … the heart of stone help?" she asked.

He frowned and a shadow of worry flickered in his eyes. "If he's still inside your mind, that wouldn't matter. It removes emotions. Not his influence."

Savina and Sean approached, their faces drawn tight with concern. The others crowded closer, forming a protective circle around her.

Savina's sharp green eyes studied Ava's face, her worry shifting into something more calculated. "What's going on?"

Ava hesitated again. But Gabriel nodded, his hand brushing hers in silent encouragement. She drew in a deep breath and forced the words out. "It's … Havok. He's in my head. I can hear him, sometimes even see him. It's like he's … right there, waiting."

Savina's expression darkened, her gaze flicking to Sean. "If he's managing to infiltrate your mind like this, it's not a simple haunting," she said. "It sounds as if there's a deeper connection. One he can use to breach your thoughts."

Ava swallowed hard. "But … what if he's using me? Could he be channeling me somehow?"

"It's possible. But for him to channel through you, he would need something powerful … something binding."

A tense silence fell over them as the implications sank in, and Ava's pulse quickened. Her mother's voice echoed in her memory, and she felt a sense of dread, as though on the brink of understanding something she wasn't sure she wanted to face.

"Like … a promised soul?" Ava asked.

Savina's gaze softened. "A promised soul holds power, yes, but it doesn't mean he has control over you. Promises and intentions can create … pathways, but they're not absolute. For Havok to truly bind your soul to his, something far stronger would need to happen, like a mutual link or binding. Only then would his influence grow beyond what it is now."

The relief Ava felt at Savina's words was fleeting. "So … he can't actually control me?"

"No," Savina replied. "What you're experiencing is a form of influence, Ava, not control. He can plant thoughts, twist your fears, and make you question reality, but he can't make you act against your will. That power is still yours. And as long as you keep your will strong, he can't take anything more than you give him. But because you were in a coma, your defenses are weakened. And the closer we get to Caprington, the more influence he'll have. We need to get to Lighthollow so I can make more potions that will help."

"We'll stay close," Sean said, his tone resolute, his broad shoulders tensing. "We're not far from the village now. We have to keep moving."

Gabriel's hand gave her arm a reassuring squeeze, his expression softening. "He won't win," he murmured, his words fierce yet calming. "You have us. And I'm right here."

Ava nodded, taking a shaky breath. She knew Havok's hold on her might be deeper than she'd realized, but with their support, she felt a flicker of hope that, together, they could find a way to break free.

The sun's final rays bled over the horizon, setting the sky ablaze with streaks of crimson and gold before fading into a bruised indigo. The snow-covered path reflected the light, shimmering like an illusion of calm. But the mountains' silence wasn't serene. It was oppressive, a heavy stillness that pressed down on them with every step.

Ava struggled to keep up, her breaths ragged and shallow as the cold air clawed at her throat. Each step felt heavier than the last, her boots sinking into the icy terrain. Around her, the others moved with grim determination. But Lighthollow was nowhere in sight.

"Shouldn't we stop soon?" Eric asked from somewhere in the middle of the group.

Sean came to a sudden halt, pivoting to face the group. His broad shoulders seemed to block out what little light remained, his expression sharp and unyielding. "We have to keep going."

"The sun's almost gone," Lance pointed out, his uneasy gaze flicking toward the encroaching darkness. "We'll lose visibility."

"I know," Sean said, his breath misting. "But if we stop now, we lose more than that. Havok's influence is growing, and not just over Ava." His eyes darted toward her, and she shrank.

Ava pulled her coat tighter around her, wishing she could vanish into its folds. *It's always me. I'm always the weak link.*

"There's a faster way," Sean continued, nodding toward a jagged ravine in the distance. Its shadowy outline loomed against the snow, an ominous cut into the mountainside. "Through the Lost Souls Necropolis."

Savina's head snapped up, her green eyes narrowing. "You can't be serious."

A shiver snaked down Ava's spine. The Necropolis. She'd heard the stories. A place where the dead lingered, their souls restless and vengeful, bound by curses. Few who entered ever returned, and those who did spoke in hushed tones of voices in the dark and shadows that moved with malicious intent.

Sean's jaw tightened. "I am serious. It'll cut hours off our journey, maybe even a full day."

"That's insane," Natalia snapped. "We'll be walking straight into the arms of death."

"It's dangerous. But we don't have a choice. Havok's reach is worse. If we don't get to Lighthollow soon, we'll lose our chance to stop him before his army gains even more ground."

Peter shook his head. "Everyone's exhausted. We need to stop."

"Do you think the Cimmerians and saberwolves care if we're tired?" Eric countered. "If they find us out here, we won't get another chance to rest."

Savina exhaled deeply, glancing at the ravine. "If we do this, no one strays. Everyone stays close, and we don't stop until we're through."

Sean nodded. "Ten minutes. Then we move."

The group settled into a shallow alcove, shielded from the worst of the wind. Lance crouched by a built fire. Natalia handed out strips of dried meat and bread, her face tight with worry as she muttered about conserving supplies.

Ava sat with her knees drawn to her chest. The crackle of the fire barely registered in her ears. Her thoughts were heavy, weighed down by the shadows of the Necropolis and the ever-present whisper of Havok at the edges of her mind.

Gabriel settled beside her, wrapping his arms around her shoulders. His warmth spread, thawing her chilled body. She leaned back against him, finding his calm breaths comforting.

"Eat." Natalia placed a small piece of bread and meat in Ava's hands. "Even if it's just a little. You'll need the energy."

She nibbled on the bread, her gaze distant, her mind caught in the shadows of what lay ahead. *The Necropolis.* Even the name curled in her chest like a serpent, its whispered stories rising unbidden, the restless dead, the hungry dark. No flame could warm the chill that name brought.

"Five minutes," Sean called, his tone sharp, brooking no argument. The words sliced through the frost-heavy air, a reminder that even their brief reprieve was borrowed.

"I hate this," she said.

"I know." He kissed her temple. "Me too."

"You can't keep using your energy on me." The words tumbled out, edged with guilt she couldn't suppress.

"What, don't think I can handle it?"

She turned to face him, frowning. "That's not what I meant. You're pushing too hard."

"I know my limits, Ava. Besides, you're more stubborn than the mountain itself. Arguing with you takes more energy than this."

Her lips twitched despite herself. "Fine."

But the brief comfort of their exchange faded as a voice invaded her thoughts, cold and cutting, winding around her mind like smoke. *You really think he can protect you? He'll leave you the moment you falter. They all will.*

Her breath caught, and she stiffened.

"Ava?" Gabriel was a thread pulling her back, but the whisper tightened its grip.

You're weak. They all know it. Even him. Havok coiled around her thoughts, dripping venom. *Especially him.*

Her vision blurred, the words digging deep, rooting themselves in her chest.

"Ava, look at me."

She wanted to, but Havok bore down harder, filling her with shadows that were too heavy to escape. She shut her eyes tight, hoping he'd disappear.

You'll fall, and they'll leave you. And when they do, you'll come crawling to me.

"I can't..." The words spilled out, shaky and thin.

"Yes, you can." Gabriel leaned closer until his forehead rested against hers. His breath mingled with hers, slow and deliberate. "Block him out. Focus on me. Fight him."

Her breath came in short bursts. His words were there, close but distant, like a lifeline she was afraid to take.

Havok's laughter cut through the haze, low and cruel. *He's lying to you. You know it.*

"Look at me," Gabriel said.

She could do this. She could beat Havok. He wasn't going to win. Forcing her eyes open, her vision sharpened enough to meet his gaze. His blue eyes locked onto hers, cutting through the chaos like the first rays of dawn after an endless night.

Havok's voice surged, but Gabriel's presence pressed against it, unyielding, a shield against the shadows encroaching on her mind.

"You're not alone," he murmured, his words firm but soft, as if speaking directly to the pieces of her that threatened to fracture. "You've got me. I'm not going anywhere."

The storm inside her began to ebb, Havok's whispers fading to a distant echo. Ava's breathing slowed, each inhale a little less sharp, each exhale a little steadier. She clung to Gabriel's words like a lifeline, grounding her in a way nothing else could.

"You're stronger than he'll ever be." His thumbs brushed against her cheeks. "Whenever he gets in your head, remember this. He's afraid of you. He knows what you can do to him."

She nodded. "I … I'll try."

"That's all you need to do." He leaned in, his lips brushing her temple, a gesture as gentle as the first snowfall. "We'll face him together."

The path narrowed as they neared the threshold of the Necropolis, the jagged edges of the mountain giving way to an archway of ancient stone. Frost clung to its surface like veins of ice, and dark ivy curled around the cracks, as if trying to hold the structure together or perhaps to seal something inside. Shadows gathered beneath the arch devouring the fading light.

Ava's steps faltered as they approached, her breath hitching. Beyond the archway, gnarled trees twisted skyward, their branches heavy with snow and shadow, forming a canopy that swallowed sound. The air grew colder, sharper, a chill that cut deeper than the mountain wind. She shivered, pulling her coat tighter.

Ava's heart quickened as whispers, faint and fleeting, seemed to drift from the depths just beyond hearing, just beyond belief.

"We're really going in there?" Lance mumbled, as if he were afraid to disturb the quiet.

"We have to," Sean said, leading the group.

Savina turned to face the group. "No one lags behind. No matter what you hear, no matter what you see, stay together. And don't touch the souls. They will latch onto you, and they will try to enter your body."

Ava's stomach dropped at the warning. Her last experience with possession was seared into her memory, the violation of her mind, the helplessness. She had no intention of letting that happen again.

Gabriel clutched Ava's hand. "Stay close to me."

The first soul drifted into view as they stepped beneath the canopy. A translucent, luminous figure hovered midair like a flame caught in suspended animation. Though humanoid in form, it was incomplete, lacking a face, features, and having only empty sockets for eyes and limp, unused limbs. More figures followed, dozens, then hundreds, suspended between the thick branches or floated in the air. Their faint glow cast eerie shadows on the snowy path.

A cold sweat broke out on Ava's skin as her eyes darted away, each flicker of movement echoing the frantic beat of her heart. "Can they talk?" she whispered to Gabriel.

"No. They're trapped. Silent."

The occasional caw of black ravens perched in the trees pierced the silence. Their sharp yellow eyes followed the group, unblinking. The first call was joined by another, then another, until the air vibrated with their harsh cries, a discordant symphony that set Ava's teeth on edge.

"Keep moving," Sean urged.

A high-pitched screech tore through the silence. Ava whipped around in time to see a soul extend a claw-like hand toward Lance. Its fingers brushed his arm, leaving behind a faint, shimmering print as it recoiled with an unnatural wail. Lance stumbled back, pale and shaken, and the group quickened their pace.

As they continued, the path became narrower, forcing them to walk single file. The arched trees seemed to close in around them, their branches forming a suffocating tunnel.

She felt a tug, a faint pull at the edge of her awareness. Her gaze drifted to the right, drawn to a bright soul that hovered off the path. It swayed gently, its hollow eyes shifting as if to meet hers. Her heart pounded as a faint whisper reached her ears, soft but familiar.

"Ava..."

Her steps faltered. The voice sounded like her mother. Her hand moved, reaching toward the glowing figure.

"Ava!" Gabriel's sharp whisper yanked her back to reality. His grip on her arm tightened, and she froze, her fingers inches from the soul. A wave of cold washed over her, and she stumbled back, her breath coming in shaky gasps.

"I ... I heard my name."

Gabriel's face was pale as he pulled her closer. "Don't listen to them. They'll say anything to get you to cross that line."

The group pressed on, their steps quicker now. The whispers faded as they reached the end of the path, but Ava couldn't shake the lingering chill that clung to her skin or the faint echo of her name.

The last soul hung suspended, like a sentinel watching their departure, its hollow eyes following them until they passed the final tree. As the eerie glow of the Necropolis faded behind them, Ava released a breath she hadn't realized she was holding. Relief washed over her, but the shadow of the Necropolis stayed, imprinted on her mind like a wound.

The world beyond felt almost too bright, the snow-covered mountains too ordinary after the nightmare they'd walked through. But the unease lingered, a silent reminder that the dead were not so left behind.

35

HALF OF SOMETHING ELSE

The small village looked frozen in time, a cluster of sturdy, weathered buildings huddled against the snowy mountainside. Lazy smoke curled from chimneys, the only sign of life amidst the silence that blanketed Lighthollow. The moon hung low, its pale light casting long, cold shadows over the empty streets. Snow crunched beneath their boots as they approached the inn, its wooden sign creaking in the chill wind.

Ava's legs felt like lead, every step a fight against the exhaustion weighing her down. Her gaze flicked toward the windows of the inn, where faint golden light spilled onto the snow.

Sean knocked on the heavy wooden door, the sound echoing in the stillness. A moment passed before the door creaked open, revealing a young bright-eyed woman bundled in a thick shawl.

"Sean," the innkeeper whispered. "It's so good to see you. Come in quickly before the cold takes you."

"Thank you, Noelle," he said.

They filed inside, the warmth pouring over Ava like a waterfall. The scent of firewood filled the air. The inn itself was still and quiet, its guests had long since gone to bed. The dying embers in the hearth of the large, stone fireplace cast flickering shadows that danced across the walls, painting the room in an ever-changing pattern of light and dark.

They all hugged Noelle and introduced Ava, Lance, and Peter. She was a young girl with light brown skin and amber eyes.

"Everyone's asleep," Noelle said. "Should I wake them?"

Savina shook her head. "No. They need to rest. I do need your help brewing something tonight."

Noelle nodded. "Of course. Just put your things in that corner and I'll bring you all some food and water."

Ava swayed, and her vision swam.

Gabriel's hand was at her elbow, guiding her toward a chair near the fire. He helped remove her backpack. "Sit. You're exhausted."

She sank onto a chair and leaned forward letting the fire warm her hands and face.

Savina had already claimed a corner of the room, her movements swift and deliberate as she unpacked her supplies onto a low wooden table. The firelight flickered against the polished glass of vials and jars, casting strange shapes across the walls.

Noelle moved beside her with the grace of a shadow, bringing steaming kettles and jars of dried herbs, the faint clink of ceramic breaking the heavy silence. Ava caught the sharp tang of lavender and rosemary.

A few minutes later, Savina approached Ava and held out a small glass vial of shimmering green liquid. The potion seemed alive, the light catching on its swirling surface. "Drink this. It will help clear your mind and restore your strength."

Tipping the vial to her lips, Ava took a small sip. The taste was unexpected, warm and floral, with a bitter edge that lingered on her tongue. A soft tingling spread through her chest, and a pulse of energy chased away the exhaustion. She let out a breath, a small smile tugging at her lips as she looked at Savina. "Thank you."

"Of course."

Noelle returned with a tray of bread, cheese, and hot broth, her footsteps light. The scent of the broth, rich and savory, wove its way through the room, mingling with the herbs and smoke. "Rooms are upstairs. Feel free to choose any on the third floor."

"Thank you," Savina said.

The group ate in near silence, the only sounds were the soft clatter of spoons against bowls and the rhythmic pop of the fire.

The broth was hot and flavorful, and Ava savored each sip as she nibbled at the bread. Once finished, she set the bowl on the table and glanced around the cozy room. "Have you ever been here?"

"A few times," Gabriel said. "This is where I met Eric."

"So, it has a special meaning."

He nodded.

The words slipped out before she could stop them. "Take any girlfriends?" The instant the question left her lips, heat flooded her cheeks. Her heart stumbled as she averted his eyes. "Sorry, that was—"

"No." His soft chuckle cut her off, a sound low and rich like the hum of a cello. "Haven't had a reason to bring anyone here … until now."

Her lips parted in surprise, but she snapped them shut as her face burned hotter than the fire. Why did she have that reaction? Was it jealousy? Or something deeper? She didn't want to analyze it too closely. What it meant to feel so tethered to him, so inexplicably drawn to him. Gabriel wasn't just someone who kept her safe. He was someone who made her feel seen, as though she could fall apart in front of him, and he wouldn't turn away. And that scared her almost as much as it comforted her. She hadn't realized how much she'd come to need him until now, when the thought of his past, of anyone else who might have occupied this space with him, felt like a sharp edge in her chest.

Gabriel stood, offering her his hand. "Come on. I'll show you to the rooms."

The stairs groaned as they climbed, the sound echoing through the stillness. On the third floor, a long hallway stretched before them, its wooden beams catching the dim glow of lantern light.

Stopping at a door at the end of the hallway, he pushed it open, revealing a small, comfortable room. The bed was made, a thick quilt folded at its foot. Across from it, a stone fireplace stood dark and cold, but Ava's gaze caught on something else, a small, private bathroom tucked to the side.

A delighted laugh escaped her lips. "A real bathroom?" She turned to thank him, but the words caught in her throat as their eyes met.

The moment stretched, fragile and electric. He leaned down, his mouth brushing hers in a kiss that was soft and unhurried, like the first fall of snow. Heat bloomed inside her, curling in her chest and spreading through her limbs as she reached up, her fingers threading into his hair.

His back hit the door with a quiet thud as his hands settled on her hips, his grip firm but reverent. He drew back, his lips a breath away from hers. "I don't think I'll ever get tired of kissing you."

"Good," she whispered. Her lips curved into a small smile as she touched the scruff of his beard. "Planning on shaving that?"

A soft laugh escaped him, his warm breath grazing against her cheek. "Yes. I was just about to get cleaned up." He kissed her once more before stepping out, leaving her breathless.

Stepping into the bathroom, Ava inhaled the faint scent of eucalyptus soap, and she closed her eyes. She turned the faucet, and the shower sputtered to life. The hot water was a blessing, streaming over her shoulders and chasing away the grime and cold that clung to her skin like a second layer.

She rested her head against the cool tile as the water pounded against her back, like it could wash away the lasting whispers in her mind. When she stepped out, clean and warm in fresh clothes, her reflection stared back at her, tired, pale, but resolute. She felt almost human again, almost whole.

But the silence of the room greeted her like an unwelcome guest. She sat on the edge of the bed, fiddling with the hem of her shirt, her thoughts louder than the crackle of the fire in the hearth.

Her gaze drifted to the door, the thought of Gabriel across the hall pulled at her like a thread she couldn't ignore. It was a comfort, knowing he was close, but it came with a shadow of doubt. Would he think she was weak if she admitted the truth, that the silence wasn't soothing. It was stifling. Was it weak to need someone like this?

Peter's absence echoed in her mind, a sharp memory of every moment he left her to face the dark alone. And like a phantom, Havok's voice curved its way into her thoughts: *He'll leave you.*

The knot in her chest tightened, hard and relentless. Maybe this was a mistake. Maybe she was asking too much.

But Gabriel's words shattered the doubt: *You're not alone.*

The idea of sitting there, trapped with her spiraling thoughts, was unbearable. She couldn't do it. Not tonight.

She stood, her bare feet cool against the wooden floor and crossed the room. The air in the hallway was cooler. She hesitated, her hand hovering at Gabriel's door. *What if he needs his own space? What if this is too much?*

Her hand faltered, almost retreating, when the door creaked open.

Gabriel stood there, his freshly shaved face gleaming, the damp strands of his hair plastered against his forehead. He was shirtless, and the firelight spilling into the hall caught the curve of his shoulders, the lean muscles of his chest. Pajama pants hung low on his hips, and Ava swallowed hard, hoping the dim light hid the flush that crept up her neck.

"Ava?"

"I ... didn't mean to bother you." She fiddled with the hem of her shirt. "I ... I don't want to be alone right now.

"Did you think I wasn't coming back?"

She shook her head. "It's not that. I just ... I don't want to smother you."

A small smile tugged at the corner of his lips. "You could never smother me." He leaned against the doorframe. "Unless I snore too loud."

Despite herself, a small laugh escaped. "I know you like time to yourself."

He took her hand, pulling her into his arms and pressed a kiss to her temple. "And I also like time with you."

Her heart skipped a beat as he led her into the room, closing the door behind them.

After the much needed rest they'd managed to steal, Ava descended the staircase into the main hall, her steps lighter than they'd felt in days. Even though she was tired, the memory of Gabriel's arms around her all night made it easier to bear the exhaustion.

The tavern buzzed with life, a stark contrast to the eerie quiet of the early morning hours when they'd first arrived. Laughter and chatter rippled through the air, punctuated by the clink of mugs. Travelers and locals alike filled the polished wooden tables, their faces alight.

To her left, the hearth blazed with golden flames. The scent of fresh bread, sizzling sausage, and spiced tea permeated the room, wrapping her in a comforting embrace. As she scanned the room, her breath caught when she spotted a familiar head of bouncing curls. Gillian. Relief flooded through her, so suddenly it nearly buckled her legs.

Gillian's wide smile broke the moment their eyes met, and she leapt from her chair, the wooden seat scraping against the floor. "Ava!" Her voice rose above the din as she rushed forward. She collided into Ava, wrapping her arms around her.

"I'm so glad you're okay," Gillian whispered. "We didn't know—" Her words dissolved into a choked cry.

Tears pricked at the corners of Ava's eyes. "It's okay. I'm here. I'm okay."

Behind Gillian, Thomas approached, his expression a mix of relief and exhaustion. "You don't know how worried we were." He pulled Ava into a brief hug.

As she drew back, Ava's chest loosened further at the sight of familiar faces. Peter and Katarina stood by the hearth, speaking in hushed tones. Link, Nicole, Anastasya, Konstantin, Ilya, Gustav, Aidan, Ronan, and Shannon all took turns embracing her.

"Gabriel!" Moira rushed toward him, throwing her arms around him. Then she pulled Ava into a hug. "I'm so glad you made it."

Aaron rested his hand on Ava's shoulder. "How are you feeling?"

"I'm fine." She gave a small smile as she wiped at her damp cheeks. Turning back to Gillian and Thomas, she asked, "Are you okay? Both of you?"

"Yeah," Thomas said, though his gaze flicked toward Gillian.

"I don't know," Gillian choked out. "I keep seeing Jeremy. Every night, he's there, like he's really alive. He … he kisses me, and it's like we're together again. But then … he starts coaxing me to join him." Her gaze dropped to the floor.

A sharp pain shot through Ava's chest, and she clutched Gillian's hand. "That's not Jeremy. It's Havok."

Gillian's eyes widened as the blood drained from her face. "What?"

"He's in your head like he was in mine," she continued, the memories of Havok scraping at the edges of her mind. "When I woke from the coma, his voice ... it was still there. He uses what you love most to break you down, to make you doubt yourself. He'll twist everything good into something dark and cruel." She paused, glancing toward Savina. "The potion. The one you gave me. It helped clear my mind. Maybe it could help Gillian too."

Savina tilted her head in thought. "It's possible. The potion strengthens mental clarity and blocks external influences. If Havok is reaching you the same way, it might give you the resistance you need."

Gillian looked between them. "You really think it could work?"

"It's worth trying," Savina said. "In fact, it might be wise for all of us to take it. If Havok is probing Ava's and Gillian's minds, there's no telling who he might target next."

A ripple of unease passed through the group.

"Savina's right," Ilya said. "If Havok is testing his reach, it's only a matter of time before he moves beyond Ava and Gillian. We can't afford to take that risk."

Link's brow furrowed, and he squeezed Gillian's shoulder. "If it helps protect us, I'm in."

Nicole nodded. "Me too."

Aaron folded his arms. "Do you have enough, Savina?"

Savina's lips pressed into a thin line as she assessed the group. "I'll need time to prepare more. Noelle, I'll need your herbs. Lavender, rosemary, and valerian root."

She nodded, already moving to fetch her supplies. "I'll gather everything we have."

As the group dispersed, Ava hesitated, her gaze lingering on Savina. "I want to learn how to make the potion. I don't want to just rely on others."

"Of course. It's a delicate process, but I'll teach you."

Gabriel's hand brushed Ava's elbow, his lips curving into the faintest smile.

"What?" she asked, tilting her head.

"You keep amazing me. The way you keep fighting, even when you're exhausted. You don't give up, not on yourself, not on us." His smile deepened. "It's one of the things I admire most about you."

A warm rush of pride enveloped her. She smiled as she turned to follow Savina.

Together, they crossed to a small corner of the room where Noelle had already begun setting up supplies. The sharp, earthy scents of dried herbs mingled with the faint tang of something bitter, as Savina measured and mixed ingredients with practiced precision.

"This." She held up a small jar of lavender, "calms the mind." She lifted a vial of thick golden liquid. "And this amplifies the potion's protective properties."

Ava watched, her fingers twitching with anticipation. When Savina handed her a mortar and pestle, she hesitated at first, but Savina's quiet instructions guided her until the mixture began to take shape. Grinding the lavender should have been calming, but her thoughts buzzed with unease. She paused mid-motion, her fingers tightening around the pestle. "Are we really safe here?"

Savina glanced at her, her green eyes softening. "Yes. Lighthollow is protected by old, powerful enchantments. The village is invisible to outsiders. It doesn't appear on maps, and even those who once knew of it wouldn't find it again without invitation."

"Then how did Gabriel find it?"

She resumed measuring out a fine golden powder. "He didn't, not exactly. Lighthollow found him."

"What does that mean?"

"Some places have a way of calling to those who need them most. And Gabriel … well, he needed this place."

A rush of gratitude toward Lighthollow enveloped her, as it was quite possibly the thing that saved Gabriel. From the Cimmerians. From the darkness. From himself.

"You have a healer's touch," Savina said, a rare smile gracing her lips. "This will serve you well. Knowing how to make something like this could save lives."

The words kindled something deep within Ava. She wasn't just surviving anymore. She was learning how to fight back. For the first time in days, a spark of hope flared. Strong. Capable. Maybe Gabriel was right. She *was* strong. And she was just getting started.

From the corner of her eye, Ava caught Ilya watching her. A shadow flickered across his face before he turned away. Did he doubt the potion's effectiveness, the way he had when Gabriel taught them the heart of stone? Unease coiled low in her chest. It had to work. She didn't know what else to do to keep Havok out of her mind. Forcing the thought aside, she focused on the steady rhythm of her hands and the faint, soothing scent of lavender.

Once she helped Savina and Noelle make enough of the elixir for everyone, Ava sank into a nearby chair, exhaustion weighing her down. She rubbed her temples, the faint scent of lavender and rosemary still clinging to her hands. Across from her, Lance, Thomas, and Gillian eased into their seats, their faces softened by the fire's warm, flickering glow. Gabriel leaned against the mantel, his quiet laughter blending with Moira and Eric's conversation. The crackle of the flames filled the silences, a soothing rhythm against the hum of low voices.

Gillian's brows knitted as she studied Ava. "You look pale. What's wrong?"

"I'm still ... weak from the coma."

"She's still in no shape to fight right now," Savina said.

Ava bristled, sitting up straighter. "So, I'm just supposed to sit on the sidelines?"

Gabriel's smirk was quick, his elbow nudging hers as he slid into the chair beside her. "You'd better."

Ava rolled her eyes but couldn't suppress the faint curve of a smile.

Nicole leaned forward, concern flickering across her face. "When will you get your strength back?"

"I don't know," she said. "It's slowly coming back, but ... it's been miserable."

"We didn't want to leave you back there," Gillian murmured, her eyes brimming with emotion. "But the Elders made us."

"It was frightening ... how easy it was for him to get inside my head like that. It felt so real."

The door to the hall swung open with a loud creak, and a spirited voice rang out. "Oh, you keep lookin' betta with age, my boy!"

Everyone turned as a thin woman with rich, dark skin and dynamic eyes strode into the room. A crescent-shaped scar gleamed in the firelight, curving from her ear down her neck. Her grin was wide and infectious as she opened her arms toward Gabriel.

"Hey, Mahalia." Gabriel grinned as she hugged him.

Pulling back, she pinched his cheeks playfully. "Still single, I see. Someone betta snatch you up before I play matchmaker."

Gabriel chuckled, his gaze flicking toward Ava. "Maybe someone already has."

The room seemed to still for a beat. Gillian gasped, her eyes darting between them.

Mahalia's brows shot up, and her grin widened as she looked Ava up and down, her approval clear. "Oh, now *this* I like. She's strong, this one. You'd best keep your eye on her."

"Stubborn, too," Gabriel quipped.

Mahalia gasped in mock horror, her hands flying to her chest. "Stubborn, is she? You must've forgotten who you're talkin' to, Gabriel. Weren't you the one who had to be dragged inside this inn your first winter here?"

Eric snorted. "Oh, I remember. He was practically freezing his ass off by the time he gave in."

Gabriel shot him a glare, his lips twitching in amusement. "Funny. Weren't you the one who tripped over your own boots trying to follow me?"

Mahalia pointed a finger at both of them, her laughter bubbling over. "The two of you are like a couple of old men bickering. If I hadn't taken you both in, you'd still be out there arguing over who could survive longer without help."

Ava raised an eyebrow. "Really? You two arguing? That doesn't sound familiar at all."

Gabriel sighed, rubbing the back of his neck. "Don't believe everything she says. She likes to exaggerate."

Mahalia leaned closer to Ava. "Don't let him fool you, love. I've got plenty of stories about the early days. Like the time he tried to cook for himself and nearly set my kitchen on fire."

Ava laughed.

Gabriel groaned. "Why do I come back here?"

"Because you love me, baby." Mahalia patted his cheek before straightening. "And because I don't let you starve. Now, let me get back to my stew before it burns. If you need anything, just holler."

As Mahalia bustled out, Gillian turned to Ava, her eyes narrowing with curiosity. "Okay, what's going on between you two?"

"What do you mean?" Ava feigned innocence, though the heat rising in her cheeks betrayed her.

"Don't act innocent!"

Gabriel cleared his throat. "I'm gonna grab some tea," he muttered, abruptly standing.

As soon as he was out of earshot, Eric snickered, leaning back in his chair. "Aww, you made him blush. Didn't think the great Gabriel could be rattled, but here we are."

Gillian's eyes widened. "Oh, my God. Something *did* happen. Spill!"

Ava hesitated, still blushing, but the corners of her mouth lifted. "We kissed. And … we're together now."

"Finally! I knew it. I *knew* something was there!"

"And now Mahalia will be planning the wedding *and* pestering you two to have kids so she can be the godmother," Eric teased.

Lance smirked. "I take it she does that to you and Joss, eh?"

"Endlessly." Eric shook his head as the group chuckled.

Gabriel returned, two steaming mugs in hand. He set one in front of Ava and kept the other, his expression calm but his ears still had a faint pink hue. "You get it all out of your system?" he asked Gillian.

"Please." She laughed. "I've only just scratched the surface."

Mahalia reappeared, balancing a tray of steaming bowls. The savory aroma of garlic, herbs, and slow-cooked chicken filled the room, making Ava's mouth water.

"Here's some stew for a brave woman." Mahalia winked, placing a bowl in front of her.

Ava blushed, dipping her spoon into the hearty dish. "I wouldn't consider myself all that brave."

"Nonsense, love," Mahalia said with a knowing grin. "Dealing with these two boys alone makes you a saint." She jerked her thumb toward Gabriel and Eric, earning a wave of laughter around the table.

As Ava glanced around at her friends, some laughing, some leaning into quiet conversations, a calm settled over her. Not just from the stew or the fire but from the sense of belonging that filled the inn. Maybe that was how Gabriel felt his first time there. Determination washed over her. Whatever battles lay ahead, they would face them together.

The fire danced low in the hearth, its golden light spilling across the walls in Ava's room. With the lights off, she snuggled closer to Gabriel on the bed, listening to their shared breaths in the stillness.

"How's the potion working?" he asked.

"I feel better. Like my mind is clearer."

"Good." His fingers traced lazy circles along her arm, calming her.

She watched him in the firelight, his profile softened by the golden glow. Her gaze lingered on the curve of his jaw, the quiet strength etched into his features, the way he seemed to carry her burdens as though they were his own. "You don't have to be strong every moment, Gabriel. Let me carry it with you."

"You already do. More than you realize."

Her fingers intertwined with his, holding on as if he might slip away. But as the silence deepened, the fear crept back, whispering in the back of her mind. What if this was all they had? What if she lost him?

"What is it?" He tipped her chin up to meet his eyes.

"I'm scared," she whispered. "Of what's coming. Of losing you … everyone."

"Me, too. Sometimes, it feels like we're just waiting for the next storm."

She closed her eyes, pressing closer to him. "I want more moments like this with you. You make me feel … stronger. Even when everything else feels impossible."

His thumb brushed over her knuckles. "You're already strong, Ava. But I'll be here, reminding you for as long as you need."

"And you? You're the strongest person I know. Even when the world turned its back on you. You were alone, but you found your way here."

He let out a deep, rumbling chuckle, a sound that vibrated through her. "I was just surviving."

"That's what amazes me about you. Your determination. The way you care so deeply, even after everything. You fight for yourself. You fight for people, for what's right, even when you don't have to. Even when it's cost you so much."

His smile faded, replaced by something quieter, deeper. "You think too highly of me, Ava."

"No," she said. "I see you for who you are. You carry everyone's pain like it's your responsibility, but you never let it break you. That's strength, Gabriel. Real strength."

His fingers tightened around hers. "You make me want to be better, you know that? To keep fighting, to keep going. Even when it feels like it's too much."

"You already are better. You're everything to me, Gabriel."

"And you're everything to me."

A faint blush warmed her cheeks. "When did you know… that you liked me?"

His eyes glinted with a playful spark. "We're already at that part of the relationship?"

She rolled her eyes.

His gaze drifted past her. "I think I first realized it when I teleported us to the Cliffs of Dover. I didn't know why I chose that place … only that I wanted to help you. And the night we went back to the abandoned town, I was terrified the Cimmerians would ambush us. And the thought of not seeing you again." He swallowed. "That's what gave me strength. Knowing I had to get back to you. You weren't just a friend to me anymore. I love you, Ava."

Her heart stuttered, his words reverberating through her chest like the soft hum of a distant melody she had longed to hear. "Say it again."

"I love you."

"I love you, Gabriel."

His mouth met hers in a gentle kiss as if time itself had slowed just for them. As his hand glided down her waist, it found its way to her thigh, tracing the smooth curves of her body with a feather-light touch. He ventured further, reaching the back of her knee, igniting a spark that burned through every nerve.

Gazing at her with dark, intense eyes, he whispered, "You are so beautiful."

Heat flooded her cheeks, her breath shallow and rapid, but her eyes remained on his. Slipping her hands under his shirt, she explored the sculpted lines of his chest, her fingers feeling the hard muscles.

Releasing a small sigh, he removed his shirt and kissed her with a fervor that left her dizzy.

She slipped off her sweater, and his gaze traveled over her, its heat sparking a flush that crept up her neck.

His lips traced a path along her jawline and down the curve of her neck, leaving a scorching trail to her stomach.

She tangled her fingers in his hair, pulling him closer until he was above her. Her heart raced, echoing in her ears as the passion coursed through her veins.

Could such a deep yearning, such a love and ache, be real? No one had ever made her feel both safe and fiercely alive, protected yet boundless, as if she could face any storm with him by her side.

With Gabriel, it was as if they were two souls that had been searching for each other forever, finally reunited. He truly saw her, understood her, and cherished her. Her love for him was an ache that both calmed and excited her heart, a beautiful paradox. He was hers, the only one to her soul, and she knew that loving him was as much a part of her as breathing.

36

TRICK

Ava stirred as the first soft light of dawn filtered through the window, casting a warm, golden glow across the room. She blinked awake, her eyes adjusting.

Gabriel lay sprawled beside her, one arm draped over his face, his breathing slow and even.

As Ava studied him, a small smile tugged at her lips. Asleep, he looked so different. Unguarded, the intensity that usually sharpened his features softened in the gentle light. She'd grown used to the way his eyes always seemed alert, ready for anything, but now he looked almost boyish, his hair tousled, and mouth relaxed. She reached out and swept a stray lock of hair from his forehead.

His arm slipped away from his face as he cracked one eye open, his mouth twitching into a smirk. "Caught you staring, didn't I?" His voice was low, roughened by sleep, sending a pleasant shiver down her spine.

She rolled her eyes, trying to hide her grin. "Caught you snoring, actually."

"Snoring? I don't snore."

"Oh, you do. Practically shook the walls."

He leaned in, his face inches from hers, a mischievous glint lighting his eye. "What can I say? I'm just good at making noise."

A blush rose to her cheeks. "Is that so?"

"Guess you'll have to find out."

"Maybe someday I'll let you prove it."

"Is that a challenge?"

Unable to contain her laughter, she grabbed a pillow and swatted him.

He laughed, a deep, rich sound that filled the room.

"You're impossible," she said.

"Yeah, but you love me."

"You're lucky," she teased.

He pulled her down onto the bed and kissed her forehead. "You have no idea."

She smiled as her fingers traced along the peaks and valleys of his muscles. Her touch lingered on the scar along his ribcage, one she'd noticed before but never asked about. "How did you get this?"

He shifted under her hand. "Being reckless. It was after I first found the Cimmerians. I fell in with a group of ... delinquents. We did dumb things. One time, I teleported too close to a jagged edge and ended up with this. Not one of my smartest moments."

Her fingertips moved to the scar on his side. "And this one?"

His body stilled for a moment. "That one's different," he whispered. "I was ordered to capture a deserter. When I got to their house, I wasn't prepared. We'd been given bad information, and they ambushed me. Stabbed me. I barely got out alive." His voice dropped, tinged with regret. "They just wanted a normal life. They knew what it meant to be a Cimmerian. At the time, I didn't. I found out later their family was killed."

Her chest ached at the sorrow in his voice. "Gabriel…"

His eyes flickered to hers, the corners of his mouth lifting in a bittersweet smile. "It's in the past."

Ava hesitated, fear curling in her stomach. "Havok knows you've been with Savina all this time. Would he…" She swallowed hard. "Would he kill you for desertion?"

"It's crossed my mind. But Havok doesn't kill his soldiers. He punishes them. He breaks them. Killing them means losing control. Torture … submission … that's how he wins."

She gasped as the image of Gabriel suffering that torment pierced her heart. "But … they never punished my mom," she whispered. "They killed her."

He placed his hand over hers. "Ava, your mom was different. Havok saw her as a threat he couldn't control. Killing her sent a message to everyone else."

"And you don't think he sees you as a threat?" Panic edged her voice. "What if he decides you're not worth the effort?"

"Havok doesn't act on impulse with someone like me. I was one of his best soldiers. Killing me outright wouldn't satisfy him. He'd want to use me, to prove something. To make an example. That's his game."

Her breath came shallow, the image of Gabriel in Havok's clutches searing into her mind. "But what if you're wrong? What if he—"

"I'm not wrong. I know Havok. His punishment is about control, not finality. He'll try to break me before he even considers killing me. And that gives us time. Time to think, to act."

The knot in her chest tightened, his reassurance doing little to ease the ache in her heart. She pressed closer to him, wrapping her arms around his waist as if she could shield him from a fate she couldn't control.

"It's okay." He kissed the top of her head.

But it wasn't. None of it was okay. "I'd do anything to keep you from that."

He pulled back, his gaze searching hers. "Why do you always put everyone else before yourself?"

"Because I've already lost too many people. When my mom died, there wasn't anyone to take care of my dad, except me. I know he can take care of himself, but I was always afraid they'd come back and kill him, too."

He studied her. "I'll make a deal. If you share your burdens, I'll do the same for you."

Her eyes brimmed with tears. "I can't lose you."

"You won't," he promised. "Not if I can help it. But you know I don't want to lose you either, right?"

"Is that why you're always playing the hero?" she asked, her lips curving into a faint smile despite the heaviness in her heart.

A quiet laugh rumbled in his chest. "I try not to. I know you're willing and capable. I guess, like you, I've lost too much, and I don't want to keep losing."

She cupped his face, her fingers brushing along his jawline. "Then let's stop trying to fight alone."

For the first time, she saw the flicker of relief in his eyes, a small surrender to the bond they shared in the quiet morning light, with their scars laid bare.

The day passed in a comforting, easy rhythm. They washed their clothes, refilled their supplies, and spent the morning exploring the energetic village. Shops lined the main street, scents of fresh bread and spices filled the air, and people chatted and laughed, their voices blending into a warm hum. Her spirits lifted with each passing hour, the energy of the place vibrant and alive. A stark contrast to the haunted silence of the abandoned town they'd teleported to.

For a moment, Ava didn't feel like they were on a journey to defeat the most powerful Enchanter. Her mind was at peace, her heart was full of joy, and her energy was being restored. As they walked, Gabriel told her of the first few weeks he spent in Lighthollow. How day by day he began to remember what it felt like to be human and not some killing machine. How Mahalia helped him, even when her husband died and she was raising Noelle alone. For the first time since his sister died, Gabriel remembered what it felt like to have a family.

As they wandered through the market, Gabriel paused by a small stall displaying polished stones and charms on thin leather cords.

"What did you find?" she asked.

He held up the charm, letting the stone catch the sunlight, its surface shimmering with flecks of blue and green, like fire caught beneath the stone's surface. "Labradorite. They say it's for protection and intuition, and they call it the 'stone of transformation.' Apparently, it's meant to keep you grounded." He paused, giving her a knowing look. "Sounds like something that might come in handy for someone who's always, you know, stumbling into trouble."

Ava gave him a mock scowl. "Me?"

He grinned, looping the cord around her neck so the labradorite rested against her collarbone. "Definitely you. This is for when I'm not there to stop you from being your usual fearless self. Not that I'm planning on letting you out of my sight anytime soon."

She laughed, her fingers brushing over the crystal. "Guess I'll have to test its limits, then."

"Just don't test them too far." He leaned in. "I'd like to keep you around."

Her heart warmed at his words, and she looked down, her fingers lingering on the stone. It was solid, reassuring, like a quiet promise she hadn't known she needed. "Thank you."

Their eyes met, and for a moment, the bustling market faded into the background. In his gaze, she saw everything he didn't say. A care that ran deep and true, a promise of protection that went beyond the charm.

After dinner, the inn's warm, cozy atmosphere settled around them. Ava, Gabriel, Eric, and Moira were deep in conversation, Gabriel's hand resting on the back of Ava's chair.

Across from them, Ilya leaned forward, his face half-shadowed in the dim light. "I think I overheard something about a Cimmerian ambush near the meadow."

Ava frowned, gripping her cup. "An ambush? When?"

"Tonight." Ilya glanced around as if to ensure no one else could hear. "One of the villagers mentioned seeing shadows in the woods earlier today, figures in black cloaks, just beyond the charms. They might be scouting, waiting for the right moment."

Gabriel stiffened. "Why didn't the villager come forward?"

Ilya shrugged. "Didn't want to cause a panic. Figured I'd tell you instead. You'd know what to do."

The room suddenly felt too warm. Ava raised her cup, taking a sip of water, but even that didn't ease the tightness building in her chest.

"Did he say how many?" Gabriel asked.

"Just shadows," Ilya said. "Could be nothing, but it's better to be prepared."

"Have you told Gustav or Aaron?" Gabriel asked.

Ava's head began to swim. The edges of her vision blurred, and the faces around her softened into a hazy, indistinct mass. Her limbs felt heavy, her body sluggish, as if her blood had turned to syrup. Gabriel and Ilya's voices became garbled, their words distant echoes.

"Ava?" Gabriel asked. "Are you okay?"

She blinked, forcing a faint smile. "I'm fine. Just … tired." Her words felt thick, clumsy, like her tongue didn't quite belong to her.

"You don't look fine.'

"I'm just hot." She pushed herself to stand, but her knees buckled, and the chair scraped against the floor. Nausea coiled in her stomach as the room spun.

Gabriel was at her side, his arm sliding around her waist. "Whoa. You're burning up."

"I'm fine."

"You're not. Come on."

The floor felt strange, like walking on clouds. "You're so … so warm."

Gabriel snorted. "Glad I can double as a space heater."

She giggled. "A really nice space heater. Like … five stars."

His arm tightened around her as they climbed the stairs. "Definitely loopy. Did you sneak something to drink?"

"Noooo." Her head lolled to the side, resting against his shoulder. "Just you. You smell nice. Like … trees."

"Trees?"

"Mm-hmm." She swayed as they reached her door, her legs barely cooperating. "And you're … very pretty. Like … ridiculously pretty."

His breath hitched in a laugh. "Pretty, huh? That's a first."

"Mm. You should be … a prince or something. With a crown."

"A prince." He opened the door and guided her to the bed. "Alright, Sleeping Beauty. Down you go."

The soft mattress cradled her as she sank into it, the blankets wrapping around her. With a clumsy reach, she grabbed his sweater and tugged him closer. "Don't go."

His hand swept her hair back from her forehead. "I'm not going anywhere. Just rest."

Her eyelids fluttered, and her vision swirled with golden light. "You're always saving me. You're … the best prince."

Gabriel's low chuckle was the last thing she heard before sleep pulled her under.

Heat engulfed Ava, heavy and suffocating, as if she were trapped inside a blazing furnace. Sweat slicked her skin, soaking her thin pajamas and trickling down her chest and legs. Her throat was parched, her mouth dry as sandpaper. Every breath burned, catching in her lungs like smoke. She tried to move, to throw off the oppressive blankets, but her limbs refused to obey, weighed down as though they were made of lead.

A wave of fear washed over her, chilling her to the bone. Was this another coma?

The thought clawed at her, panic rising like a tidal wave. Her eyes fluttered open, catching glimpses of moonlight spilling across her bed, but the world swam as if it weren't real. Her mind fought to catch hold of something tangible, something solid.

"Gabriel…" Her voice rasped. *Is he here? Is this real?* Panic surged. "Gabriel…"

"I'm right here," he said, soft yet distant, like an echo across the water.

"Hot…"

A cool hand pressed against her forehead, soothing against the inferno raging beneath her skin. "You're burning up," he murmured. Relief washed over her as the blankets disappeared, peeled back in one swift motion.

Her world tilted as his arms scooped her up. The motion jostled her enough to send nausea surging. She groaned, her head sagging against his chest as the door swung open. A sharp blast of icy air hit her face, a shock against her overheated body, and she gasped.

Her feet dangled, swaying like melted wax in his grip.

"They've found you," he said. "We have to leave. Now."

The freezing wind stirred her from the haze, sharpening her awareness. "Who?" Her voice was hoarse, broken. "What about everyone else?"

"The farther I get you from here, the harder it'll be for them to track you." His voice was clipped, emotionless, and it sent a faint ripple of unease through her.

"Put me down. I can run. I feel … better."

"You're still too weak."

"No," she protested. "Let me walk."

Reluctantly, he set her down. Her bare feet sank into the snow, and she gasped from the icy chill biting into her toes. The jolt cleared her head further, but she wobbled, her legs weak and unstable. "I need shoes."

"There's no time for that." He grabbed her hand and tugged her forward.

The inn lights faded behind them, swallowed by the dark expanse of the woods. Each hurried step deepened her apprehension.

Her foot caught on something, and she stumbled hard into the snow. Pain flared in her palms as they hit the frozen ground.

"Ava, we don't have time for this." He yanked her up with a force that made her wince.

"Gabriel … stop," she breathed. Something was wrong. He had never handled her like this, never been so cold, so unfeeling. "You're … scaring me."

He turned to her, and her breath hitched. His face was familiar, but his eyes gleamed in the moonlight, sharp and predatory. "They're coming after us. Havok is waiting for you. We have to hurry."

Panic seized her, leaving her body paralyzed with dread. "What are you talking about?"

His lips curved into a smile that was cold, hollow, and utterly wrong. "You were right to suspect me."

Her stomach dropped as clarity struck. "You're … you're not Gabriel. Get out of my head!"

"This isn't in your head, sweetheart. This is real."

"No."

His hand grazed her cheek, and a wave of nausea washed over her. "Does this feel fake to you?"

She slapped his hand away, a surge of energy sparking under her skin. Her powers, dormant for weeks, flickered to life, water pooling along her arms. It was weak, but it was something. "I'm not going with you."

"You don't have a choice," he sneered. "Havok's forces are seconds away. We're taking the Elementals. If you come with me, it all stops. No one else has to die."

She steadied her breathing. "Never."

He clicked his tongue. "Shame. But look at the bright side: when you join Havok, you'll see me every day. Well, a version of me, at least."

Her heart hammered, her mind begging for clarity. She tried to pull herself from the fog, but nothing worked. The realization hit her, sudden and sharp. "You drugged me, didn't you?"

"I had to even the playing field. But I underestimated you."

A loud crack shattered the stillness of the woods, pulling Ava's attention toward the village. Black smoke twisted upward into the indigo sky, an ominous signal of chaos. Faint screams pierced the air, raw and jagged, slicing through her like shards of glass.

"No!" She bolted toward the village, her bare feet slipping on the icy ground.

He snatched her wrist, jerking her back.

"Let go of me!" she snarled, fighting with all her strength. She drove her elbow into his ribs, a solid, satisfying impact that sent a sharp grunt from his lips.

But he didn't release her. His grip remained firm, and she staggered back. Something was off. His movements lacked Gabriel's strength, his touch unfamiliar. The truth hit her like a blow to the chest. This wasn't Gabriel.

His hand shot out, closing around her throat like a vice. The force sent her stumbling, her back slamming into a tree. Bark scraped against her skin as her breath strangled in her throat. Panic roared in her ears as her vision darkened, the edges of the world fraying black.

She clawed at his hand, her nails digging into his skin, but he squeezed harder. Stars danced in her vision, her lungs screaming for air. She had to act. Now.

She focused, her thoughts sharpening despite the haze. Water. She imagined it flooding his lungs, icy and suffocating.

He froze. His grip faltered. A strangled, choking sound tore from his throat, and he released her, wobbling back as he clutched his chest. He dropped to his knees, gasping and sputtering, his body convulsing as if drowning.

Collapsing against the tree, Ava massaged her bruised throat as she fought to catch her breath. Her chest heaved, the cold air burning her lungs as she stared at him, her mind racing.

His body convulsed once more before it shifted. Hair lightened to a dull brown, his frame shrinking, losing the solid build she knew so well. His gasps softened, replaced by a low, pained groan.

She blinked, her vision clearing enough to meet his eyes. Pale blue, wide with pain and shock.

Ilya.

37

CHOICE

"Ilya?" Dread pooled in her stomach. Leaping to her feet, she stumbled backward, but his arm snaked out, catching her ankle. She fell hard, cold snow seeping through her clothes. Her vision blurred as she tried to push herself up, but Ilya held her.

"You thought you killed me?" He got to his feet, jerking her up with a bruising grip. His fingers clamped around her neck, dragging her away from the village, the harsh moonlight glinting off his features as he morphed back into Gabriel's form, a sinister smile on his lips.

She wanted to throw up. "You aren't taking me to him." She struggled against him as a trickle of water began forming along her arms. She focused, willing it to strengthen, but it was slower than usual, her concentration slipping with each pulse of pain from her temples.

"Oh, I think I am."

A sudden blow threw him off-balance, tearing his hand from Ava, and he stumbled back.

She whirled around as two Gabriels clashed in the snow, grunts and the sickening crack of fists colliding echoing through the trees. They slammed each other against the trunks, snow crashing down around them. She couldn't tell which one was the real Gabriel. Her Gabriel.

One of the men threw a brutal punch, sending the other staggering back with a low growl.

The sharp screams from the village pierced the air, each one a reminder that lives were being torn apart. She had to get to them. Seizing the opportunity to slip away, Ava moved towards the forest's edge. The faint scent of smoke, sharp and acrid, filled her nostrils as she reached the clearing, where flames raged through the village. Through gaps between buildings, motionless bodies lay scattered in the streets, their silhouettes haunting against the firelit background. The grogginess from whatever Ilya had drugged her with clung stubbornly, her limbs heavy, but she forced herself to run, her movements slow and erratic.

"Ava!" Gabriel called behind her, weak and strained.

She froze, her heart stuttering. Turning, she saw Gabriel standing there, one hand clutching his side. Blood seeped through his shirt, darkening the fabric as it dripped onto the snow, staining it crimson. His entire frame wavered as he struggled to stay upright.

She halted, suspicion flickering to life even as her heart lurched at the sight of his pain. "Get away from me."

"It's me, I promise." He raised his free hand, palm open, his voice raw with desperation. "Please. It's really me." He sank to his knees, each breath ragged, digging his fingers into the snow for support.

"How do I know it's really you?" she demanded, torn between her urgency to return to the village and the urgency to heal him. But his eyes held the same intensity, the same depth that had always been there, no matter how dire things became.

He coughed, blood spraying the snow at his feet. "I took you to the Cliffs of Dover," he rasped, each word labored.

She took a tentative step forward. "Is he … is Ilya dead?"

"No. He got away." His gaze met hers, pleading. "Please believe me."

With a deep breath, she rushed over, easing him down to lie flat. She carefully lifted his shirt, swallowing back a surge of nausea from the deep, raw wound torn into his side. She blinked again, her vision wavering. "What … what did this?"

"A tree branch."

She concentrated, but the familiar cool sensation of water seemed to hover out of reach. Gritting her teeth, she pressed her hands over the wound, willing the water to flow. At first, a thin trickle formed. "Come on," she murmured. She could feel Gabriel's shallow breaths beneath her hands. Another thin stream of water flowed from her palms and washed over his torn skin. Finally, it took hold, knitting the wound.

Gabriel's labored breathing eased, and his expression relaxed for a brief second. "Thank you." He jumped to his feet, startling her. He offered his hand. "I swear I'm not going to hurt you. Come on."

They reached the edge of the village, as the chaos raged.

"You have to stay here," he insisted. "You can't fight in this condition." But before she could respond, he was already lunging forward, crashing into a man twice his size.

The village was a war zone. Flames and smoke devoured the buildings, thick and choking, while Enchanters on both sides unleashed powers that ripped through the air. Fireballs, lightning strikes, the roar of explosions. The building nearest them shuddered, beams snapping as it began to collapse in a cascade of splintering wood and stone.

Ava's gaze darted across the melee, spotting Thomas being hurled against a brick wall. He slumped to the ground, the bricks crumbling under his weight.

Aaron laced his fingers around a Cimmerian neck, energy draining from the young Enchanter's form as she sagged. Katarina's flash of blue hair caught Ava's attention. She leapt over a woman, slamming her into the ground with an unrelenting grip around her neck.

Ava narrowed her gaze. There was no way she was going to stand by and watch. She sprinted forward, catching sight of a young man attacking Gillian. With a swift leap, she landed on his back, water swirling around her hands as she focused, turning it into a sharp, jagged icicle. The man barely had time to react before she slashed the ice across his throat, crimson gushing as he collapsed.

She stumbled but caught herself, spinning to see Gillian engaged with another woman. With a quick flick of her wrist, Ava sent a sharp blast of water toward the woman, piercing her shoulder like shrapnel. Gillian kicked the woman to the ground.

The panicked screams from her left turned her head. A woman danced in frantic circles as flames consumed her body, the fire licking up her arms as she writhed.

Suddenly, a sharp, searing pain tore through Ava's side. Blinding flashes of red and white filled her vision. Reaching back, she felt something firm lodged in her flesh, her fingers slick with warm blood that dripped down her hand.

"Take care of Ava!" Aaron shouted.

She felt Gabriel's arm wrap around her, pulling her tight against his chest. "I have to take this out," he whispered into her ear. "Hold on. It's going to hurt." She buried her face against him, bracing herself as his fingers gripped the foreign object. With a swift motion, he pulled it free.

Agony ripped through her, forcing a scream from her lips. The ground rushed up to meet her as she sank to the snow, the icy cold seeping into her back.

"Ava, you have to heal yourself." He held firm pressure against the wound.

"I can't."

"Come on, you're not giving up on me now."

She clenched her teeth, taking shallow, rapid breaths, fighting to channel the water from her palms. The pain blurred her focus, but Gabriel held her. The burning ache ebbed as her power flowed over her wound, sealing it closed. When the pain faded, she took a deep breath and opened her eyes.

"Are you okay?" Worry etched his features.

She nodded, looking him over. "Are you?"

"Yes."

He pulled her into a tight hug before they both turned to the wreckage. The horrific destruction of the village laid bare. Familiar faces were strewn across the ground, lifeless and still. She spotted Mahalia, facedown and motionless, and her breath hitched as grief surged through her.

"It's over … for now," Thomas said. Blood spattered across his face, mingling with the dust and dirt in his hair.

"Thomas!" Moira pulled him into a tight embrace. Then she turned to Gabriel and Ava, wrapping them in a hug.

"Is everyone … okay?" Thomas asked.

Moira's face crumpled as tears streamed down her cheeks. "Nathan … and Mahalia." She swallowed. "They're gone."

Ava's heart sank as dread settled over her. Nathan's son, Lucas, would never know his father now. She pictured Cara, trying to explain to her young son why his father would never come home. And Mahalia … she'd just met the woman, but it felt like she'd known her forever.

"Here's our traitor!" Gustav bellowed as he dragged Ilya across the snow-packed road, his boots scraping against the frozen ground.

Ilya's head hung low. But when Gustav yanked him upright, the moonlight caught his face, and Ava saw a glint of defiance in his eyes.

"I caught him with the Cimmerians," Gustav growled.

"What?" Anastasya whispered, her voice thick with disbelief.

Ava glanced at Savina. "It was Ilya all along. He's been leading Havok and the Cimmerians past your charms."

"How is that possible?" Katarina asked as the group closed in around Ilya, forming a tense circle.

"He drugged me. And morphed into Gabriel to trick me."

Gabriel's fists clenched at his sides. Fury flashed in his eyes. For a fleeting moment, it seemed like he might restrain himself.

Ilya's smirk curled as he lifted his head, his gaze locking on Ava. "I knew I couldn't morph into Peter again."

Ice froze around her heart. Her knees wobbled. Bile rose to her throat and she clamped her jaw shut. She hadn't dreamed of Peter kissing her. It wasn't some sick vision from Havok. Ilya had morphed into Peter and kissed her. He'd broken her spirit, letting Havok inside her head. She felt as if he'd stripped her in front of everyone.

Gabriel lunged, his fist connecting with Ilya's jaw in a sickening crack. The impact sent Ilya stumbling back into Gustav, blood dripping from his split lip.

Ilya let out a low, rasping laugh. "Temper, temper, Gabriel. Always so predictable."

"You sick bastard," Katarina hissed.

"Oh, the games I played with you all," he sneered. "The snakes, Ava's sweet dreams of her mother…" His eyes settled on Lance, his smirk deepening. "Even your precious visions of Melissa." He turned to Gillian. "Although, these last few nights with you have been fun."

Gillian's face twisted in horror. "What?"

"You're all so easy to manipulate. Weak. Pathetic."

Lance surged forward, but Thomas and Link grabbed his shoulders, holding him back. "You bastard!"

Anastasya shook her head, eyes wide. "I cannot believe this."

Katarina's hands trembled as she stepped forward, her expression torn between rage and betrayal. "After everything … all the times we trusted you, stood by you. How could you do this?"

"Trust?" He let out a bitter laugh, blood staining his teeth. "I was never one of you. You were fools to think I ever could be. I tried to bring you with me, Katarina. You chose wrong."

Her hand snapped around his throat. Gustav released Ilya as her grip tightened, glowing tendrils of light snaking around his neck.

Ilya's eyes widened in panic, his defiance slipping into fear. He gasped, choking as the light seared his skin. Blood welled beneath the surface, staining his face as pain wrinkled his features. His legs buckled, and his body crumpled to the snow with a dull thud, leaving a dark stain spreading beneath the white.

"Katarina!" Gustav shouted. "We could have used him as a prisoner, gotten answers."

Her chest heaved, her trembling hands still glowing. "He didn't deserve to live." She turned to Peter, and he pulled her into his arms. She pressed her face against his shoulder, muffling the quiet sob that escaped.

Ava trembled, her body quaking. She stared at Ilya's lifeless form, the snow beneath him dark and tainted, the evidence of betrayal staining more than the ground. She'd been fooled twice by someone she'd thought she could trust. Someone who had smiled, fought beside them, shared their victories and defeats. The betrayal sliced deeper than she expected, leaving a hollow ache in its wake. "I can't believe … I let him get so close."

Gabriel's arms wrapped around her, his voice soft against her ear. "He can't hurt you anymore."

"But Havok will," Noelle said. She looked at Savina, her eyes shimmering with tears. "He'll come back, he always does. You have to kill him."

Savina placed a comforting hand on Noelle's shoulder. "We'll do everything we can."

"The inn suffered minimal damage," Noelle murmured, swallowing back her grief and holding her head high. "Will they come back tonight?"

"I doubt it." Moira cast Ava a glance of regret. "We had no idea. I'm sorry, Ava."

"It wasn't your fault," Gabriel said. "We all trusted him."

Savina nodded. "Everyone let's get inside. The injured need tending, and the Elementals need rest. We need to be prepared for whatever may come next."

Aaron raised his hand to the group. "And for those who are able, let's start cleaning up and tending to the fallen."

As everyone dispersed to their duties, Gabriel turned to Ava, a frown creasing his brow. "Why didn't you stay hidden?"

"This is my fight as much as it is yours."

His mouth quirked into a reluctant smile. "Stubborn."

"I know." The crushing realization of her mistake, mistaking Ilya for Gabriel, settled over her, a sickening sensation of betrayal weaving deep inside. She met his gaze. "I'm sorry. I didn't know."

"There was no way you could have known."

"But somewhere, deep inside, something told me it wasn't you … that it couldn't be."

He frowned. "After you fell asleep, I noticed something outside the village. Tracks, fresh ones, leading toward the meadow. At the time, I thought Ilya was right." A muscle in his jaw twitched. "I had to check it out, make sure we weren't about to be ambushed."

She studied his face, her chest aching at the guilt shadowing his features. "You didn't know he'd try something. That he'd use you to—" Her voice broke, and she struggled to shake the memory of Ilya's malicious grin.

"I shouldn't have left. I should've stayed with you."

She caressed his cheek. "You did it to protect us. It's what you always do."

"And it gave him the opening he needed." He let out a breath. "I swear to you, it won't happen again."

"Gabriel, don't you dare blame yourself."

His lips pressed into a thin line, his gaze dropping for a moment before he nodded. "I need to help Aaron with the cleanup." He kissed her hand. "I'll be in soon."

Her heart sank as he walked away. Even though Ilya's betrayal clung to her, a glimmer of resolve sparked within her. Havok wouldn't stop. She knew that now more than ever. And she needed to be ready.

Inside the inn, Ava joined Gillian at a round table, the low hum of murmured voices filling the space. Noelle and a few others moved through the room, passing out warm drinks and blankets. They'd survived another Cimmerian battle, but how many more could they endure?

Ava's gaze lingered on the group around her, exhaustion etched into their faces. They needed a plan. Havok wouldn't let them attack Caprington and slip away unscathed. Every strategy they'd tried had been countered, every move anticipated. He was always two steps ahead, manipulating them like pawns in a game.

"I can't believe Ilya ..." Gillian shook her head as a tear slid down her cheek. She angrily wiped it away. "How did you know it wasn't Gabriel?"

Ava turned to her, the question pulling her back into the moment. Gillian's face was streaked with dirt and blood, her bouncy curls limp and unkempt. "He didn't fight like Gabriel. He wasn't using his ability."

Savina approached, her sharp green eyes assessing Ava as she spoke. "That's because anyone who morphs into another cannot use their own power. It's one way to confirm identity." She studied Ava. "It seems the drugs have fully dissipated."

"What did he use on me?" Ava asked.

"A sleeping potion, likely acquired from someone within the village." Savina's expression darkened. "I've placed a charm over this building. If they come back, they won't see us. You can rest." She walked away tending to others.

But Ava shook her head and leaned in. "There's no rest until Havok is dead." She kept her voice barely above a whisper. "He'll keep killing people if we don't act."

"He's going to kill people whether we act or not," Thomas muttered, dragging his hands down his face.

"We've got to figure something out," Gillian said. "We can't keep losing like this."

Ava nodded. "I know. But what's left? Every tactic we try, he's already anticipated. Every defense, every counterattack … it's like he's always two steps ahead."

A tense silence stretched between them, heavy with unspoken fears and the growing realization of their predicament.

After taking a deep breath, Ava finally uttered the words, struggling but persevering. "What if…" She hesitated. "What if we surrender?"

Gillian's head snapped toward her, her face pale with shock. "Ava, you can't mean that. We're fighting to stay free, not … give in."

Ava's shoulders slumped, but her voice didn't waver. "Think about it. Havok's spies can find us anywhere. We can't keep running, and we can't keep fighting head-on. But if we pretend to switch sides, we could get close enough to him. Close enough to end this."

"That's insane." Gillian crossed her arms. "What if they don't believe us? What if they kill us on sight?"

"That's where the heart of stone comes in," Lance said. He leaned forward. "If we can perfect hiding our emotions, we might be able to convince Havok we're serious."

Gillian shook her head. "And what if they test us? Or worse, what if we really have to hurt someone to prove it? Do you think we could go through with that?"

Ava's chest tightened at the thought. "If we don't, Havok wins anyway. He'll destroy us, one by one. If this gives us even the smallest chance to stop him, then it's worth it."

"But Gabriel … everyone else…" Gillian's voice faltered. "If they don't know, they'll think we've really betrayed them."

"That's the risk." Ava swallowed hard. "If they knew, they'd try to stop us. Or worse, someone might slip and give it away. Havok would see through any deception in an instant."

Thomas nodded. "She's right. This stays between us. No one else can know."

Gillian hugged her arms around herself, her expression a mix of fear and reluctant understanding. "So, we go to him. We lie, gain his trust, and then we take him down from the inside."

As the gravity of their decision settled over them, a wave of fear, sharp and undeniable fell over Ava. But beneath it was a steady current of determination. They would do this. For the people they loved, for the chance to end this once and for all. They had to.

"Are we all in?" Lance asked, his eyes dark and solemn.

One by one, they nodded, sealing their pact in silent agreement.

38

A NIGHT LIKE THIS

Ava peeled away her blood-stained pajamas, the fabric stiff and rust-colored from battle, and threw them in the fire. She stepped into the shower, the scalding water a temporary relief against the ache that clung to her shoulders. Warm rivulets ran down her body, washing away grime and dried blood, swirling into a murky whirlpool beneath her feet. How many more times would she watch her own blood flow down the drain? How much more death would she witness at the hands of the Cimmerians?

Tears pricked at her eyes, hot and unyielding, and she sank to the shower floor, the water cascading over her like it could wash away the agony in her chest. Could she go through with the plan to take Havok down? Could she really distance herself from Gabriel? The thought alone felt like a knife burrowing deep into her heart, slashing it apart again and again.

For a moment, the urge to abandon the plan overwhelmed her. To run to her friends, to tell them to forget it all. They'd find another way. Somehow. They had to.

But she knew that was wishful thinking.

The sobs came hard and fast, tearing from her chest as she buried her face in her hands. Gabriel would never forgive her. He would hate her. Despise her. But he'd be alive. That had to be enough, even if it destroyed her.

Taking several shaky breaths, she forced herself to calm down, the tears subsiding. Her body felt heavy, her heart hollow, but she pushed herself to finish cleaning up. Wrapping a towel around her, she stepped out of the bathroom and froze.

Gabriel sat on the edge of her bed, freshly showered, dressed in clean clothes. His damp hair clung to his forehead, and his piercing blue eyes lifted to meet hers.

Her stomach dropped. How much had he heard?

She hesitated by the fireplace, gripping the towel tighter around her as if it were armor. The warmth of the fire touched her back, but her insides felt cold, raw. Struggling to keep her composure, she pushed away the tremor in her chest.

His eyes softened, full of quiet patience. "What is it?" His voice was gentle, but there was an edge of worry beneath it, subtle but there.

Ava swallowed, her throat tight. "I know it wasn't you, but … all I can see is him. That look in your eyes. It wasn't your eyes, but it felt like it was. The way his voice turned into yours, so wrong but so close. He wanted me to believe you'd betrayed me."

Gabriel stood and crossed the space between them. He touched her bare arms, his thumb skimming over her skin.

"Ava, I would never betray you. Not then, not now. You know that, don't you?"

She nodded, her lips trembling. "I do. But … in that moment, it felt so real. And now, I can't stop thinking about it." She closed her eyes against the tears threatening to spill again.

He drew her into his arms, and she inhaled his familiar scent, the faint hint of juniper washing over her, settling her heart. Her muscles began to relax, and her head found a resting place against his chest. "Stay with me tonight."

"Always."

Drawing back, Ava cupped his face, pulling his lips to hers. The towel slipped from her grasp, pooling on the floor.

His arms enveloped her, strong yet tender, as he lifted her. He carefully laid her on the bed, the mattress dipping beneath them.

Shivers rippled through her as he hovered close.

His breath brushed against her neck, warm and featherlight, as his fingers swept her hair back from her shoulders.

She stiffened, anticipation coiling low in her stomach as his lips grazed her skin. The faintest pressure, soft and deliberate, sent a trail of sparks down her spine.

The hairs on the nape of her neck stood on end as he whispered against her skin. "This is me." His lips followed the outline of her collarbone, slow and reverent, like he was trying to memorize every inch of her.

She closed her eyes, her hands gripping his sides, feeling the solid strength beneath her fingertips.

"This is me." He pressed a kiss to her lips as his hand moved to the curve of her hip, to her thigh.

Her breath caught, and her body trembled at the intensity of each sensation. A flutter of nerves settled inside her stomach, but she was ready. She wanted to give herself to him, to let him feel the love and yearning she'd kept hidden. She wanted him, needed him, and for tonight, she wanted to let herself love without fear. Would it be selfish to hold on, even if only for this moment? She knew that soon she would need to pull away, to close herself off, but not now. Now, she wanted him with all she had.

Her hands trembled as she slipped her fingers beneath the hem of his shirt, lifting it over his head. Gabriel helped her, the shirt falling forgotten to the floor. Her fingertips skimmed over the contours of his chest, tracing the firm lines of his skin.

Each touch sent a shockwave through her, burning something deep within. She savored the moment, committing every detail to memory. The way his muscles tensed under her touch, the quiet hitch in his breath when her hands lingered.

Taking a deep breath, Ava calmed herself as her fingers slid lower, grazing against the waistband of his pants. With a gentle pull and a racing heart, her breaths came in short, shallow gasps.

Gabriel's hand caught hers, his gaze locking with hers, blue eyes intense and searching. "Are you sure?" he whispered.

She nodded. "I've never been more sure."

He kissed her, his lips so soft. So urgent. Slowly, his hand ventured lower, trailing a path of fervor, causing her to quiver.

Finally, as they gave themselves to each other, the world around them faded, leaving the heat of his touch and the quiet rhythm of their hearts beating in unison. Every breath, every touch, every whispered promise held them close, binding them in a moment of peace and passion in a world that felt so often broken. She surrendered to him, letting his love, his presence, and his unyielding strength anchor her. For this fleeting, precious night, there was no war, no fear. Only the truth of them, raw and unguarded, as they held onto each other as though the dawn might tear them apart.

39

OF LOVE AND LOSS

The soft rise and fall of Gabriel's breathing filled the quiet room like the tide pulling Ava back to shore. The first faint light of dawn crept through the curtains, brushing over his features. She lay still, her head resting on his chest, the steady thrum of his heartbeat beneath her ear.

She watched him sleep, his face softened by the gentle morning shadows. His dark lashes brushed his cheeks, and a faint smile lingered on his lips, as if even in sleep, he could feel her there. Her eyes traced the lines of his face, committing every detail to memory. The strong curve of his jaw, the roughness of faint stubble, the gentle crease between his brows that softened in sleep.

How could she ever let go of this? A painful knot of longing tightened in her chest, a bittersweet ache that resonated deep within her soul.

Closing her eyes, she savored the contrast of softness and rugged strength in his skin against hers. For a moment, she let herself pretend this could last, that they could stay like this forever, untouched by the world outside.

Her fingers brushed his cheek, grazing his skin. She wanted to keep this sensation, to memorize the feel of him. The memories of last night washed over her. She hadn't known she could feel like that, completely seen, completely loved. The way he'd touched her, like she was the only thing that mattered in the world. She swallowed hard, the ache in her throat almost unbearable.

I'm going to lose him.

The thought struck her like a blow, sharp and unforgiving. She had let herself have this one night, this one perfect, fleeting moment with him. But now, she had to let him go. She couldn't keep him close, not when the plan required her to distance herself. To deceive him, to make him believe she didn't care as deeply as she did.

Tears pricked her eyes, but she refused to let them fall. She couldn't afford to break now. She couldn't risk waking him, couldn't bear the questions in his eyes if he saw her like this.

As she began to pull away, his arm drew her closer, holding her firmly. The gesture wrenched her heart, and she nestled into the comfort of his shoulder, breathing him in, the scent of juniper and the faintest hint of earth.

She couldn't help herself. Leaning up, she pressed a soft kiss to his jaw. As her lips skimmed his skin, he shifted, his eyes fluttering open as a faint, sleepy smile played on his face.

"Good morning," he murmured, his voice rough with sleep, sending a shiver through her.

"Hi," she whispered.

He lifted his hand to brush a stray lock of hair from her face. "I could stay like this with you forever." His fingers skated down her arm, leaving fire in their wake.

"Me too."

His fingertips moved along her shoulder and down her back, tracing a soothing rhythm that made her pulse quicken. "How'd you sleep?" he asked with a mix of tenderness and mischief.

Her mind felt hazy, unable to complete a single thought. "What?"

He chuckled. "Should I stop?" he teased, his hand caressing her waist as he leaned closer, his breath a whisper against her skin.

"Gabe…" she hesitated, her cheeks warming.

He paused. "What is it?" Concern flickered in his eyes. "Are you hurt?"

She shook her head, chewing her lip. "Was … did you … I mean…" She swallowed. "Did you like it?"

Amusement softened his gaze as his lips curved into a gentle smile. "Did I enjoy it? Ava, I don't think I've ever felt anything more perfect."

Relief washed over her, and a shy laugh escaped. "Good … I just … don't know what I'm doing."

"You were amazing." He lifted her chin, his gaze holding hers. "And it wasn't just that. Being with you, it's more than I could ever say."

She let out a quiet sigh of relief, a smile breaking across her face. "I … I loved it, Gabriel. I … didn't want it to end."

His lips were on hers, tender and loving and perfect. Her body melted into his as he held himself above her. A rush of heat ignited within her, the thrill of him pressing against her, his breath mingling with hers.

The taste of his lips and the softness of his touch set her blood ablaze, building with every moment. As their kiss deepened, desire surged, consuming her. Her cheeks flushed, her breath caught, and electric sensations danced over her skin, leaving her trembling beneath the unrelenting intensity. Time slowed to a crawl, as they nestled in each other's arms.

"I love you, Ava."

Her heart swelled, her throat tightening with emotion. She pressed her forehead to his, their breaths intertwined. "I love you."

A bittersweet finality settled over her as they held each other, their bodies entwined. In his arms, with his heartbeat against her skin, she let herself believe in the fragile hope of forever, even if it only existed in this fleeting moment.

Scattered debris lay strewn across the once-peaceful village, a haunting reminder of the night's violence. Charred timbers jutted out from the snow like jagged bones, while fragments of fabric and remnants of lives torn apart littered the ground. Silence hung heavy in the air, broken only by the quiet scrape of shovels against packed snow and the hushed murmurs of villagers and allies working side by side, each gesture a small attempt to reclaim normalcy from the ashes.

Ava knelt beside an elderly woman, helping her gather fallen branches. Her fingers, numb from the cold, moved methodically, even as the weight of the morning pressed down on her heart. Even though she was strong enough to warm herself, she didn't. She didn't deserve it. Each face she passed was etched with exhaustion, a haunted look in their glassy eyes, telling stories of grief unspoken.

The inn still stood, scarred but standing, its chimney trailing thin wisps of smoke like a beacon in the devastation. She would always remember the inn as a place of love. A place where she gave her heart to a man who was everything to her.

Her gaze found Gabriel across the courtyard. He was helping a group of children gather wood, his presence calming them, his smile softening their frightened faces. The children's laughter, tentative but bright, cut through the bleakness, a reminder of hope and resilience. Just yesterday, she'd walked through these same streets with him, sharing stolen glances and quiet moments. But now, all that vivacity had been replaced by shadows. Havok had taken that from them, and he would keep taking until there was nothing left. The thoughts tore at her until she inhaled a deep breath. Breaking apart each word as though they were nothing. Just words. Nothing. Like Gabriel taught her.

She lifted a charred piece of wood, its rough edges still warm, and tossed it onto a growing pile. The scent of ash lingered, clinging to her skin, mingling with the icy bite of the air.

Gillian shoveled snow and sifted through what was left of someone's home. When Gillian's gaze met Ava's, she offered a small, weary smile.

"Feels like I'm digging through memories," Gillian murmured.

Ava lowered her shovel. "What makes someone do this? How can anyone be so full of hate?"

Gillian bent down, picking up a small, soot-streaked child's toy. A wooden horse with one wheel missing. She stared at it, brushing the ash away. "I keep thinking… what if this were us?"

"We'd fight just the same," she replied, feeling the words tremble on her lips. "And we'd rebuild. But seeing it here … like this…"

"I didn't realize … how much more we'd have to carry after last night." She let out a sigh, her hands shaking as she held the broken toy. "I don't want to give in to him. I don't want to surrender."

Ava's heart ached at the thought of giving up Gabriel, of the impossible choices looming before her. "Neither do I. The thought of … hurting Gabriel, it makes me sick. But it feels like we're out of options. Havok will get what he wants, and they can go free."

She tossed the toy in a pile. "Like Gabriel will ever let Havok take you."

"He'll have to." She swallowed the oncoming tears.

"When … when are we turning off our emotions?" Gillian asked.

"I don't know."

They worked in silence, the quiet sounds of shovels filling the void.

Gillian stopped her.

"What?" Ava asked.

"Moira's vision." Gillian glanced around to make sure no one was listening. "She saw this … you and Thomas joining Havok. How are we supposed to keep it from them? They'll know. They'll try to stop us. You know they won't let us surrender."

Thoughts raced in Ava's mind as guilt and fear twirled inside her. "I … I don't know. What if it doesn't even work? What if Havok kills them all anyway?" The thought clawed at her insides, relentless and suffocating.

She glanced at Gabriel and her heart stopped, seized by an agony that ripped her apart from the inside. Tears pricked at her eyes, hot and aching. She couldn't breathe, each attempt scraping her lungs like shards of glass.

Her vision blurred, the world around her spinning, shapes and colors melting together into a frantic swirl of white, red, and gray. Gabriel's face flickered in and out of focus, a reminder of everything she had to protect, everything she might lose. She clutched her chest, gasping, the sound of her own strained breaths drowning out the murmurs around her.

"Ava?" Gillian's voice was distant, muffled, as though coming through water.

Ava's knees buckled, and she collapsed, shutting her eyes tight, hoping to block out the chaos, the fears slashing her mind.

The ringing in her ears grew louder, drowning out everything but the relentless thud of her heart, pounding in frantic rhythm. She was going to die. Her heart was going to explode.

A warm, soothing voice pierced the panic. "Ava," Gabriel said. He sounded so close, so real. "Breathe."

She couldn't. She didn't want to open her eyes. She didn't want to look at him, to see the face that she would betray. The image of him lying still, cold, lifeless. She couldn't bear it. She didn't want to crumble, not now, not with him so close.

"You're okay." His words seemed delicate, ready to break at any moment.

His hand reached out, resting on her shoulder, his touch calming her and bringing her back from the storm in her mind. "Ava, I'm right here."

The tenderness in his voice, the urgency, forced her to open her eyes. She caught a glimpse of him through her tears.

His gaze held her captive, radiating strength and a silent promise that calmed her racing heart.

"We're going to make it," he said. "I'm not going anywhere."

As dusk settled over the village, everyone gathered at the forest's edge, where a clearing under towering, solemn trees had been chosen as a resting place for the fallen. Snow drifted from above, cloaking the ground in a white blanket that seemed to absorb every sound, lending a quiet reverence to the scene. Each body was wrapped in linen, and villagers moved forward with stones or crystals. The offerings, personal and simple, were placed atop each wrapped body as symbols of resilience, remembrance, and hope.

Ava almost couldn't stand to watch, to be there, knowing that any of them could be next. She took several deep breaths.

Noelle stepped forward, her head held high as she placed a deep purple amethyst, its vibrant color standing out against the white snow atop Mahalia. A powerful symbol of the love and respect she held for her, a lasting tribute to her spirit and the way she impacted everyone around her, including Ava, who had just met her.

Gabriel blinked back tears, his jaw tense as he watched Noelle. Ava squeezed his hand. He glanced down, meeting her eyes, and the tear that rolled down his cheek tore her apart. She wrapped her arms around him and held him.

Sean placed an emerald stone on Nathan's shrouded body, a symbol of hope and rebirth. He rejoined Shannon, Aiden, Ronan, and Moira.

As the final words faded into the soft sounds of nature, the group dispersed, a hush settling over the village. Gabriel stayed close to Ava, his thumb caressing her knuckles as they walked back, their steps crunching through fresh snow. She let her gaze drift across the snowy path, her mind tangled from what they'd seen, what they'd lost, and the haunting idea of more battles to come.

Peering out the window, Ava watched the snow drift down, heavy flakes covering the village below. The world outside was blanketed in quiet stillness, a strange contrast to the storm raging within her.

The faint crackle of the fire was the only sound as Gabriel coaxed it to life. When the fire steadied, he moved to her, his arms winding around her from behind.

She turned to face him, her eyes locking onto his. His composure faltered, but he didn't hold back. He let her see everything, the sorrow etched deep in his features, the grief that darkened his gaze, the anger simmering beneath it all, and beneath that, the love he held for her, raw and unguarded, tangled with the fear of losing her.

"Thank you," he said. "For being here. For everything."

A sharp pain lodged in her heart. She closed her eyes, leaning into him, their breaths falling into a fragile rhythm.

The day's grief seemed to recede in his quiet embrace, but guilt threatened to swallow her whole. But she couldn't pull away from him. Even if it was to protect him. But right now, she couldn't. Right now, she needed to hold him as much as he needed her.

He swept a strand of hair from her face, his fingers lingering on her cheek for a moment. His touch was gentle, tentative, as though she might slip away. Then, he leaned down, his lips brushing hers in a soft, tender kiss. It wasn't urgent but aching, filled with comfort and longing, a shared solace that whispered all the words they couldn't say.

"I need you," he whispered. "I can't bear the thought of you—"

Softly, she pressed her fingers to his mouth, silencing him. The words were too much, too close to the truth she couldn't let him know. Instead, she kissed him again, her fingers tangling in his hair, pulling him closer. When his hands found her waist, guiding them to the bed, she didn't resist. Her heart was screaming at her to remember why she had to let go, but her body refused to listen.

He shed his shirt, then hers, his skin hot against hers as he pressed against her. With slow kisses, he seemed to be etching her into his memory. Every touch was careful, deliberate, a silent promise in the face of the storm closing in around them.

They sank into each other, their movements unhurried, filled with a need that wasn't just physical but healing. In his arms, she let herself forget for a moment the plan, the lies, the sacrifices. His soft touch, the quiet gravity of his nearness, cradled her in a fragile peace she didn't want to lose.

As they lay tangled, the world outside felt distant, no sound but the quiet rhythm of their breathing. She rested her head against his chest, listening to the beating of his heart, a sound she would carry with her when the time came to let go.

Ava made a silent vow to hold on to this moment. No matter what lay ahead, she would carry this with her, the love, the strength, the quiet resolve they shared, as they faced the coming shadows.

40

UNFORGIVING

The fire crackled under the heavy gray sky, its heat spilling over the group as they huddled close, their breaths mingling in the chill air. Ava's strength had returned, though they hadn't faced a single danger since they left Lighthollow, which scared her.

Shadows flickered across Gillian's face, and she let out a frustrated groan. "This is so hard."

Ava, Thomas, Lance, and Gabriel sat with her, each working to practice the heart of stone technique, severing emotion from thought, a skill that, Ava realized, demanded more discipline than anything she'd ever attempted. She tried to focus, pulling her thoughts inward, but Gabriel's presence beside her tugged at her like a gentle current. For two weeks now, she'd tried, unsuccessfully, to put distance between them, hoping to steel herself against the separation she knew was coming. But each time she tried, the idea set her heart racing, a tidal wave of dread pressing down on her chest. Instead of pushing him away, she found herself clinging more to each quiet glance, each brush of his hand. She knew it was selfish. She was sinking deeper, drowning herself in him. She was in the middle of the ocean and forgot how to swim.

Thomas rolled his eyes. "You're amazing with manipulating minds, G. Try using that on yourself."

Gillian managed a small smile. "I wish it worked like that."

"You'll get it," Gabriel said. A hint of amusement flickered in his gaze as he scratched at his growing beard, a constant source of frustration. He'd grumble about it every morning, and she found herself biting back a smile every time he did.

"I'm scared that the second I see Jeremy, I'll fall apart." She stared into the fire.

Gabriel nodded. "You have to prepare for that. You *will* see him. And he may fight you. Or they may torture him in front of you."

Ava flinched as the words sank in, her breath catching in her throat. For a fleeting moment, her mind conjured the excruciating image. Gabriel, bound, hurt, his strength stripped away. Would they torture him? Would they let him go? Or worse, would they manipulate him, pull him back into their fold, and make him one of them again? The questions crawled through her mind, writhing and relentless, like worms burrowing into dark corners she didn't want to face.

"You can do this, Gillian," Lance said, breaking Ava's spiraling thoughts. "Do it for Jeremy. For Melissa. We're all here for you."

But Ava knew he wasn't just speaking to Gillian. His words reached her too, pulling her back to the present, grounding her in the fight they couldn't afford to lose.

Gillian nodded and took a deep breath. "You're right."

Gabriel's eyes darkened, and a fierce determination set his features as he looked at each of them in turn. "Good. Then let's try again. Jeremy is dead."

They all watched as Gillian's face stayed still, no emotion betraying her pain.

His gaze shifted to Ava, his eyes meeting hers with a flash of challenge. "Your mother was a Cimmerian who abandoned you."

Ava forced herself to hold his gaze, her expression blank, even as his words cut deep. She focused, steadying her heart's rhythm, keeping her face neutral. She would not let him or anyone see her falter.

One by one, he moved to each of them, hurling brutal truths, unearthing their deepest fears, testing their resolve. The firelight danced over their faces, casting long shadows and softening the sharp edges of their pain, a testament to their growing strength as they held their composure together.

Over the next few days, they grew stronger, their control sharpening. Each session brought them closer, uniting their hearts in an unspoken bond.

As the cold settled deep around the camp, Ava slipped into the tent she now shared with Gabriel. His familiar scent, a mix of juniper and earth that eased the tension in her chest.

Gabriel lay back, one arm behind his head, his eyes closed, though a soft smile touched his lips as she entered. He opened one eye, catching her staring, and held out his arm in invitation.

Her heart fluttered as she crossed the small space, settling against his side. He pulled her close.

She nestled her head on his shoulder.

Their breaths fell into a gentle rhythm, each heartbeat a quiet reassurance.

"I'm scared," she whispered.

His fingers traced light circles on her back. "Me too. But whatever happens, we'll face it together."

She shifted, looking up at him, her heart twisting, knowing they wouldn't face it together. "Tell me something good. Something to look forward to."

A faint smile played on his lips. "All right. Someday, when all this is over, we'll find a place by the sea. Where the only sound is the waves. A little house, maybe a garden. And you, surrounded by green and life." His thumb brushed over her cheek. "That's how I want to see you. Somewhere peaceful."

Her heart swelled with the image. It was a vision she hadn't dared to imagine.

He pressed a gentle kiss to her forehead, a soft promise. "One day," he murmured, "You deserve that, Ava. We both do."

"Do you really think we'll get there?"

"I have to believe we will." He pulled her tighter against him, as if he could shield her from every dark path that awaited them. "You're my future, Ava. And as long as I'm breathing, I'll make sure we see that day together."

She closed her eyes, letting his words wrap around her, softening the ache in her chest. When it was over, she would find him again. "When things get hard, what will you hold on to?"

He was silent for a moment, his fingers stilling on her back. "I'll hold on to this," he whispered. "The way you look at me, the way you make me feel like I can be better. Stronger. I'll hold on to everything about you."

"Even when I'm afraid?" she whispered.

"Especially then." He tilted her chin, meeting her gaze with a quiet intensity. "I don't need you to be fearless, Ava. Just ... here. With me."

His hand traced gentle patterns along her arm. She shifted closer, feeling the solid press of his body against hers, the ache of longing rising. He leaned in, brushing his lips over hers, the kiss slow and filled with an intensity that made her heart race. For a moment, the world outside the tent disappeared, leaving the two of them entwined.

A distant cough broke the silence, and Gabriel tensed, glancing at the tent walls, the thin fabric separating them from the others. "Wish we had ... somewhere better than this," he murmured against her ear.

She let out a small laugh. "Me too." The desire to forget where they were, to be lost in the two of them, was almost overwhelming.

"We'll make up for it someday." His thumb brushed her lips. "Somewhere where we don't have to be so quiet."

Her heart ached with both want and affection. She leaned into him, letting the moment stretch as long as it could, feeling the intensity of everything they couldn't say aloud. The frustration, the closeness all simmered between them as they held each other.

Under the thick, clouded sky, they trudged through miles of snow-covered ground until they reached a looming tunnel, its entrance like a mouth ready to swallow them whole.

Ava stilled, remembering the last tunnel she ventured through with the snakes. But Ilya made her think there were snakes, and he was dead.

Taking a deep breath, she went inside with Gabriel beside her.

The darkness suffocated her along with the heavy and damp air. As they walked, the cool stone walls seemed to close in around them, and the stale, earthy smell of decay lingered in the air. Ava kept her eyes fixed forward, but she couldn't shake the prickling unease creeping along her spine.

Emerging from the other side, Ava tensed as a strange heaviness settled over her. The light was gray, muted, and the air felt thicker, clinging to her skin as if laced with unseen shadows. She couldn't explain it, but something about this place felt wrong, like death was waiting out of sight, hidden behind the bare trees or within the mist that drifted over the ground.

"Another trick of the Cimmerians," Gabriel said. "They don't want outsiders to be here."

A low, thunderous roar drew their attention, growing louder as they moved forward, each step. Snow began to fall in delicate flakes, adding a creepy quietness to the scene, and soon they reached the source of the sound: rapids, crashing over rocks and foaming white as they plummeted into a gorge. The violent torrent misted the air, obscuring the depths below. The river stretched wide and furious, an uncrossable divide between them and their path forward.

Savina studied the churning water, turning to Aaron, Sean, and Gustav. "We can't cross this. We have to go around."

"Why not?" Ava asked. "I can control the water. Just give me a chance." She was sure she could do it.

Aaron stared at her. "It's too treacherous."

"Who knows how long this river goes on?" Thomas muttered. "This could take days."

"Yeah, I agree," Link said. "Ava can help us cross."

"No more discussion," Aaron commanded.

The group grumbled in response. The thought of losing even more time set a fire in Ava. They were tired, their supplies running low again. They couldn't waste more time. She scanned the edge of the river, her eyes landing on a rock jutting from the rushing water. All she had to do was leap onto that rock and force the rapids to calm, just long enough for everyone to pass.

"Ava," Gabriel warned. "Don't even think about it."

But she'd already made up her mind. As the group moved along the riverbank, Ava exchanged a quick look with Thomas and darted toward the water.

"Ava, no!" Gabriel's voice chased after her, but she was already leaping, her heart in her throat. For a split second, she felt weightless, then her hands gripped the rough rock. The world seemed to hold its breath.

Until the stone gave way.

She plunged into the river, the icy water cut into her skin like knives. The water slammed into her like a wall, stealing the breath from her lungs. The relentless force of the current dragged her under, crashing her against rocks and swirling her in every direction. She fought to resurface, her lungs burning as she was thrown again and again beneath the waves. Finally, she managed to break free for a moment, gasping, only to be pulled back under. Desperation clawed at her, and she seized a low-hanging branch, securing herself against the relentless pull of the water.

With every ounce of strength, she focused on calming the river, feeling the raw power of the water fight against her control. "Cross! Everyone, cross!" Blood trickled from her nose, a searing pain thrummed in her temples, and her muscles trembled from the effort. She couldn't hold on much longer.

The moment her grip slipped, the water reclaimed its wrath. The force tore her from the branch, and she tumbled, colliding against rocks downstream. Her head struck something hard, and everything went black.

When she came to, her body was being pulled across the water as a hand gripped her arm. She coughed, water spilling from her lips as she gasped for air. Blinking through the haze, she looked up and saw a line of identical Erics, his clones forming a human chain from the cliff to where she lay. They passed her from one to the next until she was laid out on the snow.

Eric shook his head. "You'd better be glad one of us can duplicate ourselves to drag you out of there. You owe me."

Gabriel rushed to her side, cradling her. "Are you trying to get yourself killed?"

"No." She met his gaze with defiance. "I just wanted to get us across."

"And you nearly cracked your skull open in the process."

Faces hovered over her, their expressions ranged from worry to annoyance.

Ava's head pounded, her vision still hazy. "Why … couldn't I breathe underwater?"

Aaron glared at her. "I told you the water was too treacherous. You need to start listening. Don't you realize the closer we get to Caprington, the worse it's going to get? Nothing is going to work in our favor."

"It worked fine," she muttered, though even she knew it sounded ridiculous.

Eric groaned. "You're impossible."

Savina approached. "No more heroics, Ava." She placed her hands over Ava's head, and a gentle warmth spreading as the throbbing pain eased.

"Thank you," Ava murmured as she struggled to stand. The lingering chill from the river froze her, but she focused on warming herself from within.

"Everyone sticks together," Aaron commanded. "Nothing here is forgiving."

Ava took a step forward, but Gabriel grabbed her arm. His eyes were hard, searching her face. "What were you thinking?"

She hesitated, wanting to deflect, but she saw the fear beneath his anger. "I was thinking about getting us across. If you could teleport us, I wouldn't have had to do that."

"You know I can't teleport here." His tone was clipped, the worry still in his eyes. "And you saw what just happened."

"At least I did something."

He tilted his head. "What's really going on, Ava? Why are you so angry?"

She pulled her gaze away, trying to mask the turmoil inside her. "I'm just … tired. Tired of all of this. We've been walking for weeks, and it feels like we're marching to our deaths. Look at us! How are we supposed to defeat Havok and his entire army?"

"Ava, we have a plan. The Elders are prepared, and I'll do whatever it takes to protect you."

"I don't want you to do whatever it takes to protect me, Gabriel. I can't stand the thought of you getting hurt. Or worse."

Realization dawned in his eyes. "Are you … giving up?"

"No, I'm—" She swallowed hard. "I'm being realistic."

"Ava, what are you thinking?"

"Nothing."

"Don't lie to me." His hands cradled her face, forcing her to look at him. "I know you, Ava. I know when you're hiding something. What are you not telling me?"

Her stomach churned as nausea threatened to take over. She wanted to run, to escape his piercing gaze, but she couldn't move. She couldn't breathe.

"Talk to me." His quiet voice was filled with an urgency that matched the storm in his eyes. "Whatever it is, we'll face it together. But you have to tell me."

Tears pricked at her eyes, but she blinked them away, forcing a weak, unconvincing smile. "I'm not planning anything, okay? I'm … overwhelmed. That's all."

"You're lying. And I don't know why, but I do know this. Whatever you're thinking of doing, don't. Don't shut me out, Ava. Not now. Not when we need each other most."

"Just let it go, Gabriel."

"I can't let it go. Not when it's you."

"We should catch up to the group." She averted his gaze and began trailing behind them.

They walked in silence, the muffled crunch of snow beneath their boots the only sound between them. She stiffened when his hand slid into hers, intertwining with a quiet resolve that made her heart ache.

And though her love for him made her want to confide everything, the image of him in danger, risking his life for her, made the words stick in her throat. She would rather bear the brunt of the plan alone than risk him discovering it, knowing he would never let her go through with it.

As they descended further, the snow thinned, revealing dead, frostbitten grass beneath their boots. Ahead, a faint glow illuminated the horizon, casting flickering shadows over a distant black fortress surrounded by specks of firelight.

Ava's heart thudded as she took in the looming castle.

"Caprington," Savina whispered, her voice heavy with foreboding.

Gabriel's eyes locked with Ava's, and a painful silence hung between them.

RIPPED APART

They had endured endless miles in blizzards, under the relentless stretch of cloudy skies, through the bitterest cold, haunting nightmares, comas, and heartbreak. But as they reached the hill overlooking the immense, forbidding black castle of Caprington, none of that mattered. The sight of its towering, jagged walls ignited a singular, fierce desire in each of them: destroy Havok's forces or die trying.

They huddled under the cover of ancient trees on the castle's edge, the air heavy with the scent of cold earth and pine. As the sun dipped behind the distant peaks, casting dark shadows across the clearing, Ava, Gabriel, and the other Elementals gathered around Aaron, Savina, Gustav, and Sean, who were deep in whispered discussion. Each Elder's face was hard with determination, their voices tense murmurs as they laid out the final plan.

Aaron's gaze swept over them. "We don't have the advantage of time or numbers. Havok's forces will spot us quickly if we're not careful. Our best chance lies in a precise, ruthless plan: get in, extract our people, and get out before Havok can mount a counterattack."

It won't work, Ava thought.

Savina unfurled a map across a fallen log, tracing a slender path with her finger. "The main entry points are heavily fortified. However, there's an old, narrow passage near the eastern cliffs. We'll have to go single file, and it may be tight, but it's likely our best chance to slip in undetected."

Gabriel leaned in. "Once inside, we'll still be outnumbered. The passage leads near the dungeons, but we'll have to fight through the main hall to reach it. We should split into two groups: one to draw Havok's forces away, creating a diversion, and another to head straight for the captives."

It won't work.

"Are we certain we have enough power to hold off Havok's soldiers?" Gustav asked, concern creasing his brow. "If Havok realizes we're creating a diversion, he'll strike, and that team could be crushed in minutes."

Aaron's expression darkened. "That's the risk we're taking. If we can hold his forces' attention long enough, it'll give the rescue team a window to reach the cells. But," he paused, his gaze moving over the group, "that means the diversion team will be bearing the brunt of Havok's forces."

Ava exchanged glances with Thomas, Gillian, and Lance. They couldn't fight. They wouldn't fight the Cimmerians. They couldn't afford any more losses. And Havok wouldn't believe them that they surrendered if they killed Cimmerians

Savina placed a reassuring hand on Gustav's arm. "We've survived worse. If we work together, we can make it through." She looked at each of them, her eyes fierce with conviction. "Our magic is our strength, but so is our unity. We must be relentless and fast. The moment the captives are free, we retreat to the woods, assuming we can shake off any pursuit."

Ava swallowed. "And what if we don't? What if Havok corners us before we can get our friends out?"

"If it comes to that," Sean said, "we'll need to be prepared to surrender. But remember, surrender doesn't mean defeat." His eyes met each of theirs, hard with unspoken understanding. "If we're forced to yield, we'll have other chances to strike from within his ranks. But we won't get that chance if we're all cut down here."

The group fell silent, absorbing Sean's words.

Gabriel set his jaw. "I know what it's like to live among the Cimmerians. Surrender might keep us alive, but it would be hell for anyone who survives it." He glanced at Ava, his hand tightening around her own, as if he could shield her from the harsh truth. "I won't let them break anyone here."

Savina's gaze softened, but her voice was firm. "No one wants to surrender, Gabriel. But if it's the only way to save as many lives as possible, then we'll make that choice. This mission requires more than just strength. It requires sacrifice. We're here for each other, no matter what happens."

Gillian's face paled. "So … we'll go in, knowing we might have to let them capture us?"

Aaron nodded. "Only as a last resort. We don't want to give Havok that power. But if it means keeping everyone alive, we may have to make that choice."

Gabriel's eyes gleamed with purpose, his focus locked on Ava. "I'll keep you safe. Whatever it takes."

As she looked at him, his words cut through her. But he didn't realize she was doing whatever it took to keep him safe. Her pulse quickened, and she forced herself to turn her gaze to the rest of the group. She knew he meant it. He would risk anything for her, even his own life, if it meant protecting her. But the weight of that promise crushed her, knowing that she might have to go against him to protect him.

She wanted to tell him the truth, to let him in on the secret plan she and the Elementals had already formed. But her heart rebelled against it; she couldn't bear to see his reaction, to see him realize she was prepared to risk herself in a way he'd never allow.

Savina folded up the map. "Then we have our plan. Stick together, stay focused, and be ready to adjust at a moment's notice. This is our best shot."

One by one, each of them nodded, acknowledging the danger and the sacrifice that lay ahead. There was no turning back now.

Aaron's eyes lingered on the castle in the distance. "We'll surround the perimeter and clear as many guards as possible. Gillian, see if you can manipulate the minds of the guards to turn on each other. We need every advantage we can get."

Gillian gave a small nod, and she squared her shoulders.

Savina added, "And I'll add a layer of pain illusions. Once they begin screaming, it'll be our cue to advance. Everyone needs to stay sharp. No one makes a move until the Elders signal."

They fanned out, planning a covert approach to Caprington's land.

Ava's heart hammered in her chest as she moved into position with the others. She would carry this burden alone, knowing she was protecting him in the only way she knew how.

As they waited in tense silence, the castle loomed against the night sky like a creature poised to strike. The black walls towered over them, stark against the snow-dusted mountains and thick, gray clouds. Flickers of torchlight threw eerie shadows across the icy lake nearby, and a chilling stillness blanketed the air.

Ava glanced toward Gabriel, fighting the impulse to reach out for one last touch. But her vow to protect him by keeping him in the dark held her back. She clenched her fists, the soil cold and damp beneath her fingers, her pulse quickening.

I'm protecting him.

The sound of heavy footsteps broke her focus. "Thought you could sneak up on us?" A harsh, mocking voice cut through the quiet.

In an instant, her heart plummeted. She whipped around, finding herself face-to-face with a line of Cimmerian soldiers, their faces hard and steadfast. For a single, breathless moment, time seemed to stop.

Then chaos erupted.

Ava thrust her arms forward, torrents of water surging from her palms, crashing into the soldiers like a tidal wave. Guards tumbled into the icy moat, their shouts muffled by the roar of rushing water. Thunder growled above, the storm Aidan had summoned raging to life. Bolts of lightning split the sky, casting the battlefield in stark, brilliant white flashes.

The Cimmerians surged forward in relentless waves. Ava's breath hitched as she caught glimpses of her friends, locked in their own desperate battles. Gillian stood rigid, her hands trembling as she forced a cluster of guards to fight each other, their faces contorted with terror. Explosions tore through the air as Link's bombs scattered fiery debris into the enemy ranks. The acrid stench of scorched earth mingled with the sharp tang of fear, thick in the cold, damp air.

A jagged blade slashed toward her. Ava ducked, heart pounding, sidestepping the attack and responding with a blast of freezing water. The soldier's legs froze in place, ice crawling up his boots, locking him in mid-stride. She moved, sweeping her gaze over the chaos.

She couldn't kill them. Her attacks were calculated, precise. She froze limbs, shattered weapons, disarmed without deadly force. Every time a Cimmerian fell, it wasn't from her hands. It was to slow them down, to protect her friends.

But there were too many.

From the corner of her eye, she saw Gillian struggling, a soldier grabbing her from behind. The man's grip was iron-tight, and Gillian's face contorted in concentration as she tried to subdue him with her powers. Ava reacted without thinking, sweeping her arm forward. A pressurized jet of water shot through the air, slamming into the soldier and sending him stumbling back. Gillian gasped, pulling free, and their eyes met for a fleeting moment of gratitude.

All around her, the battle teetered on the edge of disaster. Lance and Thomas fought back-to-back, their weapons flashing as guards pressed closer. Natalia moved like a specter, singing under her breath, her eerie melody leaving Cimmerians crumpling in her wake. But even she tired, her movements slowed, her face pale and strained.

Suddenly, everything went silent.

The battle around her froze mid-motion, as though someone had pressed pause on reality. Snow hung suspended in the air, weapons halted mid-swing, and enemies hung in a silent tableau.

Ava's breath caught as she turned, and Gabriel stood before her.

His face inches from hers, eyes blazing as he gripped her shoulders. "I don't have much time. I stopped everything, just for a moment."

Her heart ached with pain. She wanted to tell him. But the words wouldn't come.

"Whatever you're planning, Ava—don't," he said, his voice raw with fear. "Don't throw yourself away. Not for me, not for anyone. I need you here."

His lips pressed hard against hers, a kiss filled with love and desperation.

She clung to him, trying to hold onto this moment.

Then, rough hands ripped them apart, and the world jolted back to life, time resuming its chaotic, relentless pace.

— 42 —

MADE OF STONE

Rough arms closed around her like a vice, and a hand clamped over her mouth. "This brings back memories, doesn't it?" Xavier whispered, his breath tickling her ear. "I remember how you tasted ... delicious." He brushed his lips against her neck.

A wave of disgust washed over her, but she forced herself to stay calm.

Gabriel locked his eyes on hers, fury etched across his face. Breaking free from his captor, he lunged forward, but Xavier's shadow engulfed him, halting him mid-step. With a flick of his wrist, Xavier sent Gabriel crashing to the ground.

"Pointless to resist," Xavier sneered. "I wonder if you're as sweet as your little blonde friend." He grinned, vile satisfaction radiating from him.

Gabriel lunged for Xavier again, his face a mixture of fury and desperation.

Her breath caught when a nearby guard's blade sliced into Gabriel's side, a dark stain spreading across his shirt.

The urge to scream, to rip free from Xavier's hold and rush to his side overwhelmed Ava.

But she couldn't. She had to steady herself. She had to turn off her emotions. Her pulse hammered as she tried to pull the pieces of her composure together, gripping the heart of stone, forcing herself to feel nothing.

Stay calm. Don't let him see anything.

Her fingers clenched at her sides, her mind echoing Gabriel's own words about keeping her emotions locked down. Every instinct screamed at her to react, to struggle, to fight. But she met Gabriel's eyes, barely allowing herself to acknowledge the pain there, the desperation, the unspoken plea.

Stop fighting, she wanted to say.

Xavier's voice slithered into her ear. "You can thank me later for teaching him his limits." He pulled her even closer, his grip like iron around her arm.

Ava forced her breathing to slow, fighting to still her pounding heart. She willed herself to become as unfeeling as the storm around them, swallowing down the waves of emotion that rose each time she saw Gabriel falter. It was just a technique, a mask she had to wear if they were going to survive this.

Gabriel, blood-streaked and breathing hard, glanced up, his gaze locking on hers. She resisted the urge to flinch, to reach out, and instead let the void she'd created between her emotions and her thoughts grow. She had to stay calm, for both their sakes. And from the look in Gabriel's eyes, he knew what she was doing.

She remained impassive, allowing the stone to encase her heart, cold and unyielding. If she broke now, she would betray everything they were trying to protect.

For him, she told herself. *I can do this for him.*

She met Gillian, Thomas, and Lance's gazes instead, nodding ever so slightly. They stayed still, portraying nothing, just as they had planned.

"We won't fight," Thomas said.

"Good." Xavier shoved Ava forward, keeping her close, his grip leeching all warmth from her skin.

Behind her, Gabriel struggled as they restrained him again, his growls of anger like low thunder rumbling in her ears. She stared straight ahead on the distant castle.

They marched across the long, narrow bridge spanning a dark, icy moat. The water below churned, its surface shrouded in mist, but Ava spotted familiar faces—Aidan, Ronan, Shannon, Anastasya—lifeless on the ground, scattered like fallen leaves. Their vacant eyes haunted her, but she didn't react.

As they entered the castle, they were enveloped by cold, towering stone walls, their breath clouding in the chill. The flickering torches cast a sickening glow on the polished floors, and the metallic scent of blood and iron hung heavy in the air. Shouts and jeers erupted from the gathered Cimmerians lining the corridor, their sneers echoing off the vaulted ceilings, a symphony of malice and hatred.

The group was led down the hallway, its narrowness pressing in around them, toward an open hall where Havok's throne loomed at the center, elevated and domineering.

Ava's gaze fixed on Havok, seated like a shadowed king on his throne, a dark grin pulling at his mouth as his black eyes landed on her. His presence dominated the hall, blotting out the light with an aura of dread. Beside him stood Jeremy, Kira, Maggie, and Melissa—each one's expression calm, unsettlingly resigned. Melissa's green eyes flickered with something familiar, a flash of recognition, but it vanished. Jeremy stood, his once-soft face now hardened, as if carved from stone. Ava didn't see Joss. She couldn't react. She had to keep her composure. Guards surrounded them.

Xavier loosened his grip on and moved back, leaving a prickling emptiness where Gabriel's warmth should have been.

Ava hated hearing Gabriel's ragged breaths. Her instincts urged her to rush to him, to press her hands to his wound and let the healing flow. But she couldn't. She couldn't blow her cover.

Havok rose from his throne. "I'm so glad to see you all." His dark smile widened as he turned to Savina. "It's been far too long, my little shadow."

Savina's face contorted in a mix of fury and heartbreak. "Let us go, Havok."

He let out a hollow laugh, taking a step down from the throne. "Oh, Savina. Did you really think I'd let you walk away? Another fight? How tiring."

"Afraid we'll conquer you again?" Aaron's voice was defiant.

Havok's smirk deepened, his gaze never wavering. "Yes, your little 'conquering' lasted all of what—minutes?" His voice turned sharp. "Give me the Elementals, and I'll spare the rest of you. Stay out of my way, and I'll consider it a fair exchange."

A wave of anxiety gripped Ava, but she remained emotionless. She opened her mouth to respond, but Savina beat her to it.

"You'll never take us willingly," she hissed.

With a flick of Havok's wrist, Savina collapsed to her knees, gasping in pain.

Clenching her fists, she suppressed the urge to run to her side, feeling her friends' eyes on her as they struggled with their own impulse to act. Taking a breath, Ava swallowed the lump in her throat. The words tasted like ash on her tongue. "We join you, Havok." Her voice carried through the hall, cold and deliberate, cutting through the tension like a blade. Gasps rippled from the captives behind her.

"Ava, don't," Gabriel murmured so softly that only she could hear.

Havok's grin widened, intrigue lighting his dark gaze like a predator circling its prey. "Well, now. This is unexpected. But why?" His black eyes pierced her, searching, as if already savoring the truth he expected to find.

She met his gaze with icy precision, forcing herself to breathe. "They're weak," she said, each word measured and cutting. "They've done nothing but betray me. You were right."

A sick satisfaction gleamed in his eyes. "And the rest of you?"

Thomas stepped forward, his face blank. "I join willingly."

Then Lance. "Yes."

Gillian, her head high. "I want to join."

"They're lying, Havok!" Aaron shouted. "Can't you see it?"

Glancing in Aaron's direction, Havok waved his hand, a flicker of power sending Aaron hurtling backward. He crashed onto the stone floor with a sickening thud, a chorus of gasps echoing from the captive Enchanters. Havok lifted a hand, silencing their cries with an effortless command. "I wouldn't try anything. My man Benjamin has already negated your powers. You're helpless and, frankly, outnumbered."

Havok's gaze danced over Ava, Thomas, Lance, and Gillian, as if savoring each declaration as if tasting something exquisite. "Fascinating." His movements were deliberate as he closed the space between himself and Ava, each step echoing in the cavernous hall. "And what of ... my traitor here?" His gaze flicked to Gabriel, and a shadow of cruelty passed over his features. "Or did you forget I was in your mind?"

She forced her face to remain impassive, even as her heart fractured. She couldn't falter. "I used him. I needed information, so I made him trust me."

"Did you now?" Tilting his head, he regarded her with a predator's focus, his dark eyes glittering with malice. A wave of icy pressure invaded her mind. A probing, searching force that coiled, testing her defenses. With calculated care, she allowed the surface of her thoughts to crack, enough to let him in. She guided him along the path, letting him glimpse only what she needed him to see: her resolve, her anger, her supposed surrender. The truth, shrouded in half-lies, unfurled before him like a carefully placed snare.

Havok's lips curved into a faint, knowing smile. "Interesting," he drawled, his voice dripping with dark satisfaction. "You are your mother's daughter. Fierce. Ruthless. Cimmerian blood flows through you as hers once did." He stepped closer, his gaze locking onto hers with unrelenting intensity. He bent close to her ear. "I have big plans for you."

A chill coursed through her, but she kept her composure, even as her pulse pounded in her ears. Gabriel's gaze burned into her, though she couldn't bring herself to look at him. She could feel his unspoken question. *How could you do this?*

Stay strong. It's the only way.

Havok's attention shifted back to Gabriel. "And now, you. Do you have anything to say for yourself?"

"I want to return," Gabriel said, his voice firm despite the ragged edges of pain.

Ava's heart stuttered, and for a moment, her carefully constructed mask nearly slipped. She snapped her gaze to him, disbelief flooding her chest. *What are you doing?*

Havok's brow arched, his amusement growing. "Ah, my prodigal soldier returns," he drawled, circling Gabriel like a wolf. "After all these years, I assumed you'd forgotten where you belong."

"I didn't forget," Gabriel replied, his tone measured. "I lost my way."

"How touching," Havok sneered. "But forgive me if I'm skeptical. After all, your *companion*"—his gaze slid to Ava, the disdain in his tone unmistakable—"claims to have used you like a pawn. So tell me, Gabriel, are you really that weak? Or are you lying?"

"I trusted the wrong people. That won't happen again."

"Won't it?" Havok pressed, his eyes narrowing. "You abandoned everything we stand for. And now you crawl back? Why?"

Gabriel didn't flinch. "Because I understand now. Power is the only thing that matters, and you taught me that. I lost sight of it, but I'm ready to prove myself."

Havok's smirk warped into something darker. "Prove yourself? Oh, you will. But first, let me remind you of what happens to deserters." He waved to the guards. "Take him to the cells."

The guards moved forward, grabbing Gabriel by the arms.

"Wait." Eve's voice cut through the hall, laced with venom. Her dark eyes glinted, the edges of her lips curling into a wicked smile as she sauntered toward Gabriel. Her long black waves caught the faint light, swaying with every deliberate step. "I knew you'd come back to me," she purred, her fingers brushing along his jaw with a possessive familiarity. "You've always been mine."

Ava's breath hitched, every muscle in her body tensing as Eve leaned in closer. *No. Don't.*

Eve's lips pressed against Gabriel's, slow and deliberate. For a split second, the room seemed to hold its breath, the world narrowing to that one excruciating moment.

Gabriel didn't recoil, didn't stiffen. Instead, he tilted his head, leaning enough to make it convincing. His hands stayed at his sides, motionless, every movement calculated, controlled.

A sharp pain stabbed Ava's stomach, and her heart hammered against her ribs. She remained still, biting down on her cheek to keep her expression neutral. *This is part of the plan.* The thought repeated like a mantra, but the sight of him, so close to Eve, so calm, sent her mind reeling.

When Eve finally pulled back, her lips curved in triumph, Gabriel's smirk mirrored hers, but it was cold, empty. His gaze flicked to Ava, so fleeting it might have been imagined, but in that moment, she saw it. The mask cracked, just for her. Something unspoken passed between them, something only she would recognize.

"Well, that was romantic." Havok rolled his eyes. "Take him away. I'll deal with him later."

Two guards seized Gabriel by the arms. He stumbled, his knees nearly giving out, but he straightened, his jaw tight as he fought to remain steady. He stayed silent, but as he passed Ava, he stared at her. His eyes were a storm of emotions, disbelief, hurt, anger.

She wanted to speak, to explain, to beg him to understand.

But she couldn't. And she didn't know when she'd see him again.

Gabriel's jaw tightened, his gaze cutting away as he was forced forward, but the echo of his disapproval burned in the space between them. It clung to her like a shadow, haunting her even as the door closed behind him.

A figure moved forward, Savina, her face pale but resolute. Her voice, heavy with exhaustion and sorrow, cut through the tension. "You only wanted the Elemental Enchanters. Let the others go."

"Oh, Savina," he crooned. "You really think I only want the Elementals? No. I want all of you." His gaze swept over the prisoners, his grin widening. "To torture every single one of you, the way you all tortured us. That's how it works. Did you honestly think I'd let this go?"

Savina's composure wavered, her lips trembling. "Then you'll have to fight us."

Havok leaned in, his hand resting heavily on her shoulder. His voice softened, a sick affection threading through it. "My pride. My little shadow." He leaned down, his mouth close to her ear. "But you abandoned me."

A small gasp of pain escaped Savina, her mask cracking as she looked up at him, tears gathering in her eyes.

He lowered his head, saying something Ava couldn't hear.

Whatever it was, it shattered Savina, and her eyes filled with a desperate pleading. "No… You promised you wouldn't."

Havok's gaze turned back to her, colder than death. "You brought this on yourself. You and Colden. I warned you, yet you defied me." A dangerous nostalgia colored his tone. "If only you'd stayed."

Savina staggered to her feet, her breath labored, but her gaze was defiant. "You will not win, Havok. You will not take them."

Her face strained as she attempted to draw on her powers, her jaw clenched in concentration, a vein pulsing on her forehead. But a thin trickle of blood slid down from her nose, her efforts thwarted by Benjamin's negation spell.

"Your powers are useless here," he murmured. "I'd hoped it wouldn't come to this. I really don't want to do this. But you betrayed me." He raised his hand, fingers poised, but Aaron pulled Savina behind him, his stance protective.

Havok smirked, and two Cimmerians seized Aaron, ripping him away from Savina's side. Their hands slipped from each other's grasp, desperation flashing in Aaron's eyes as he struggled against his captors.

He took her hand in his. She trembled, gasping for breath as her face twisted in agony.

"No!" Aaron cried as he fought against the Cimmerians holding him. He watched as Savina's body fell limp in Havok's arms, her gasps growing weaker until her eyes fluttered shut.

Anguished cries surrounded Ava, but she let the heart of stone protect her from the sight of Savina's lifeless form.

Havok's face fell, a flicker of sadness passing over his features as he eased her to the floor. For a brief moment, it was as if he truly mourned her loss. He removed his cloak and covered Savina's body. "Take her to the sepulcher," he ordered, his tone colder than ice. "She is to have a proper burial."

"Savina!" Aaron wrenched free, rushing to her side. He gathered her into his arms, his hands trembling as he touched her face, tears streaming down his cheeks. "How could you? How could you kill both your children? They loved you."

Havok's mask slipped back into place, his expression hardening with fury. "And they betrayed me. I had no choice."

"There's always a choice," Aaron spat. "You will burn for this. A thousand deaths, and it still won't be enough to make you pay."

Havok flicked his wrist, signaling the guards to pull Aaron away. He turned back to the room. Some of the hostages wept, their shoulders shaking, while others glared at him with a fierce, unbroken defiance. The air was thick with despair and fury, both heavy and suffocating, as if even the walls bore witness to their helplessness.

Havok sneered, his lips curling into a mocking smile. "If you all swear your allegiance to me, you will not be tortured." His words fell like stones into the silence, each syllable laced with chilling indifference, making it clear that mercy was a game to him.

A tense silence filled the hall, the question hovered like a storm cloud.

Eric stepped forward. "I will swear my allegiance." His words were steady, betraying no fear, though his eyes glinted with a subtle, hidden determination.

Peter cleared his throat, glancing at Katarina beside him before nodding. "We will."

"Excellent," he said, his tone dangerously smooth, like oil over fire. His gaze lingered on each of them, savoring the sight of their submission. "Take the others away."

The guards seized Moira, Natalia, Aaron, and the others, and led them away. The room emptied, leaving only a handful behind.

"I'm so pleased," Havok said. "I have rooms prepared for each of you, but first, a quick stop in our lab."

Thomas's brows knit in confusion. "For what?" His voice was wary, a hint of dread creeping into his tone.

"For a little memory alteration." The words seemed to hang in the air, chilling each of them to the bone. The implication was clear. Whatever loyalty they pledged, Havok intended to make it permanent, by any means necessary. "I know you've all pledged your allegiance to me, but this cements that."

A robust guard with black, curly hair seized Ava's arm, pulling her forward, and she caught sight of other guards securing the Elementals, along with Eric, Peter, and Katarina. They were herded down a cold, dimly lit corridor, the walls close and suffocating, until they entered a small room bathed in soft yellow light. The unexpected warmth of the light contrasted with the sterile chill of the room, unsettling her further. Ava's heart pounded, but she kept her face blank. With Benjamin, the power-negator, among them, there was no way out.

As the door shut behind them, the guards lined the walls, forming an immovable barrier. The room felt impossibly cramped with their presence, especially with the four ominous, dentist-like chairs arranged in the center, each one equipped with thick, leather straps. Ava's throat constricted, but she forced herself to remain composed.

"Is this really necessary?" Thomas asked. "We want to be on Havok's side."

A man with slick black hair and piercing green eyes stepped forward, exuding a detached, clinical menace. He wore a white lab coat, the only stark figure against the muted room, like some grotesque parody of a doctor. "Yes, well. Havok can never be too certain." His gaze swept over each of them, cold and assessing. "I'm Klaus, and I'm here to take your memories away," he added with unsettling cheer, as though they were patients about to undergo a routine check-up.

One of the guards shoved Ava into a chair, and the leather straps tightened around her wrists and ankles, pressing her against the cold metal frame. She forced herself to keep her breathing even as the others were being restrained beside her. Across the room, Peter stood rigid, the fear in his eyes unmistakable. She gave him a quick, reassuring look, though the moment felt hollow in the face of what they were about to lose.

Klaus moved to Gillian first, lifting her arm and preparing a syringe filled with a clear liquid that glinted in the light.

Ava averted her gaze, shutting her eyes, every muscle in her body rigid. She couldn't watch. This was the price of their plan, but it bore down on her chest, each heartbeat a painful reminder of what she was giving up. Memories of her father, of Gabriel, of everything that made her who she was, swirled in her mind, slipping through her fingers like sand.

The thought of Gabriel struck like a raw wound, a sharp ache that hollowed her out. She clung to the memory of his touch, the strength of his arms, his voice, always grounding her. His eyes, deep with quiet intensity, flashed in her mind, and she felt the ghost of his lips on hers, igniting a reckless spark in her heart. She didn't know who she'd be after this, didn't know if she'd even recognize herself. But she held onto him, grasping at every fleeting detail as if he could tether her to the person she used to be.

A firm grip on her arm snapped her back. She opened her eyes to Klaus standing over her, a syringe in hand, his face cold and expressionless. "This won't hurt at all. But you will feel … numb, exhausted." He secured a tourniquet around her arm. The needle gleamed as he tapped it once, then slipped it into her vein.

The prick was sharp, the liquid icy as it flowed into her bloodstream. Her heart hammered, memories rushing in like a flood. She focused on Gabriel, his laughter, his smile, the way he made her feel seen, understood. But the edges of her thoughts began to blur, the weight in her limbs dragging her down. The warmth of his arms, the blue of his eyes, the sound of his voice. They all started to fade, slipping further from her grasp. Her vision dimmed, her mind spiraling into an inescapable haze as the heaviness swallowed her whole.

A shadow fell over her as Klaus leaned in, his eyes intense, fingers pressing against her temples. Suddenly, a voice, not spoken aloud but echoing in her mind, almost resonant, filled her thoughts.

Klaus was speaking to her mind. *You are an Elemental Enchanter. You have the power to control water. Use it to defeat the Cimmerians and Havok. Keep up the ruse. You must make him believe you have lost your memories. You all are the answer to end this.*

As Klaus's words echoed in her mind, a glimmer of hope flickered within her. He wasn't there to erase anything. He was guiding her, arming her with instructions rather than taking them away. This wasn't a memory erasure; it was a façade, a chance to deceive Havok from within.

As Klaus released her and moved to Thomas, she let her head slump, feeling the effects of the drug wash over her, but she clung to the message, the command that felt as if it had come from somewhere beyond the physical realm. Her body felt leaden, her vision dimming, but her purpose crystallized in the silence that followed.

Her mother's words, whispered to her in dreams, came back to her, weaving through the fog like a guiding light: *Join them. If you don't, everyone will die. Convince the others to swear their allegiance, and they will kill Havok.*

This was their destiny.

ACKNOWLEDGEMENTS

To all of my readers and fans. Your incredible support does not go unnoticed. I couldn't do this without you.

To all the musicians I have ever listened to and who continuously inspire me.

To Jennifer for your support, encouragement, and laughter. To my girl Paige. There are not enough words to say how awesome you are. I could not accomplish writing without you. A thousand times thank you. To Chani for all of your editorial advice and support. To my awesome betas and street team. You rock! To Angie and Rachel. To Nicole for being my friend.

To my mom; my dad; Patrick, Morgan, and Alison. You are incredible and I love you all.

PLAYLIST

Walking Blind – Aidan Hawken

Rain – Breaking Benjamin

Going Under – Evanescence

Disintegration – Jimmy Eat World

Everybody Lies – Jason Walker

Over – Jimmy Eat World

Silver Springs – Lykke Li

Hey Jupiter – Tori Amos

Almost Lover – A Fine Frenzy

The Mess – The Naked and Famous

Winter Sun – Dishwalla

Figure 8 – Ellie Goulding

Black Tangled Heart – Silverchair

Dead In The Water – Ellie Goulding

Fine Again – Seether

Never Let Me Go – Florence & the Machine

Snow Angel – Tori Amos

Dark Roman Wine – Snow Patrol

Holding a Heart – Toby Lightman

Skin – Zola Jesus

Elastic Heart – Sia

Losing Your Memory – Ryan Star

Kiss Me – Ed Sheeran

Don't Deserve You - Plumb

The Only One – Evanescence

Made of Stone – Evanescence

ABOUT THE AUTHOR

Carrigan Richards is the author of *Pieces of Me* and the *Elemental Enchanters series*. She graduated from Kennesaw State University with a degree in English. She lives near Atlanta with her dog.